Icon of Gold

Teresa Crane

LITTLE, BROWN AND COMPANY

A *Little, Brown* Book

First published in Great Britain in 1997
by Little, Brown and Company
Reprinted 1997

A CIP catalogue record for this book
is available from the British Library.

ISBN 0 316 88198 8

Typeset in Palatino by M Rules
Printed and bound in Great Britain by
Clays Ltd, St Ives plc

Little, Brown and Company (UK)
Brettenham House
Lancaster Place
London WC2E 7EN

Icon of
Gold

PART ONE

Suffolk
Winter 1952

Chapter One

The leading horses, hooves thundering on the wet turf, took the final fence bunched dangerously tightly together. Their riders, bright silks sodden, urged them fiercely with voice and with whip. The punters were on their feet, roaring them on, their enthusiasm undiminished by the steady drizzle of fine rain that enveloped the course. A horse pecked, stumbled, regained its feet: but balance was gone, and the jockey's seat was lost. He came off lightly as an acrobat, hit the turf rolling, just as the tired back markers crashed through the brushwood of the fence. A sharp hoof lashed. No one but the fallen man himself heard the crack of breaking bone.

Adam Sinclair, bareheaded in the drifting rain, was yelling with the rest of them. 'Come on! *Come on!*' The grey to win, that was all he needed. That lovely grey to win and he would recoup all this afternoon's losses at a stroke –

The loose horse was causing trouble, threading through the leading group, running flat out and uncontrolled, wet mane flying. Round the last bend two runners were pulling ahead; the long-legged grey and a sturdy chestnut.

Adam stopped shouting. His hands were clenched: in the cold and the rain he was sweating.

It was a two-horse race now, the rest of the field despite the riders' frantic efforts were falling behind. It had been a gruelling run, at least half the field had fallen and those gallant animals that were left were labouring. The two leaders, ears flat, tails streaming, battled down the last straight towards the post, their diminutive riders standing in the stirrups urging their mounts to the last heartbursting effort.

Come on! *Come on!*

The grey was faltering, the long, graceful strides becoming uneven. Slowly, inexorably, the smaller chestnut was pulling ahead.

The crowd's excitement reached a crescendo. Encouraged, the handsome grey put in one last brave effort, regaining a little of the lost ground. But still, when they swept past the finishing post there was a clear half length between them.

Adam screwed up his betting slip and let it drop to the sodden mud beneath his feet. 'Shit!' he said, very quietly, '*Oh, shit!*'

'Bus is stoppin'.' Three pairs of interested eyes peered into the dreary and blustery November afternoon that sulked beyond the fly-specked window of the shop-cum-post-office of the hamlet of Aken, an unnoteworthy spot a mile or so inland from the windswept sweep of the Suffolk coastline. 'First time tha'ss bothered this week,' the speaker added, drily. The stink of the paraffin stove used to heat the shop easily overcame the smell of bacon and biscuits and the flat, musty aroma of the sacks of beans and lentils and flour that more usually permeated the place.

In the lane outside the gears of the ancient single-decker vehicle clashed and it pulled away, rattling, leaving a solitary figure standing by the roadside; a tall, slim young man in city clothes, a small grip in one hand.

The youngest of the trio of watchers, a woman of perhaps twenty-five with a baby on her hip, stood on tiptoe to get a better view. It was not often that tall, dark, presentable strangers turned up in Aken. Not since the Yanks had left the area after the war, anyway. 'A foreigner I'd say, from the look of him.'

The young man stood for a moment, looking around him, hesitant, one hand to the brim of his hat, holding it against the gusting wind.

'Anyone comes from Thorpness they're a foreigner round here,' Mrs Hamilton, the postmistress, said, her voice dryer still.

'Tha'ss 'cos they are.' The old man who was propped comfortably against the counter tranquilly relit his pipe. 'Strange folks at Thorpness. Strange folk. Never held wi' 'em meself.'

The woman cast an exasperated look at him. 'Don't be so daft, Tom Blowers.'

He smiled a sly, brown-toothed smile.

'He's comin' across.' The young woman settled the fidgeting child more firmly. 'Hush up, now, Jimmy.'

The stranger hesitated for a moment outside the door, then pushed it open. The bell jangled discordantly, and fell to an echoing quiet. Three pairs of questioning eyes met his.

As, courteously, he took off his hat a lock of heavy black hair fell across his forehead. 'I'm sorry – I wonder . . .?'

They watched him, waiting. 'I'm looking for Sandlings Cottage. Mr and Mrs Kotsikas –' The accent was immediately and unmistakably recognisable as American, but with some underlying inflection. His pronunciation of the Greek surname with which so many locals professed to struggle was unthinking and easy.

There was a short, interested silence, then, 'Up the road a bit,' the old man said, jerking his head. 'Turn left, then left again at the bike.'

'I – beg your pardon?'

Mrs Hamilton took pity on him. 'Mrs Kotsikas leaves a bicycle at the end of the track that leads to the cottage. For gettin' down to the village when she needs to. Turn right out

of the door here, follow the road up for a mile or so. There's
a narrow lane, on the left. There's no signpost – that doesn't
go anywhere, you see. Just on to the heath and to a couple of
houses. About a mile on down there's a dirt track. Tha'ss
where she leaves the bike. You can't miss it. Just keep
walkin' till you come to the cottages.'

'I see.' He ducked his head a little awkwardly. 'Thank you
Ma'am.'

'You're welcome.'

Turning away he stopped. 'Oh – do you sell cigarettes?'

'Players and Woodbine.'

'You wouldn't have Three Castles?'

She raised faintly caustic brows. 'Players and Woodbine,'
she repeated.

'Of course – I'm sorry – I'll take twenty Players, please.'
He paid for the cigarettes, tucked them into the inner pocket
of his overcoat – his good quality overcoat, Mrs Hamilton
noted – picked up his small bag, settled his hat firmly on his
head. 'Thank you again.'

Mrs Hamilton nodded. The girl with the baby, unac-
countably, blushed as his eyes met hers. The old man eyed
him, dourly impassive.

A gust of wind disturbed the stuffy atmosphere and then
the bell jangled again as the stranger shut the door behind
him.

'Well, well,' said Mrs Hamilton, with impenetrable
equanimity.

The old man said nothing. A cloud of pipe smoke
enveloped them both. Mrs Hamilton tutted.

The younger woman was at the window watching the tall
figure trudge up the lane, shoulders hunched against the
wind. She sighed a little as she turned away. Those eyes!
Like a film star's! Honestly – just like a flipping film star's!
Made you feel really weird just to look at them. That Mrs
Kotsi-whatever had better keep her visitor away from the
village girls, that was for sure. Too many parents around

here remembered the Yanks. She smiled a little, wryly. She had a few memories herself.

'Half a pound of best back, please, Mrs Hamilton.'

Nikos Kotsikas had been cold in New York. Very cold; especially at the beginning, when he had first arrived from Greece. He had seen that busy metropolis brought to a standstill by snowdrifts that engulfed automobiles and immobilised the public transport system. He had walked in a Central Park of sculpted ice and sub-zero temperatures. He had scurried back to his grandmother's elegant centrally heated apartment through blizzards as blinding as any in the Arctic.

He never remembered being as bone-cold as he was now.

The wind blew in bitter gusts direct from the North Sea – the sea that, grey as the skies above it and white-capped with wind-lashed spume, lay perhaps a mile behind him, crashing with constant and primeval force on to its long shingle beaches, visible occasionally through gaps in the leafless hedge that lined the narrow, deserted road. The sky was vast, and dense with billowing slate-grey cloud. He hooked his bag on to his shoulder and shoved his hands deep in his pockets. As he pushed doggedly on he found, somewhere in the back of his mind, the cherished picture forming; clear, quiet sea blue as sapphire, backed by the warm, still, bee-humming mountains that were lapped with groves of orange, lemon and olive, and whose crests rose against a crystalline, sunlit sky. He had not been back to Greece since his father had spirited him out of that war-torn land after the terrible death of his mother just before his sixteenth birthday. In the ten years since he had been to many places and seen many things. But he had never forgotten. He glanced about him. Nothing could be further from that warm and glittering beauty than this. The wild, sandy heathland was winter-dark, the gorse windswept, the bracken dry and brown, the branches of the birch trees slender, fragile-looking, bare against the threatening sky.

Where the hell was everybody? Surely *someone* must live in this God-forsaken place?

The lane narrowed further. Ahead he could see a left-hand turn, little more than a roughly tarmacked track, leading through a stand of battered and insignificant-looking scrub-like trees. This must be it. He turned into it, the distant sea now on his left, churning still, cold-looking and constantly restless. For a moment the huddled trees broke the force of the wind a little and he was able to catch his breath. Then he was in the open again, head down, collar around his cold, aching ears.

Turn left again at the bicycle. At the *bicycle* for Christ's sake?

Ten minutes later he found it; an ancient pre-war machine, battered, its black paintwork chipped and muddy, a wicker basket, very much the worse for wear, strapped to its sit-up-and-beg handlebars. It was propped against the hedge beside a narrow sandy cart track that struck off east in the general direction of the sea. In the twenty minutes or so since he had left the shop he had not seen a soul. A few large, wet flakes of snow flew in the wind. Well, it couldn't be far now, surely? Warmth and shelter and a friendly face. It was a seductive thought; just now, he told himself grimly, he'd settle for a barn if it got him out of this wind. What's more, he was hungry. He'd give a year of his life for a cup of hot coffee and a doughnut; and as so often happened the simple, homely thought unexpectedly triggered memory and he found himself remembering the New York apartment that had been his home for so long. Home. The very word all but choked him with grief and with a crushing homesickness that brought with it a pain that was almost physical. Stop thinking about it; he had to stop thinking about it. He had to forget, to start afresh. Over and over he had told himself that during the long voyage across the Atlantic. But the treacherous memories would not let him go.

The tragedy had struck so suddenly and so hard that at first he had been almost anaesthetised against the pain; it

was later that it had hit him. As now, uncalled for and
unwanted the vivid recollections would catch him unaware
and he could not escape them. He could see, could smell,
could actually for a moment feel around him the charming,
peaceful apartment with its waxed floors and polished furniture, its quiet-ticking clocks, its books and its pictures. A
sanctuary of harmonious warmth and comfort in the winter,
peacefully fanned and shaded in the sweltering New York
summer, the rooms graced and ordered by his grandmother,
as she had graced and ordered everything she had touched,
including Nikos' own life. The gentle scoldings, the wisdom,
the laughter and the loving care. The music.

His eyes were suddenly hot with tears, and not for the
first time he found himself taking refuge in a passion of
almost childish anger. It wasn't fair! It wasn't! She hadn't
been that old. Why should she have died so horribly?
Cancer. He hated the very word. Hated to recall what it had
done to her, she who with her soft voice and slow, gentle
smile had, until the disease had struck so suddenly, never
lost the beauty of her youth; on the contrary she had been
one of that rare breed of women upon whom the years actually bestow more than they take. The thick, well-cut silver
hair had still shone, the unusual gold-green eyes that had
passed from mother to daughter and thence to Nikos himself
had still been clear. The strong, serene bone structure of her
face had been flawless. It had often amused him and – yes –
been a source of pride too, to see men's eyes turn upon his
grandmother as she walked into a room or a restaurant. The
one thing that New York recognised in its women was class;
and Susan Constandina had certainly had that.

His face was cold, flayed by the wind. Clinging wet flakes
of snow were suddenly driving in from the sea. But it was
neither the wind nor the snow that was blurring his vision.
Impatient and embarrassed he knuckled away the tears. For
Christ's sake – this was England! Everyone knew that men
didn't cry in England.

The uneven track dipped a little, leading down into a hollow where the wind was at least a little less fierce. He lifted his head, scenting the air. Wood smoke.

The squall had died as swiftly as it had arisen, and the snow had stopped. Ahead, through the tossing trees, he saw the ancient tiles of a low moss-grown roof, and a chimney from which the wisp of fragrant smoke issued, to be rent and torn by the wind. This, surely, must be it?

He stood, appalled.

The place looked derelict. The windows were filthy and uncurtained, the tiny garden an overgrown riot of weeds, brambles and nettles through which a disintegrating brick path meandered. The only sign that the place was inhabited at all was the wind-blown smoke.

He rapped at the wooden door with his knuckles.

Nothing happened.

He tried again, and when still there was no reply he lifted the latch. The door opened on to a large, dark and incredibly untidy room. A fire burned in a small, filthy grate. Every surface was cluttered, an armchair was piled with old newspapers. Light filtered through the uncurtained and extremely dirty window.

'Cath? That you? 'Bout time. Tha'ss cold as a witch's tit out there – you'll catch your death on that beach one o' these days . . .' A man's voice, irascible and with the cracked cadences of age in it. Nikos stood, embarrassed and uncertain, as an elderly man shuffled across the room, peering short-sightedly towards the open door.

'No. I'm – I'm sorry, Sir. My name is Nikos Kotsikas. I think I must have missed my way –' *Turn left at the bicycle? A joke? Some joke!* 'I'm looking for –'

'She in't in. She's took the damn' dogs down the beach,' the man interrupted him brusquely, in fact downright rudely. 'Daft female she can be. Roamin' that beach at all hours. She'll catch her death. I'm allus tellin' her –' He was a full head shorter than Nikos, wore dirty corduroy trousers a size or two too big for him and an assortment of worn and ragged woollen jumpers and cardigans of indeterminate colour that would, Nikos thought, have given grief to a scarecrow. He, like the room itself, smelled rank and unpleasant. He turned his back, shuffled towards the fire. 'You're in the wrong house, boy,' he said. 'Next door. Tha'ss where you should be. Next door.'

'Next door?' Nikos was puzzled. So far as he had seen there had been no other house.

The ancient head jerked. 'Go round the back. You'll see. But I told you– Cathy in't in. She's down the beach.'

'I see. Well – thank you very much . . .' Awkwardly Nikos hesitated for a second. The old man neither turned nor replied. Thankfully Nikos opened the door and escaped into the fresh air; for a moment even the bitter wind was welcome after the foetid atmosphere inside.

The brick path, he now saw, went on past the door and round the corner of the house. He hefted his grip on to his shoulder and followed it.

The house he was looking for was not, he discovered, strictly speaking 'next door' to the old man's, but back to back with it. The second cottage faced the distant sea, and the sandy track resumed its way from a small rickety gate out on to the scrub-cloaked heathlands towards the dunes and the wild shore beyond. The surprisingly large garden was contained by a low flint wall and though at least, unlike its neighbour, it gave some impression of being cultivated, at this time of year and in this fierce and salty gale it looked bleak indeed. The gnarled branches of an old fruit tree creaked and groaned. A wooden bird table had blown over and lay half buried in a bed of tough-looking sharp-thorned rose bushes. Small paths meandered from nowhere to nowhere amongst leafless, lifeless plants and shrubs. A seat was set beneath a sagging latticed arch, forlorn and incongruous reminder of the days of summer.

The house, like its partner behind, was small, with a

couple of lean-to additions, the low tiled roof moss-covered, the windows stained with salt spray. It was obviously very old, and had settled into its sandy foundations like a bird into a nest. The doorframe, like the frames of the windows, was distorted and angular. Upon the door, weather-beaten but legible was a small painted sign – *Sandlings Cottage* – the border of the sign and the two capital letters decorated by tiny paintings of small sea creatures.

Nikos lifted the latch.

The room in which he found himself was virtually identical to the one next door. It was also almost as cluttered and untidy, though undoubtedly – and thankfully – cleaner and fresher smelling. There were books everywhere. A half-finished pencil sketch was pinned to a beam, and a sketch pad and pencils were tossed on an ancient-looking and squashily comfortable sofa. There was a heap of shells and stones sitting, inexplicably, in the centre of a small tea table, next to a glass-shaded oil lamp that had obviously been pushed aside to make way for them. Sand and little bits of dried seaweed were scattered across the polished surface. A pair of shoes lay where they had apparently been kicked off beside one of the armchairs. An unwashed mug sat in the hearth. A cheerful fire danced in the basket of the blackened grate. The room was warm; but not simply from the warmth of the flames. There was colour everywhere. Bright cushions were scattered haphazardly across the shabby sofa and chairs – jade, and blue and deep terracotta. The curtains were the yellow of lemons in sunshine, the plaster walls around the beams were a slightly paler reflection of that same colour, applied with a careless hand. The ceiling was low.

'Hello?' He shut the door behind him. Sudden silence fell. 'Hello?'

The wind whistled through the chinks in the door; sparks glowed in the chimney. He crossed the room, pushed open a small latched door that opened into a surprisingly spacious lean-to kitchen with a big pine table and a cast-iron cooking range that gave out a wonderfully cosy heat. The room was as untidy as the sitting room, and as empty of life. The big old sink held a couple of dirty plates and a cup and saucer. He heard the wind singing in the chimney of the range. On the table was a wooden board, on it a chunk of cheese and half a loaf of what looked temptingly like home-made bread. He'd eaten nothing since a quick – and awful – sandwich at Liverpool Street station before he'd caught the train. He cut a piece of cheese and bit into it. It was mouthwatering; flavourful and strong. He carved himself another piece, took a chunk of bread to go with it. He guessed they wouldn't mind his helping himself whilst he waited. For wait he was going to. No way in the world was he leaving this cheerful warmth to go back out into that fearsome weather.

The bread and cheese finished he helped himself to a glass of water, then wandered back into the sitting room, subsided into a deep and comfortable armchair in front of the fire and reached for his cigarettes.

Catherine Kotsikas turned the piece of driftwood in her fingers, fascinated by the smooth, waterworn texture, the surreal, twisted shape. She ran a finger along it, for the moment completely absorbed and all but unaware of her surroundings. A sudden gust of wind buffeted her, almost knocking her from her feet. She slipped the piece of wood into her pocket, where it joined a motley collection of stones and shells and looked up. 'Paddy! Sandy! Here! Come on! Time to go.' The two dogs, one a huge and shaggy animal with feet like plates and a great feathered tail and the other, much smaller and of equally indeterminate breed, that at the moment looked like nothing so much as a drowned rat having been soaked to the skin in his determined efforts to catch and savage a wave, blithely ignored her. 'Sandy! Will you come here!' The woman waited for a moment, hands in pockets, watching the dogs as they dashed back and forth into the cold water. She pulled a face, casting wry eyes to the stormy heavens. 'Talk to yourself, Cathy, talk to yourself,' she said aloud, succumbing to a habit she knew tended to engender tolerant mirth amongst friends and raise the eyebrows of strangers. She turned and started to tramp up the sliding shingle slope, her Wellingtons sinking ankle-deep in the smooth stones. 'OK. Do as you like. I'm going,' she called to the dogs, above the wind.

The smaller animal lifted his head alertly and watched her for a moment. Then, ears flopping and tail flying like a flag in the wind he scampered after her. Big Paddy, more reluctantly, followed, turning to look back at the crashing breakers before finally making up his mind and trotting docilely to her. Cathy pulled up the hood of her shabby duffel coat and tightened her scarf. The wind at her back whipped the escaping strands of curling brown hair about her face. The little dog danced about her feet, excited by the wild weather, whilst Paddy ambled behind, sniffing every gorse bush and clump of grass. Cathy battled her way to the top of the beach, where the sandy track back to the cottage began. As she topped the rise the wind was fiercest; a moment later as she and the dogs dropped down into the lee of the dunes the sudden quiet was almost eerie, the air comparatively still. From here, for now, she could no longer see the sea, but its restless, rhythmic crash followed her as she struck inland. There was snow in the wind. The cottage would be warm, and empty, and blessedly quiet; and she had done her working stint for the day. Now she could please herself; crumpets in front of the fire, with the wireless and a book. She smiled to herself as she stuffed the straying hair back into her hood and strode on.

Nikos, long legs stretched to the fire, was half asleep when he heard her coming. He jumped awake as the catch on the door rattled and the door opened a little, held against the wind. 'There you are, Sands – in you go –' a woman's voice. 'I'll just take old Paddy back to Bert. Shan't be a sec. Do try not to make too much mess, you little tripe-hound!' The door slammed shut again.

Nikos leapt from the chair. A scruffy and extremely wet little dog rocketed into the room, shook itself violently, spraying water and sand particles indiscriminately about the place, saw the intruder and immediately showed a set of small, perfect, razor-sharp teeth.

Nervously Nikos backed away. 'Good dog. Good boy –'

Sandy's lip curled further in a far from encouraging way, and he growled in his throat.

'Nice dog,' Nikos said, not very convinced this was the case. His grandmother had always held extremely strong views on what she saw as the risible habit of allowing dogs the free run of a house. She considered even the most inoffensive of them at best a nuisance and at worst a mess-making and destructive health hazard. Nikos had not realised until this moment how much of that attitude had rubbed off on him. 'Good boy.'

Sandy, thoroughly enjoying this unexpected opportunity to show his worth as a guard dog, let go a shrill, hair-raising crescendo of barking.

Discretion overcame valour; Nikos backed carefully through the kitchen door, slamming it firmly shut as the small dog, his dander up with a vengeance, launched himself at it, barking like a mad thing. Nikos listened to the claws that scrabbled furiously at the wood and offered up a small prayer of thanks that his father and stepmother did not favour Alsatians as pets.

A moment later he heard her voice. 'Sandy, for heaven's sake! What are you up to? I could hear you next door!' Cathy stopped. A man's overcoat lay tossed on the sofa. The kitchen door, that she knew she had left open, was fast shut. Sandy, ecstatically overwrought, leapt three feet in the air and dragged his claws down the painted wood. 'Is there someone there?' The question was sharp, but by no means frightened. 'Sandy – come here! This minute!' There was a

small silence. 'That's better. Now, do as you're told and stay!'
She lifted her voice. 'You can come out. He won't hurt you
unless I tell him to.'

Very gingerly Nikos opened the door. She stood, severe
and attentive, damp curling hair tangled about her head,
shapeless wet duffel coat steaming in the heat of the fire. The
dog, panting, sat by her stockinged feet; her Wellingtons lay
discarded by the door. Sandy shifted a little, growling deep in
his throat. She nudged him with her foot. 'Shut up, Sands.'

'I'm sorry,' Nikos said, watching the animal warily, his
hand still prudently holding the door, 'the door was on the
latch. I hoped you wouldn't mind –?'

Her face had changed. Her eyes, wide and oddly slanted,
had lit to a startled smile. 'Nikos! It *is* Nikos, isn't it?'

'I'm afraid so.' Nikos was diffident. 'I'm sorry – I guess
you weren't expecting me –'

'Nikos!' she said again. 'What on earth? Oh, Sandy, do
belt up! Nobody believes you, you daft animal!' The dog
had taken the opportunity to shrill into frenzied barking
again. 'It's a friend.' She hunkered down to him, hand affectionately on the ruff of his neck. She shook him a little.
'Enough!'

'He had me convinced,' Nikos said.

The dog subsided. Flickered a last glance at Nikos. Licked
Cathy's hand.

She stood up, smiling a wide, sudden, open smile. 'He
wouldn't hurt you. Honestly. He doesn't know how. But he
makes a good show, doesn't he?'

'He sure does.' The words were heartfelt. Still a little warily Nikos stepped into the room. She came to him, took his
hands and, very easily, brushed his cheek with her lips.
'Welcome. Where's Leon?'

He looked at her blankly.

'Leon.' She cocked her head amusedly. 'Your father. My
husband. I assume he came with you?' Then in sudden
uncertainty, 'He is with you?'

He shook his head. 'No. I'm sorry. I – don't know where he is.'

She looked at him for what seemed a very long time. Then she took a breath, slow and quiet. 'Don't tell me. He didn't meet you off the boat?' The inflection of the words was only barely questioning.

Nikos shook his head again.

She sighed once more, exasperatedly, turned to pull a heavy curtain across the door against the fierce draught. 'Oh, Lord, that man! I *knew* I should have –' she stopped, shaking her head.

'The boat docked late last night, as scheduled,' Nikos said. 'There was no sign of Pa. I waited till midmorning this morning and then called the London office –'

'And Miss Hooper didn't know where he was?'

'No. She wasn't too sure where he might be, or when he'd be back. She couldn't suggest anything but for me to get my luggage stored in Southampton and make my own way here. So that's what I did. I'm sorry – since there's no telephone here I couldn't warn you. Miss – Hooper did you say her name is? – said she'd tell Pa when he came back from wherever he's disappeared to . . .'

She had picked up a long poker and was stirring the fire back into life. She straightened. She was smiling, but like the smile her voice was strained. 'Leon can be so infuriating. The man never lets anyone know where he is! Oh, Nikos – I'm so sorry – he must have got held up –'

'Or he forgot.' Despite his best efforts Nikos himself could hear how forlorn and childish that sounded. He bit his lip .

'Oh, no! Of course not!' She shook her head, gently scolding, and reached to touch his arm. 'Of course not!' she repeated, quietly. 'Nikos, you know your father. The words "a law unto himself" were coined for him! And he is a very busy man. It's terribly difficult to keep up with him. I can't do it – I've given up trying. I sometimes think he can't keep up with himself.' She was drifting about the room, half-heartedly

tidying as she went. 'There's so much happening – the business expanding – the house in Greece – you know how he
is – he's so full of energy, he gets so utterly involved with
whatever it is that he's engaged in at any one time that I truly
believe he sometimes doesn't know what day of the week it is!
He has absolutely no sense of time: he just expects the world to
fall into step with him. He does it over and over again. A couple of weeks ago he was supposed to come home for the
weekend and he simply didn't turn up. When he did – three
days later – it was in Athens at some meeting or other. Poor
Miss Hooper – who's a brick if there ever was one – didn't
know where he was then, either. We've both given up worrying about him I'm afraid.' She was aware she was overdoing it;
but the gleam of misery in the boy's eyes had touched her to
the quick. Damn Leon and his bloody selfishness! How could
he hurt the boy like this, and at such a time? She smiled a little,
trying to lighten the atmosphere. 'I blame it on his war. He
seems to have this urgent need to remain incommunicado at
all times. You'd think he'd never heard of the telephone. And
as for putting pen to paper –' She glanced about the room,
upon which her efforts, such as they were, had made little
impact, and gestured vaguely. 'Oh, dear. I do wish I had
known you were coming. I'd have tidied the place up a bit. I'm
afraid Sandy and I get a little sloppy here on our own.'

'Don't be silly.' He smiled a slow, shy smile. 'It's nice,' he
said, and was quite surprised to discover that he meant it.
'It's very different. I like it.'

She could not resist sudden laughter. 'How very diplomatic of you.' She looked at him, keenly. 'You don't have to
pretend, you know. I know it must be a bit of a shock. It's in
the middle of nowhere, it isn't anything like what you've
been used to, it's messy to boot and the weather's awful.
This part of the world is a bit of an acquired taste at the best
of times. I'm sorry, I really am. A couple of days in London
with Leon to acclimatise yourself and get the lie of the land
would have been better.'

He smiled again, and again her heart went out to him in sympathy. 'I guess.'

'No guessing about it. I'm actually amazed that you found me at all. This place isn't exactly on the beaten track.'

The smile widened, still shy but responding to her spontaneous warmth. 'I'm real proud of myself, actually. A New Yorker on the loose. Trains and buses and instructions from the local shop and here I am – well –' he pulled a wry face, 'I suppose I have to include the old guy next door in that.'

'Oh, dear.' The simple words were heartfelt. She could not contain her amusement. 'You've met Bert? Honestly – you have to take my word for it – he isn't as bad as he seems. He takes delight in appearing disagreeable, but he's a good friend. I'm very fond of him.'

Sandy had decided that his duty was done. He ambled to Nikos, sniffed his trousers, settled himself proprietorially on his foot.

Cathy dumped a pile of sketches on to a small desk, clearing a space on a table by the fire. 'Do you like crumpets?'

He looked at her blankly. Her hair was drying, curling untidily as it did so. There was, he noticed, a small streak of silver over her left temple. 'Crumpets,' he repeated. 'I – don't know. I don't think I've ever had them.'

She picked up a long toasting fork from the hearth and handed it to him. 'Then now's a good time to start, don't you think? You toast, and I'll butter.'

'You're very like your mother,' she said, later, looking at him thoughtfully over the rim of her teacup.

He glanced at her, surprised. His own cup of tea stood barely tasted beside him. Not even two heaped teaspoons of sugar had made the stuff anywhere near palatable.

'I've seen photographs,' she said gently, in explanation. 'She was very beautiful.'

'Yes. She was.' He was suddenly still, the remarkable eyes veiled. *The shouts, the screams. The smell of his father's blood. The taste of his tears.* Abruptly he reached into his pocket. 'Do you mind if I smoke?'

She shook her head. 'Of course not. No, thank you,' she added as he offered her a silver cigarette case, 'I don't.' She cast a not unsympathetic glance at the cooling tea. 'I'm sorry I haven't got any coffee. I'll get some next time I'm in Aldburgh. I can try the village shop, but I don't hold out much hope.'

'Oh, please – you mustn't let me put you out . . .' He was awkward again, a gauche child on his best behaviour in a stranger's house.

'It's no trouble.'

He smiled, tiredly. 'I liked the crumpets.'

'Well, there you are, then. We'll make an Englishman of you yet. Next thing you know you'll be talking about the weather.' Sobering she leaned to him and touched his arm. 'Nikos, I truly don't know how to say this – but I am so very sorry. About your grandmother. I know from Leon how very close to her you were.'

He turned his head sharply from her, looked into the fire. The dull ache of grief was always there, ready to be stirred fiercely to pain.

'It's all been a dreadful upheaval for you.'

He shrugged.

'Do you mind?'

Still he would not meet her eyes. 'Mind?' he asked.

'That your father sent for you.'

The limpid eyes turned to her at last. 'What else would I do?' he asked, simply. 'I had nowhere else to go. After *Ghiaghia* –' he stopped, swallowed, '– after Grandmother died –' he struggled for a moment and could not go on. He looked back at the fire, but not before she had seen the glint of tears.

There was a long moment of quiet. Cathy put her cup down and stood up. 'Well,' she said, briskly, 'why don't I show you your room? You must be exhausted. Try to get some rest before supper. The room's Adam's actually – my son's – like the proverbial bad penny he turns up from time to time so I always keep it ready. There are some clothes of his you can borrow if you'd like – you're much the same stamp.' She led the way to a wooden door, that opened on to a steep little stairway. 'Careful. It's a bit dark.'

He picked up his bag and followed her up the stairs and into a fair-sized bedroom. The wind buffeted at the window, rattling the panes and the bright curtains moved in the draught. The room was furnished simply; a sturdy old wardrobe, a chest of drawers on which stood a couple of photo frames and a flowered china jug and bowl, a big, comfortable-looking bed covered with a soft, rose-coloured eiderdown. Book shelves, heavily laden, lined one wall and a battered cricket bat was propped in one corner. The curtains were flowered in rose and blue and there was a large rug of the same colours on the polished floor. A fire lay ready laid in the tiny cast-iron grate. His stepmother struck a match and set it to the newspaper. In a moment wood and coal were crackling and scented smoke curled up the chimney. 'I'm sorry. You must find it all a bit primitive,' she said.

'It's charming.' He felt suddenly and overwhelmingly weary. Outside, an early darkness was falling.

Cathy laughed a little. 'Not the word Adam would use, I'm afraid. My son thinks I'm mad not to sell and move somewhere more civilised – by which he means London, of course. Your father, as I'm sure you know, feels much the same, though he indulges me.' She watched as he put his bag on the bed. 'Nikos – do you mind? About Leon and me?' She shrugged a little. 'I'm sorry. That's not very diplomatic, is it? But I'm no good at beating about the bush.'

'Mind? Why should I mind?' Again he was avoiding her eyes.

'Leon told me that your grandmother was upset. That we married so suddenly. That we didn't invite you.' She watched him for a moment. 'It may seem odd – it was odd,

I suppose – but we didn't invite anyone. Not even Adam. It was my fault. I –' she spread her hands, 'I didn't want a fuss. It was the second time for both of us. I just felt it was an intensely personal thing. It was very selfish, I see that now. I didn't mean to upset anyone, I promise.'

'It doesn't matter.' It had at the time. It had mattered very much indeed. It had been the beginning of an estrangement all the worse for not being openly acknowledged. 'It was a long time ago.'

'Four years,' she said. Four years. Four strange and often turbulent years since she had finally – and against her better judgement – succumbed to Leon's ardent and single-minded pursuit of her. Four years, and in truth she knew him no better now than she had then. And now, here was the son, so unlike the father, through no fault of his own disturbing her peace and invading her precious privacy – she knew the thought to be unworthy, tried to stifle it. Where the devil *was* Leon that he hadn't met the poor boy and taken him to London as had been planned? The man was impossible; self-centred and unreliable. Sympathy for this young lost soul easily overcame the small stirrings of resentment. 'Rest a while,' she said, 'I'll be downstairs if you need anything. Perhaps you'd like to come down for a drink later?'

'That would be nice. Thank you.'

Was he always so wearingly polite? She thought of her own son's casual and cheerful offhandedness and wondered, not for the first time, why the young always had to be so extreme. 'There are some woollies and some heavy trousers in the wardrobe. I'm sure Adam won't mind if you borrow them. They'll be warmer and more comfortable for you. It's a bit late now, but tomorrow, if you'd like you can take a bath. It's in the kitchen –' She laughed at his startled expression. 'I know it sounds primitive, but you'll see. It's less uncivilised than it sounds, and since the electricity arrived last year a great deal less than it was!'

'I'm sure it is.'

She hesitated at the door. 'Is there anything I can get you now?'

He lifted his head. His smooth olive-skinned face looked suddenly drawn, the extraordinary eyes were tired and red-rimmed. 'No, thank you.' She had turned to leave when he added, 'I'm sorry – it's silly I know but I don't know what to call you.'

She smiled over her shoulder. 'As you know, I'm Catherine. Leon calls me Kati. Everyone else – even Adam – calls me Cathy, though he will occasionally resort to "Ma" under stress. So why not make it "Cathy", since I don't somehow fancy "Step-ma"? Now – get some rest. I'll see you later. Supper will be about eight.'

She left the room quietly. Nikos sat quite still for a long time, listening to the wind and to the crackle of the fire.

Where the hell was his father? Why hadn't he been at Southampton to meet him as he had promised? What was he *doing* alone in this God-forsaken place? Why had things changed so terribly? Why couldn't they have stayed as they were?

Once again the anguished grief and homesickness, that in his stepmother's presence he had stubbornly held at bay, rose in a wave that this time engulfed him entirely.

In weary misery he buried his face in his hands, and his shoulders shook.

Chapter Two

Nikos woke the next morning to an eerie silence and a heavy head, that thumped painfully as he rolled on his side to look at the clock.

Ten o' clock.

'Christ!' He sat up. Winced. Rubbed his forehead, hard. He shouldn't drink whisky. He knew it. He especially shouldn't drink whisky when he was tired and emotional.

'You might as well have another,' Cathy had said, watching him sympathetically and nursing her own small drink. 'It might help you to sleep.' And so he had, and it had. And now he regretted it, in spades.

He swung his legs over the side of the bed and pulled himself to a sitting position before hauling himself gingerly to his feet and crossing to the window to open the curtains. Dense fog billowed to the panes, drifting ominously around the house, writhing through the bare boughs of the trees. In contrast to the wild wind of the day before, the air was still, and dank. Everything was sodden; water dripped from leaf and branch. Through the shifting, murky veil he glimpsed the sheen of the waters of the marshes that lay behind the house. 'Sandlings is a water-house with a vengeance,' Cathy had said the night before, smiling. 'The sea in front and the marshes behind. It's one of the things I love about it.'

He had watched her curiously. 'What about the Greek house?' he had asked. 'When it's finished will you and Pa live there?'

The curl of her eyelashes had hidden the expression in her eyes as she looked down into her glass. 'Some of the time, I expect.' Her voice had been cool, neutral. 'I don't want to give up my own life entirely.' Her glance had flickered to his and then away 'The painting may not pay much but I do love it. And my publishers are in London . . .'

He had already seen and admired the sketches she had done in preparation for the children's book that she had been commissioned to illustrate. 'So you won't sell this house?'

'No.' The word was swift, almost sharp. She softened it with a quick smile. 'No, I won't. My grandfather left it to me. I've always loved it. It's my home.'

As, despite what happened there – perhaps even because of it – the Greek house is Pa's. He had not spoken the words aloud. Resting his aching forehead on the window and staring through the wraith-like trees to that glint of water he thought now, as he had thought several times since his arrival, how strangely mismatched his volatile and quintessentially Greek father and this English wife of his appeared to be. Artistic, cheerfully and openly disorganised, apparently utterly self-sufficient, she seemed to care little or nothing for those things that Nikos knew had become his father's icons; power, position, money; the drive to succeed. Leon Kotsikas had lost everything in the war: a beloved wife, most of his family, his home and at the end very nearly his own life. Nikos still possessed the letter his father had sent him from the hospital in England where he had been recovering from wounds sustained in fighting the communists who had been trying through armed revolution to impose Red rule upon Greece. *'One day this war will end. One day Greece will be whole again, and free. And I will rebuild, from*

*the ruins, our home and our family, and our name will be strong
again –'* He knew the words by heart.

'Huh!' his American grandmother had said, drily dismissive, *'Greek histrionics! He was born a peasant, and he will die
one.'* Even three years after the death of her much-loved only
daughter she still could not forgive the man whom – quite
unjustifiably, Nikos knew – she held responsible. She had
never cared for her son-in-law.

Nikos straightened, shivering a little. Christ, it was cold!
He slipped his shirt on, picked up the trousers and jumper
he had left on the floor the night before. He pulled them on,
pushed the sleeves of the jumper up to his elbows; Cathy
had been right, he and Adam must certainly be of a height,
though it seemed that Cathy's son was broader in the shoulder. He glanced at a photograph that stood on the dressing
table, of a handsome, smiling, fair-haired young man of
about his own age. He picked it up, studying it. There was,
so far as he could see, little of Cathy about him apart from
the thick and untameable hair, so presumably he took after
his father. She had told him a little last night; Adam's father
had been killed in one of the last German raids on London in
1944, leaving Cathy with a fifteen-year-old boy to bring up
alone. She had brought him here, to Suffolk, until the war
had ended the following year and had then sold the London
house to finance his education and to supplement her own
income. Adam worked in the City – his mother was vague
about his exact occupation – 'He changes jobs so often it's
hard to keep up with him. But he seems to make a lot of
money.' She had pulled a small, smiling face '– and spends it
as fast. Shades of his father!'

Nikos sighed and put the photograph down. Earning a
living; another problem to be faced. The one thing he had
not been sorry to leave behind was his job in New York; a
mundane nine-to-five clerical post in a large bank that had
kept the wolf from the door but had not exactly inspired or
stimulated. He now had the small inheritance left to him by

his grandmother and he had hoped that this would give him the chance to decide for himself what to do for a living. But his father – forceful, flamboyant and rarely one to take into account anyone's opinion but his own – had simply assumed that he would join him in the business he had set up a few years earlier. Some people, Nikos supposed, would jump at the chance; the business seemed to be extremely successful and was expanding all the time; Leon's latest venture was into shipping, his reason being, he said, characteristically, that he was tired of relying on others to transport Kotsikas cargoes. Grief-stricken and lonely after his grandmother's death Nikos had not argued. Now he half wished he had. Now, too late, he was beginning to question his own weakness in allowing the father he had not seen in ten years to order his life as if he were the child that Leon still apparently thought him. He, Nikos, was an American citizen, his American grandmother had seen to that. He could have stayed in the land of his adoption, his mother's land, and ignored or defied his father's high-handed decision that it was time for him to join the business that bore his name. But though Nikos' nationality was American his blood was Greek and the call of the family was strong. So he had returned.

And his father had not been there to meet him.

He glanced out of the window again at the fog, that seemed to be getting thicker with each passing moment, at the dripping trees, the untidy, sodden garden. His head was still hammering. And there wasn't any coffee.

He sat on the bed, pushed his feet into his shoes, lifting his foot on to a chair to tie the laces so as to avoid bending too far and having the top of his head come off altogether.

Cathy was in the kitchen, making bread, the wireless playing quietly beside her. This was one of the few domestic chores she really loved. The kitchen was warm and peaceful. Sandy was stretched companionably with his back to the comfort of

the range. With tranquil patience she kneaded and turned
the smooth dough. She acknowledged it as a failing, but she
knew she was quite simply incapable of doing nothing. She
had never acquired the knack of total inactivity. The moment
her hands were not occupied her tiresome brain took over,
and could occasionally put her through hoops far more
wearing than physical exercise. This simple, mindless, pro-
ductive activity was to her, like walking with the dogs, or
pottering in the garden, the very essence of relaxation.
Mozart helped. The music, measured and beautiful, filled
her mind and washed it clear of thought. The fog beyond the
window stood between her and the world, halting the eye
and deadening sound, mysterious, ghostly. The house could
have been floating in cloud. She loved these East Coast fogs,
that crept so stealthily from the sea, that enveloped and isolated the cottage. She had never, even as a child, been afraid
of darkness; had always, indeed, considered it to be posi-
tively friendly. It was light that was the danger; if no one
could see you what possible danger could there be? You
could hide in the fog.

Leon, bred in warmth and in sunshine, hated it of course.

She sighed, her hands for a moment stilled, the moment
spoiled. Where the hell was he? Why – *why*? – hadn't he met
his poor, brave, bewildered son off the boat as he had
promised he would? How could one man combine in his
character the exasperating and contradictory extremes that
Leon could? Kindness and cruelty. Compassion and cavalier
indifference to the feelings of others. Passionate loyalty and
cold-blooded self-interest. The man was impossible. And at
the same time hopelessly engaging. No one knew that better
than Cathy, and she would not deny it. She had succumbed
herself to his charm that heady summer five years ago when,
convalescing at a nursing home in nearby Aldburgh he had
met her, decided almost upon the instant and despite her
protestations that she was to marry him, pursued her with
that single-minded resolution that she now knew to be

inherent in him, and within four months had made her his wife. Not so much a whirlwind romance, she had often told herself later, a little wryly, more a tornado. They had had a blissful and passionate ten days' honeymoon at the cottage ending in a single and spectacular quarrel during which she had proved that, when direly provoked, she had a temper to match his, and he had performed the first of his disappearing acts, simply walking out of the house and coming back two weeks later with a huge bunch of roses, a bottle of Champagne, no apology whatsoever and the news that he had used the small sum she had lent him when they had married to set up in business in London. Since the subject of the row had been her firmly reiterated refusal to leave Suffolk and move to the capital – a stand she had taken from the start but which he had, despite promises, arbitrarily expected her to relinquish once she had become his wife – she had expected further trouble, but it had not come. 'You are right, *koukla mou*,' he had said, kissing her, 'as you always are. London is no place for you. You stay here. You stay where you are happy. It breaks my heart. You know it.' He had grinned widely, black eyes dancing, 'But think – each time I return –' a great, wide-shouldered man with the muscles of a wrestler he had swept her into his arms as if she had been a child and kissed her again, '– we have a new honeymoon!'

She put the smooth, elastic dough into a large bowl, covered it with a damp cloth and set it at the back of the stove to rise. Almost without thinking she reached for the kettle. With tea off the ration at last there need be no scraping and saving and re-using the sodden dregs from the teapot; another small sign that life was truly getting back to normal. She set the kettle on the hotplate, turned and leaned comfortably against the warm range, looking out pensively into the drifting fog.

She had come much later to the conclusion that Leon's change of heart had been dictated more by shrewd practicalities than by any desire to indulge her. He had swiftly realised, she suspected, that whilst he was involved in the enterprising and cutthroat business of making money the fewer people who knew exactly where he was and what he was doing the better, and that included his unnervingly honest wife. Not that he didn't love her; he did, she knew it. It was odd that, even after all that had happened since, she knew it still. Even after the broken promises, the long absences, the other women, she knew he loved her. The strange and unhappy thing was that she was no longer sure that she loved him, or even if she ever truly had. Oh, she was fond of him and, yes, she was still attracted to him physically. Most women were. Even now, at fifty, Leon Kotsikas had about him an almost animal energy that was impossible to ignore and hard to resist. She turned to take the steaming kettle from the range, smiling a little grimly; since his swift and early success many had not tried to resist. Money was the greatest aphrodisiac of all.

'You're getting cynical in your old age,' she said aloud, shaking her head, pouring the water into the warmed teapot.

'I – beg your pardon?'

She turned, startled. Nikos stood in the doorway, leaning against the doorjamb, his dark hair rumpled, his eyelids drooping. Her artist's eye noted, as it had from the first, the extraordinary and quite unstudied grace of the boy. A heart-breaker, this one, if ever she'd seen one. Yet, oddly and rather endearingly he did not himself seem to know it. She laughed at his question. 'I'm sorry. It's a terrible habit. I'm afraid I talk to myself. Out loud. Everyone tells me it's the first step on the road to lunacy. They're probably right.'

He grinned and shook his head. Winced a little. 'Oh, I'm sure not.'

She surveyed him, trying not to show that her sympathy was tinged with amusement. 'Oh, dear. Is it bad?'

He blinked as if thinking about it.

She reached for the kettle again. 'I know you don't like tea. But try it weak, and black, just for now. As soon as the fog lifts a bit I'll pop down to the village shop. They must have something approximating coffee.'

'Oh, no – please – I really don't want you to put yourself out – you've been so kind already –'

'Don't be silly. I need to go to the Post Office anyway. They keep my letters for me – it doesn't seem fair to drag the postman all the way out here, and Bert never gets any mail – Leon just might have deigned to drop us a note and tell us where he is –' she paused as he dropped his gaze from hers. 'Oh, Nikos, please don't. I told you last night you mustn't take it personally. There's an explanation. You wait and see.'

'I guess,' he said. But he did not sound convinced.

The fog lifted around lunchtime, though the day was grey and very overcast and mist still shrouded the heathland.

'I wish you'd let me go,' Nikos said for at least the fourth time as Cathy wound her long woollen scarf about her neck.

'Don't be silly. You snuggle up and have a snooze around the fire. I'll be back in no time.'

'But –'

'But nothing.' She pushed him gently into a chair. 'Just do as you're told. I won't be long.'

In truth it was a relief to step out of the house alone and, having ascertained that Bert did not want her to pick anything up from the shop for him, to set off up the sandy lane towards the bicycle. 'Shape up, girl,' she scolded herself. 'You're in danger of becoming some kind of bloody recluse! The poor boy can't help it – it isn't his fault if his father's a thoughtless self-centred sod.' She grinned a little. There were advantages to talking aloud. In her time as a nurse in a military hospital during and for some time after the war she had picked up a vocabulary she rarely used in public but that afforded her, just occasionally, the most enormous and succinct satisfaction in private. She tossed her purse into the basket, clambered aboard the bicycle and wobbled down the lane, the heavy machine taking a moment or so to right itself.

Once steady however, its very weight carried it on down the slight slope. She took her feet off the pedals and stuck her legs out straight, laughing like a girl. *'I'm singin' in the rain – da de da de da de da –'* She was still humming to herself as she turned, more decorously, into the lane that led to the village. 'Afternoon, Mrs Burton.' The woman, waiting at a bus stop, nodded a dour greeting. Cathy could feel her eyes follow her down the road; she resisted the sore temptation to take her feet off the pedals and sing again.

The small shop was empty. 'Afternoon, Mrs Hamilton.'

'A'ternoon.'

'Coffee,' Cathy said. 'Do you have some coffee?'

'Got some somewhere. Don't get much call . . .' Mrs Hamilton, a large lady with tightly crimped grey hair rummaged on a shelf, turned with a bottle in her hand. 'This'd be fer the young man, would it?'

'Er –' Cathy eyed the bottle uncertainly. 'Yes. That is – I'm not sure this is exactly –'

'Tha'ss all there is,' Mrs Hamilton said, stolidly. 'Oh, an' there's a letter, come this mornin'.'

'Thank you.' Cathy picked up the bottle. Coffee and chicory. Oh, dear. 'Better than nothing I suppose,' she said.

'Pardon?' Mrs Hamilton emerged from behind the Post Office counter carrying an envelope.

'Nothing. Talking to myself. Terrible habit.'

The woman's eyes wrinkled into a small, sly smile. 'You know what they say –?'

'Yes,' Cathy said, cheerfully, 'I do.' She took the envelope and looked at it. Not Leon's writing, but Adam's. She paid for the coffee, took it outside, put it in the basket and tore open the envelope. She read the single page in a glance, let out a small, explosively exasperated breath and read it again. 'Oh, Lord.' She opened her purse, rummaged in it for pennies and pulled open the heavy door of the telephone box that stood outside the shop.

*

'What do you mean he's got my bedroom?' This seemed to have been the first thing that she'd said actually to engage Adam's interest. In the background she could hear a hubbub of activity, a buzz of voices, some laughter.

'What I say. I've had to put him in your room. Oh, don't be daft, Adam – where else could I have put him?'

'But he'll be gone by the weekend.' The words were couched as a statement rather than a question.

'How do I know? I've no idea where Leon is or when he'll be back – he could be in Greece, or New York or Timbuktu for all I know! You don't propose that I should throw poor Nikos out on the street, do you?'

'There are hotels, aren't there?'

'Adam!'

'Oh – I'm sorry, Ma. It's just that I really did want to see you –'

'Why the sudden rush?' She did not realise quite how sharply she had said it until the silence at the other end of the line lasted just a little too long. 'Adam?'

'It just seems ages since I've seen you, that's all. And I could do with a bit of a rest.' The nonchalance was, possibly deliberately, overdone.

'Why? What's the matter?' Motherly concern overcame irritation.

'Nothing. Just a bit tired, that's all. There's a lot going on. I can't often seem to get away.' He let the words sink in before adding, 'But don't worry. It doesn't matter.'

'Couldn't you make it the weekend after next?'

"fraid not. I'm booked up. And the following one too.'

She wavered. 'We-ell – I suppose –'

'Couldn't this Nikos sleep in the sitting room?'

Couldn't you? She left the words unsaid. It was, after all, as Adam had already pointed out, his room. 'I suppose he could.'

'You do want me to come, don't you?'

'Of course I do. It's just that – darling, it's Thursday

already! I just wish you'd given me a little more notice, that's all.'

This time the silence was noticeably hurt. 'You've always told me,' her son said quietly, 'that Sandlings was my home.'

'It is! Of course it is! Whenever you want it –'

'– providing I give you notice.'

'No!' She had lived with Adam's father for long enough to know that, not necessarily intentionally, she was being manipulated; but this was Adam, her Adam, and there was nothing she could do about it.

In the background she heard someone call Adam's name. 'A minute,' he called back, and then into the phone, 'look, sorry, I'm going to have to go.'

'So – are you coming at the weekend?'

'If it's OK.'

'Of course it is. If Nikos hasn't left by then I can make up a bed for him downstairs.'

'Fine. I'll see you sometime Saturday morning. Got to go – 'bye, Mum.'

''Bye, Adam.' The phone was already dead. She held it for a moment, looking sightlessly at the printed instructions as to what to do with Button 'A' and Button 'B'.

She loved Adam dearly.

And she knew him too well.

She wished the suspicion were not strengthening by the moment that his desire to see her so suddenly and so urgently might have as much to do with money as with filial devotion. It had happened before.

She sighed a little, pondering, then as she turned to leave, more in hope than expectation, pressed Button 'B'. Nothing happened. 'OK,' she said, with a shrug. 'It was worth a try.'

Sandy greeted her, as usual, with hysteria. Nikos came from the kitchen, opened his mouth to speak. Cathy forestalled him. 'I know, I'm sorry I've been longer than I said – there was a letter from Adam and I had to ring him from the phone box. I'm sorry – I hope you don't mind – he wants to come down for the weekend. It means you'll have to sleep on the floor for a couple of nights – oh, here's the coffee –' she pulled a rueful face as she handed it to him '– it's that awful stuff with chicory I'm afraid, but it was all they had. Thinking about it you'll probably hate it even more than the tea. Oh, Sandy, do calm down! You're enough to try the patience of a saint sometimes!' She straightened. 'Trust Adam to jump this on me with no notice! We're going to be a bit of a houseful I'm afraid.' She laughed a little, 'All we need now is for Leon to turn up –' She stopped.

Nikos' face was a picture. There was a small silence. Then he stepped back and pushed the kitchen door wide open. Cathy stared. The table was heaped untidily with boxes and bags, all of them inscribed with the famous name of Fortnum and Mason. There was a crate of wine, two bottles of whisky and a magnum of Champagne. Beside the Champagne rested two exquisitely wrapped small parcels.

Cathy looked at Nikos.

He nodded, half-apologetically. 'He has,' he said. He hefted the bottle of coffee in his hand and shrugged. 'He arrived about ten minutes after you left.'

She looked around. 'But – I didn't see a car. Where is he?'

Nikos' grin was sudden and infectious. 'He's gone into Aldburgh,' he said. 'To buy some real coffee.'

Leon came back an hour or so later bringing not only coffee but a huge bouquet of flowers for Cathy, a bone for Sandy that was almost as big as the dog himself, a carton of Nikos' favourite cigarettes and an enormous heavy knitted jumper of the kind the local fishermen wore. He swept into the house laughing, kissed Cathy fiercely, sent Nikos reeling with a friendly slap on the back and dumped the things he was carrying on to the already precarious pile on the kitchen table.

Cathy stood at the door watching him, unable despite her

best efforts to prevent laughter. 'Leon! Where on earth have you *been*? '

He took off the jacket of his suit, threw it carelessly on to Sandy's dog-haired chair, reached for the pullover. 'Later. I tell you later. First things first –' he hauled the garment over his head and emerged, his strongly springing silvering hair tousled, grinning. 'Always I forget how bloody cold this place is. Is a nightmare.'

'It's healthy,' she said. 'And tell us now. I know your "laters".'

He spread his hands innocently, looking beyond her to Nikos. 'You see how she nags me?'

'*Leon* –'

'Later,' he said firmly. 'I told Nikos. It wasn't my fault. I radioed a message to the ship. He did not receive it. I shall make enquiries. No harm is done – he is here. Now –' His dark face lit again. He rummaged amongst the things on the table and pulled out the two wrapped presents. 'Here.' He tossed one over Cathy's head to Nikos, who caught it one-handed, then reached for Cathy's hand drawing her towards him. 'For you, my Kati,' he said, and kissed her cheek.

She took the proffered package. 'A Greek –' she said, lightly '– bearing gifts.'

He threw his huge head back and laughed expansively. 'No need to beware of me, *koukla mou*. Open your present.'

Nikos had come to the door behind them. In his hand he held a gold watch, the bracelet glittering even in the dull November light. 'Pa. It's just great. But – you really shouldn't have –'

'Why not? I can't greet my son with a gift?'

'But such a gift! It must have cost a bomb!'

Leon shrugged.

Cathy stood, turning the pretty package over in her hand. 'Open it.'

The watch was exquisite, with a tiny, beautifully marked face, the casing studded with small diamonds, and a narrow

gold bracelet. The catch too was set with diamonds, a delicate masterpiece in itself. 'It's beautiful,' she said.

'Yes.' Leon beamed. 'I think so. Like my Kati. Put it on.'
She unbuckled the worn leather strap of the plain and work-
manlike watch she always wore and laid it on the table.

Leon took the new watch and slipped it about her wrist,
fastened the delicate catch, the large, spatulate fingers surprisingly deft. 'It's really beautiful,' she repeated, quietly,
and kissed him, softly.

'You like it?' The power of his personality was focused
for a moment entirely upon her, his eyes bright with the
pleasure of giving. 'You like it, truly? There was another – if
you prefer –?'

'No. No, I really do like it.' She dropped another light kiss
on his cheek. 'Thank you.'

He turned, picked up one of the bottles of Champagne.
'So! Now we celebrate! Being together at last. The three of
us –'

'Ah,' Cathy said.

Leon lifted bushy brows. '"Ah"? What's this "ah"?'

She laughed. 'This "ah" is Adam. There was a letter at the
Post Office this afternoon. I spoke to him on the phone. He
wanted to come down for the weekend. I said yes. I'm sorry,
I didn't realise –'

Leon let out a roar of laughter that Cathy thought just
might have been audible in the village shop. 'So we're sar-
dines in a can? So what? Good! It will perhaps keep us
warm! And I was going to talk to Adam anyway. I have
some ideas. We can do business, I think –'

Cathy took breath to speak, but did not. 'Ah,' she said
again, with dry and different emphasis.

Leon tapped the side of his nose with his finger. 'He has a
brain, your Adam. And he has some contacts I might find
useful. It will be good to talk.'

'I'm sure it will.' Cathy went to a cupboard and produced
three glasses. 'I'm sorry – they don't match, and they aren't

exactly delicate. But I guess the Champagne will taste just as
good.'

'*Christos!*' Leon was laughing again. 'No Champagne
glasses? I bring some from London next time I come.'

'For heaven's sake, Leon, don't be so silly. What would I
do here with Champagne glasses?'

The cork popped. Leon carefully poured the foaming,
sparkling liquid into the bizarre assortment of glasses, one a
tumbler. His dark and intent eyes met Cathy's. 'Life is going
well, *koukla mou*,' he said, softly. 'There will be more
Champagne, I think.'

'If there is we can drink it as well from these as anything,'
she said, equably, and raised her glass. 'To you both. And to
the future.' She glanced at Nikos. 'A new start,' she said,
with an impulsive, smiling warmth. 'I do hope you'll be
happy with us.'

There was a small, oddly awkward moment of silence.
She cocked her head in characteristic way, looking directly
into his eyes. 'Nikos?'

'Yes,' he said, and lifted his own glass to hers. 'I'm sure I
will be.'

Early on Saturday morning Leon picked Adam up from
Ipswich, and by the time they got back to the house they
were already talking business. Cathy had laid the big kitchen
table for breakfast and bacon, eggs and sausages were
cooked and waiting on the range. The mouthwatering smell
of fresh bread filled the house.

'Mmm. That smells good.' Her son put an arm about her
shoulders and kissed her.

She smiled and put a hand on his, acknowledging the
greeting. 'Breakfast is ready.' She turned to where Nikos
stood, a little shyly, his back to the window. 'Adam – this is
Nikos, Leon's son.'

'Hi.'

'Hello.' The two young men shook hands. Cathy watched

them, smiling; they made a striking contrast, the one slim and dark, indefinably foreign-looking, the other broad-shouldered and fair, the very image of the Anglo-Saxon. She pulled out a chair. 'Right everyone – breakfast. Sit yourselves down – there's coffee or tea –'

'Kati?' Leon's voice was sharp.

She looked at him in surprise. 'What?'

'Your watch. Where is it?'

She lifted her arm. 'My old one is on my wrist,' she said collectedly, 'and my beautiful new one is where it belongs, safe upstairs on the dressing table, away from cooking and washing-up water and the million and one accidents of everyday life.'

'I wanted you to wear it,' he said, still unsmiling.

'And I shall.' She was coolly soothing. 'On special occasions, as befits such a special thing. Don't be silly, Leon, how can I wear something so delicate and precious every day?'

'I want you to,' he said again, with ominous emphasis.

Nikos, a little alarmed, looked from one to the other. Adam, undisturbed, carved himself a doorstep of bread and spread it thickly with yellow butter.

Cathy's mouth set stubbornly. 'It's my watch. And I don't want to damage it; and you know I would –'

'I buy you another.'

'Leon, *no* –'

Leon grabbed Nikos' hand, none too gently, and held it up. 'Nikos wears his.'

'Nikos doesn't cook, clean, make beds, wash up, cart the coal, walk the dogs and chop the wood,' she snapped. 'Now don't be so ridiculous, Leon. I love the watch, I really do. But this one is much more sensible for everyday wear. Now do stop making such an issue of it. Sit down and eat your breakfast.'

For a moment the air was charged. Then, suddenly, Leon shrugged and laughed in genuine amusement. 'You're stubborn as a mule, woman!'

'So I've been told. I wouldn't know.' She grinned suddenly, the wide, subversive grin that Nikos was coming to realise was so characteristic of her. 'I don't know any mules. Adam – tea or coffee?'

She was at the sink washing up, the three men, plates scraped clean, and mounds of bread and marmalade demolished, sitting about the table with a fresh pot of coffee when the subject of the Greek house came up.

'How's it going?' It was Adam who had brought up the subject. 'Have you been out there lately?'

Leon gestured enthusiastically, almost knocking his cup over. 'Is going very well.' He shrugged, using his big hands expressively to denote a certain reservation. 'There are a few problems, here and there. How could there not be? Building materials are not easy to come by. The men, if I'm not there –' again the expressive hands '– they are Greek. They would rather fish, or tend their olive trees. But I come and I go, they never know when. I praise the good work and the bad I tear down with my own hands and they do it again. I pay them well. And they know me, know how far to go. A good job, I want. A special job. It will be a beautiful house.' Nikos, watching, saw his eyes flicker to Cathy's back. The dishes clattered in the big, chipped butler sink. 'The whole village thinks Leon Kotsikas has taken leave of his senses. A garden I'm making. A garden with flowers, and even with grass. For Kati.' He chuckled. 'No one in the village has such a garden. They ask me: "What is this garden? Can you keep goats in it? Do you grow beans? Can you eat flowers?" I say, "My wife loves flowers. Flowers she shall have."'

Cathy neither turned nor spoke.

'Where is the garden?' Nikos asked. 'Is it down the mountain, on the terraces below the house?'

Leon took his eyes from Cathy's back. 'Yes. That's right.'

'I remember,' Nikos said, softly. 'The view's wonderful.

Out across the valley and with the sea in the distance –' he hesitated. 'Mother used to love that view.'

Cathy's hands stilled in the bowl. Then, resolutely, she scoured another dirty plate.

'Just exactly what are you doing to the house?' Adam reached to pour another cup of coffee.

Leon rested his chin on a huge fist. 'After Nikos' mother – died – Nikos and I had to leave the village. The Germans were after us, the communists too. The house, and its neighbour, stood empty for years, and in any case the Germans had damaged both badly. In Greece a neglected house falls quickly to ruin. It –' he hesitated, searching for the word, '– it decays. The weeds and the vines grow, the walls crumble, the roof falls. And so it was with my house when I returned. It was a simple house, you understand. A village house like all the others. I bought the house next door and I began to repair, and add, making the two into one.' He grinned. 'The village thinks I am rich.' He shrugged a little, enjoying the joke, 'Perhaps I am, a little. So – I add another storey, and a balcony, I turn the animal rooms downstairs into bedrooms – they are the coolest place in the house, for they are buried in the rock of the mountain – I make a kitchen – my Kati will not have to cook outside as the other women do, or take her meat to the oven of the village baker – and I bring the water from the spring into the house –'

'Sounds like quite a project,' Adam said.

'It is my home,' his stepfather said, quietly. 'It was the home of my father, and his father and of many before him. I do it for us and I do it for them. And I do it properly, in the traditional manner, built as the people of my village have always built. It is a symbol.'

Cathy turned slowly, drying her hands on a tea towel. Leon looked at her. 'You'll come to see it soon?' he asked. 'In two months, perhaps three, you will need to decide on the colours you wish.'

'Yes,' she said, her tone utterly noncommittal.

If Leon noticed he said nothing. He leaned back, stretched. 'Nikos – I go to the shop for a paper. You'd like a ride?'

'Sure.' Nikos stood, smiled at Cathy. 'Thank you. That was great.'

She nodded, smiling.

Adam watched as father and son donned jackets and hats and left. Cathy tossed him a tea towel. 'Make yourself useful.'

He stood up and began to wipe the plates, stacking them on the table. 'Do I gather you aren't exactly as enthusiastic about the Greek house as Leon is?'

She sighed. 'It's going to be lovely. I know it is. And the location is utterly beautiful. When I was there last year – when Leon finally brought himself to go back – it was spring. The wild flowers were everywhere. The mountain-sides looked like a garden. There really is a stunning view. And I've seen Leon's plans for the house. It really is going to be very nice.'

'But?'

'You know "but". But I love it here. But this is my home. My life is here.'

'Your life is with your husband. Isn't it?' The words were not entirely unsympathetic.

She did not answer him directly, but cast a quick, questioning look. 'Would you want me to go?'

He did not hesitate. 'Why not? The world's getting smaller every day. Time will come when you're no further from London on a Greek island than buried out here in wildest Suffolk. I honestly don't know how you can stick it out here anyway. Ma, Leon's making lots of money. He can give you a good life. He wants to –'

She turned, studying him, shrewdly. 'Has Leon been talking to you?'

His fair skin had flushed just a little. 'He – did mention it. On the drive from the station.'

'He asked you to persuade me?'

'Not exactly.' He was guarded; he busied himself with the cloth again.

Anger stirred. 'It's my decision, Adam, and I'll make it.'

'You don't have to tell me that.' The words were so rueful that they brought sudden laughter to them both.

She sobered quickly, reached to clear the last things from the table. 'You don't understand. It's not just leaving here. I'd be moving to a different culture, living amongst people I don't know or understand, and who certainly wouldn't know or understand me. Oh, the ones I've met are charming; but then those are Leon's associates, very different, I suspect, to the inhabitants of a village halfway up a mountain on a Greek island. These people don't take kindly to outsiders.'

'I wouldn't have thought that would bother you? You like being alone.'

'There's a difference,' she said quietly, 'between being alone on your own ground and by your own choice and being alone surrounded by strangers. I should have thought even you could have worked that one out. I don't speak the language –'

'You could learn.'

Cathy turned on him. 'Adam, will you stop it! I've told you – it's my business, no one else's.'

'Yours and Leon's I would have thought.' He was gentle.

She was perilously close to temper, not least because, in fairness, she knew he was right. 'It's certainly none of yours!'

He shrugged, picked up the plates and opened a cupboard door. Cathy, hastily, slipped under his arm and closed it again. 'It's all right. I'll put them away.'

'Honestly Ma.' His smile was amused. 'Don't you ever tidy up?'

'Not often.' She was unimpressed. 'Do you?'

He studied her face for a moment. Then, 'Come on, Sandy,' he said to the dog, who had been watching proceedings interestedly from his chair. 'Lets go and get some air in our lungs.' He took a heavy jacket from the back of the door. The dog was down in a bound and at the door, tail wagging, head cocked, bright eyes on Adam's face. Adam turned back to Cathy. 'You married Leon, Ma.'

She said nothing.

'He's a great bloke. And he works like a Trojan –'

'Don't tell him that,' she said, quick and dry. 'He might try to sell you a horse.'

'Don't be clever,' he said. 'You know what I mean. Leon's been through a hell of a lot. I just feel he deserves your support, that's all.'

She was silent for a long moment. 'He really has got to you, hasn't he?' she asked at last, her eyes puzzled.

'Nope.' He opened the door and cold air swirled around the warm kitchen. The dog shot out like a bullet from a gun. 'I just think you should give it some serious consideration, that's all. Seems to me that most women would jump at the chance.'

'I'm not –!' she stopped, gritting her teeth.

'All right. I know. You aren't most women.'

She was certain that the trace of tolerant weariness he allowed to sound in his voice was deliberate; for an awful moment she feared she might slap him, like the graceless child she sometimes perceived him to be. 'Don't you patronise me, Adam Sinclair!'

'I wouldn't dare, Ma,' he said, straightfaced. 'I truly wouldn't dare.' The latch clicked softly and precisely behind him as he closed the door.

She turned to the table, picked up a plate and for a brief and silly second contemplated dropping it on to the unforgiving stone flags. Then, very carefully, she placed it back on the pile. 'Sorry plate,' she said. 'It isn't your fault.' She tilted her head back and quietly addressed a crack in the ceiling. 'Bugger it,' she said conversationally and with what she considered admirable restraint. 'Bloody bugger it.'

Chapter Three

Trouble erupted between Leon and his son as swiftly and unexpectedly as a summer storm can be bred from a clear, warm sky. The first Cathy knew of it was the sound of raised voices in the kitchen as she came in from a Sunday morning stroll through the woods with the dogs. She had delivered Paddy back to his owner and had spent her usual ten minutes humouring the old man's pessimism about the weather, the state of the country and of life in general. She let herself in through the front door still smiling to herself and stopped, listening, surprised. Nikos' voice was raised, passionate and angry.

'Germany? *Germany*? Pa – you've been doing business in Germany? You've been taking German money? I don't – I can't! – believe it!'

Leon's deep voice rumbled; Cathy could not make out the words. She took off her coat, and carrying it over her arm pushed open the door of the kitchen. The three men sat, as she had left them, around the kitchen table. She noted, wryly, that the breakfast dishes had simply been cleared into the big sink and left there. As she entered Leon was saying, 'It's over, Nikos. Over! You can't live your life in the past –' None of the three moved as Cathy pushed open the door. Nikos' dark face had paled, his lucent eyes were blazing with anger.

Adam sat back in his chair, a cigarette held lazily between his fingers, clear blue gaze moving interestedly from father to son and back again.

Nikos came to his feet, the legs of his chair scraping loudly on the flags of the floor. He leaned forward, facing his father, his weight resting on his hands upon the table. 'Over? No, Pa! It isn't over. Have you forgotten? Have you forgotten what they did to us? To our country?' He paused, almost choked with emotion, 'Have you forgotten what they did to Mother?'

This time it was Leon who came to his feet with a roar of anger and a torrent of furious Greek. Adam leaned forward and put his chin on his fist, watching, his face inscrutable. Nikos, in face of his father's fury, blanched further, but held his ground, replying swiftly and shortly in the same language, his face defiant. Leon reached a massive hand across the table and caught his son by the shirt front, hauling him forward. Sandy, excited by the turbulent atmosphere, danced around his legs, barking shrilly.

'Leon! For heaven's sake!' Cathy dropped her coat and caught at Leon's arm. 'Stop it! What on earth's going on? Sandy, do shut up!'

The dog took no notice whatsoever; if anything the frenzy of his barking increased.

Cathy's own nerves had taken quite enough over the past couple of days. She bent to the dog, picked him up by the scruff of the neck and dumped him in his chair. 'Enough!' She turned. 'Leon! Let the boy go. Where the hell do you think you are? In some backstreet bar in Athens?'

There was a long, perilous moment of quiet. Then, slowly, Leon released his grip and straightened. Nikos pushed himself back from the table. Father and son stood eye to eye. Cathy could see that despite his every effort, despite the stubborn lift of his chin, the younger man was trembling. She felt a sudden, overwhelming sympathy. Surely the boy had been through enough recently without this?

Leon, still watching his son, lifted a warning finger. 'Never say that again, boy. Never tell me that I don't remember what happened to your mother. I watched. As you did.'

It was quite deliberately brutal. Nikos shut his eyes for a second. Cathy, looking away from the naked pain in the young face found her attention suddenly caught by Adam. He was still watching intently, his bright, forget-me-not eyes moving from one face to another. His face betrayed nothing.

Leon pressed relentlessly on. 'Your mother, God rest her soul, would be the first to know that life goes on. It's over. It's finished. A new war begins. A war to survive. A war to succeed. A war to show the world that we are not broken. And, yes –' Nikos had opened his mouth to speak, '– I will use any means to win that war. Any means, you understand?' He slipped his hand into the open neck of his shirt and lifted something into the light, something that glinted gold as it swung and turned in his fingers. Cathy was very familiar with the small, weighty medallion that Leon always wore. She knew, too, its provenance. 'Your mother gave me this. It was her last gift to me. You know it well. The Holy Virgin, to protect me. One day it will be yours; it is the thing that binds us to her, the only thing we have of her.' The exquisitely worked miniature golden icon spun and settled, sheened in the quiet light. 'May she strike me dead if I have forgotten what happened!' He let the icon drop, and his fist hit the table with savage force. 'But that isn't the point! It's time you grew up, boy. It's time you were away from the influence of women. Your mother, God rest her, is dead. And so, now, is your Grandmother.' He stabbed a finger forcefully. 'It's time you joined the world of the men. Time you joined me in making the name of Kotsikas a name to be reckoned with. And if that means dealing with Germans – if it means dealing with the devil himself – then you'll do it. And you'll smile while you do it. Is that understood?'

A heavy silence hung in the room.

'Did you hear me?' Leon's voice was suddenly very quiet.

'I heard you.'

'And is it understood?'

Nikos' voice cracked a little as he spoke. 'It's understood.' Blindly he turned and walked to the back door.

Only Cathy, who had moved near to the door, saw the tears. She put out a hand. 'Nikos –' He walked past her. In the quiet the snick of the doorlatch as it shut behind him sounded very loud.

Wordless, Cathy picked up her coat, pushed one arm into a sleeve, struggled into the other, reached for a heavy jacket that hung on the back of the door and, with scarcely a glance at Leon, followed.

She did not see the quick lift of Adam's head, nor the narrowing of her son's eyes as he looked after her.

'The boy is soft,' Leon growled.

Adam considered for a moment. 'Yes. I think he probably is.' He smiled his most tranquil smile, reached into his pocket. 'It's not his fault. He'll get over it. Cigarette?'

Outside Cathy looked around. There was no sign of Nikos. 'Nikos? Nikos!' She listened intently; heard nothing but the cold wind that soughed in the trees and the distant crash of the waves upon the shingle beach. She buttoned her coat, turned the collar up about her ears and set off down the track towards the sea.

She saw Nikos as she breasted the dunes and caught her breath as the full force of the spray-laden north-easter struck her. He was hunkered on to his heels, his arms crossed on his knees, his head bowed. His damp hair was wild and he was panting for breath; obviously he had run all the way from the cottage. She scrunched through the shifting shingle to him. He did not lift his head. 'Here.' She had to raise her voice above the sound of wind and sea. She put the jacket about his shoulders; shoulders that, suddenly, were shaking. She straightened, stood looking out at the grey, wind-whipped, white-capped waves. Beneath the wild and natural sounds she could hear his sobs. Her own eyes stung. Still looking out to the distant, smudged horizon she laid a hand lightly on his damp head; a contact, a warmth, a small touch of comfort. After a moment she felt his cold hand come up and clasp hers, but his head remained bowed and still the sobs shook him. She lifted her face to the wind, steadying her own nerves, trying to ignore the almost painful compassion that threatened to overwhelm her. The last thing he needed, she told herself fiercely, was for her to cry with him. The last thing he would want at the moment was her pity.

It was a long time before she felt him calm a little. Fine rain was flying in the air. She crouched beside him. 'Put your jacket on.' She held it for him as he slipped his arms into the sleeves. His eyes were blurred and swollen with tears, his face drawn. His breath still caught in his throat in small hic-coughing sobs. 'Nikos, don't,' she said, softly, her arm about his shoulders her mouth close to his ear. 'Please don't.'

He leaned against her like a tired child. The wind buffeted, died a little, buffeted again. The sea washed tirelessly against the stones. She held him, tightly, willing warmth and strength into the taut, shaking body. He laid his head upon her shoulder, his eyes fixed on the long, rolling breakers that crashed and swirled upon the beach, foaming upon the patches of sand, shifting the smooth round stones of the shingle. When he started to speak at first she could barely hear him; then his voice got stronger. 'We were hiding on the mountainside above the house. Pa was badly wounded – he was caught in an ambush – his leg was smashed to pieces – you must have seen the scars – Mother insisted – she *insisted* – that if she were in the house alone they wouldn't suspect –'

The terror when the convoy of trucks and motorcycles had driven up the rocky track to the village, when grey-clad soldiers had poured from them, shouting orders, crashing on closed doors with their rifle-butts. The noise; women screaming, men shouting, the sounds of blows, the occasional shot. It had never left him. The panic – that he still sometimes experienced in dreams – as the brutal threat had surged up the mountainside, closer and closer—

'– she made me go and join Pa. We could see the yard of the house.' He stopped.

'Nikos, don't. Don't think about it.' She knew the story; just once, after a serious bout of drinking, Leon had spoken of what had happened. Nikos had been just sixteen years old. Her arm tightened about him.

'They came to the house. She stood in the yard. She was very small, and very beautiful. There were five of them.' He was trembling like a leaf.

His crippled father's huge, peasant's hands had held him, one hand over his mouth. 'Do you think she wants to see you die too?' Leon had been weeping in anguish at his own helplessness.

'She didn't make a sound. Not once. Not when they –' he chewed his lip, '– not when they hurt her. Not when they killed her, after they had used her.'

Leon's strength had easily overcome his boy's struggles. He had turned Nikos' head into his chest, his grip like a vice, to prevent him from watching. Nikos remembered now the smell of his father's body, the great gouts of blood that were pumping from the re-opened wound in his thigh. Could feel in his own body, as he had on that awful day, the shaking of Leon's huge, wasted frame.

He lifted a tired, tear-marked face and turned to look at her. 'How could he?' he asked, simply. 'How *could* he?'

Cathy was quiet for a long moment. Then: 'He's right in a way, you know. It's over. It's past. We can't forget, of course we can't. But it's time perhaps for forgiveness –'

He shook his head, fiercely and silently.

'Oh – not the men who did it. I understand that. But, Nikos, the wounds have to heal. What we must do is to try to make sure it can't happen again. And hatred won't do that.'

'Grandmother hated them.'

Ah. Cathy said nothing.

'She – I think she hated Pa too.'

'Oh, surely not?' The words were gentle.

He shook his head. 'You didn't know her. She was a very strong woman. A very good woman, but very single minded. And where she loved she loved with her whole heart. Mother was her only child. She never forgave Pa for what happened, not even when he agreed that I should go to America to live with her.' He had stopped shivering, his weight was heavy against her. The sobs had died. 'I miss her,' he said, very quietly. 'I miss her so much.'

Cathy inclined her head to his, laid her cheek on his damp hair. 'Of course you do.' Her bare hands were frozen, her face stung from the wind and the salt spray and she could feel the chill of the wet stones on which she sat creeping through the heavy material of her slacks. Yet for all the discomfort she had no desire to move. They sat so in silence for a long time. Then, very slowly, he lifted his head from her shoulder and turned to look at her. Her brown hair was wild and wet, her face pinched with cold. Her eyes, hazel green and oddly slanted, that from the first moment he had met her had reminded him of a cat's, held his; disturbed, suddenly, and questioning. She made to pull away from him.

He caught her hand.

'Nikos –'

Very gently he carried her hand to his face, bowed his head to rest his forehead on her loosely clenched knuckles.

'We must get back,' she said, quietly, at last.

'Yes.'

'They'll wonder what's happened to us.'

His eyes lifted to hers. He let go of her hand. 'Yes,' he said again.

They walked back to the cottage, oddly careful to keep their distance, not to catch each other's eye, both wrapped in a slightly unnerved silence that each would have been hard put to explain.

Leon was alone in the kitchen when they got back, sitting at the table reading a two-day-old newspaper. He glanced up as they entered, but said nothing. Nikos shrugged out of the wet jacket, held out a hand. 'Sorry, Pa. You're right, of course.'

Leon's face lit to a smile. He took the hand, shook it fiercely, threw his other arm about his son's shoulders.

Cathy put the kettle on the stove. 'Where's Adam?'

'Lighting the fire in the other room.' Arm still around Nikos Leon reached for her, hugged her to him.

She kissed his cheek affectionately. 'Mind my ribs, you great bear. Now for goodness' sake, the pair of you, get out of my kitchen while I clear up. I'll bring you coffee in a minute. I've got lunch to cook.'

Over the traditional Sunday roast the subject of Christmas came up. 'Come to London,' Leon said. 'We stay in a hotel – all of us –'

'Oh, Leon, no. Please – not at Christmas. Christmas is a time to be at home –'

'But it makes so much work for you!'

'I don't mind. You know I don't. I love it. Christmas should always be celebrated at home. It's what Christmas is all about. Look – I'll tell you what – why don't we spend Christmas here, and then perhaps go to London for New Year?' She glanced at Adam. 'Would that suit you?'

Adam shrugged. 'OK by me.'

'That's settled then,' Cathy said, firmly.

Leon laughed. 'It looks that way.' He glanced back at Adam who was looking at his watch. 'What time train do you want to catch?'

'I'd thought the four o'clock. I've got a date at seven.'

'You're meeting Lorraine?' Cathy asked.

He looked up in surprise. 'Oh, no. Didn't I tell you? We split weeks ago.' He laughed. 'There've been two more since then.'

She shook her head, reaching for his empty plate 'I can't keep up with you.'

'You know what they say; there's safety in numbers.'

'Don't you ever feel like settling down?'

'Good God no!' The words were so heartfelt they brought a shout of laughter from Leon. Cathy collected the plates.

'Let me.' Nikos came swiftly to his feet. He took the plates from her and carried them to the sink. He had said little during the meal. Cathy had felt his eyes upon her once or twice, but each time she had glanced at him he had looked away. She suspected that, now the high emotions had calmed, he was embarrassed that she had witnessed his tears. She hoped he would not let it spoil the real friendship that had started to grow between them. 'Thank you,' she said, smiling.

He ducked his head and flushed a little; still would not meet her eyes. Cathy cut several large pieces of apple pie, handed them around, a little irritated with herself as she realised that now it was she who was avoiding Nikos' eyes, she who was careful not to touch his hand as she handed him his plate; she who found herself pushing from her mind the memory of those odd and perplexingly disturbing moments on the beach when the link of their cold hands had seemed to verge on more than the simple offering and accepting of comfort. The very thought was ridiculous; the boy had become over-emotional, and now he understandably felt awkward about it. That was all. He'd get over it; and all the easier, she added to herself dryly, if she managed to behave like the extremely sensible and grown-up person that she usually was. She tapped his wrist, to gain his attention. 'Nikos? Custard or cream?'

She was pleased, later in the afternoon, when Nikos opted to go for the drive with his father when he took Adam to the station. It was good that the two of them should spend some time with each other. And it meant a couple of hours' peace for her. Apart from the angry words of the morning she had enjoyed the weekend, and despite the tiff about moving to Greece had especially enjoyed having her son's company for a couple of days. She and Adam had once been very close; she supposed it was inevitable that as he had grown to manhood and moved away the relationship should have changed. Yet at least it did seem that this time he really had wanted simply to see her. He had not, as she had felt so sure he would, asked for money. She felt guilty at the thought.

'Some mother I am, Sandy.' She rubbed the dog's rough ears, laughed at his expectant face. 'Oh, no. We're staying right here in the warm. And, yes, I know the house is a shambles, but it can wait, so there. I've got a book to read.'

An hour or so later she closed the book, stretched, yawned, grimaced at the dying fire. She looked around her. The room, which rarely at the best of times could be described as tidy, was now in a state of utter disorder. She had made tea before the men had left, and the used cups and saucers still sat on the table. A pile of newspapers had somehow managed to distribute themselves about the room and the bedclothes that Nikos had used were stuffed inelegantly behind the sofa. Sighing she stood up, surveyed the mess, hands on hips. Sandy cocked his head on one side, watching her. 'You aren't by any chance my fairy godmother in disguise, are you?' she asked him, a little gloomily. The dog's tail thumped, and he looked hopeful. 'No. I didn't think you were. So I suppose I'll just have to do it myself.' She stacked the dirty cups and headed for the kitchen.

Oddly, once started, she actually discovered some enthusiasm for the task. Though often untidy the little house was rarely this chaotic; bringing some order to it was somehow more satisfying than usual. She made up the fire, turned on the radio and set to. Within less than an hour she had finished downstairs and leaving it looking pleasingly neat and comfortable she decided, virtuously, to take her crusade to the bedrooms. Adam's room was relatively tidy, and all that needed doing was for the bedclothes to be changed. Her own room was something else again; Leon, she thought, exasperatedly, could cause havoc in a room by simply walking through it. His clothes were everywhere, his suitcase open on the unmade bed, two pairs of shoes lay on the floor where they had dropped and the dressing table harboured brushes, combs, a handkerchief, a cutthroat razor, a handful of small change and Leon's leather wallet. She picked it up, puzzled. There was no need to open it to tell that it was all but empty. Yet in all the time she had known him she had never known him not to carry money – usually a lot of money – and always in this wallet. It was an expensive leather affair with his initials tooled in gold, about which she had often teased him, as indeed she had about the size of the sum he usually carried with him. Only half in jest he always answered in the same vein; once a peasant always a peasant – money in the bank is good, money in the pocket is better. For every friend it loses you it will make another two. She weighed the wallet in her hand and shrugged amusedly; it certainly looked as if Leon had been buying friends –

The idle thought stopped her in her tracks. And with it came another, a sudden, clear recollection; on Friday night Leon had tossed this same wallet on to this same dressing table. And it had been full. She was certain of it. She stood for a long moment looking down at the thing; then she opened it. Two worn ten-shilling notes were tucked in it; nothing else. Buying friends. The phrase was in her head now and would not be dismissed. She shook her head. 'Two and two make four,' she told herself aloud, sternly. 'Not six, or eight. Stop jumping to silly conclusions.'

From the garden outside came the sound of voices, and laughter. She looked out of the window. Leon and Nikos were coming down the path. As she watched Leon shouted with laughter and punched his son's arm in play. Laughing too, Nikos pretended to stagger at the force of it. She smiled as she watched them; they were like a couple of children in a school playground. Then as she turned to go downstairs to greet them her eyes fell on the empty wallet again, and the smile faded.

Full on Friday, empty now. Having left the house only once – to pick Adam up at the station – her husband had certainly bought something; something very expensive.

Remembering, vividly, the conversation about the Greek house – upon which subject Adam had never advanced an opinion before – she wished she could rid herself of the quite possibly scurrilous suspicion that the expensive item

that her less than scrupulous husband had bought had been
her son.

'Why so quiet, Kati? Is something wrong?'

Cathy glanced up to find her husband's eyes fixed quizzi-
cally upon her. Curled into a chair in front of the fire, a book
open and unread on her lap, she had been staring thoughtfully into the flames. 'No. Nothing's wrong.' Even she could
hear the lack of conviction in her voice.

He raised bushy, questioning eyebrows. 'You're still angry
with me for not meeting Nikos from the boat?' He cradled
the glass of brandy he held in his big hand, watching her.

'No. Of course not. Well – I still think it was pretty awful
of you, but since Nikos seems to have forgiven you there's
no point in my keeping on about it, is there?'

'No. There isn't. So – what is it?'

She hesitated.

'Kati?' He was insistent. 'There's something. I can tell.'

She closed the book with a snap and sat up. 'Yes, there is –
well, that is – I don't know –'

'Tell me.'

She looked at him for a long moment, then spoke suddenly and quickly. 'While you were out I went upstairs to
tidy the bedroom. I found your wallet. It's empty.'

He said nothing, but his eyes were wary. He sipped his
drink. Then, 'So?' he asked.

'So – on Friday night there was a lot of money in it. Where
did it go?'

'Is it any of your business?' There was a spark of anger in
his face.

She leaned forward. 'No. Not unless you gave it to Adam.'

The silence this time was long.

'Did you?' she asked, bluntly, watching him.

'And if I did? It's my money. Why shouldn't I help your
son out of a little difficulty? What's the matter with you,
Kati? Do you begrudge him the money?'

Very containedly she stood and walked to the sideboard, poured herself a small brandy, turned to face him. 'Would you like to rephrase that?' she asked with precarious calm.

He shrugged. 'What else can I think?'

'Think? I sometimes wonder if you ever bloody think! Leon – he's gambling again! Isn't he?'

Again the shrug.

She fought and won the battle to stop herself from shrieking at him like a fishwife. Nikos had gone to bed only half an hour before, and his room was above the one in which they were talking. 'Leon, you know how I feel about Adam and his gambling –'

'You're too protective. Let the boy – the man – have his fun –'

'*Fun?* Is that what you think it is? Leon, gambling isn't fun to Adam. Any more than it was to his father –'

'Ah,' he said. 'We come back to that.'

'His father was a compulsive gambler. I've told you. It ruined him. It ruined us. I won't have Adam go the same way!'

'Kati, why must you always fly to the extreme? Adam has got himself into a spot of bother, that's all. I offered to help him out. He told me he was through with gambling –'

'If you believe that you'll believe anything. Leon, don't try to pretend naiveté with me! While you encourage him he'll never be through with gambling. And to go behind my back like that –'

He stood, angrily. 'Enough. Enough! The transaction was between me and Adam. He's a grown man. You must allow him his freedom.'

'Freedom to destroy himself? As his father did?'

'Don't be so melodramatic.'

She tilted her head and swallowed the brandy at one gulp, slammed the glass down on the sideboard. 'It isn't melodrama.' Her voice was clipped and flinty with anger. 'It's the simple truth. I've lied to you, Leon. I've lied to everyone. I've lied above all to Adam.'

He was watching her, suddenly intently, a dangerous

gleam in his dark eyes. 'Lied? To me? What do you mean?'

She walked past him, stood, arms folded across her breasts, looking down into the fire. 'My husband didn't die in an air raid,' she said at last, very quietly, and turned to face him, to meet his eyes. 'He killed himself.'

Leon stared at her. She waited. He said nothing.

'Did you hear me?'

'I heard you.' His voice was totally expressionless.

'Have you nothing to say?'

'I heard you,' he said again. 'I don't know if I believe you.'

Temper finally overcame reason; in a flash of fury she lifted her hand to slap him. He was quicker than she was. He caught her wrist in a painful grip, shaking his head slowly. 'Oh, no, my Kati. Not even you. No one strikes me. Now. Explain.'

She stood silent, trembling with anger, until he released her wrist. He turned and poured another brandy, offered it to her. She took it, the anger draining from her. 'It's true. Danny did commit suicide. It just so happened that Adam and I were here in Suffolk at the time – it was during the last bad bout of air raids, and we thought it safer for the boy here. It wasn't hard to conceal from him what had happened. It was wartime. People were dying every day.'

'Why did he do it?'

She sighed. 'I'm not sure I ever knew. The gambling had got the better of him and he knew it. He wasn't strong. He was facing ruin. Perhaps worse.' She shrugged a little. 'As I say, he wasn't a strong man. There was something missing in him. He was handsome, and charming, and feckless as hell. But he was – unbalanced.' She raised her eyes to his. 'Now do you see why I'm angry? Now do you see why I don't want you giving money to my son – to Danny's son? Especially behind my back?'

'Yes. I do.' He stepped to her, put an arm about her shoulders. 'Kati, I'm sorry.'

She sighed, tiredly. 'Promise me you won't tell him.'

'I promise.'

'And promise me you won't encourage his gambling.'

'I promise that, too.'

She stood in silence, her forehead pressed against his broad shoulder. 'Leon?' Her voice was muffled.

'Yes?'

She lifted her head. 'What did you ask for in exchange for the money?' She studied him, saw the faint lift of colour in his swarthy skin. 'You did ask for something, didn't you?'

He did not reply.

She waited for a long time before stepping from the circle of his arm. She sat down again in the armchair, leaned her head tiredly back against the cushion and closed her eyes. 'Leon, do you think you can buy *anything*? Do you think everything and everyone is for sale?'

He sat in the chair opposite her, leaning forward, elbows on knees, rolling the glass between the palms of his hand. 'Frankly? Yes. I do. It's a lesson that life has taught me.'

'It's a very sad one.'

'Perhaps.' In the quiet the coals collapsed in the hearth. 'Kati?'

Cathy opened her eyes.

'I make you a promise. A solemn promise.'

'Oh?'

'I will watch over your son for you as if he were my own. I'll keep him under my eye and to the best of my ability I'll keep him out of trouble.' Born of long practice, Leon knew well how to phrase a promise that would not be so binding as to prevent future manoeuvre.

Cathy did not notice the ambivalence. 'Thank you,' she said.

'Now, will you make me a promise in return?'

She waited, a little warily.

'When the spring comes, and the house is finished, will you come with me to see it?'

He reached a hand to her. After only a moment's hesitation she took it. 'Yes,' she said, 'I will.'

Chapter Four

Leon returned to London, taking Nikos with him, a day or so later, and Cathy, not entirely sorry to be left to her own devices, settled back into her quiet life. As the winter turned colder and snow settled across the flat East Anglian sandlings she worked on the sketches for the book, walked the wild shore with the dogs, and for a couple of weeks, as Christmas approached, slipped tranquilly back into her self-contained ways. Before Leon had left they had arranged that she would join him in the capital for a couple of days in mid-December, to combine a visit to her publishers, Christmas shopping and a trip to the theatre to see the new Agatha Christie play *The Mousetrap*. Until then Sandlings was hers again and she was content.

The trip to London, embarked on initially as something of a chore, turned out to be hugely enjoyable. Half a dozen finished illustrations duly delivered and gratifyingly received, she spent a day in the West End shopping, returning to the hotel where she was staying with Leon worn out but triumphant to the point of smugness. 'All done,' she announced, kicking her shoes off and throwing herself on to the bed. 'Christmas is in the bag. Literally.' She gestured to the heap of paper carrier bags she had dumped on the floor.

'Several bags, in fact.'

Leon came to sit beside her, touched her hair, winding a curl about his finger. 'Not quite,' he said, smiling. 'Tomorrow I want you to run an errand for me.'

She turned on her stomach, groaning. 'Oh, Leon, no! Don't be so mean! I refuse – I refuse! – to go near another shop. Not even for you. You'll have to do your own Christmas shopping, so there!'

'But I insist, *koukla mou*. Tomorrow you go shopping again – for yourself. Tomorrow night we go to the theatre. Then we meet the boys for supper at the Savoy. I want you to buy yourself a dress. And shoes. And anything else you want. It is my Christmas gift to you. Buy something extravagant. Spend what you wish. Not to walk the dogs on your wild and windy beach but to visit the theatre with your husband, and to have dinner with your two handsome boys.'

Cathy sat up, hugging her knees, contemplating the not unattractive thought. 'It's a terrible waste of money,' she ventured.

Leon shook his head. 'No. I told you; it is my gift to you. And if you never wear it again it still will not be wasted.' He cupped her chin in his hand and tilted her head to study her face. 'Will you do as I ask?'

She opened slanted, innocent eyes. 'Don't I always?'

He shouted with laughter at that. She watched him, smiling, held out a hand. 'Yes, I'll do as you ask. It'll be a terrible strain, but I expect I can face it. Dragging round the shops and spending money on myself! Honestly – the things you ask a girl to do!' The mockery was gentle.

He opened her hand, kissed the palm.

Light-heartedly she blew the kiss back to him. 'Come on. I'll let you buy me dinner. I'm starving.'

Twenty-four hours later she surveyed herself in the mirror in mild, not to say comic, astonishment. 'Good God. Poor Sandy would have a fit if he could see me now. He'd run a mile.'

'You look wonderful.' Leon came up behind her, smiling.

'It'll look very neat with my Wellingtons, don't you think?'

'It's a great shame you don't have them with you,' he agreed, straightfaced.

She turned and laid her arms lightly about his neck. 'I'm glad you like it.'

'It's perfect.'

The dress was of taffeta, with a scooped off-the-shoulder neckline, a slender, belted waist and a flaring calf-length skirt. It was the colour of a peacock's tail, glinting blue and green as she moved. 'I feel dreadfully guilty. It really was extortionately expensive.'

Leon picked up the matching stole from the bed and placed it around her shoulders. 'For tonight there is no such thing as expensive. Tonight we enjoy ourselves.' He adjusted his black tie and brushed the lapels of his dinner jacket. She regarded him approvingly. 'You look pretty damned smart yourself.'

Smiling broadly he held out a crooked arm. She laid her fingers lightly on it. 'Cinderella, off to the ball.'

'With her handsome prince.'

She sketched a laughing curtsey. 'But of course.'

Cathy enjoyed every moment in the theatre, from the hum of excitement that died to quiet expectancy as the curtain rose, through the intrigues of the cleverly plotted play that was proving to be so popular, to the denouement that sent people out into the foggy streets discussing it still. The Savoy was thronged with after-theatre diners and drinkers. Leon steered her through the crowd to where Nikos and Adam and a quite stunningly attractive young woman awaited them at a reserved table, upon which already stood an ice-bucket containing an almost empty bottle of Champagne. The two boys rose to greet them. The girl, dressed in a strapless affair of rustling black taffeta with a huge, bouffant skirt, matching elbow-length gloves and earrings that swung and glittered as she moved, sat demurely, batting long, interested eyelashes at Leon as they were introduced. Cathy suppressed an amused smile. Even without trying Leon did have the most dramatic effect upon young women. Adam put a casually possessive hand on the girl's bare shoulder. 'This is Dorothy. Dot, meet Cathy and Leon.'

Wide blue eyes flickered to Cathy, then fixed firmly on Leon. 'Lovely to meet you.' A breathy, little-girl voice. The eyelashes were working again. This time Cathy did grin as she offered her cheek for her son's kiss.

Adam, holding her by the shoulders, put her from him and looked at her in what could only be described as uncomplimentary astonishment. 'You look great. What happened to the duffel coat?'

'I checked it in at the cloakroom. I didn't want to appear overdressed. Don't look so damned surprised,' she added with mild asperity, 'I may be your mother but I'm not quite ready for the bathchair yet.' She settled herself, rustling satisfactorily, between the two young men, smiled at Nikos. 'Nikos. How are you?'

'I'm well. Thank you.' Nikos, too, was looking at her with bright and flatteringly appreciative eyes. 'You do look –' he hesitated, '– wonderful,' he said.

'Make the most of it.' She leaned to him, lowering her voice, 'I turn into a pumpkin at midnight.'

Nikos had drunk at least half of a large bottle of heady Champagne rather too quickly. 'Not before you dance with me, I hope,' he said, equally quietly.

To her own astonishment she felt her cheeks warm a little. 'Of course. If you'd like.'

Leon had sat beside Dorothy, his arm across the back of her chair. 'More Champagne,' he said, 'and then we eat.' He smiled expansively around the table. 'Tonight is a celebration.'

'What are we celebrating?' There went the eyelashes again, and the little, breathy voice. Adam winked at Cathy.

Leon patted the black-gloved arm. 'Don't worry, my dear,' he said, heavily playful. 'We'll think of something.'

It was a long time since Cathy had spent such a diverting evening. True to form Leon flirted outrageously with Dorothy, who, pouting and giggling and using the eyelashes to good effect, appeared to swallow the performance whole and without the benefit of salt. Where, Cathy found herself wondering, did Adam find them? Adam himself, far from being put out, appeared to enjoy the pantomime hugely. He was in high spirits and on very good form, entertaining his companions with caustic and Cathy could only assume well-informed gossip about their fellow diners, many of whom he appeared to know well. Nikos, meanwhile, danced atten-dance on his stepmother in a way that both amused and flattered her. The food was excellent, the surroundings splendid. She had been to this most famous of hotels once before, with Danny, but that had been during the war and the time of the 'five shilling menu', when shortages and rationing had restricted the fare, air raid precaution had marred the lovely interiors and the elegance of evening dress had been exchanged for military uniform. Now, at last, after the years of austerity that had followed the war, restored and renovated the place was its dazzling self again, a glam-orous magnet for the rich and the famous and for those who aspired to riches and fame. She caught Leon's eye. He raised his glass and toasted her wordlessly. A dapper young man had stepped to the microphone. The dance band swung into a nostalgic 1930s medley. Dorothy was tapping her foot. *'I'll be seeing you in all the old familiar places –'*

'I want to dance.' Dorothy was looking not at Adam but at Leon.

Adam took her hand, shook his curly head, laughing. 'Don't be daft. Leon's a Greek. He only dances with plates and hankies. Come on, Dotty my love. You'll have to make do with me.' He drew her on to the floor and they slipped easily in amongst the other dancers; as handsome a pair, Cathy thought, not without pride, as any there.

'Would you care to dance?' It was Nikos, quietly, beside her. He looked at his father. 'Would you mind?'

Leon waved a large, beringed hand expansively. 'Of course not. Enjoy yourselves. That's what we're here for.' His eyes moved to a table not far from theirs. 'I've seen a man I need to talk to. Go dance. Have fun.'

Nikos took her hand to lead her to the floor. His fingers were cool, and for a surprised moment she fancied that they trembled a little in hers. He danced well, smoothly and with style. She relaxed to the rhythm of his movements, following his lead, allowing herself simply to slip into a music- and Champagne-induced trance of enjoyment. They did not speak. The tune changed; the singer, she thought, dreamily, really was very good indeed. Seductive. That was the word. '*Embrace me, my sweet embraceable you –*' Nikos' arm tightened a little about her as he led her into a graceful series of turns. She closed her eyes, smiling, opened them again to find him looking down at her, watching her intently, his unusual eyes reflecting the sparkling light from the candles on the tables that surrounded the floor. He pulled her to him, suddenly and fiercely, rested his cheek lightly on the top of her head. This time there could be no mistaking his trembling. It communicated itself through his body and through the grip of his hand.

The last note died. The music stopped. There was a ripple of applause; people started to walk from the floor. As Cathy started to move Nikos caught her hand. 'Please,' he said, 'one more?'

She hesitated.

'Please.'

The band had swung into a quickstep. Cathy could see Leon standing at a table nearby, talking to a man she did not know. Catching her eye he smiled, lifted a hand, then turned back to his conversation.

'Cathy, please?' Nikos' voice was soft. Adam and Dorothy were still on the floor. Adam grinned at her as they swung expertly past.

She put her hand on Nikos' shoulder, felt his arm about her once more, and again they danced, gracefully, in perfect step and in silence.

When they got back to the table Leon was still deeply engrossed in his conversation, and Adam and Dorothy were executing a flamboyant tango on the dance floor. Nikos held the chair for her, then sat beside her, picking up his glass of wine, his eyes on the dancers. 'How's Sandy?' he asked, unexpectedly.

She smiled. 'Naughty as ever.'

'And the cottage?'

The smile widened. 'Untidy as ever.'

The slight, odd tension that had held him relaxed. He looked at her, returning her smile. 'And Bert?' he asked, pulling a ruefully comic face.

She laughed outright. 'As cantankerous as ever.'

He leaned forward on his elbows, cupping his glass in two hands, his face thoughtful. 'It's funny. I think about it a lot. Sandlings – the sea – those windy, deserted beaches –'

'And the sky,' she said. 'Don't forget the sky.'

'I don't.'

'So –' she turned her head to look at him, '– what's so strange that you should think about it?'

He shrugged a little. 'To be frank – I was appalled when I first arrived. I'm a city boy, pure and simple. Remember, I've lived in New York for almost ten years. You could say I grew up there. The thought of living somewhere like you do wouldn't have appealed to me at all.'

She was watching him with real curiosity in her eyes. 'And now?'

He shook his head. 'I don't know. It's just that, sometimes, in a busy street or a crowded tube I suddenly find myself thinking, that's all.'

'Of the space, and the peace, and the quiet?'

He hesitated only fractionally. 'Yes. I guess so.'

She laughed. 'But not of the inconvenience, the draughts, of bathing in the kitchen and the fact that if the wind gets up above a brisk breeze the newly installed electricity gives up and uninstalls itself.'

He laughed with her. 'No.'

The tango had come to a passionate and triumphant conclusion. Talking and laughing, people were returning to their tables. Leon had finished his conversation and was weaving his way back towards them. 'You must come down for the weekend,' she said, impulsively. 'Let me show you the area properly. There are so many beautiful, wild places. There are wetlands and woodlands and some lovely villages. My favourite is a place called Dunwich. You won't believe when you see it – it's tiny now, just a little coastal village – but in the Middle Ages it was a thriving port. The whole city has been taken by the sea – I've a map at the cottage –'

'Oh, Lord!' said Adam's voice from behind her. 'Do I hear Cathy cantering off on her favourite hobby horse?'

Smiling, Cathy put up a hand to cover his, that he had laid lightly on her shoulder. 'Don't be rude, darling. People will think your mother didn't teach you any manners.'

'May I?' Nikos asked.

She glanced at him, surprised by an odd note of urgency in his voice. 'Of course.' Still holding Adam's hand she laid her other hand on Nikos'. 'It's your home. You're welcome any time.'

'Speaking of which –' Adam slid into the chair next to his mother, reaching for the wine bottle and speaking across her to Nikos. 'How's the new flat?'

Cathy turned her head. 'You've found a flat?'

'Yes. Well, that is, it isn't exactly mine. An American friend offered for me to use it while he's out of town for a few months, while I look for a place of my own. It was a real stroke of luck, actually. It's a pretty smart place.'

'Where is it?' Cathy smiled a greeting as Leon rejoined them.

'In Kensington. Prince's Street. Very near the Albert Hall.'

That caught her attention. 'Lucky you! My only complaint as a country bumpkin is that I rarely get a chance to go to a concert or the opera.'

'Move to London,' Leon said, promptly. 'We'll buy a flat. You can listen to Mozart and – what's-his-name? – the man Mahler – every night. And twice on Sundays.'

Cathy laughed. 'And walk Sandy round the Serpentine? I don't think either of us would much enjoy that.'

Leon shrugged good-humouredly.

'You like Mahler?' Nikos asked, seriously.

Adam groaned. 'Oh, Lord! Nikos, be a good chap, don't get her started! Dunwich is bad enough.'

'It's just –' Nikos hesitated.

Cathy accepted a glass of wine. 'What?'

'They're playing Mahler at the Hall the night after next. *The Sixth* – I saw the posters.'

'Tragic!' said Adam, and snorted with laughter at his own laboured witticism. Dorothy looked at him in undisguised puzzlement, which only made him laugh more.

Cathy nudged his foot under the table. 'Adam! Behave yourself!'

'Yes, Ma.'

'I wondered –' Nikos looked around the table, 'I could perhaps get us all tickets? You could come back to the flat for supper afterwards.'

Dorothy looked vaguely alarmed. Adam raised wry eyebrows. Leon shook his head, smiling. 'Ah, no, my boy. Not even for you. Take Kati. A good idea. Take Kati and I will treat you to supper afterwards.'

Nikos looked at Cathy. She shook her head. 'Nikos, I'm sorry – it's a lovely idea, and thank you. But I'm going home tomorrow.'

'Stay another couple of days.' It was Leon, easily. 'Why the rush? You fly up here, fly round and then fly back like a frightened little bird! Seriously – why not stay? Your precious sandlings won't disappear while you're away. Your precious cottage won't fall down –'

'It might,' she said.

'– your ill-behaved Sandy is keeping the equally ill-behaved Bert company. Stay. Visit a museum. Go to the Tate and look at the pictures.' He spread his hands. 'You like such things. Then, on Thursday night Nikos will escort you to the concert, which you will both enjoy the more for not having Philistines like us around.' His bright, dark eyes took in Adam and the openly relieved Dorothy. 'I will then take you both for supper and on Friday you will take the train back to your –' he paused for effect '– country retreat, having in the meantime pleased me, yourself and Nikos. An early Christmas treat. And a chance to see that there are at least some advantages to living in London.'

'Don't be sly, Leon,' Cathy said. 'It doesn't become you.'

He laughed. 'Tell me, though. Doesn't that sound agreeable?'

'It sounds wonderful.' Cathy herself only half understood her own reluctance. 'But –'

'Please?' Nikos said, softly.

'But nothing.' Leon folded his arms. 'Is settled. Adam – tell me again the name of the man you spoke to last week who seemed interested in the Athens project?'

As they spoke Nikos leaned to her. 'I'm sorry. If you really don't want to come on Thursday, please say so. Don't feel you must.'

'Oh, don't be so silly. Of course I want to come. As Adam pointed out, I'm a Mahler bore.'

'He was a brilliant man. A wonderful conductor, and a powerful composer. My grandmother –' he stopped, blinked a little.

'What?' She was gentle. There was a sudden gale of laughter as Leon spoke and Adam replied smartly.

'She met him. When he was chief conductor at the Met. She was devoted to him, and to his music.'

'Your grandmother was fond of music?'

His face lit to a sudden, dazzling smile. 'She lived it. Breathed it. She was a very accomplished pianist.'

'I didn't know that.'

The dark lashes lifted, the disconcerting golden eyes met hers. 'You'll come? Please?' The lids dropped again, long, dark-skinned fingers toyed with his napkin. 'To be honest – it's stupid I know – but it's the first time I've been able to think about facing Mahler since –'

'I'll come. Of course I'll come.'

The unguarded delight in his face was a reward in itself.

'So –' Leon leaned across the table. 'Kati. You stay?'

'I'll stay,' she said. 'Just for another couple of days.'

'What I don't think I know,' Dorothy said, enunciating rather over-carefully, 'is exactly what we've been celebrating?'

Adam winked at his mother. 'Not having to go to a Mahler concert,' he said, gravely. 'That's enough for anyone to celebrate.'

The night of the concert was foggy, the streets and alleys of the city enveloped in a choking, soot-laden smog that muffled sound and bemused the senses. Cathy and Nikos met in the foyer, Cathy a little flustered, 'I'm sorry I'm late. Stupidly I came by taxi – it took for ever to get here! It would have been much quicker by tube.'

Nikos, who had been waiting a full half hour, shook his head. 'It doesn't matter. I've only just got here myself as a matter of fact. The whole of London seems to have come to a standstill. Let me take your coat.'

Cathy shrugged it from her shoulders. 'Leon has booked a table for ten o'clock at a little restaurant just along the road – the "Pescatore". He'll meet us there. It's all right – don't bother to check it in. Let's find our seats. There isn't a lot of time . . .'

The concert exceeded even Cathy's expectations. It had been so long since she had attended a live performance she had almost forgotten the pleasure, the enthralling feeling of involvement that it could engender. The concert could have been planned with her own preferences in mind; Bruckner in the first half, Mahler in the second. The massive, dramatic Sixth, known popularly as the 'Tragic' Symphony, stirred her almost to tears. As, afterwards, they stepped on to the wet pavement and into the filthy, billowing smog the music still echoed in her head and in her heart. 'That was wonderful. Thank you.'

'Don't be silly. I loved it. I hate to admit it but I don't like going to concerts alone. Music is something to be shared.'

Cathy pulled her collar up around her ears, slipped her arm through his. 'You used to go with your Grandmother?'

'Oh, yes. Two, three times a month.' Their footsteps echoed dully. Traffic crept past, headlights yellow in the wall of fog. People hurried by, scarves muffling their faces in an effort to keep the smoke-laden stuff from their lungs.

'You must miss her very much.'

'Yes.'

She cocked her head to look up at him. 'It will pass, you know,' she said, gently. 'I know how bad it feels now, but it will ease.'

'Yes. I suppose so.' The sadness in his voice caught at her heart.

They walked on in silence for a while. The shop windows glowed eerily in the foggy darkness. When Cathy spoke her tone was lighter. 'Tell me – did you have a girlfriend in New York?'

Nikos smiled, noncommittally. 'A couple.'

'But no one serious?'

He shook his head.

'Not ever?' She half wished she had not started the conversation, could not imagine why she had.

He hunched his shoulders. 'One, I guess. But it didn't work out. Is this the place?'

The restaurant was warm, cosy and intimate, a refuge from the chill, sooty dankness outside. 'Ah – *Signora* Kotsikas – there is a message –' The proprietor, small, dark and mildly harassed as his tables began to fill with after-theatre diners, led them to a small table in an alcove. '*Signor* Kotsikas – he telephoned –'

'Oh, no!' The words were exasperatedly resigned.

'– he has been unavoidably delayed. He will join you perhaps for coffee. Please –' he held the chair for her. 'You would like an aperitif? I bring a menu. If I may recommend – the *carbonara* is very good –'

Seated, they smiled at each other across the table. 'Your father –' Cathy began.

'– is impossible,' Nikos finished for her, and laughed. 'I guess we'll just have to talk amongst ourselves until he arrives.'

Cathy sipped her Martini, savouring it. 'Oh, I expect we can manage that, don't you?'

She was right. In the hour and a half that followed, before Leon finally joined them, at no time did the conversation flag. On the contrary, the *carbonara* cooled on their plates and the discreetly hovering waiters went unnoticed as they talked, of everything and anything except, by what seemed to Cathy later to be an odd, mutual pact, the personal. The subjects ranged from the light to the serious, from a partisan argument about the relative dancing skills of Fred Astaire and Gene Kelly, to the results of the recent election in Greece, that had brought to power Field Marshal Papagos. They agreed that the likelihood of a lasting armistice in Korea was unlikely and that with the testing of Britain's first atom bomb and America's first hydrogen bomb the world had by no means become a safer place. Cathy told Nikos – at his insistence – the denouement of *The Mousetrap* – 'I'm not a theatre-goer, I'll never see it, so it really doesn't matter. It's just that if the greater part of London knows I might as well too, don't you think?' And still, as if bound by some unspoken rule they avoided anything close to intimacy. When Leon finally arrived they were discussing the burning issue of the day; the trial and conviction of Christopher Craig and Derek Bentley and the subsequent death sentence meted out to Bentley, Craig at sixteen being too young to be subject to capital punishment. Cathy, passionately opposed to the death penalty, had taken the case to heart. 'They surely won't hang him. He didn't do it. There's never been any question. Craig shot the policeman –'

'"Let him have it,"' Nikos mused, sipping his coffee. 'What did he mean? The gun? Or the bullet?'

'It doesn't really matter, does it? Oh, yes, of course it does, I know that. But to hang someone on such a chancy piece of evidence – to hang someone at all in this day and age – is barbaric. It's judicial murder.'

'There surely has to be some kind of sanction? Some kind of deterrent?'

'I don't think it does deter. It's a vicious and inhuman punishment that has no place in a civilised society. I don't want someone killed on my behalf, no matter what he's done.'

'You really do feel strongly about it, don't you?'

She laughed a little self-consciously. 'Sorry. Yes, I do – ah – Leon! At last! Where have you been?'

Leon kissed her cheek. 'Lost in the fog.' His smile somehow managed to belie the words. 'How was the concert?'

'Wonderful. Why won't you ever tell me where you've been?' The question was mild.

He seated himself beside her, spread his hands. 'I had to see a man, that's all. Business, *koukla mou*, business.' He lifted a hand to a hovering waiter. 'Coffee please. And a large brandy.' He leaned back in his chair, looking from one to the other. 'Now. Tell me about this wonderful concert.'

*

The next morning, still in the midst of one of the worst killer smogs in memory, Cathy made her way to Liverpool Street station and the train for Suffolk. To her surprise Nikos had offered to escort her, an offer that Leon accepted on her behalf despite her protestations that she could manage alone. Nikos stood now on the platform, talking through the open window. 'You're sure you'll be all right at the other end? You've got an awful lot of parcels and things.'

She laughed. 'Nikos, for goodness' sake! Of course I will. I'll take a taxi. You're as bad as Adam! I'm not a decrepit old lady, you know. Not yet, anyway. And I have a tongue in my head.'

A whistle shrilled, steam shrieked from the engine, the couplings creaked and clanked and the train began slowly to move. She leaned from the window and kissed him affectionately on the cheek. The train picked up speed. He walked with it. 'Did you mean what you said? May I come down to the cottage for a weekend?'

'Of course. Any time –'

'Thanks. I will.' He stopped, his hand lifted in farewell. She leaned from the window for a moment, waving, then settled into her seat and reached for her newspaper.

On the platform Nikos stood for a long time after the train had disappeared into the murk, looking after it. The station smelled of fog and of steam. People bustled about him; someone cannoned into him and hurried on without apology.

Turning at last he hunched his shoulders, shoved his hands in his pockets and went back out into the foggy streets of London.

Chapter Five

On more than one occasion during the next few days Nikos Kotsikas found himself questioning, quite seriously, if he were taking leave of his senses. He could neither sleep nor eat, his concentration was shot to pieces. He was restless as a sick child.

He could think of nothing – absolutely nothing – but his father's wife.

They had danced together, they had spoken together and they had sat side by side listening to the majestic music of Mahler; and since the moment the train taking her back to Suffolk had steamed from the station he had not been able to get her out of his mind. Her face and her voice haunted him. He could see every single thing about her as clearly as if she were constantly beside him; the smallest of her mannerisms was burned into his memory. The way she cocked her head to one side as she spoke; the wayward hair that refused to lend itself to the sleek and controlled styles of the day. Her sudden, flashing smile. Her silly habit of talking to herself. Her laughter, and her friendly generosity.

Of which he knew he was in danger of taking a terrible advantage.

In vain he tried to rationalise his feelings; he was still

grieving at the loss of his grandmother, he was unsettled and uncertain of the future. From the start Cathy had shown nothing but kindness and understanding. It was natural he should be drawn to her, had been drawn to her since first they had met.

The train of thought always ended in bleak self-derision; he knew he was lying to himself. This was no comfortable, natural, filial devotion. From the moment he had first seen his stepmother, rain-soaked, windblown and utterly unafraid, he had thought her beautiful. From the start her honesty and humour, her freeness of spirit had enchanted and attracted him. Her open and ready acceptance of him as Leon's son had made it all too easy to get close to her; she, of course, had perceived no danger and by the time he had seen the peril of the situation it had been too late; the truth was that he was infatuated, and helplessly so. The terrible, enraging, enchanting thing was that, impossible as the whole situation was for him, he did not truly care. He had of course read – with the healthy scepticism of one who had never suffered it – of that lover's condition where the simple existence of the loved one, no matter how unattainable, no matter how painful the circumstances, was a constant source of joy. The thought had always seemed to him to be irrational to the point of stupidity. Now, suddenly and ridiculously, here he was behaving like nothing so much as the hapless hero of a sixpenny romance. Confused as he was, yet still the mere thought of her could light the day. He took every possible opportunity to bring her name into a conversation. He was obsessed with the thought of seeing her again. And she had invited him to the cottage.

Time and time over he suppressed the thought. He must not go, and he knew it. In two weeks or so Christmas would be here. He would see her then, safely, in company with his father and Adam. He should stay away until he drove down with his father, as arranged, early on Christmas Eve. If he went before, if he saw her alone, he knew the chances were that he would make a fool of himself and embarrass her. God alone knew what she would think of him if she suspected his feelings; just thinking about the possibility made him cringe. The only sane thing to do was to stay away from her. The strongly idealistic and romantic streak in him could savour that, exquisitely painful as it was. He believed he would die for Cathy – kill for her even – but he knew she would – must – never know. Nikos in his most impressionable years had had instilled into him an almost Quixotic view of womanhood, and in his stepmother he truly thought he had found its embodiment. As the week that followed the concert passed he persuaded himself that he could keep this most private and perilous of secrets safe from the world. Safe from Cathy herself. He would watch her, and guard her and keep his distance. He could never bring himself to hurt or upset her. He would not – could not – deny himself his dreams but he must be careful never, ever, to see her alone, most especially not at Sandlings.

In that, however, as in so many other things, he had failed to take into account his autocratic father.

The first thing Leon did, with not so much as a by-your-leave, was to move in with his son. He needed, he announced, a base; hotel rooms, however well appointed, were not always the most convenient or comfortable of places. The apartment in Prince's Street was pleasant, conveniently situated, and there were two bedrooms. The solution, therefore was obvious. Nikos' fainthearted suggestion that his father might like rather more privacy than this arrangement afforded was brushed aside. Sooner or later Leon would find accommodation of his own in the capital. For now he was too busy. This would do. He moved in the weekend before Christmas.

On the following Monday, two days before Christmas Eve, a stranger turned up at the small office in Bayswater that was the modest headquarters of Kotsikas and Company. As it happened both Leon and Nikos were there checking a bill of lading when Miss Hooper, the sharp-faced, middle-aged and fiercely efficient factotum of the business put her head around the door. 'A – gentleman – to see you, Mr Leon.'

Leon raised his eyebrows amusedly at the more than obvious hesitation. 'What sort of – gentleman?'

'A Greek gentleman, I believe. He won't give a name.' Miss Hooper either missed or ignored the mischievous imitation of her own tone. 'Will you see him?'

Leon slanted a laughing look at Nikos.'Yes, Miss Hooper. We will see him.'

The man erupted through the door in a torrent of ebullient Greek, stopped when he saw Nikos, his black eyes suddenly and, Nikos thought, rather oddly, wary.

'Yannis!' Leon leaped from his seat, came around the desk, thumping the smaller man on the back. 'Yannis, welcome! Why didn't you telephone?' He too spoke in Greek.

Yannis shrugged a little. His eyes were still on Nikos.

Leon reached a hand to his son. 'Nikos, come. Meet a very old friend. Yannis Vasilios. We go back many years. He met you once as a child. In the war. Don't you remember?'

Smiling, Nikos shook his head.

The wary eyes had lightened. '*Nikos!*' the stranger exclaimed, with as much native enthusiasm as if it were his own son who had stepped from the past.

'That's it. Nikos. My son. Grown to be a man and come to join us.'

Nikos took the proffered hand and shook it. The man, though small and built not unlike a skinned rabbit, had a grip of iron. The thread of a long scar ran, white against the brown skin, across the right cheekbone of his thin face to the corner of his mouth. Even dressed in a shabby city suit he looked exactly as Nikos imagined a pirate would.

Leon turned to Nikos. 'Yannis works with me from time to time in Greece.' He turned back to the newcomer. 'What news?'

There was a sudden, slightly precarious silence.

'Nikos –' Leon covered it with easy charm, slipping now back into English '– do me a favour. Ouzo. Go get us another bottle of ouzo. This deserves something stronger than coffee.'

Nikos hesitated for a moment, trying to suppress resentment. This was not the first time his father had treated him like an office boy, at beck and call to run errands and not to be included in the real business of the office. 'There's a bottle in the drawer, isn't there?'

His father, who had turned back to Yannis did not even look at him. 'The usual Off Licence, on the corner. He gets it in for me.' He glanced at his watch. 'You'd better hurry. He closes in fifteen minutes, thanks to the ridiculous Anglo-Saxon licensing laws.' He laughed a little, talking now directly to Yannis, 'I tell the man often; no Greek would stand for it! Now – tell me – how is the family?'

Tight-lipped Nikos reached for his coat, which hung on a hook on the back of the door. He had already worked with his father for long enough to know that argument would serve for nothing. As he closed the door he heard them take up the conversation once more in Greek. 'There's news?' his father asked. Nikos did not hear the reply. Throwing his coat on as he went he crossed Miss Hooper's little office without so much as a glance at her – which raised a pair of thin, caustic eyebrows – and ran down the narrow, rubber-covered, dark stairs and out into the street.

By the time he returned with the ouzo he had regained some equanimity. As Cathy herself had pointed out, Leon's instinct always was to secrecy. He had spent too much time in a dangerous world at war where trust, even between father and son, had to be earned and respected. It would come. In time, it would come. He pushed open the door to the office.

'– the others – they aren't far behind us, I think – we should hurry,' Yannis was saying. As Nikos entered he looked up sharply, slid from the desk where he had been perched and smiled broadly. Both men already held a glass, half-full of the water-clouded spirit so beloved of Greeks. An almost full bottle stood on the desk. The air was thick with cigarette smoke. Nikos crossed the room and pointedly stood the bottle he carried beside the one already there. He slipped out of his coat.

'Well done.' Leon reached beneath the desk, produced a glass. 'One for you, my boy. The rest we'll take home to finish tonight, the three of us.'

Nikos blinked. Looked from one to the other.

Leon, in characteristic gesture, spread his hands innocently. 'Well, of course, our good friend must stay with us?'

Nikos took a long-suffering breath. 'Of course.'

'And then – tomorrow –' Leon was pouring the drink with suspicious care, not looking at his son, '– tomorrow, there is a small change of plan.'

Nikos waited.

His father came around the desk, handed him the glass. 'Tomorrow,' he said, 'Yannis and I must fly to Athens.'

The younger man stared at him.

Leon smiled blithely and lifted his glass in a toast before swallowing its contents in one go.

'You can't,' Nikos said, flatly.

Leon's huge head turned to him. The smile had gone.

'Pa, you can't! It's Christmas! Cathy's expecting us the day after tomorrow! You promised her we'd go down early in the car to help with the shopping!'

'I told you. A small change of plan. It is important. It is business. It cannot be helped.'

Nikos said the first thing that came into his head: 'Cathy will kill you.'

Leon let out one of his roars of laughter. 'No, my boy. You forget it is the messenger, the bringer of bad news, that suffers. Kati will kill *you*!'

'Well, thanks.' The words were grim.

'Now, now.' His father laid a conciliatory hand on his arm. 'I'm joking. Kati will understand. And – I tell you what – I give her you instead.'

Nikos' head came up sharply. 'What the hell do you mean?'

'You are right. I did say we would go to Suffolk with the car early to help her to shop. So – you be my ambassador of goodwill. You take the car and go. You help with this shopping. Perhaps Adam can get a couple of days to go with you? With two strong young men about her, why would she need me?'

Nikos was fighting the most contradictory turmoil of emotion it had ever been his misfortune to endure. 'You know Adam can't come,' he said. 'We've already spoken about it, remember? We suggested he travelled down with us. He can't. He's got some all-important office party or something. He's coming late on Christmas Eve.'

'Then, I tell you what.' Leon beamed. 'Tomorrow Yannis and I leave for Greece, you leave for Suffolk, and our good Miss Hooper tidies up the office, files some things and then goes home for a few days. We all meet again after Christmas. Everyone is happy, yes?'

Nikos looked desperately from one to the other. Yannis' scarred face was blandly expressionless, as if he had been stricken suddenly deaf. 'Pa – everyone is happy, no! I mean it. Cathy will be *furious!*'

'She will recover.' Beneath the jollity was an adamantine base of solid rock.

The inference of his father's earlier sentence was only now seeping into Nikos' appalled brain. He fixed Leon with the bright golden eyes of his mother. 'After Christmas?' he repeated. 'Pa – you aren't saying you won't be back for Christmas, are you?'

The familiar, graceless evasiveness was in the smile and the gesture that accompanied it. 'Of course not. At least –' the smile again '– I hope not.'

Nikos groaned and ran his hands through his hair.

'I will try.' The words were infuriatingly soothing; reassurance to a child.

Not without difficulty, Nikos held his temper. 'What exactly is this "business"? At least let me tell Cathy that.'

'Is not possible to talk about it. Is not settled.' Leon leaned forward, poked a spatulate finger into the air. 'But is most important. Most vital for the company. If we lose it –' he shrugged '– who knows? We fight to get established. We must be prepared to make sacrifices. Kati will understand, I tell you. Now –' giving his son no time to reply he reached into his pocket and pulled out a set of keys which he tossed to Yannis, who caught them one-handed. 'The keys to the apartment. You go now and have a bath and a rest. Nikos and I will finish here and join you later. I cook for us. Wait –' he reached for the ouzo Nikos had bought, handed it to the other man. 'Take it with you.' He winked. 'Don't get drunk before we get home. Tonight we will have a real Greek night.'

Yannis made his farewells and left. As the door shut behind him Nikos opened his mouth.

'No!' Leon held up a broad hand. 'Enough. What must be done must be done. Is a pity, I know. But for now, business comes first. Later, it will be different. Tomorrow I go with Yannis, you take the car to Suffolk to help Kati. With luck I will be back in two days and all will be well. If not, we will spend New Year together, as we planned.' He picked up the papers they had been looking at. 'Come. The sooner started the sooner finished. No argument, Nikos. One day you will thank me.'

Nikos looked at him in something close to despair. 'Yes, Pa,' he said.

Leon cooked moussaka, oily and dripping with cheese. The diminutive Yannis consumed it as if he had not eaten in a week, washing it down with what looked to Nikos enough retsina wine to sink a battleship. 'You don't change, my friend!' Leon laughed. 'Always you ate for two men!' and they fell again, as they had all evening, to reminiscence.

From the start of the war they had been in the Resistance together, fighting the occupying Axis forces in the mountains. In those dark, inspirational years they had shared adventure and hardship, desperation and the heady taste of victory, and then the bitterly bad times that had followed what for the rest of the world had been the end of the conflict but for Greece had meant the self-inflicted wound of civil war. Both had lost loved ones in circumstances that hardly bore recollection. Now the patina of time, the need to look forward, to reconstruct, was filling in the cracks, smoothing the jagged edges of hatred, but still, sometimes, in the grim humour a savage and unforgiving thread twisted through the fabric of their conversation. Nikos, outside of the fellowship of their shared experiences and privately half absorbed with his own demons listened, and learned. The wine was followed by more ouzo. Leon sat, elbows on table, his unbuttoned shirt collar revealing a neck strong and muscular as that of a man half his age. As he reached once more for the bottle the icon on its gold chain swung and glinted in the lamplight. Nikos blinked eyes that suddenly were not focusing terribly well.

Yannis looked at him solemnly. 'A hero, your father, you know that?'

'Pah,' said Leon.

'A hero. Saved my life.'

'No more than you did mine, several times. Shut up, Yannis.'

Nikos drew himself back from memory. 'What happened?'

Leon leaned his great frame back in the chair, picking at his teeth with a wooden toothpick. The golden medallion glinted again. 'The idiot got himself captured by the Communists. They decided that perhaps they should put him up against a wall and shoot him.' He grinned. 'Looking back perhaps it wasn't such a bad idea; but at the time I didn't think so. So I – changed their minds for them.'

'How?'

'With a little help from a couple of sticks of dynamite and a machine gun. I was young and impulsive in those days.' The smile this time was wolfish. 'And I had scores of my own to settle.'

Yannis' hand had gone to his scarred face. 'It was some fight,' he said, fond recollection in his voice. He put his elbow on the table, rested his chin on it and closed his eyes. Within seconds he was snoring.

'Enough, old friend!' With the callousness of long-established friendship Leon slapped him on the shoulder, jumping him awake. 'Come. We have a busy day tomorrow.' He hauled the smaller man to his feet, supporting him as he staggered a little. 'We toss a coin for the bed. It will be like old times.'

Yannis shook his head like a terrier coming out of water, blinked at Nikos, 'You should be proud of him, boy,' he said. 'He is a hero of Greece.'

Leon punched his shoulder, ungently. 'Shut up, man, and come and get some sleep.'

Yannis reached for the almost empty ouzo bottle, grinned inebriatedly into Leon's face. 'Shame to waste it.' Clutching it to his chest he followed Leon to the bedroom door. At the door he turned and lifted a hand to Nikos. '*Kalinihta sas.*'

Leon smiled. 'Good night. Sleep well.'

'A hero. I mean it. Saved my life.'

'Will you stop buggering about and get in here!' A huge hand caught him by the collar and hauled him into the bedroom. Leon's grinning face appeared around the doorjamb. 'Goodnight, Nikos.'

Nikos lifted a hand.

The door shut. He heard voices and laughter, the clatter of a glass. He put his head in his hands, staring sightlessly into his empty glass. He sat so for a very long time listening to the quiet murmur of their voices. There was a crash, more laughter, then silence.

Fate.

'*Tempt not the stars, young man, thou canst not play With the severity of fate* –' Where the hell did that come from? He had an uncomfortable feeling that it had something to do with a broken heart.

Beyond the door Yannis snored, peacefully.

Nikos pushed back his chair, turned out the lamp and went, sleepless, to bed.

The next morning, tired, dehydrated and with an ouzo-induced headache pounding behind his eyes, he watched as his father and Yannis climbed into the taxi that was to take them to the airport. It had turned suddenly and unseasonally warm and a heavy, soaking drizzle fell steadily. Before following Yannis into the car Leon clasped his son's shoulders, kissed him on both cheeks. 'Good boy. Look after Kati for me. Tell her not to fret; she will have the best present her Leon has ever bought her. Tell her that.' A moment later the taxi pulled away from the kerb and slid into the dense London traffic, and he was gone.

Nikos shook his head slowly. A present, for God's sake? How could Leon know his wife so little?

The black Austin Princess was parked a little further down the road. Five minutes after his father had left for the airport and Athens, Nikos was nosing through the Knightsbridge traffic heading in the opposite direction.

The December afternoon was already darkening to an early winter dusk as he turned the car into the narrow tarmacked track that led across the heathland to the cottage. He had driven slowly, deliberately taken time out of the journey to lunch in Colchester and to do some shopping of his own. The shops were warm and crowded, decorated for the season. At last the grip of post-war austerity was loosening;

there was a feeling of optimism abroad, the feeling that with the ascension of a popular young queen to the throne a new era was about to dawn. A new Elizabethan Age, well earned by a population that had at one time stood alone during those dark days of war and who since had endured the make-do-and-mend hardship of a country all but bankrupted by the conflict that had torn Europe apart for six dreadful years. Now, at last, things were changing, and in his new young queen, her handsome husband and two sturdy and attractive children the oft-quoted 'man-in-the-street' saw a symbol of a brave and bright future. The Coronation was still almost six months off, yet newspapers, magazines, shop displays were full of it; 1953 was to be a fresh start for the nation.

The headlights picked up Cathy's bicycle, propped against the leafless hedge. Nikos negotiated the sharp corner slowly and carefully; the car bumped and rocked down the uneven surface of the track, which was barely the width of the vehicle. The only place to park was near a small gap in the hedge perhaps a hundred yards from the cottages. Nikos found it, manoeuvred into it and turned off the engine, reaching into the glove box for the torch he had remembered at the last moment to bring. Wind buffeted the car. A dull light shone from the uncurtained window of Bert's cottage, emphasising the gathering, inhospitable darkness. In the distance, above the wind, the sea crashed and roared its winter song. The smell of woodsmoke was strong on the salt air.

Cathy, dressed as ever in practical slacks and a heavy pullover, was decorating the sitting room in preparation for the festivities. A fire burned brightly in the grate. Nikos stood for a moment amongst the wind-tossed shrubs of the garden just outside of the pool of light thrown by the window, watching her. Brightly painted home-made paper chains looped from the beams, the room was full of evergreen – holly, ivy and fir, tied with ribbons. In the far corner a small Christmas tree stood, awaiting attention. Cathy was standing on the table trying to attach a wired contraption of silver and gold to the ceiling. As he watched she gingerly lowered her arms, watching the thing suspiciously as it dangled precariously above her. She wagged her finger at it warningly, said something; it promptly fell down, draping her head and shoulders. He heard her explosion of laughter through the window. She sat on the table, swinging her legs, disentangling herself. Sandy, who had been watching her interestedly suddenly sensed the intruder, leapt to the window and broke into a frenzy of barking. Cathy turned her head sharply.

Nikos went to the door, rapping loudly. 'Cathy? It's OK – it's me – Nikos.'

Sandy's hysteria increased. He heard the bar being taken down, the rattle of the latch, and then there she was, silhouetted against the lamplight, looking at him in delighted disbelief. 'Nikos? *Nikos!* What are you doing here? I wasn't expecting you till tomorrow –' her eyes went past him into the dark and windswept afternoon. 'Is Leon with you? Oh, Sandy do shut up. And stop trying to lick poor Nikos to death! Anyone would think you hadn't seen him for a year! Come in out of the cold, my dear.' She stepped into Nikos' arms and gave him a quick, hard hug, caught his hand to pull him into the warm, softly lit room. 'I was just putting up some decorations. Christmas isn't Christmas without decorations, is it?' She hesitated, her hand on the door, her face questioning.

'Pa isn't with me,' Nikos said, and then, cursing himself for a coward even as he spoke added, 'he – sent me on ahead. To give you a hand.'

She closed the door, held out her hands for the heavy coat that he was shrugging from his shoulders. Her face was bright with pleasure. The cottage smelled as he remembered it, of fresh bread and woodsmoke. Sandy gave one more ecstatic and gravity-defying leap and then sat panting at his feet, flagged tail wagging. Cathy took his coat into the kitchen to hang it on the back of the door, talking as she went, 'Will he be coming with Adam tomorrow? I spoke to him yesterday – Adam, that is – he's catching the six o'clock from Liverpool Street.' She reappeared at the door, smiling. 'I know it's silly, but I can't tell you how much I'm looking forward to having us all here together. I've managed to get an *enormous* chicken from the farmer up the road – well, it looked enormous running around with its feathers on, I hope it doesn't shrink too much without them. We can go and pick it up tomorrow morning. And there's an order to fetch from the grocer's at Aldburgh as well. If Leon and Adam can be here by, say, half past sevenish we could perhaps have something to eat and then pop down to the village pub for a drink – they usually sing carols on Christmas Eve. I did wonder – I mean, you don't have to if you don't want to of course – but I wondered if we might even go on to the midnight service at St Peter's? It's silly – hypocritical, I suppose – neither Adam nor I set foot in church from one year's end to the next, and you and Leon are both Greek Orthodox, I know, but, well, Christmas is different, isn't it? It would be so very nice –' She stopped. Nikos was standing, awkwardly, in the middle of the room, making no attempt to answer her nor to sit down. Cathy stood for what seemed like a very long time, studying his face. 'Nikos?' she asked at last, very quietly. 'What is it?'

He opened his mouth. Closed it again, gestured helplessly.

'Leon?' she asked, the word only barely a question.

He nodded.

'Where is he?'

'He's had to go to Athens. On business.'

'I see.' She was still very quiet, apparently perfectly composed. 'When?'

'This morning.'

'This morning,' she repeated, and took a long, controlled breath. 'The day before Christmas Eve.'

He said nothing.

'And did he deign to explain what this – business – might be? Or when – or indeed whether – he plans to honour us with his presence within the next week or two?'

'He –' Nikos stopped.

'Yes?' She had walked past him, was standing at the table tinkering with the decoration she had been attempting to fix to the ceiling, that Nikos could now see was a complex construction of wire, cotton and gold and silver milk bottle caps.

'He said he'd try to get back.'

'It's a ten-hour flight to Athens,' she said.

'Yes.'

She glanced at him, 'Ergo –' the word was heavily sarcastic '– it's a ten-hour flight back.'

He could not meet her eyes.

'In which case, even at my most optimistic, I can't imagine that your father is likely to spend Christmas in the bosom of his family. Can you?' The lightness of the words was belied by the fingers that systematically twisted and destroyed the glittering metal discs. 'I'll kill him,' she said at last, conversationally. 'If he ever has the gall to show his face here again I'll kill him. Slowly.'

'I said you'd say that.'

She looked at him again. 'Oh? And what did he say?'

He shook his head, miserably. 'He said you'd kill me. You know – the messenger. The bearer of bad news.'

Her expression softened at that. 'Oh, don't be silly.' She came to him, put her hands on his shoulders, leaned to him a little, affectionately. 'It isn't your fault.' She let out a long breath, tamping down fury, containing and coming close to defeating bitter disappointment. 'It's Leon's loss if he can't see what's important and what isn't. And anyway –' she lifted her head and smiled, with a glint of that irrepressible humour that he so loved '– look at it this way: at least it means that you and Adam won't have to fight about who gets a chicken leg. It's an ill wind that blows no good at all as they say.'

He stood rigid beneath her hands, his arms hanging gauchely at his sides. Desperately he wanted to hold her, to gather her to him, to lay his face on that unruly mop of hair. He did not move. 'Pa said to tell you –' he began.

'What?'

'– that he'd bring you back the best present you've ever had.'

There was a long and dangerous silence. Then: 'Did he now?' Cathy said, lightly. 'Well, that should be an experience. For one of us at least.' She moved away from him, to the sideboard where stood bottles and glasses. Without asking she poured him a large brandy, and one for herself. Putting the glass in his hand she raised her own. 'Absent friends,' she said, drily.

And present loves. At the back of his mind during the drive from London had been the thought, almost the hope, that seeing her would break the spell. All of his adult life had been spent in a sophisticated metropolis, loved and cared for by a woman of elegance and good taste who had done her level best to cut him off from what she quite openly regarded as his regrettable peasant background. Understated good looks, fastidious grooming, impeccable manners, cool self-possession; these were the things for which every self-respecting woman strove and for which any man with any pretension to culture would look. Untroubled and unconventional disregard for such self-evidently admirable qualities had had no place in Susan Costandina's well-ordered world. Lately Nikos had more than once found himself wondering, flinching a little from the thought, what his grandmother would have made of Cathy, with her impulsive, unguarded laughter, her off-hand attitude to her appearance, her apparent inability to enter a room without immediately reducing it to casual disorder. He had seen her wrenching a comb through her tangled hair after a walk on the beach then simply giving up the unequal battle, tossing the thing to one side and winding the damp, unmanageable mass into an untidy bun with one hand whilst searching all over the kitchen for a hairclip with the other. Her clothes were tough, and warm and comfortable and in general accorded not even a token nod to the fashions of the day. Almost invariably as now, he noticed – there would be an absent-minded smudge of paint or ink on her face or her forehead. Even in London he had noticed that she never painted her practically short, square fingernails. She was of medium height and medium build. There was a dusting of freckles across the bridge of her nose. Her face, devoid of powders and creams, was almost gypsy-brown from the salt air. The only even slightly remarkable thing about her were the slanting, hazel eyes with their give-away laughter lines. She was more than twenty years older than he, though he often found himself forgetting that; she was ageless, and he loved her. Worse; as he stood, glass raised, watching her, he knew with a twist of almost physical pain that he wanted her. She was his father's wife. In even thinking such a thing he was breaking a taboo as old as the civilisation in which he lived, and he knew it. He touched his glass to hers. 'Absent friends.'

She took a long swallow of the spirit. 'I have an idea.'

'Oh?'

She touched his chest with her index finger. 'You get some logs in and make up the fire.' Up came her thumb, gesturing back towards the kitchen. 'I'll rustle up something for supper. We'll eat in front of the fire, then with a little help from Mahler and a lot of help from this –' she held up her glass '– we'll decorate the Christmas tree. Leon may be here, or Leon may be there, but at Sandlings, come hell or high bloody water it's Christmas and we're damned well going to celebrate accordingly. OK?' She smiled, too brightly.

'OK,' he said.

'And then afterwards, if you'd like, we could play chess. Or cards.' The grin this time was more natural. 'Or Ludo, if we've partaken a little too freely of the cup that cheers, so to speak.'

'I think I should warn you,' he said, 'that I play a mean game of Ludo.'

'Good.' She nodded solemnly. 'I do like a challenge. The logs are stacked round the back of the house. Supper will be ready in half an hour or so. We'll break into the Christmas goodies and have a feast.' She walked to the kitchen door, turned back. 'Oh – and if we do play Ludo –'

'Yes?'

'– bags I green.' She disappeared into the kitchen.

For Nikos the evening was enchantment and torture in about equal parts. Whilst Cathy banged and clattered in the kitchen, singing carols all the while perhaps just a touch too loudly and a touch too defiantly, he carefully unpacked the delicate glass ornaments for the tree from the cardboard box Cathy had deposited on the table. Fragile and delicate as spun sugar they were, his stepmother told him, relics of her own childhood, brought out each year, and inevitably each year suffering a casualty or two until now there were perhaps only a couple of dozen left. 'At least twice as many survived a world war,' she said, swinging a sparkling glass icicle from her finger, 'but Adam's cackhandedness is something else entirely. Remind me not to let him anywhere near them. They're impossible to buy nowadays.' They ate companionably in front of a roaring fire, and played Mahler, scratched but still magnificent, on an ancient wind-up gramophone. The little tree decorated and finished with tiny bows of shining silver ribbon and an ancient fairy doll with a tarnished tinsel wand, they eyed the chess set, shook their heads in unison and opted for the Ludo. The brandy by now was finished, and cheerfully unrepentant Cathy opened another. She seemed to have been overtaken by a mood of absolute and reckless gaiety. She cheated outrageously, urging Nikos to do the same, changed the rules twice and still managed to lose, which she appeared to find intemperately funny. When one of the counters fell to the floor and Sandy with a nonchalant flick of his tongue ate it, they decided to call it a day.

Cathy stretched, pushed her hand through her hair. 'You go on up. I'll clear up down here.'

'Are you sure?' He ached to touch her, ached to have her arms about him. He stood up, moved away. 'Why don't you leave it? We could do it in the morning.'

She yawned. 'No. Off you go like a good boy. Busy day tomorrow.'

'Fine.' He hesitated. 'Well – goodnight, then.'

Cathy was collecting the counters and board. She flashed him a quick smile. 'Good night. Sleep tight.'

He walked to the door at the foot of the stairs. Opened it. Stopped. Turned back to her. 'Cathy, I'm really sorry. About Pa, I mean.'

She stilled for a moment. Shook her head. 'I told you. It isn't your fault. I suppose I shouldn't have expected anything else. Shouldn't have . . .' she trailed off, shrugged.

He watched her for a long moment. She turned away, busied herself with the battered box.

Long after he had heard her climb the stairs and go into her own bedroom, long after all sound had ceased and the house, lulled by the distant sound of the sea on shingle, had settled to the darkness and quiet of a country night, long after he had smoked his last cigarette he lay sleepless still. When at last he fell to a fitful doze his dreams were darkly disturbing and on waking it shamed him a little to remember them.

Chapter Six

'Something tells me,' Cathy said with mild and disarming honesty the next morning, eyeing her plate of cornflakes doubtfully, 'that I drank just a tad too much brandy last night.' She bent over to deposit the soggy remnants in Sandy's bowl. The dog slurped them up delightedly. Cathy poured herself another cup of tea, and yawned. 'More toast?'

Nikos shook his head. 'No, thanks, I'm fine.'

She eyed him sympathetically. 'I'm sorry. This isn't going to be much of a Christmas for you, is it?'

'Oh, don't be silly!' His denial was quick. He smiled. 'I'm enjoying it already.'

Cathy smiled, got up and began clearing the table. 'We'll soon put a stop to that. Before we go shopping we have to call in next door. That'll take the grin off your face if nothing else does.' Seeing his faint wince of protest she laughed outright. 'Oh, don't worry – poor Bert isn't nearly as bad as he tries to make out. He's a dear old codger underneath.'

'Really?' Nikos did not hide his scepticism. 'How far do you have to dig?'

The cottage next door was just as squalid as he remembered it. He stood awkwardly just inside the door as Cathy badgered and scolded the old man into providing them with a list of things he needed from the town. 'You are the limit, Bert, honestly you are! I told you days ago I was going into town this morning. You were supposed to have the list ready!' She sat herself down at the table, cleared a space with a careless sweep of her arm and accepted the stub of pencil and scrap of crumpled paper Bert offered her. 'Right. Fire away.'

Bert shrugged, shuffled shapelessly back to his sagging armchair. 'I dunno. Nothin' you can't get me at the village shop I s'pose.'

'Some things are cheaper in town,' Cathy said, undaunted and unimpressed. 'Paraffin, for instance. How are you fixed for paraffin? And what about those cough lozenges you said eased your chest last time I bought them? Mrs Hamilton doesn't keep those . . .' It took ten minutes to extract a small list of necessities from the obstinately recalcitrant old man – an exercise that to Cathy's amusement Nikos later compared to the pulling of teeth. At last Cathy sat back and, laying down the pencil, glanced around the cluttered room. Big, rough-coated Paddy leaned beside her, his nose resting on her knee, eyes blissfully shut as she scratched his head. 'Honestly, Bert, you are a miserable old humbug!' she said, cheerfully. 'It's Christmas Eve and you've not got so much as a sprig of holly about the place.'

Bert grunted, his small eyes gleaming with something close to relish. 'Holly? Don't talk rubbish, girl. You'll be wantin' me to go carol singin' next! Bloody Christmas. Bloody waste of time more like.'

'Bloody Scrooge you mean. Dickens must have had you in mind, you know that?'

'Dickens who? I don't know no Dickens.' The old man cackled, drily. Nikos got the distinct impression that, with variations, this was an oft-played and well-known game to them both.

Cathy leaned her elbows on the table. 'I think you might have been too much even for him, you disreputable old bag of bones,' she said, the amused affection in her smile echoed in the tone of her voice.

Another cackle. 'You're probably right, girl. You're probably right.'

She rested her chin on her hands, watching him. 'Bert?'

'No,' he said. 'Told you once, told you a dozen times. No.'

'Just for dinner. Just for Christmas dinner. I hate to think of you in here on your own on Christmas day –'

'Christmas day, Michaelmas day, next Tuesday twelve-month, what difference does it make?' The old man was no longer laughing. His expression was mulishly stubborn. 'I got me wireless an' I got me dog. Tha'ss good enough for me the rest of the year, why not on Christmas?'

'You're an obstinate old idiot.'

Quite seriously, he nodded. 'Aye.'

'At least come in for a drink.'

He jerked his head in the direction of the kitchen. 'Got me home brew, thanks all the same.'

'I *know* you have!' By now Cathy could not but let her exasperation show. 'I mean – oh, you know what I mean!'

All at once the narrow shoulders shook and the walnut face wrinkled further to a triumphant grin. 'Temper, temper, girl,' he said.

Cathy threw back her head and laughed. 'You're impossible,' she said, 'I really ought to give up on you, you know that?'

Still the triumphant glint of amusement. Another shrug. 'Please yerself.' Paddy had left Cathy and ambled over to his master. 'Giddown,' the old man said. The dog settled peaceably at his feet, nose on paws. 'Yer needn't think yer'll be gettin' too much exercise in the next couple of days,' Bert addressed the dog 'Our next door lady'll be too busy enjoyin' this Christmas of hers to think about you.'

'Not true.' Cathy stood, tucked the note into her purse. 'In fact I'll probably take them both out this afternoon.' She walked to where he sat, stood looking down at him for a moment. When she spoke her voice was quiet, 'Bert, please? Won't you reconsider? Won't you please just pop in for a while tomorrow?'

Nikos watched as the old head tilted to look up at her. Suddenly, and to his surprise, he sensed the almost tangible bond of affection between them. A veined and mottled hand, brown as the earth and still remarkably strong-looking reached for Cathy's for a moment. 'Leave it, love,' the old man said. 'I'm all right. I've never thought much to Christmas, an' that's the truth.'

Cathy sighed, shook her head a little. 'Well you aren't going to get away with it entirely,' she said. 'I'll pop in at about one with some chicken and a piece of pudding. No neighbour of mine's going to ignore Christmas altogether, so there!' She turned, joined Nikos at the door.

'That husband of yours comin' to join you?'

The question was unexpected. Cathy hesitated a moment. Then, 'No,' she said, lightly, 'he's away. On business. But I've got the two boys.'

The old head shook. 'Some people in't got the sense they was born with,' the man said, then, with that small spark of malicious amusement again, 'but then he's a foreigner, in't he? No accountin' fer foreigners.' His smile as he looked at Nikos was beatific.

Cathy went back to him, kissed his leathery cheek lightly and shook a finger at him. 'You're a wicked old man who doesn't deserve a friend in the world, you know that?'

'In't got one. Not so far as I know.' He stirred the big, raw-boned dog with his foot. 'It's Paddy here. You don't fool me, girl. Think I don't know he's the one you come to see?'

Outside, walking through the rising wind to the car Nikos shook his head. 'That's one very peculiar old man.'

Cathy laughed. 'He's all right. He just enjoys being awkward, that's all. It's one of the few pleasures left to him. That and his home brew. By the way –' they had reached the car; she opened the door and climbed in '– if he ever gets round to offering you a glass decline gracefully. It's lethal stuff.'

Nikos slid behind the wheel. 'I still think he could show a bit more – well, gratitude, I suppose.'

'He does. He just shows it in a funny way, that's all. We both understand.' Her smile was warm. Her arm was brushing his. For a moment her nearness almost stopped his breath. He wound down the window and stuck his head out to reverse up the narrow, uneven track, a difficult task at the best of times. Wind blustered into the car. In the few minutes the awkward manoeuvre took he had almost regained control of himself. He wound up the window. 'Wind's getting up.'

He heard her laughter, looked at her questioningly. 'I told you you'd finish up talking about the weather!' she said, delightedly. 'It's an essential part of learning to live with the English. But yes, you're right, it is. As a matter of fact we've already had some quite bad gales this winter. But it's mostly all right. It's only when it combines with a high tide that there's any danger.'

He had reached the corner and was backing around it on to the wider track. 'Danger?'

'From flooding. It floods occasionally around here. But it's not usually much. Who was it used to say, "*Mind my bike?*"' she added, apparently inconsequentially.

He took his foot from the accelerator and turned to glance at her, blankly.

'Someone on the wireless. A comedian,' she added, helpfully. 'Arthur Askey, or someone. Perhaps he used to park his bicycle on an awkward corner as well?' She pointed.

He slammed his foot on the brake. The bicycle, inches from the nearside front bumper, rocked a little as the bumper touched the hedge against which it rested. 'Sorry,' he said. 'This damned track isn't the easiest thing to back up, I have to say.'

'If it rained you probably wouldn't be able to manage it at all,' she said, cheerfully. 'It's a quagmire in bad weather.

Why not leave the car up here on the wider lane? It's not far
to walk and would make life a lot easier. It's OK,' she had
her window open and was watching the ditch and the dense
hedge her side, 'you're round. All you have to worry about
now is the odd tractor or horse and cart coming the other
way.' Again that sudden, wide smile, and his heart turned
over. 'Now you know why I ride a bicycle.'

It took best part of the morning to complete their errands, but
by lunchtime they were back at the cottage with, as Cathy
pointed out, enough provisions to see them through a fairly
lengthy siege. While she delivered the purchases they had
bought for Bert, Nikos carted the bags and boxes from the car
to the cottage and piled them on the kitchen table. When
Cathy came back, while she was busy in the kitchen stacking
cupboards and filling the larder he cleared the fire in the sitting room and lit it, listening to her movements in the kitchen,
the sound of her voice as she hummed a Christmas carol; and
for a moment, sitting back on his heels watching as the small
flames curled and licked about the kindling, he was utterly
and oddly content. He had never taken such pleasure from
anyone's company. He loved the bright, snug feel of this little
house, Cathy's home, upon which her personality was
stamped so strongly. He loved to feel her near, to know that if
he turned his head he might see her standing at the kitchen
door, or walking towards him with that beguiling smile. Just
for this instant all guilt, all anguish faded, and it was enough
that he was here with her, that he loved her, that he had at the
very least her friendship and affection. Darker thoughts,
darker desires for a moment faded, unconsciously – and had
he but realised it dangerously – tamped down as the now
fiercely burning flames were smothered beneath the logs and
coal that they would eventually consume.

'Cheese sandwiches OK for lunch?' Cathy had appeared
at the door.

'Fine.'

She went back into the kitchen. 'I was wondering,' she called, 'if you'd like a bath while I take the dogs out this afternoon? That would give the water plenty of time to reheat and I can have mine when you go to pick Adam up from the station.'

He put the guard in front of the fire and joined her. She was buttering bread and the kettle hummed on the stove. 'That would be great,' he said.

'I know it's a bit of a fiddle,' she said, 'but it's really rather fun when the kitchen's all warm and cosy like this.' The bath, as he already knew, was neatly and ingeniously fitted beneath a hinged wooden top which, covered in bright cushions, served a double purpose as a seat when not in use. It was filled through a length of hosepipe from the sink and emptied through a pipe that ran through the wall to a drain in the lean-to lavatory next door; a simple but perfectly workable arrangement that was one of the many things about the cottage that Nikos knew would probably at one time have appalled him, yet now seemed not only acceptable but a positive part of the charm of the place. He accepted his sandwich. 'You're sure there'll be enough water for us both?'

She patted the huge stove affectionately. 'Oh, yes. This old thing heats enough for an army. Enjoy a soak. I'll stretch my legs and give the dogs a good run.'

He laughed. 'Stretch your legs? You've been on your feet all morning!'

She looked at him in genuine surprise. 'But that was in the town. That was on pavements and in stuffy shops. That's the very reason why I want to get out on to the beach, don't you see?'

He watched as she made tea for herself, coffee for him. 'You really couldn't live in a city, could you?' he asked after a moment.

'No.' The answer was uncompromising. She leaned across the table and put his cup down beside him. 'I couldn't. Not permanently. Not now.'

Nikos spooned sugar slowly and thoughtfully into the dark liquid, not looking at her. 'And Greece?' he asked, quietly. 'When the house is finished will you be able to live in Greece?'

Cathy was quiet for a very long time. He glanced up at her, fearing he had offended or upset her with the direct question. She shook her head, unsmiling. 'Same answer, I think. Not permanently.'

'You know that Pa –?' he stopped, shrugged, wishing, too late, that he had not started the conversation.

She sat down, quartered her sandwich very neatly and precisely, lifted her eyes to his. 'Nikos,' she said, patiently, and for the first time he glimpsed the depth of the anger beneath her calm, 'at the moment what your father does or does not want, does or does not intend to do is –' she hesitated '– shall we say is not my most pressing concern. I have a home. It's here. Leon knows where I am. Which is more,' she added, drily, 'than I can say about him. When he comes back from wherever he is, which I suppose at some point he will, then we'll talk about it.' Seeing the faintly disconcerted look on his face she smiled, lightening the moment, 'That'll be after I've thrown a fit and a few plates, of course, rather than before.'

The conversation stayed with her as she walked the windy beach, the dogs dashing to and fro about her heels, pouncing on the waves and occasionally on each other in a flurry of high spirits. In her determination to keep busy, not to let the festival be spoiled, she had hardly herself realised the strength of her resentment at this latest betrayal – for that was certainly how she saw it – of Leon's. Once again she heard Adam's words when he had spoken of the Greek house: *'Your life is with your husband, isn't it?'* She bent and picked up a smooth, heavy pebble, hurled it with all her strength out into the grey, churning sea. Heavy clouds had built up, the afternoon was darkening and there was rain now in the wind. Blindly she walked on. Your life is with

your husband. Your life is with your husband, that is, when
he cares to tell you where he is and what he's doing. And,
come to that, who he's doing it with. Your life is with him
even if over and over he blandly and brutally and apparently without thought tramples on your heart and on your
self-esteem and thinks he can make up for it with a casual,
expensive trinket. 'Sandy, come away from there!' The little
dog was up on the dunes, that were thick with sea holly and
riddled with rabbit holes and was busy excavating, damp
sand flying from beneath his scrabbling paws. Cathy stood
for a moment, the wind in her face, looking around her.
Resentment burned deeper. This was where her life was.
This was where she belonged. If the charming, ruthless,
womanising, unreliable man she had married could treat
her so cavalierly here, how much worse might not her situation become if she agreed to abandon her independence
altogether and follow him to Greece?

The rain was steady now and suddenly very heavy, blow-
ing in from the sea, sheeting in torrents across the beach.
She whistled sharply. The bedraggled dogs came to her, even
their high spirits a little quelled by the downpour. 'Come on,
boys. Enough's enough; we'd best get back before we
drown.'

Nikos had thoroughly enjoyed his bath. As Cathy had said
the kitchen was warm and cosy and there was no shortage of
hot water. He had taken the liberty of helping himself to a
drink. He lay in somnolent comfort listening to the rain that
drove against the window. His earlier, perhaps perverse,
feeling of contentment had returned. He sipped his whisky,
leaned his head back, his eyelids drooping. The glass tilted
and he jumped awake, half laughing. He sat up, tossed back
the last of the drink and reached for the towel.

He was dried, half dressed and rubbing at his damp hair
when he heard the front door open and close, and Cathy's
voice called, 'Hello, Nikos? It's only me.'

Shirtless and still holding the towel he stepped to the door and opened it. 'It's OK. I'm finished. Oh, good Lord!' The last words came in laughter.

Cathy stood, unbuttoning her sodden macintosh, dripping indiscriminately on polished floorboards and rug. She looked like a drowned rat, her drenched hair plastered to her head, water dripping down her neck and running down her face. 'My hat blew off,' she said crossly, 'and I couldn't catch it. And what good it is having two dogs with you when they let your hat get away without so much as trying to fetch it I don't know! Call yourself a dog?' This last was addressed to Sandy who, wet as his mistress, had leapt on to his chair beside the fire and was peaceably licking himself dry. 'I'd take you back and change you for a cat if I could be bothered, you knuckle-headed know-nothing pooch! And what do you think you're laughing at?'

'It's not a what it's a who! A very wet who!' Nikos could not contain his laughter. 'You should see yourself! Here –' he threw the towel around his neck, came to her and helped her out of the saturated coat. The rain had been so fierce it had driven through the shoulders to dampen her pullover. She dragged it off over her head, still muttering ill-temperedly.

'Bloody trousers – look at them – I might as well have been paddling!' She scrubbed at her wet face with the jumper, lifted her head, eyed him repressively. 'Nikos, it really isn't that funny!'

'I know, I know.' Watching her, bedraggled and grumbling like a wet child, an unexpected and completely uncontrollable surge of tenderness engulfed him and his laughter died. He felt for a moment that his heart had stopped. He could not take his eyes from hers. There was a sudden long moment of silence. Cathy's movements stilled. He took the towel from around his neck, and instead of handing it to her said softly, 'Turn around.' Her disconcerted gaze held his for a moment longer, then, very slowly, she turned her back to him. With infinite gentleness he began to rub at her soaked and dripping hair, massaging her scalp through the damp thickness of the towel. He felt her relax, leaning against him. She lifted her head a little; he sensed that she had closed her eyes, mesmerised. Sandy, his own ablutions complete, settled himself into his chair, put his nose on his paw and watched them with tranquil interest. The room was very quiet.

He felt the change in her, the sudden tension that gripped her and pulled her from him. As she turned abruptly back to face him his fingers tangled in her hair. She put up a hand to steady herself; her cold hand on his warm skin was like an electric shock. His hand was still in her hair. More than anything he had wanted in his life before he wanted to kiss her.

She ducked her head; he disentangled his fingers. She took the towel from him and buried her face in it, rubbing her head roughly. He stepped back. When she finally emerged from the towel there were two high spots of colour on her cheeks. She did not look at him. 'I'd better go up and change into something a little less likely to give me pneumonia.' She tossed the towel on to a chair and, very straight-backed, walked to the door that led to the stairs. As she disappeared through it, closing it very quietly behind her he put his head back, closing his eyes for a second and running a hand through his dishevelled hair. After a moment he spun on his heel, snatched up the towel and went back into the kitchen. He leaned for a long moment on the table, palms flat, head bowed. 'Fool!' he whispered quietly, through gritted teeth 'You fool!' and then, as the extent of the damage he had self-evidently inflicted sank in, his hand hit the table, hard, 'Oh, Jesus, you *fool!*' The words were soft, and savage, and verged on despair.

Upstairs, very composedly, Cathy went about the business of changing her clothes; studiously avoiding meeting her own eyes in the mirror as she did so. Even when, warm and dry in fresh slacks and jumper she picked up a hair brush and began to drag it, painfully fiercely, through the damp tangle of her hair she did it looking out of the window to where the marshes behind the cottage glinted like

polished pewter in the grey afternoon. It had stopped rain-
ing. She turned to put the brush on the dressing table; and
this time could not avoid her reflection in the mirror. Steeling
herself she faced it, steadily. Her cheeks burned. Her eyes,
about which the years had pencilled the fine lines of laughter and of tears glowed as if lit by a candle. The usually
unremarked streak of silver in her hair looked like a carelessly applied splash of paint.

Nikos had wanted to kiss her. She had felt it, sensed it,
known it as surely as if his lips had actually touched hers.

But worse – much worse – she had wanted it too. She
could not deny it.

Shaken to the core she stared at that face that suddenly
seemed the face of a stranger. She could not have been more
shocked if the solid, trusted ground beneath her feet had
suddenly and treacherously yawned to a chasm. A series of
apparently unconnected incidents flickered in her memory.
Nikos, crying on the beach, his hand in hers, her face on his
spray-damp hair. The almost imperceptible trembling of his
fingers as he had led her on to the dance floor at the Savoy.
His body against hers as they had danced. The enchantment
of Mahler. Had she encouraged him? *Had she?* She stared,
long and blankly, at the reflected stranger. Then, 'Mince
pies,' she said aloud, with a kind of manic calm. 'I've got to
make the mince pies.'

For one sweetly terrible moment she allowed herself to
wonder what his kiss would have been like.

She looked at her watch. A couple of hours and Nikos
would leave to pick up Adam from the station. Then they
would no longer be alone and everything would return to
normal; this crazy looking-glass world that she seemed so
suddenly to have stepped into would revert to its usual
rational and manageable self. 'Mince pies,' she said again, a
lunatic mantra, an invocation of common sense. 'I've got to
make the mince pies. Adam's coming. Adam likes mince pies.'

*

Nikos drove into Ipswich in the foulest mood possible. The past hour or so had been the most difficult of his life. He and his stepmother had been excessively and courteously careful not to catch each other's eyes, not to come near each other, not to speak of anything that touched on the personal. He had tasted and complimented her on her mince pies, she had asked him polite questions about his Christmases in New York with his grandmother. Every few minutes he had glanced at the clock, willing the hands to move. In the end he had left at least half an hour too early. He stood now waiting at the barrier as the train steamed in, watching for Adam's tall figure amongst the crowds, for the first time actually pleased that Cathy's sometimes graceless but often diverting son was coming to join them. If he were honest he could not have said that he very greatly cared for Adam; the least that could be said was that he would probably not have gone out of his way to make a friend of him if it had not been for the family connection, and he suspected that Adam felt the same. But after this afternoon's disaster – for that was certainly the way Nikos saw it – the devil himself would have been welcome to ease the atmosphere between himself and Cathy. One thing was certain: under no circumstances could he, Nikos, allow himself to be left alone with her over the next couple of days. Adam did not know it, he found himself thinking a little grimly, but he had just acquired a shadow for the duration of the holiday.

The station, and the crowds, were festive. People hurried past carrying bags and parcels, happy to be home at the start of the unusually long Christmas break. A small Salvation Army band played Christmas carols; a child shook a tin, collecting money. Nikos dropped a sixpence in it, then looked up to see Adam striding along the platform deep in conversation with another man, a small, thin-faced man in a shabby overcoat and a dark trilby hat. Adam was carrying a couple of parcels under his arm. Just before he came to the barrier he stopped, hunting in his pocket for his ticket. The smaller man stopped with him, still talking earnestly, gesturing with thin hands, as if giving directions. Adam nodded. The other man slipped something into Adam's pocket, smiled and winked and then disappeared into the flow of people going through the barrier like a fish into a muddied stream. Adam lifted his head and saw Nikos, lifted a hand in casual greeting. A few minutes later they were in the car and heading through the town. Nikos got the impression that Adam was in high spirits, pleased with himself; an impression confirmed when Adam, lighting a cigarette, said, 'Well – it looks as if Christmas in the country might not be quite such a pain after all.'

'Oh?' Nikos' eyes were on the road. He felt the man beside him stretch a little, making himself comfortable, his arm across the back of Nikos' seat. It was one of the things he envied Adam – this effortless ability somehow to take charge of his surroundings, to treat any place or situation as if it were his own natural domain. Nikos had never seen him ill at ease, or awkward.

'Met a guy on the train.' Adam put his head back to expel a long stream of smoke. 'There's a meeting. On Boxing Day. At Huntingdon.'

Nikos glanced at him, blankly. 'A meeting? What sort of meeting?'

Adam laughed. 'A race meeting. Over the sticks. The guy on the train was a bookie.' He patted his pocket. 'He gave me his card.'

Nikos glanced at him. 'Boxing Day?' he said. 'You can't go anywhere on Boxing Day!'

Adam looked at him in genuine surprise. 'Why ever not?'

'You – you're supposed to be here for Christmas. Cathy will be terribly disappointed if you disappear on Boxing Day –'

'Oh, don't be daft. She's got Leon and you to keep her company – unless you'd like to come along, of course?'

'She hasn't,' Nikos said.

'Hasn't what?'

'Cathy doesn't have Pa. He isn't here. He isn't coming.'

There was a long silence. Adam let out a very soft whistle. 'Well I'll be damned. The old bastard! Where is he?'

'In Athens I think. Somewhere in Greece at any rate. A man turned up a couple of days ago. There was some sort of deal – I don't know. Anyway it seems it couldn't wait. Pa flew to Greece yesterday. There's no way he'll be back in time to join us.'

'The old bastard!' Adam repeated, and this time there was a trace of admiration in his tone. He turned again to look at Nikos in the flickering light. 'Is that really where he's gone?'

'What do you mean?'

'You're sure there isn't –' Adam stopped, shrugged '– a little hanky panky going on?'

Nikos' hands tightened on the steering wheel. He waited for a moment before saying, shortly and simply, 'If you mean is he with another woman then no, I don't believe he is. I was there when the arrangements were made. It isn't a woman. It's money.'

'Fair enough, fair enough.' Adam was conciliatory. 'I just wondered, that's all. We all know Leon has a way with the ladies.' He sat in silence for a moment, watching through the window as the lights grew fewer and the car sped on into the dark countryside. 'Boy oh boy,' he said at last, 'I'll bet she was mad.'

'She was.'

'I wouldn't want to be in Leon's shoes when he does turn up.'

'No.'

'He'd just better bring her back something extra special, I guess.'

'If he does she'll throw it at him.'

'That bad?

'That bad.'

Nikos sensed the other man's shrug. 'Oh, well. That's their

problem, isn't it? I don't see why it should stop me from having a bit of fun on Boxing Day.'

'Adam –!'

Adam interrupted, an edge of fierceness in his voice. 'Listen – this happy family Christmas in the country wasn't my idea in the first place, if you remember? It's Wednesday bloody night. The damned weekend is tacked on to the holiday. I won't be back in London until Sunday. I've got to do *something* to stay sane in this God-forsaken hole. I'm going racing on Boxing Day and that's that.'

They had covered a couple of miles before Nikos broke the slightly hostile silence that had fallen between them. 'This Huntingdon place,' he asked, tentatively. 'Is it far? Could we get there and back in an afternoon?'

Adam turned his head to look at him. Nikos kept his eyes on the road ahead. He sensed the other man's sudden, sly smile. 'Yes,' Adam said. 'We can. Quite easily.'

Chapter Seven

With a skill that Nikos, whilst resenting it, could not help but admire, Adam set about charming and manipulating his mother from the moment he stepped over the threshold of Sandlings. 'Leave it to me, old boy,' he had said in the car. 'Just leave it to me. We'll be at that meeting on Friday or my name isn't Adam Sinclair. You'll see. But just leave me to broach the subject, OK?'

It did not harm his cause that Cathy was so openly glad to see him. She threw her arms about him and hugged him. 'Happy Christmas, darling.'

'And to you.' He bent to kiss her, straightened, looking around the room. 'The place looks great. It's something I always remember about Christmas – the way you always made things look so good, even during the war.' He set the parcels he carried under the tree, turned back to her, put an arm about her shoulder. 'Damn' shame Leon couldn't make it after all.'

'Yes.'

'Never mind. We'll manage.' He lifted his head, scenting the air. 'Something smells good.'

She smiled. 'Supper. It's waiting.' She glanced at her watch; the serviceable old one, Nikos noticed, not the beautiful thing that had been his father's gift to her. 'I wondered, after we've eaten, if you'd like to come down to the carol service at St Peter's? Only if you aren't too tired,' she added quickly. 'If you'd rather stay here –?'

'Not at all, not at all. Christmas comes but once a year and all that. And I know Christmas Eve has always been your favourite part of it. We'll do whatever you want, eh, Nikos?'

Nikos nodded.

Cathy slipped her arm through her son's. 'Come and eat. I want to hear all about where you've been and what you've been doing. Are you still seeing Dorothy? What was the trip from town like? Were the trains very crowded?' Not once since the two young men had entered the room had she so much as glanced at Nikos. In an unhappy silence he followed them through to the kitchen. He was called on to make very little contribution to the conversation during the meal; Adam's entire attention was focused on his mother, and she made little or no attempt to involve Nikos in their exchanges. The meal finished, Adam insisted that he and Nikos should wash up whilst Cathy got ready to go out. On their own in the kitchen he tossed a tea towel to Nikos, winked and stuck up a thumb. 'It's in the bag.'

Early as they were, the church was already crowded. The ancient building was ablaze with candles and dressed and decorated with the verdant greenery of the season. There was a crib in the porch, the figures freshly and garishly painted. An ancient organ, inexpertly played, wheezed its way through a piece that Nikos did not recognise. Several people greeted Cathy and Adam as they walked in and found them- selves a seat; a few covertly curious glances were thrown in Nikos' direction. He was not surprised when, reaching a pew where there were a few spaces Cathy pointedly drew Adam with her as she made her way along it, leaving Nikos to fol- low, and thus putting Adam between them. He sat in the whispering, shuffling crowd isolated and alone. All but unaware of his surroundings he brooded, mentally cursing his father for his selfishness, himself for his foolishness,

Adam for involving him in a cruel sham that, whatever he said, could only, in the end, upset Cathy. He stumbled through the service, standing, sitting, kneeling when everyone else did, making no attempt to join in the carol singing. Adam, beside him, blond head shining in the candlelight, virtuous as a choirboy, cheerfully sang every word. When the service came to a close they joined the slow procession that moved to the door. Christmas greetings were exchanged, introductions were made; he smiled and nodded and shook hands politely. Then at last they were back in the car and driving home, Nikos at the wheel, Adam beside him singing Christmas carols at the top of his voice, Cathy a quiet presence in the back.

Back at Sandlings Adam made a beeline for the whisky bottle. 'I've been a good boy for quite long enough. Cathy, you'll have one with me?' He was already pouring. 'Nikos?'

Cathy accepted the glass. Nikos shook his head. 'Not now if you don't mind. I've got a bit of a headache. I think I'll turn in.' It had already been decided that this time Adam would sleep downstairs.

'Would you like an aspirin?' Almost for the first time that evening Cathy met his eyes. Hers were concerned. He shook his head. 'No. Honestly, I'll be fine. I'm a bit tired, that's all.'

Adam held up the bottle. 'Sure a drop of this won't help?'

'No, thank you.' Nikos stood awkwardly in the middle of the room. Normally Cathy would wish him goodnight with a brush of her lips on his cheek or a light touch of her hand on his arm. 'I'll see you in the morning, then.'

'It is the morning,' Cathy said, quietly. 'Christmas morning.' Softly she came to him, stood on tiptoe to kiss his cheek. 'Happy Christmas, my dear.' Her voice and her eyes were perfectly steady.

He stepped away from her sharply. 'Happy Christmas. And to you, Adam.'

Adam lifted a hand in acknowledgement, turned to stir the fire to life. Blindly Nikos opened the door that led to the staircase, stood leaning in the darkness for a moment before reaching for the light switch. Through the door he heard Adam's voice: 'I say, I don't suppose we could break into the mince pies, could we? I'm starving.'

Cathy murmured an answer. He heard the kitchen door open; slowly he climbed the stairs and left them together.

In the sitting room Adam munched his mince pie, licked the crumbs from his fingers and poured another drink. 'If there's one thing I miss about living at home it's your cooking.'

Cathy turned from where she had been standing staring pensively at the little, glittering tree with its glass baubles and pretty bows and its heap of brightly wrapped parcels. 'Find yourself a nice girl and settle down,' she suggested, a little absently, her eyes still abstracted.

Adam snorted with laughter. 'Don't be daft! Where would I find a girl that could cook? Most of the ones I kick around with don't know a boiled egg from a lamb chop!' He threw himself down in an armchair, stretched his long legs out to the fire.

She snapped from her reverie, ruffled his hair affectionately. 'Thanks for coming to the service. I did enjoy it.'

He tilted his head, smiled his wide, disarming smile. 'So did I. It reminded me of when I was a kid. We always used to go, didn't we?'

She smiled. 'Yes. We did.'

Adam leaned forward, his elbows on his knees, glass held between the palms of his hands, his blue eyes bright. 'Do you remember what else we always used to do?' His gaze flickered to the Christmas tree and back. 'We always used to open a present, remember? When we came back from church. We used to save the rest for the morning, but we always used to open just one.'

She laughed a little. 'So we did. That started when you were a very little boy. It was because you used to get so excited that you wouldn't sleep unless you were allowed to choose one to open.'

He jumped up, put his glass on the mantelpiece. 'Let's do it! Open mine.' He reached to the stack of parcels and pulled one out. It was beautifully and obviously professionally wrapped. Gently he pushed her down into the armchair and knelt in front of her, the parcel in his hands. 'It's like old times, isn't it? Just you and me together?'

She took the pretty package, turned it over in her hands. 'Yes, it is. This looks too lovely to spoil it by opening it!'

'The girl in the shop did it for me. Go on – open it! Please?'

The boyishness of it made her smile. 'All right.' Very carefully she picked at the bow that held the thing together.

Adam fidgeted impatiently, laughing. 'Just tear it!'

She tore the paper from a long, narrow box which when opened proved to hold a pair of elbow-length black silk gloves and a pretty silver and turquoise ring. 'Oh, Adam, they're lovely!'

'They're to go with the dress you bought. The one you wore to the Savoy. You looked so gorgeous. I just thought these would finish the outfit off.'

'They will.' She pushed up the sleeve of her jumper and pulled one of the gloves on, slipping the ring on her finger over the top of it, spreading her hand to study it. 'Incongruous, but elegant!'

He took her hand and kissed it. 'Well you are, when you let yourself be.' He laughed, and corrected himself. 'Elegant that is. Not incongruous. I told you – you looked absolutely gorgeous that night. Dotty Dotty thought so, too.'

'*Your mother*,' Dot had actually said, '*seems to be the only woman in the room who isn't wearing gloves.*' The remark had fortuitously slipped into his mind when, having left his Christmas shopping, as always, to the very last moment, and having not given the slightest thought to his mother's present he had spotted both the gloves and the ring in a shop window display.

Cathy dropped a kiss on to the top of his head. 'They're lovely. Really lovely. Thank you. Now –' she pointed. 'Your turn. Pick a present.'

'Any present?'

'Of course.'

'Even one that isn't there?'

She frowned a little, puzzled. 'What do you mean?'

He nibbled his lip, looking, as he well knew, so like the little boy he had once been that her heart turned over. 'I wanted to ask a favour.' He flashed her a quick, mischievous smile. 'A Christmas favour. Do you mind?'

She hesitated only for a moment. 'Of course not.'

'It isn't just for me. It's for Nikos too.'

She relaxed. Not money then. Not this time.

'Well? May I have my Christmas favour?'

She slipped the ring from her finger, peeled the long glove from her arm. 'Of course you may.'

'Promise?' He was insistent.

'Promise.' She folded the slip of silk back into the box, lay the ring carefully upon it, lifted her head to smile at him. 'What is it?'

They spent Christmas Day very quietly and remarkably pleasantly. Adam having got his way over the race meeting was in good temper, and in his company the strain between Cathy and Nikos seemed to have eased. They slept late, opened presents over an early sherry then Cathy shut the two young men out of the kitchen while she prepared Christmas lunch. Before they ate she took a plated helping of chicken in to Bert, who accepted it with his customary splenetic gracelessness and then surprised and touched her by handing her a packet ill wrapped in brown paper. 'Why, Bert! What is it?'

'Open it and see, daft woman.'

The gift was an emerald green woollen scarf. Delightedly she wound it around her neck. 'It's lovely! Thank you.' She bent to kiss his cheek.

His dark skin grew a shade darker. 'That'll keep you warm while you walk the dogs, p'raps.'

After lunch they left the dishes on the table, opened

another bottle of wine and went into the sitting room to listen to the new queen's first Christmas speech. 'Poor thing,' Cathy said afterwards. 'So young. And so many responsibilities.'

'And all that boodle.' Adam was sprawled in his armchair, replete, his eyes closed. 'Sort of makes up for it, don't you think?'

Cathy punched his arm. 'Don't be so cynical. And don't go to sleep either.'

He opened his eyes, his expression injured. 'Why not? That's what Christmas afternoon is for.'

'That's what Christmas afternoon is for *after* the washing up is done, not before. I'm going to try out my new scarf and walk Sandy to the beach and back. I won't be long. The washing up –' she smiled and pointed to the kitchen door '– is thataway.'

Nikos scrambled to his feet. 'I'll do it.'

Adam had closed his eyes again. 'If you insist.'

'Adam!'

'It's all right. Really.' Nikos followed her into the kitchen. She reached for the heavy waxed jacket that hung behind the door. As she shrugged into it he, with unthinking and automatic good manners, reached to help her. His hands were still resting on her shoulders when she turned to face him. The wireless droned in the other room. Adam snored. Infinitely gently Nikos turned up her coat collar and handed her the green scarf. 'Enjoy your walk.'

'Yes.' Their eyes held for a moment, openly and intently. Cathy shook her head a little. 'Here, Sandy,' she called briskly, and, the dog dancing about her excitedly she turned away. Nikos stood for a long time after she had gone, looking at the closed door, his heart hammering in his chest. That fleeting moment of contact, that tiny movement, and he was lost again. All the defences so painfully constructed over the past twenty-four hours were destroyed. He wanted her. He had to face it. And he had to get away, before he tried to do something about it; before he caused a complete disaster.

They played cards later, cribbage at first at sixpence a game
until Adam declared this to be too tame and instigated a
game of poker in which he took flamboyant risks and played
for the pennies and ha'pennies they were staking as fiercely
as if they had been guineas. At midnight Cathy leaned back
in her chair pushing the last of her pile of coppers to her son.
'You've cleared me out. I'm for bed.'

'One more round?'

She shook her head. 'No fear. It's bed for me.'

After she had left them Adam neatly stacked his winnings
in piles on the table. Nikos watched him. Sensing it, Adam
lifted his head, his brilliant forget-me-not eyes gleaming with
the excitement of the game. 'A good omen,' he said, indicating
the money, 'I feel lucky.' He rubbed his thumb and forefinger
together. 'Tomorrow's going to be good. You still on to come?'

Nikos' hesitation was infinitesimal. The last thing he
wanted to do was to go with Adam. The last thing he could
do was to stay here alone with his stepmother. 'Sure,' he said,
'I'm still on.'

In the event, once they got there, Nikos found himself enjoying the afternoon. The atmosphere of the meeting was festive,
the weather had turned cold and bright, and whilst he could
not match Adam's fervour when it came to the racing he nevertheless could not help but be caught up in the noisy
excitement as the horses thundered towards the post urged
on by the vociferous punters. As it happened, in the end,
Adam's presentiment of luck turned out to be well founded,
though not before a couple of bad results had hit his pocket
hard. Nikos had taken a few pounds to the meeting, ready to
lose, part of the payment, as far as he was concerned, for the
afternoon's entertainment. Adam on the other hand gambled
to win. His reaction to a loss was to double his stake next
time, and the longer the odds the better. It was an unlikely
outsider that changed his luck. He distributed the large roll of
notes between several pockets, slipped a fiver in his shoe as

extra insurance – everywhere there were notices warning of the activities of pickpockets – and, grinning, took a large swig from his hip flask. 'Right. Two more to go.' He studied the card he held, 'I fancy the grey. "Roll on Home". That'll do me. A pony on the nose. Join me?'

Nikos shook his head, laughing. 'Too strong for me. I'll stick to ten bob each way.' He took the proffered flask, sipped from it, shook it. It was almost empty. 'You're running low.'

Adam shook his head, put his hand in his pocket and produced a second flask. 'Not a chance.'

'Roll on Home' came in at fifteen to one. Adam promptly lost half of his considerable winnings on the last race but was still cock-a-hoop and almost feverishly excited as they made their way back to the car. 'Tell you what. How about a celebration?'

Nikos glanced around the rather drab countryside in which the racecourse was set. 'What do you suggest? Chase a few sheep?'

'Cambridge. It's on the way. Pubs'll be open by the time we get there.' He winked, patted his pocket. 'Who knows? Might find ourselves a couple of fillies up for the Maiden Stakes.'

The noisy crowd in the pub was predominantly male. Adam pushed his way through to the bar, came back with a couple of whiskies. He stood nursing his glass, practised eye roving the smoky room. 'Not much on offer here. Hold on a minute. I'll have a word.' He sidled back into the crowd. Nikos lit a cigarette and watched him. Adam leaned across the bar, beckoning. The harassed bartender ignored him. As if by magic a crumpled brown ten-shilling note appeared in Adam's hand. The barman's attention was engaged. He moved to where Adam stood, leaned across the counter, listening, nodding, speaking rapidly. The note disappeared over the bar. Adam rejoined Nikos. 'Drink up,' he said, cheerfully 'We're in the wrong pub.'

Fog wisped in the darkness, and their breath clouded the

air. 'Leave the car here,' Adam said, 'it isn't far. Just round the corner.'

The street was quiet. There was movement in a doorway. Beneath a street lamp, that shed its shroud of light through the thickening fog, two young women stood talking. A cigarette glowed and died, a spark in the darkness. 'Adam –' Nikos said.

'Hello girls.' Adam's bright hair, fog-damp, sparkled in the light of the lamp. 'Happy Christmas. Fancy a drink?'

It was eight o'clock before Cathy really started to worry. As darkness had fallen a heavy bank of fog had rolled in from the sea, blanketing the countryside. Even the sound of the sea was muffled. She had listened to a play on the radio, then had switched to a concert on the Third Programme, that played quietly in the background as she picked unenthusiastically at the carcass of yesterday's chicken. She had not drawn the curtains; the thick, hushed darkness outside seemed to invade the house. The weather report had said the fog was widespread. That must be why Nikos and Adam were late. She tried not to think of the lethal combination of poor visibility and the general insobriety of the season. She gave up on the chicken, eyed the depleted plate of mince pies and decided against them too. She wandered to the window, leaning to the pane, cupping her hands about her eyes to peer out. She could see absolutely nothing; the wall of fog was impenetrable. She turned back to the warmth and light of the kitchen. Sandy, curled in front of the stove, watched her every movement. 'They won't be long now,' she said to him, reassuringly. 'I'm sure they won't be.'

The dog's small tail thumped twice and was still.

'I could pop next door and check that Bert's all right.'

Sandy cocked his head on one side.

The wireless had slipped a little from the station, and was hissing and crackling. She adjusted it. Looked at her watch. 'He'll be in bed, I suppose. Oh, dammit, where the hell *are* they?'

In the dripping silence beyond the window the North Sea fog continued to roll in and blanket the flat East Anglian landscape.

The room was untidy, the furniture threadbare; the whole house smelled of badly cooked food and overused lavatories. The two girls, who had introduced themselves as Babs and Irene, lived on the top floor. The air was heavy with cigarette smoke, the ceiling yellowed with it. One of the bottles of gin that Adam, on the girls' instructions, had bought when they left the pub was already empty, the other well on the way. The girls were drinking it with orange, thick, sticky and sweet. Nikos turned his head from the smell of it on Irene's breath as she buried her face in his neck and guided his hand inside her unbuttoned blouse. The other girl, Babs, was naked to the waist, sprawled on Adam's lap, his hand up her skirt. Adam whispered something. Babs giggled.

'Come on, darlin'.' Irene wriggled, her hand groping at the buttons of Nikos' trousers. 'Come on, Yankee – let's use the bedroom first.' She raised her voice. 'That OK, Babs?'

'Wa'ss'at?' Babs' untidy blonde head lifted. Her voice was slurred.

Irene jerked her head towards the door. 'OK if the Yank an' me use the bedroom first?'

Babs hauled her skirt up a little higher, turned back to Adam. 'Do what you like, Reen love. Big Boy here ain't gonna wait for no bedroom from the feel of it.' She laughed huskily.

The other girl slid a little unsteadily from Nikos' lap, stood up and unbuttoned her skirt, letting it slip to the floor. She was wearing laddered stockings and a suspender belt that even in the dingy light looked none too clean. Her blouse hung open, revealing her large, soft breasts. She held out a hand. 'Come on, then, darlin', come and see what Reenie's got for you –'

Nikos could stand it no longer. The self-disgust that he had been battling welled in him like a physical sickness.

'Adam – it's bloody nearly ten o'clock! Cathy'll be worried sick.'

'What?' Adam's tousled head lifted. He blinked.

Nikos stood up, buttoning his trousers. 'We've got to go. God only knows how long it will take us to get back –'

Irene was watching him, eyes suddenly narrowed, mouth hard. 'You what?'

'We've got to go,' he repeated, desperately. 'Adam –'

'Oh, no you don't.' Irene shook her head.

Babs wrapped her arms about Adam's neck. 'What's he on about, Gorgeous?'

'Oh, come on, Nikos!' Adam's hand slid down Babs' naked back. 'Don't be such a spoilsport. We promised the girls a good time –'

'That –' Irene said, softly, her eyes still razor sharp on Nikos', '– isn't all we was promised.'

'Adam!' Nikos was struggling into his jacket. 'Come on. We have to go.'

'An' I say no.' Irene grabbed his arm. 'What the 'ell do you think you're doin'? Playin' games are we? You want ter go? Then go. You ain't nothin' ter write 'ome about, don't you think it. But –' her hand came out, flat, palm up, 'you bloody pay for what you ordered. I ain't goin' back out in that bleedin' fog tonight. An' I got a livin' to earn like any other girl.'

'Adam, for Christ's sake –'

Adam pushed Babs from his lap and stood up. The girl slid to the floor like a sack, sat, half-naked and blinking aggriev-edly. ''ere –!'

'Nikos –' Adam was dishevelled but patient. 'Don't be such an ass. You agreed. You were as ready for it as I was –'

''e was quick enough to put 'is 'and up my skirt,' Irene put in drily.

'I've changed my mind.'

'Well, you haven't changed mine.' Adam's voice was edged with anger now. 'You bloody well know what we agreed.'

Nikos gripped his arm. 'It's thick fog out there. It's already nearly ten. Think of Cathy. Your mother. She'll be frantic –'

''is mother?' Irene was so incredulous she almost laughed. 'Now I've 'eard everything! 'is bleedin' *mother?*'

Nikos was hunting through his jacket pockets. The hunt produced three crumpled notes; two pounds and a ten shilling. He proffered them to Irene.

'What the 'ell is that supposed to be?' she asked, conversationally.

'I'm sorry. It's all I have.'

'Well it ain't good enough.' She planted her hands on her narrow, bare hips.

Nikos picked up his coat, turned to Adam. 'I'm going. You either come or you don't.'

'And how the hell am I supposed to get home if you take the car?'

'That's up to you.'

'Oh, for Christ's sweet sake!'

'Are you coming or not?' Nikos was dogged.

'You ain't goin' nowhere,' Irene said. She had planted herself in front of the door. 'Not till I've got my money.'

'An' me,' Babs said from the floor. She nodded slowly and drunkenly. 'An' me,' she repeated.

'Give it to them,' Nikos said.

'What?'

'The money. Give it to them. I'll pay you back. But I'm going. Now.'

Adam stared at him for a moment, about to speak; but whatever he saw in the other man's face gave his angry words pause. He shrugged, reached for his jacket. 'You crazy bastard.' He pulled out a roll of notes, counted some out. Irene crossed the room, hand held out. He handed her the money. She curled her fingers in graphic encouragement. He peeled off another couple.

'I'll pay you back,' Nikos said.

'You'd fucking well better.' Oddly enough, a sudden touch

of caustic amusement overlaid the anger of the words. 'With interest.' He picked up his overcoat, flicked a finger to his forehead. 'Good evening, ladies.'

'Fuck off,' Irene said, pleasantly, 'an' good riddance.'

'Where they goin', Reen?' Babs looked from one to the other in inebriated puzzlement. 'Where's Gorgeous goin'?'

''ome to mother,' Irene said, 'believe it or not.'

The journey was as much of a nightmare as Nikos had feared it would be. Visibility for most of the way veered from a few yards to zero. The route was unfamiliar. Trying to use the headlights simply made things worse; reflecting off the fog they simply created a wall so thick that it might have been made of solid brick. They crawled along, following the kerb where there was one, which on this mostly country road was not often, and for most of the time, despite the map they carried, only vaguely aware of their exact whereabouts. For a long time, as they pulled out of the city and guessed their way almost blindly on to the main road that led across country to the coast neither of them spoke except briefly and to the point about which might be the best route to try to follow. Once fairly certain that they were on the main easterly road that would, in time, take them home Nikos tried to apologise. 'I'm sorry. I just couldn't stand it. It was all so – squalid.'

Adam yawned. 'Scrubbers always are, didn't you know that?' He was remarkably sanguine. Nikos sensed his grin in the dark. 'You might at least have let me have a go before you threw a fit, though.'

'I'm sorry,' Nikos said again. His head was thumping and his eyes ached with strain as he tried to probe the wreathing fog. Hammering in his blood he could feel Cathy's fear, her worry. For her son. Perhaps, a little for him. He had never felt so guilty – or so dirty, so utterly soiled – in his life. Time crept by, and the car crawled on. Would they never get there? He felt like a swimmer desperately needing to reach the safety of the beach and battling against an outflowing tide. Beside him

Adam breathed softly and deeply. He had gone to sleep, mindless and guiltless as a child. Nikos gritted his already aching teeth and drove on into the cold and damp void of the fog.

They reached Sandlings at two-thirty in the morning. All the lights were on, glowing dimly through the fog. Adam was unsteady on his feet, fuddled by sleep and the beginnings of a hangover. Nikos supported him as they felt their way down the track to the cottage. As Nikos pushed open the front door and pulled the heavy curtain aside Sandy erupted into his usual frenzied house-dog routine, but calmed immediately when he saw who the intruders were. The fire was dead and the room was bone-chillingly cold. Cathy was curled, fully dressed, on the sofa, her head resting awkwardly on her arm. The wireless spat and hissed atmospherics, the station having long closed down for the night.

She woke up instantly; Nikos actually felt the split second when overwhelming relief became fury. 'Where the hell have you two been?'

Adam flinched a little, spread conciliatory hands. 'Sorry.'

'Sorry? *Sorry?* Is that all you've got to say for yourself? I've been worried *sick*! Are you going to tell me, fog or no fog, that it's taken you –' she glanced at her watch '– getting on for ten hours to get here from Huntingdon?'

Adam shook a fair, apologetic head. 'No. I'm sorry. We – I – had a good day. Won a bit, you know? We stopped off in Cambridge to celebrate.'

'Without a thought for me.' Her eyes had flickered to Nikos. He lowered his own, unable to meet her anguishedly savage gaze. There was a moment's silence. 'I thought you were both dead,' she said, suddenly very controlled and quiet. 'Or at least badly injured. I thought there must have been an accident. I thought – I feared – the police would come . . .' she stopped and swallowed fiercely.

Adam huddled into his overcoat. 'Look. I'm sorry, I really am. But here we are, and we're fine, and can we talk about it in the morning? I'll grovel then, I promise. We went into Cambridge, we had a couple of drinks, picked up a couple of girls –' again those artless spread hands. 'You know how it is. Time flies.'

'When you're enjoying yourself.' The tone of Cathy's voice had changed entirely. Glancing at her Nikos thought he had never seen her eyes so icy cold. They were looking directly at him; once more he could not for his life hold them with his own.

'And then, honestly, it has taken hours to get home. The fog's really bad.'

'So I gather from the reports on the wireless.' Her voice, usually so warm, was still clipped and chill. 'Well, since you've now deigned to turn up I suppose I can go to bed. Nikos – have you nothing to say for yourself?'

He had not spoken since they had come through the door. He glanced at her, helpless. In the deadly cold of the room his face was flaming. 'I'm sorry,' he said, and he himself could hear the total emptiness of the words.

'So am I.' For a brief, bleak instant they might have been alone. Nikos, looking into her face, thanked God devoutly that they were not.

Adam, his fuddled brain and tired body a little revitalised by the walk from the car and the cold of the room looked from one to the other; even he, without getting near to understanding it, sensed the tense atmosphere between them.

The moment was gone. 'You're not children,' Cathy said. 'You're two grown men. You'll do as you like. Just next time don't leave me here worrying myself to death about you.' She turned from them and stalked to the door that led to the staircase. Her hand on the knob she turned back for a moment. 'Happy Christmas,' she said, acidly, and left them.

'Ouch,' said Adam, not too concernedly. 'Bloody hell – it's cold as charity in here. Colder. Fancy a brandy?'

Chapter Eight

They were fog-bound for two days; even as the two young men packed their bags and left after Sunday lunch it still shrouded the heathland, blanketed the dunes and wreathed eerily through the scrubby, dripping trees. By then Cathy had, at least outwardly, recovered her equilibrium and Adam had just about got over a thumping and well-deserved hangover. On the day after their trip to the races both young men had slept until after noon. When they had finally surfaced apologies were proffered once more and this time, temper having cooled, had been received more graciously; yet a subdued Nikos was certain that whilst Cathy's anger with her son had more or less entirely dissipated he discerned in her attitude towards himself a certain frostiness that no amount of carefully cheerful conversation could conceal. In the event he was glad to leave; by no means, from his point of view, could the visit have been termed an unmitigated success.

'Be careful. The fog's still very thick.' Cathy accompanied them up the track to the car, hugged Adam, dropped a swift, cool kiss on Nikos' cheek. 'Give my love to your father,' she added drily, 'if you can find him.'

'Thanks for Christmas.' Adam was eager to be off. London

and its pre-New-Year diversions beckoned. 'We'll see you in a few days' time, at New Year.'

'Let's wait and see. Leon might be in Australia by then for all we know. A vaguely made plan to spend New Year in London with his family would hardly be enough to hold him if something more profitable beckoned, now would it?'

'He'll be back,' Nikos said, quietly, 'I'm sure he will.'

Cathy smiled a bright, unconvinced smile. 'We'll see. Now, off you go. And take care.'

She watched as the black car slid into the drifting mist and disappeared, the sound of its engine dying, leaving a silence broken only by the distant fog-muffled sound of the sea. She stood for a long time, quite still, before, shoving her hands into her pockets and hunching her shoulders against the cold, she turned and walked back slowly to the quiet, empty cottage.

The telegram arrived the following day. It came whilst Cathy was taking her regular walk on the beach with the dogs; when she got back it was to find an agitated Bert waiting at the door clutching a yellow envelope. 'Came soon after you left.' The old man watched her with a touching anxiety as she tore it open. 'Boy wouldn't wait. Said if you wanted to reply you'd have to do it from the Post Office in the shop. Bad news, is it?' Bert belonged to a generation that, having gone through two world wars, would never associate a telegram with anything else.

Cathy scanned the scrap of paper again. 'A matter of opinion,' she said, tartly, then, glancing up and catching his concerned expression reached to him quickly and touched his arm reassuringly. 'No, no. Nothing to worry about. It's Leon. He's back.' She glanced back at the brief message with an acrimonious eye. 'It seems I'm summoned to join him in London for the New Year celebrations.'

'Will you go?'

She did not reply for a moment. Then, 'I don't know, Bert,' she said, 'I really don't know.'

He eyed her, his genuine relief for her already giving way to his usual caustic cantankerousness. 'You'll go, girl,' he said, 'an' yes, I'll look after the dog for you. Just don't expect me to spoil the little brute the way you do, tha'ss all.'

She spoke to Leon from the phone box outside the shop later on that afternoon. Yes, she would join him; but on one point she was adamant. She would not stay in Nikos' flat.

'But, Kati, why ever not?'

'Because it isn't fair on Nikos. And it wouldn't be fair on me. We have to talk, Leon, and I don't want to do it in front of an audience.'

'Talk?' He was all innocence.

'Talk.' The word was curt. 'You know what I mean.'

'Ah, Kati, Kati, you aren't still angry because I didn't come at Christmas?'

'Aren't I? I thought perhaps I was.'

He sighed a long-suffering sigh. She could almost see his eyes being cast to heaven in exasperation at the perversity of women. She controlled a lift of anger. 'Book us into a hotel. Or I won't come. I mean it.'

'Of course, of course. If that's what you want, that's what you shall have. I promise you, *koukla mou*, your Leon will make it up to you. Anything you want, you shall have. I have bought you a present. To go with your dress. And for the boys, gold cuff links, with their initials –'

'I gather the trip to Greece was a success?' The words were dry.

'Yes. It was.'

'Well, you can tell me all about it when we see each other, can't you? I'm really keen to know what it was that was so much more important than our Christmas together.'

There was a sudden, small, guarded silence. 'It was business, Kati, just business.'

'I see.'

'Listen – catch the midday train tomorrow, yes? By then I will have made all the arrangements, I promise. I will meet you at the station. And don't forget to bring your pretty dress. Adam has invited us to a party with some of his friends on New Year's Eve.'

'OK. Leon, I have to go, my money's running out. I'll see you tomorrow, at Liverpool Street.'

'The midday train. And Kati – I'm sure you will like your present –' the money dropped noisily into the box; Leon's voice was cut off by the purring tone.

Cathy eyed the buzzing receiver repressively. 'I'm sure I will,' she said, acidly.

'It's lovely,' she said, with truth but no great enthusiasm.

Leon, standing behind her, met her eyes in the mirror. 'You like it?'

'It's lovely,' she said again. The glittering pendant on its golden chain caught the light as she moved.

'You'll wear it tomorrow night?'

'Of course. If you'd like me to.' She reached to undo the catch.

'Let me.' Leon released the catch, lifted the pendant, swinging it, before putting it into Cathy's hand. 'You see? I thought about you.'

Cathy tilted her head, looking up at him, unsmiling. 'Did you? Did you really?'

'But of course!' He spread his hands in the familiar gesture. 'Can't you see that I did?'

She stood up abruptly and walked to the window, stood for a moment looking out across the roofs and towers of a London that was still in the process of restoration and reconstruction after the devastation of the wartime blitz.

'Kati?' Leon asked quietly from behind her.

She turned. 'Leon, why can't you understand? Why can't you understand why a – a bauble like this –' she held out her hand. The pendant glittered on her open palm '– can't make up for what you did? You left without a word or a thought. You simply abandoned the plans that we had made and went off on your own. You won't tell me where you went or what you did –'

He sighed, patiently. 'I told you. I was in Athens. Doing business.'

'What sort of business? And why over Christmas? Why couldn't this – business – that you're so mysterious about have waited for a couple of days? Oh, for heaven's sake!' She shook her head fiercely. 'We've been over and over it. You know how I feel.'

'Then why don't you try to see how I feel?' There was a rising edge of temper in the words. 'Do you think I wanted to spend Christmas away from you? Don't you think that if I could have made other arrangements I would?'

'I don't know. I truly don't know!' Her voice was rising to match his.

'Well, you bloody well should! For Christ's sake, Kati, if you would come up and live in London with me such mis-understandings wouldn't arise –'

Her head came up sharply in challenge. 'You mean that if I'd been in London you wouldn't have gone?'

He stood breathing heavily, said nothing.

'Exactly!' she snapped. 'All you mean is that if I'd been here you'd have come home and expected me to pack your bag for you before you left. You still wouldn't have told me what you were doing or why. You still wouldn't have given a damn that our Christmas would be spoiled –'

'I keep telling you, woman –' he roared.

'I *know* what you keep telling me. You were in Athens. Doing business. What business? And with whom?'

He hesitated. 'Shipping business,' he said. 'With an old friend. He – he's in financial trouble. That was why I had to go so quickly.'

She was watching him steadily. 'I don't believe you,' she said, flatly.

His mouth tightened.

'Leon – you think I don't know when you're lying?'

'I'm not lying, woman.'

She walked quietly to him, reached for his hand and guided it to the open neck of his shirt, where the heavy icon hung.

'Swear it,' she said.

He fingered the icon. Said nothing.

'Well,' she said very quietly after a moment, 'I think that proves something, don't you?'

'You don't understand,' he said.

'No. I don't. We should get ready. It's nearly time for dinner.' Her voice was very cool.

He made a visible effort to calm himself. 'I went briefly to the house,' he said. 'It will be ready, I think, by the spring. We will go to Greece for Easter. It is a great festival. You will enjoy it. It will make up for Christmas.'

'Perhaps,' she said, and left him to guess to which – or even to how many – of his statements the word applied.

The New Year's Eve 'party' to which Adam had invited them turned out to be a rather splendid ball held in one of the grander hotels overlooking Hyde Park. He and Nikos joined Leon and Cathy for dinner first; they were to join a party at the ball later. Cathy glanced around. 'No Dorothy?'

'Who? Oh – Dotty.' Adam grinned, shook his head. 'Fallen by the wayside I'm afraid. She was getting a gleam in her eye that was making me nervous.' He winked. 'I like the gloves.'

Cathy laughed. 'So do I.'

The meal was good, and the atmosphere festive and relaxed. Neither Cathy nor Leon were sulkers, and though the differences between them remained, superficially at least they were at ease with each other. Adam was his usual extrovert self; only Nikos was quiet, though since that was his nature no one but Cathy noticed just how quiet. He sat and he listened, smiled in the right places and consumed a large quantity of wine. Nikos had come to a decision, and tonight was the night he intended to implement it. He paid no special attention to Cathy, made no great input to the conversation. His time would come and he would say what he had to say. After that, things would be in the lap of the gods, though he had no great faith in their goodwill.

They moved into the ballroom, and found their table. A great clock, decked in silver and gold, ticked on one wall. There were silver and gold balloons in a huge net strung above the dance floor. The candlelit tables held bowls of streamers and novelties, and there were hats and masks and tiny Union Jacks. People were already on the dance floor.

'Champagne,' Leon said.

'Lots of it.' Adam was wearing a cardboard top hat at a jaunty angle. 'Ah – there they are –' He stood, waving a hand. A large group of young people who had just entered the room steered their way through the tables towards them. There were introductions and handshakes, kisses for Adam from the girls. Cathy caught only half the names: there was a Henrietta, a Jennifer and a Phyllis, two Davids and a Quentin, after that she lost count and could not have put a name to a face anyway. They were a handsome bunch, the young men dapper in their evening suits, the girls in taffeta and lace, bright-lipped, slender-waisted, bare-shouldered in heels so high Cathy wondered how they could walk on them, let alone dance. She found herself sitting next to a girl in green whose permed blonde hair gleamed like a metal helmet in the lights and who punctuated everything she said with a trill of pretty laughter. Fortunately, since by now the noise levels were such that it was difficult to hear what anyone was saying anyway, she did not appear to require any response apart from the odd nod and smile, so Cathy obliged with nods and smiles and sipped her Champagne and found to her surprise that she was beginning really to enjoy herself. She danced with Leon, and with Adam and with a couple of the other young men. By the time the huge clock had ticked round to eleven o'clock she had drunk enough Champagne to tempt her to risk dancing with Nikos, something she had told herself sternly earlier that she would not do; but in the event he did not ask her so the decision did not have to be made. Perversely she found herself a little piqued. She caught his eye, smiled, and then wished she had not; his eyes held hers for a long, disturbingly intent moment before he reached in his pocket for his cigarette case, extracted a cigarette and lit it, long lashes downswept and with not the trace of an answering smile. An odd, quarrelsome anger stirred. It was she who had cause to be put out, surely, not him. Adam's words, that she had spent days putting from her mind, sounded suddenly and clearly in her head. '*We went into Cambridge, we had a couple of drinks, picked up a couple of girls –*' Well, that was what young men did, wasn't it? As she had already asked herself a million times: what business was it of hers?

She reached for her glass and drained it, smiled charmingly at the young man who immediately refilled it for her. 'I say – would you like to dance?'

'I'd love to.' She gave him her hand, allowed him to draw her from her seat; felt rather than saw the sudden flicker of Nikos' eyes. Damn him. She stepped into the young man's arms, smiling warmly into his face, and they drifted into a graceful waltz.

The clock ticked on, the Champagne continued to flow and the glittering, elegant crowd chattered, laughed and danced their way towards 1953.

Nikos watched the clock and sipped his Champagne.

Cathy was dancing with Leon when the Master of Ceremonies called for quiet, a few minutes before midnight. 'Ladies and gentlemen – I ask you to charge your glasses . . .' They made their way back to the table where the rest of the party was gathering. All over the room the sound of popping Champagne corks competed with a buzz of conversation and laughter. '. . . a year that is to see the

Coronation of our young Queen, God bless her, a year in which this great country of ours will celebrate the dawn of a new Elizabethan era –'

Adam winked at his mother. 'What a load of –' he stopped himself in time, grinned '– baloney.'

She slapped his arm lightly. 'Ssh!'

The room had fallen quiet. The clock's hands moved together. From a radio on the stage Big Ben's chimes struck the hour.

Pandemonium broke loose. Amidst the cheers streamers popped, toy trumpets and whistles were blown, the great net released its silver and gold balloons on to the crowd below. Leon reached for Cathy, kissed her. *'Polla Kronia*, my Kati. Happy New Year.'

'And to you.' She put an arm about his neck, hugged him for a moment, then was pulled away by Adam.

'Happy New Year, mother dear –' Everyone was kissing, calling greetings. A young man whose name Cathy did not know kissed her soundly. 'Happy New Year –' The band had struck up the Conga. An excited, laughing line was forming on the dance floor.

Cathy felt a touch on her arm. She turned. Nikos bent to her, kissed her not as others had, but long and softly, and with an aching hunger that almost stopped her heart. 'I love you,' he said, his mouth close to her ear, the words for her alone in the noisy celebrations around them. 'I love you more than I have ever loved anyone or anything in my life before.' Startled she tried to pull away from him, to look into his face, but for a moment he held her fast. 'Don't say anything. Please. I don't want you to say anything. I don't want you to answer. I just want you to believe me; I just want you to know. I love you. I'll always love you.' He let her go then, and as he did so someone caught her hand, swung her away from him. The Conga line was weaving past. *'Aye, aye, Conga, Aye, aye Conga –'* Cathy found herself, her hands on Adam's narrow waist, being led around tables, up on to the stage, down again, out of one door, along a corridor, and then, to cheers from the onlookers, back through another, the line coiling around the dancefloor, breaking into two, turning back on itself.

'I love you. I love you more than I have ever loved anyone or anything in my life before.'

She ought to be horrified. She ought to be angry. She was neither.

'I love you. I love you more than I have ever loved anyone or anything in my life before.'

It did not occur to her to doubt what he had said. On the contrary; with a certainty that was absolute she knew it to be true. It had been there for her to see, to sense, since the first time she had touched him. She glanced to where he sat, his long, dark fingers curled loosely about the stem of his glass, unsmiling, openly watching her; and her heart turned over. More than anything she wanted to go to him, to hold him, to ease the misery in his eyes. To tell him – to tell him what?

The band was playing faster and faster, the line was breaking into small, wildly jigging groups. Balloons were being batted from hand to hand, or popped beneath stamping feet.

The answer came directly on the heels of the question. To tell him, *'Yes, I love you, too.'* To tell him, *'Don't worry. It's all right. As long as we don't do anything about it, it's all right. Our secret. We don't have to share it with anyone but each other.'*

The music had stopped at last, people were trooping back to the tables. Above the clock on the wall the figures '1953' had been unveiled, glittering in red, white and blue.

He was her husband's son, and young enough to be her own.

He was beautiful, and he loved her.

It dawned on her suddenly that, bizarre as the situation was, what she felt, predominantly, however inappropriate it might be, was happiness. Pure happiness. And for this one moment she could not bring herself to crush or deny it. Tomorrow she could be shocked, at herself and at Nikos.

Tomorrow she could be stern and practical. Tomorrow she would certainly see the chasm that yawned at their feet and step back from it.

For tonight, just for tonight, she wanted to hold safe this fragile, almost painful happiness that his words had kindled. And she wanted him to know of it. He at least, surely, deserved that. She could not bear to hurt him; to reject him out of hand would be sheer cruelty. There was tomorrow for that. It could surely do no harm to talk to him, just once, to acknowledge his feelings and her own, and then, gently, to abrogate them. *'It's all right,'* she told herself again. *'As long as we don't do anything about it.'* And knew in her soul as she thought it what a flawed assertion it was.

The crooner was back on stage; the band swung into a dreamy popular waltz. 'Ladies and gentlemen,' trumpeted the Master of Ceremonies, 'a Ladies' Excuse Me – take your partners please –'

Cathy held out a hand. 'Nikos? You haven't danced with me all evening.'

He held her carefully and in silence at first. Then: 'I'm sorry,' he said, 'I've shocked you. Embarrassed you.'

'No.'

'I just had to tell you, that's all. I had to. And I thought – here – with everyone around us –' he hesitated. 'Do you want me to go away? I could go back to America. Or perhaps to Greece. Pa's talking of opening an office there –'

'No,' she said again. She tilted her head to look at him. 'Nikos. Look at me.'

Reluctantly his eyes met hers.

'It's all right,' she said, softly, 'Nikos, it's all right. No one can help feelings; it's what we do about them that matters. We aren't doing anything wrong. And we won't. You know we won't. So it's all right.'

The golden eyes had widened. He missed a step, stumbled a little, regained his balance. 'We?' he asked.

She allowed herself, just for a moment, to study his face, to watch the gleam of understanding become a flash of joy.

'We?' he asked again. 'You mean –' he paused and then continued, carefully '– you mean you understand what I feel for you?'

'Yes.'

'And –' he could not bring himself to ask the agonising question he wanted to ask '– you aren't angry with me?'

'Of course I'm not.' The dance floor was crowded; they could barely move.

He had relaxed, drawing her to him. He laid his cheek against her hair. 'Cathy, I love you.'

'Ssh!' Gently reproving she squeezed his hand.

They danced in silence for a long time. Cathy closed her eyes, mesmerised by the feel of his body against hers, the touch of his hand, the sense, the smell of him. The words he had spoken were folded and tucked safely into her memory; a memento, wrapped in tissue and stored away from prying eyes, a private pledge to be treasured, but never, never to be claimed. They must never do this again, of course. Certainly not. But just for now – it could surely do no harm –?

Someone tapped her on the shoulder. She recognised the trilling laughter of the girl in green. 'Excuse me – may I?' The girl was tiny, barely to Nikos' shoulder. She smiled up into his face.

'Of course.' Cathy extricated herself from Nikos' arms. His hand clung to hers for the smallest of moments before she turned from them and wormed her way through the throng back to the table, where her husband waited.

She and Nikos had no chance for private conversation after that, yet oddly enough it did not seem to matter. Their glances touched occasionally, they exchanged pleasantries in the course of general conversation, but the dark under-current that ran between them and for the moment at least bewitched them both was too deep for anyone else to sense or divine. When the party broke up a couple of hours later she kissed him goodbye quite naturally. Only as they were leaving, when Leon, well into his cups, clapped a huge arm about her shoulders saying, 'Come, Kati. Home with your husband. We must start this New Year the way we mean to continue –' did she discern a flicker of something in the lucent green-gold eyes as Nikos looked from her to his father that momentarily disturbed her, that woke her, so to speak, from the dream into which his declaration of love had lured her.

Suddenly her head cleared. For Christ's sake! What had she done? What had she said? What had she inferred?

'Tomorrow, my boy,' Leon was saying, 'you sleep as late as you wish. On Friday Kati goes home and you and I start work again.' He clasped his son's hand. 'We have much to do. Happy New Year to you, Nikos. Pray it will be a good one for Kotsikas and Son!'

Nikos said nothing.

Leon made love to her that night, swiftly and with passion, and then as swiftly fell asleep beside her.

Only then, staring sleepless into the darkness as he snored gently beside her, and remembering that sudden, dark flash of anger on Nikos' face as he had looked at his father, did she truly realise what she might have done.

On the day after New Year's Day Cathy ran away, as fast as a ticket to Suffolk could take her. She had neither seen nor spoken to Nikos since the ball. She was torn between longing to see him and a desire never to get near him again. She needed to go home. She saw Leon off to the office, packed her bags and ordered a taxi. She arrived at Liverpool Street station at five minutes to ten.

Nikos was waiting for her.

He stood by the barrier, scanning the faces of the thinning crowds; too late she saw him, he was already coming towards her.

'What are you doing here?'

'Waiting for you.'

'Nikos –!'

'I had to see you. I had to.'

'How did you know which train I was catching? You didn't – you didn't ask your father?'

'Of course not. I simply came first thing, and waited. I'd have waited all day if needs be.'

'Leon's expecting you at the office.'

'I know.'

'What will you tell him?'

He shrugged.

They stood in helpless silence. Around them the station bustled; a whistle screeched, a train belched steam and the couplings clanked as it pulled away.

'I want to come and see you,' he said.

'No!' She was panic-stricken. 'Nikos, no! You know you mustn't.' She walked past him, fast, towards the barrier. 'I have to go. The train leaves in five minutes.'

'Don't go. Catch the next one. Talk to me.'

'No. I can't. Nikos – please!' She showed her ticket. Nikos produced a platform ticket and passed through the barrier with her, hurrying beside her as she walked along the platform.

'You said "we",' he said.

'What?' She struggled to open a door. He reached past her, turned the heavy handle, stood back for her to enter the carriage. An elderly woman sat in a corner seat, reading a newspaper. Nikos took Cathy's bag, put it up on the luggage rack, let the leather window strap slip before he stepped back down on to the platform and shut the door. 'You said "we",' he said again, through the open window. His face was drawn. He looked very tired and very young. 'On New Year's Eve. You know what I mean.'

'Yes. I know.'

'I want to come and see you. I have to talk to you.'

She reached to touch the hand that rested on the window.

'You mustn't. My dear, you know you mustn't.'

The woman in the corner was watching them, an avid glint of interest in her eyes.

'Please.'

'No.' She was stubborn.

'I'll come anyway. You can't hide from me for ever.'

'I'm not hiding –'

'What are you doing then? Do you know? Do you understand what you're doing to me?'

She was silent.

Someone ran past, jumped into the next door carriage. As the door slammed a whistle blew.

'I love you,' Nikos said. 'I mean it. And I won't let you go. I can't. I will come. In a week or so. And then, if you don't want to see me you can send me away. But I will come.'

The train was moving. He lifted her fingers to his lips then stepped back. She stared straight ahead. A poster depicting an impossibly pretty mother with two impossibly rosy children invited her to visit Clacton for fresh air and fun. The mirror above it was cracked. The woman in the corner rustled her newspaper, her eyes flickering to Cathy's face and away.

Cathy leaned back and closed her eyes. Home; she needed to go home.

Chapter Nine

The year started with a cold spell; at the end of the first week and into the beginning of the second Sandlings was snowed in, a not uncommon state of affairs in January along that exposed North Sea coast. To Cathy it was almost a relief; quite happy to be cut off from the world she worked long and absorbing hours, concentrating with single-minded determination on the task in hand and filling what spare time she had in reorganising and redecorating her favourite room in the cottage, the kitchen. She had been planning this project for some time, and had purchased paint and materials months before. It had been her lifelong habit, when disturbed or uncertain, to apply herself to some satisfying physical task or activity. Cleaning and scrubbing, splashing paint on walls and furniture, sewing curtains and cushions served a dual purpose – the first the simple pleasure of seeing the bright transformation of her special room and the second the assurance of a good night's sleep at the end of an extended and physically tiring day. She tried not to think of Nikos, and for the best part of the time at least was successful. Only occasionally did her defences slip and she found herself remembering those words he had spoken as the year had turned. And even then, at this remove, and in these different and so dearly familiar surroundings the whole business took on something of the air of a dream; he could not, surely, have meant what he had said? It wasn't possible. Firmly she pushed to the back of her mind the memory of his intense gaze, of the misery in his eyes when she had left him at Liverpool Street. He was a child. Her stepson. A lonely young man in a strange country, clinging to the first warmth and kindness he had encountered after the loss of his grandmother. He would by now, she was certain, be regretting his impulsive behaviour. What Nikos needed was a girl of his own age, a fling of the type at which her own son seemed so adept.

And even as she thought it she was uneasily aware of how much she disliked the idea.

At first she had half expected a letter, but the days and then the weeks slipped by and none came, reaffirming her own certainty that Nikos had come to his senses and was regretting his passionate but possibly Champagne-induced declaration. She would, she resolved, remain buried in the country for as long as was likely not to draw notice or comment, and then, when a meeting with Nikos was unavoidable – which it undoubtedly would be sooner or later – would simply act as if nothing untoward had passed between them. The poor boy must be suffering agonies of embarrassment. It was up to her, sensibly and with care, to ease the situation for him.

Thus she reasoned, safely and sanely, during those busy waking moments when despite her resolution she found herself thinking of him. But there were other occasions when, snuggled beneath the huge, soft eiderdown, drifting in the quiet darkness between waking and sleep, her unguarded senses conjured other pictures, other possibilities. And in that hidden core of her that she supposed some would think of as her soul she was forced to face the fact that whatever Nikos' state of mind her own desires were neither as straightforward nor as irreproachable as she would like to believe.

Leon spent most of that first month of 1953 in Greece.

Obviously whatever business it had been that had taken him from her at Christmas was both ongoing and successful. Cathy received the odd note, the odd postcard, quickly scrawled and, as always, actually divulging very little. The snow cleared and once more the fog crawled in from the sea. The day came, three weeks or so after she had started, when she stood, hands on hips, and surveyed with satisfaction the greens and blues and lemon-yellows of her refurbished kitchen. That night she opened a bottle of wine in celebration, sat by the fire sketching and listening to Mahler on the ancient wind-up gramophone and almost convinced herself that there was no better way to spend an evening.

In the darkness outside, the sound so familiar that Cathy hardly took account of it, the cold sea continued its endless, attritive assault on the long and vulnerable coastline, the tide creaming and thundering in, reaching with watery fingers greedily to the dunes, to retreat at its appointed time, seething and with its appetite unsated.

'Bad weather on its way I reckon.' Tom Blowers tranquilly tamped down his pipe, lit it, sucked on it noisily.

'Wind's gettin' up a bit.' Mrs Hamilton was rearranging a shelf of tins. 'They've been havin' it bad up north. Gales and whatnot. Low pressure everywhere, they said on the shipping forecast. Bad time with the tides high.'

The old man nodded his head. 'At least the wind's in the southeast. That should keep 'em down, not whip 'em up. We're safe enough.'

The door bell jangled. Mrs Hamilton looked round. 'Afternoon, Sally. Hello, young Jimmy. How are you?'

The baby on the young woman's hip gapped a wide, toothless smile.

'Pound of flour, Mrs H., please,' the girl said. 'An' half of best back. Afternoon, Tom.'

The man nodded, dourly.

'Bit breezy out there.' The young woman moved to the

window, peered out. 'Hello – there's the Yank again – Mrs Kosti-whatnot's stepson.' She leaned closer to the window. The tall figure who had stepped off the Friday afternoon bus turned his coat collar up, pulled the brim of his trilby down against the wind and pushed his hands deep into his pockets. 'Reckon he knows where he's goin' this time.' Nikos had set off up the lane, walking fast. The girl watched him for a moment, a trace of wistfulness in her expression.

'Run out o' back I'm afraid,' Mrs Hamilton said. 'Streaky do?'

'What?' the girl turned from the window. 'Oh – yes – OK – if that's all you've got –' She felt in her pocket. 'Me Mum's given me some sweet coupons for the baby – you got anythin' in?'

Cathy was aware of the freshening wind as she sat, board on lap, sketching a collection of delicate, sea-worn shells. The book she was illustrating was a children's fantasy set in a mythical kingdom beneath the sea; her efforts of the past three or four weeks were now truly bearing fruit – another couple of weeks and she should have a portfolio well worth presenting to her publisher.

Sandy lifted his head, cocked it sharply, looking at the door. The wind blustered again. The dog growled a little in his throat.

Cathy did not look up. 'Don't be daft, Sands. It's only the wind.'

The window rattled a little, and a gust whistled in the chimney.

Sandy growled again, jumped from his chair and trotted to the door, looking expectant.

Cathy glanced up, laughed. 'If you expect me to let you out in that you've got another think coming. You get that wind up your tail and I won't see you for a week, you little tyke –' She stopped. Over the sound of the wind and of the radio that was playing quietly in the corner, and muffled by the heavy, draught-excluding curtain, she fancied she had heard a rap on the door.

Sandy yapped, shrill and excited.

Puzzled, she set her sketches on the sofa beside her and stood up. As she pulled aside the curtain there was another, sharper knock. The wind whistled through the ill-fitting door. She opened it.

The fresh gust that entered with her visitor billowed the curtain and sent papers flying about the room. Nikos slammed the door behind him and leaned on it.

There was a very long moment of silence.

'What the hell are you doing here?' Cathy asked at last, very quietly.

Nikos said nothing. He took off his hat, ran his fingers through his flattened hair. He looked wretched, his face was thin and haggard, the Mediterranean-dark skin almost blue with cold, the usually brilliant eyes ringed with tiredness. Right up until the moment he had lifted his knuckles to the door he had not been certain he could follow through his decision to see her.

'I asked a question.' No trace of the turmoil that the unexpected sight of him had triggered sounded in her voice. She clenched her hands against their trembling, schooled her face.

Still he did not speak. His eyes, tormented and searching, held hers. With a sudden brusque movement she turned from him, began to pick up the scattered sketches.

'Cathy – please?'

At the sound of the whispered words, at the depth of pleading contained in them her movements stilled and she stood, rigid and silent, her back to him.

He came to her, standing very close, but not touching her. *'Please!'*

She felt his distress as if it had been a physical pain in her own body. Defeated, she turned, and his arms went about her.

'Don't cry,' she said, quietly and desperately, into his shoulder, 'Nikos, please, don't cry –'

The sobs continued to shudder through his body. His arms were clamped painfully tightly about her, his face was buried in her hair. Gently she freed her arms, lifted them about his neck, drew his head down on to her shoulder, her own sudden, helpless tears mingling with his. 'Darling Nikos, please don't cry.'

The sobs subsided a little. Still he caught his breath unevenly, like a desolately weeping child. Her hand lifted to his hair. It was soft, and thick, smooth as silk in her fingers. She lifted her head. At first his lips were gentle, salt-tasting and trembling on hers. Then inexorably, his arms tightened about her and his mouth bore down on hers. In the space between one moment and another she knew she was lost; all her pious excuses, all her efforts to deceive herself in that second she accepted for the sham they were. His mouth still on hers he shrugged the coat from his shoulders and threw it into the corner. Then his arms were about her again, and now she could feel the urgency of his body, an urgency matched by her own. She pulled away from him. 'Nikos –!' She might as well have tried to stop the rising wind with her breath. His hands were at the buttons of her shirt, and then her breasts were bare and his mouth was at her nipples. She threw back her head and cried out. His long-fingered hands, that she had watched so often, gripped her waist, clamping her to him; eyes closed he teased her with teeth and tongue. Once more, half-heartedly, she attempted to pull away from him. He lifted his head. 'No!' the word, like his face, was fierce. Still holding her to him he straightened, stood breathing heavily, looking down at her. She stood quite still, her shirt open, tears still running down her face. 'I love you,' he said. 'Cathy, I love you. You're the most beautiful, the most perfect woman I've ever known –'

She shook her head, dashed a hand across her eyes.

'Yes.' Suddenly he was calm. Calm and very sure. Her body was warm, and soft and trembled against his. At last he knew – was utterly certain – that he was not alone in this madness that had taken him. The wind, that had died a little, suddenly gusted against the window again, and as it did so the small lamp in the corner went out abruptly and there was a sudden silence in the room as the radio died, the electricity cut off. He lifted a hand to Cathy's wet face. 'Yes,' he repeated, softly. His eyes were intent. 'Cathy, I don't care if it's right or wrong. I can't care any more. I only know it's so. I love you. I have never and will never love anyone the way I love you.' Very gently he brushed his fingers across the smooth, taut skin of her breast. 'And you are beautiful. You are perfect. But that isn't why I love you. I love you because I can't help it. I love you because you are in my soul and my soul would die without you.'

She was watching him as if mesmerised, almost unaware of her own nakedness.

'I love you and I want you.' He let a small silence linger. 'And I believe you want me,' he said, softly.

She ducked her head, would not reply.

He took her chin in his hand and lifted it so that she had to look at him. 'Tell me. Tell me the truth. Do you want me to go?'

She stood in a stubborn, desperate silence.

'Answer me, my darling. Do you want me to leave? I will, if that's what you want. I won't force you, if that's what you're hoping for – ah!' His fingers tightened on her arms as she made a sudden, furious movement. 'Don't be angry. I'm only trying to be honest. To force you to be honest. Tell me. Do you want me to go?'

She closed her eyes. 'No.' It was barely a breath.

'You know what will happen if I stay?'

She hesitated.

'Cathy?'

Her eyes flew open. Angrily, almost defiantly, 'Yes,' she said.

His hands slid down her arms and took hers. Very gently, his eyes never leaving her face, he drew her to the door which led to the shadowed stairwell. The afternoon was darkening. The wind blustered about the house, a primeval force, isolating and enclosing them. At the foot of the stairs he turned her to face him. 'You're sure?'

'No,' she said. 'No, I'm not. How could I be? You're –'

He put his hand to her lips, stopping the words. 'Forget who and what I am. Do you love me?'

'Yes.' The word was anguished.

'Then for now that's all that matters.'

'It's wrong!'

His certainty would not leave him now. 'How can it be?' he asked, simply, and drew her with him, up the dark stairs.

Nikos had not so far abandoned conscience that he could make love to her in his father's bed. He drew her into Adam's room. She stood trembling and allowed him gently to undress her.

'Open your eyes,' he said.

Cathy shook her head.

'Please.'

She opened her eyes. She was shivering with cold. Chill draughts whispered through the small room. Nikos moved to the fireplace and set a match to the ready-laid fire. Flames licked and flickered, light as well as warmth. He turned back to face her. Automatically she put up her hands to cover her breasts.

'No,' he said, quietly. 'Please – I want to look at you.'

'Nikos!'

'Please,' he said again, gently stubborn. 'I told you. I think you're beautiful.' He was loosening his tie, unbuttoning his shirt.

She was genuinely bewildered. 'But I'm not!' she whispered. 'Can't you understand; that's what frightens me. I'm *not!*'

'To me you are. You always will be. No matter what happens. No matter how old you get –' he saw her flinch at that, came to her, naked, and took her hands, gripped them firmly. 'Cathy, don't! I know how much older you are than I am. There's nothing we can do to change that; but it doesn't matter, don't you see? I *like* it that you're older. I love it. And you *are* beautiful.' He bent to her, brushed her lips with his. His skin was warm and smooth as silk; she could feel his body's arousal. She shuddered again, but this time not from the cold. When he laid her upon the bed it was her mouth that became suddenly urgent, her hands that clung, pulling him to her, trying to cover her own body with his. Laughing softly he resisted her, forcibly unclasping her hands from about his neck and stretching her arms wide upon the bed. 'Oh, no,' he said, very quietly, 'I've waited too long for this. Lie still, woman –' His mouth was on her breasts, his hand smoothing her belly, slipping to the cleft between her legs, that had already flooded, awaiting him. 'Don't think. Feel. Let me love you. Let me show you how beautiful you really are.'

Tenderly and fiercely he loved her, all the pent-up needs and emotions of the past few weeks expressing themselves through his fingertips, his tongue, and at last, all restraint abandoned, through the sudden, savage thrusting of his body in hers. As the warmth of him erupted in her, convulsing him, he cried out and clung to her. Like a flower in sunshine she opened to him. His body still and heavy upon hers she tasted the salt on his cheek. In gentle silence she held him; and as the wind howled like a banshee about the house and the firelight flickered upon the ceiling, they slept.

Waking, Cathy had absolutely no idea how long they had lain there. It was full dark, and the fire was low. The room was cold. Nikos had curled himself up beside her, his head on her shoulder. As she moved a little he stirred, immediately aware of her even in his sleep. In the faint light from the fire she studied his face. Relaxed and calm, the sweep of his lashes shadowing the high, smooth cheekbones, she thought she had never seen anything so beautiful; she ached with love for him. As she watched, the eyelashes fluttered and lifted. He smiled. 'Hello.'

'Hello.'

He put up a hand to touch her cheek; she took it in her own and kissed it.

'You're cold,' he said, softly.

'Yes.'

'I'll make up the fire.'

'Yes.'

Neither of them moved.

'I love you,' he said.

'And I you.'

He smiled.

She kissed him, butterfly-light, on his mouth, his chin, his closed eyelids. 'Fire,' she said.

She watched as, lissome and naked, he rolled from the bed and crossed the room, bending to the fire. The grace of the movement all but stopped her breath. As he shovelled coal on the glowing embers a sudden billow of smoke blew into the room. He leaned back from it. 'Hey, what's that about?'

'Wind's veering about a bit I expect. It always makes the chimney smoke.' Cathy was still watching him. She held out a hand. 'Come back to –' She stopped. Sat bolt upright. 'Oh, shit!' she said, quietly, her face screwed up in exasperation, and then again, explosively, 'Oh *shit!*' She buried her curly head in her hands for a moment, then, scrambling from the bed, reached for her clothes and started to throw them on. 'What's the time?'

He was watching her in astonishment. 'What's the matter?'

'Bert.' She struggled her arms into her shirt, 'Oh, blast it, I can't see what I'm doing –'

'*Bert?*' His voice was incredulous. 'Oh, come on –'

She stopped her hasty dressing, came to him and flung her arms about his neck, kissing him. 'I'm sorry. I didn't tell you.' She smiled a little, touching his lips with a finger. 'I didn't get much chance if you think about it. Bert's very unwell. I think it's flu. I've been looking after him. And now – oh, blast it – when did the electricity go off?'

He looked at his watch in the glow of the fire. 'A couple of hours ago I guess.'

'I'll have to pop next door. I won't be long –'

'Let me come –' He reached for his trousers.

'No. You stay here. There's really nothing you can do. I

promise I won't be long.' She ran into the other bedroom, came back struggling into a thick jumper. 'I'll just make up his fire, light his lamp, make him a cup of tea. Try to make him comfortable. His temperature was up at lunchtime. I tried to persuade him to come in here with me, but the stubborn old devil wouldn't –'

He raised his eyebrows. She sucked her lip, flushing a little.

'– I'll be right back.' She kissed him lightly. He held her tightly to him. 'Make yourself comfortable. The kitchen will be warmest. The stove roars away when the wind blows.' She turned to the door.

'Cathy?' His voice was soft.

She turned back to him.

'Do you regret – what just happened?'

She studied his face for a moment in the softness of the firelight. 'No,' she said. 'How could I?' and disappeared into the darkness.

When she slipped back through the front door, windblown and drenched, a little over half an hour later it was to a room tidied and candlelit. The fire roared and danced. She took off her duffel coat and looked around her in delight. Beethoven played on the gramophone; the 'Pastoral'. Through the open door of the kitchen she could hear Nikos humming to the music. A glass oil lamp had been lit and stood upon the kitchen table. The smell of frying bacon was delicious on the air. She crossed the room, stood at the kitchen door. He glanced over his shoulder at her, his smile lighting his face. 'You told me to make myself at home. I took you at your word.' He was standing at the stove, manipulating the huge black frying pan. Two tumblers of whisky stood upon the table. 'The kitchen looks great.' He indicated the glasses with a movement of his head. 'I poured you a drink.'

She smiled. 'Thanks. And thanks.' She picked up the glass, sat at the table, nursing it in her cupped hands, watching him.

'How's the old feller?'

Cathy shook her head. 'Not good. I finally persuaded

him into bed. I'll pop back later. I'm worried about him.'

He turned, studying her face. 'You want to fetch him in here?' he asked, genuinely concerned. 'I could help –'

'He won't. He simply won't.' She shook her head. 'You know what he is. We can't forcibly evacuate him, now can we? He'll be all right. I just have to remember to keep an eye on him.' Her eyes went to the window as another gust of wind rattled it. 'It's getting a bit wild out there. I hope we aren't going to get the bad weather they've had up north. It's a nuisance about the electricity. With no radio we're stuck with no news or forecasts.'

He laid a plate of bacon and eggs in front of her, dropped a kiss on to the top of her head. 'Then there's no point in fretting, is there? We've more important things to think about.'

She caught his hand, held it to her cheek. 'I'm not sure I want to think. I'm not sure I can.'

With their hands still linked he sat down. 'Then we won't,' he said, softly. 'Not now. Not yet. I can stay until Sunday – if you'd like me to, that is?'

She smiled her answer.

'There'll be plenty of time to talk. For now – eat your supper.' He kissed her fingertips, one by one, 'I want to make love to you again.'

They made love on the floor by the light of the fire, and then he held her, relaxed and sleepy, his back against the sofa, looking into the flames. The room was warm and softly lit by the candles; an enchanted haven made more intimate, more cosy by the sound of the wind and sea in the darkness outside. With his cheek resting upon Cathy's curly hair, Nikos let contentment fill him. Tomorrow they would face the future. Tomorrow, or the day after. For now he could think of nothing but the fact that the agony was over; she loved him. And for the moment, that was enough.

The next morning the cold wind, north-westerly now, had if anything strengthened a little. Towards lunchtime, hand-in-hand and heads down against the wind they went down to the dunes and watched the churning, foaming waves as they crashed on to the strand. 'It's coming up awfully high,' Cathy said. 'And there's an hour or so to go before it turns.'

'Will it be a problem?'

She shook her head. 'Probably not. The tides are always high at this time of year. Goodness, it's cold!' She shivered a little and leaned to him, laughing, 'Come on. Let's get back.'

Snug in the warmth of the kitchen she made soup for Bert, and a pie for herself and Nikos, humming softly to herself as she moved about the room. Nikos sat at the table and watched her. Every now and again she caught his eye, and smiled, warmly; absurdly a little shyly. Each time she passed him she could not resist touching him, gently, on his shoulder, or his cheek or his hand. The smallest of contacts were a pleasure in which they both delighted. Before they ate their own lunch Cathy took the soup in to Bert. The old man was still very poorly, the leathery skin of his face flushed unhealthily, his narrow frame wracked by coughing. 'Perhaps I should get a doctor,' Cathy said, worriedly.

'Don't talk silly, girl.' He stopped, breathing heavily and noisily. 'What you goin' ter do – get out in that lot on yer bike?' He jerked his head towards the window. 'No point in both of us finishin' up with pneumonia. Anyway – I got no doctor. No one'd come.'

She tucked the bedclothes around him, checked the Thermos of hot tea she had made for him. 'Well, I've got one. And if you're no better by tomorrow I'm going to call him.' She banked up the fire, set the guard in front of it, turned to face him. 'Bert, I wish you'd come next door with me. You could be comfortable upstairs in bed –'

'I'm comfortable upstairs in me own bed. I've told yer. No.'

She felt a small and she supposed shameful twinge of relief. 'OK. If you won't you won't. I'll be back this afternoon.'

Bert grunted.

Outside she stood for a moment in the roaring wind,

straining her eyes and ears towards the sea. By her reckoning the tide must be up about now. The sound of it was wild. Despite her easy reassurance to Nikos earlier she listened for a moment, a little uneasily, before letting herself in to the warm, quiet cottage.

Nikos was waiting for her. 'I love you,' he said.

That afternoon, unexpectedly, they had a visitor. The loud knock on the door startled them both. Nikos was sitting on the sofa, Cathy curled up on the floor at his feet, her head on his knee. The gramophone played quietly. They had been talking, but had fallen silent, listening to the music when the hammering on the door made them both jump. In guilty haste Cathy scrambled to her feet. 'Who the devil's that?'

Nikos shrugged, shook his head.

Cathy threw back the curtain and opened the door. 'Mr Becket! What are you doing here? Come in –' she stepped back, holding the door against the wind.

A burly figure dressed in the dark blue overcoat and cap of the coastguard service stepped into the room, took off his cap to reveal a bushy cloud of silver-grey hair. 'Afternoon, Mrs Kotsikas.' He struggled a little with the name, looked at Nikos. 'Afternoon, sir.'

'My stepson,' Cathy said, and to her horror found deep colour rising in her face. Flustered, she slammed the door against the wind, hurried to the gramophone and took the needle from the record. 'What can we do for you, Mr Becket?' she asked into the sudden quiet.

'Just called round by way of a warning, Ma'am. Tha'ss a high tide this evenin' and the wind's risin'. It don't look good.'

She turned. 'You think it might break through?'

'Just bein' careful, Ma'am. There's flood warnings up an' down the coast. Where possible people at risk are bein' warned, tha'ss all. Just in case, like.'

'What's happening?'

He shrugged. 'All's well so far. The defences held the early tide, but that wind's comin' somethin' fierce now and swung onshore. There's been very little ebb. Could be a surge this evenin' –'

'We're on higher ground here. The cottage has never flooded.'

He put his cap back on, turned to the door. 'Like I say, Ma'am, just thought you should know, tha'ss all. Some people have decided to move inland for the night. Just in case, like.'

Cathy shook her head. 'We've nowhere to go. And we couldn't anyway –'

Both men looked at her.

'Bert,' Cathy said to Nikos. 'We can't leave him while he's so poorly.' She turned back to the coastguard. 'There can't be that much risk, can there?'

The wide shoulders shrugged again. 'Like I say – there's no knowing. There's trouble everywhere. Seems there's a ship gone down off the Irish coast. The *Princess Victoria*. Passengers and mail. Terrible loss of life, they say. Hardly any survivors at all.'

Cathy shook her head. 'That's terrible. We hadn't heard. The electricity's off. We've no wireless.'

The man glanced round, and a warm if weary smile lit his broad, weather-beaten face. 'You certainly look snug enough,' he said. 'You say old Bert's not well?'

'Yes. Flu, I think. We couldn't move him. Even if he would, which he wouldn't. He won't come in here, let alone go anywhere else,' she added in a tone rueful enough to bring another smile.

'Tha'ss old Bert right enough.' The man turned to the door. 'Well, I'd best be goin'. I'll try to come by again if there's any definite news.'

'Oh, please – won't you stay for a cup of tea?'

He shook his head. 'Kind of you, Ma'am, but no, I'd best be off. Haven't been by old Mrs Ransome's yet. If anything does give her place'll be the first to go.'

Cathy opened the door, into the bluster of the wind. 'Well, thank you for coming.'

'My pleasure, Ma'am.'

'Is there any real danger, do you think?' Nikos asked as she shut the door behind the coastguard.

She shook her head. 'I shouldn't think so. Even if the walls did breach, as I say, it's happened before, and the water's never reached the cottage. Best thing to do is batten down the hatches and ride it out.' She came to him, touched his cheek as he tilted his head to look up at her. 'I love you.'

That evening an all but unprecedented combination of circumstances – wind, tide, a monstrous surge pushed from the gale-lashed Atlantic to the cold waters of the North Sea – sent a tidal wave raging down the embattled east coast that no puny man-made sea defences could stand against. Lincolnshire, Norfolk, Suffolk, Essex – one by one as the wind and the tides rose the coastal flatlands were inundated. Huge waves crashed and battered their way into town and village, flooding streets and houses, tossing boats like flotsam against the quays. Breach after breach sent the swirling water inland. It was the wildest night in living memory, and one that was to exact a ghastly death toll and leave many shocked and homeless.

As full dark fell and wind and sea howled menacingly Cathy and Nikos sat silent in front of the fire. They had made love again, to the sound of the rising storm. Cathy leaned against Nikos; his hand rested on the smooth skin of her breast inside her shirt.

'Does anyone know you're here?' she asked.

'No.'

'No one must.'

'No.'

'And –' she struggled for a moment '– Nikos, you know that you mustn't come again.'

'Don't be ridiculous,' he said, very calmly.

There was a long silence. 'It's impossible,' she said, quietly, at last. 'You know it is.'

'No. I don't. I won't.'

'Nikos –'

'Shut up,' he said, gently. 'Shut up, my darling, and listen to the wind.'

The inexorable surge reached them later that night; the defences, here as elsewhere, were hopelessly inadequate. When the sea finally broke through Cathy and Nikos, having decided to stay downstairs for the night, were dozing on the sofa. They heard nothing as the waters raged foaming through the breach then spread, silent and dark across the unprotected fields and wetlands. Only as a sullen dawn broke, grim, cold and windlashed, did they realise that Sandlings, together with its huddled companion cottage next door, was cut off, a tiny island in a vast watery landscape that spread as far as the eye could see. Trees stood in the salty water, or in some cases lay partly submerged, blown down by the gale; flotsam bobbed on the swirling tide. Track and lane had disappeared, marked only by the top few inches of hedge that stood above the flood. Water lapped at the edge of the garden and had come to within a foot of Bert's front step. But the few feet of elevation had stood them in good stead. They were marooned, but safe. There was nothing to do but to sit it out.

'Perhaps the gods mean us to be together for a little while,' Cathy said, surveying the flooded landscape from the bedroom window.

Nikos put his arm about her shoulder. 'Perhaps the gods mean us to be together for ever,' he said.

Cathy did not reply.

C h a p t e r   T e n

Neither of them realised the extent of the disaster until Bill Becket reached them again, this time by boat, soon after day-light. On first waking to the grey, gale-swept morning, and before his arrival they were understandably preoccupied with their own situation; but a hasty check on supplies and fuel quickly reassured them. For the moment at least even the water supply seemed to have held up. Cathy took the news to Bert, who seemed a little improved and was, as usual, glee-fully pessimistic. 'Next tide'll get us. Mark my words.'

The coastguard, wet, cold and tired, was relieved to find them safe. 'It's been one hell of a night, an' tha'ss the truth, eh, Jack?' His companion, a young constable who looked exhausted enough to drop, nodded. Becket, sitting at the kitchen table, a steaming cup of tea in front of him, rubbed his face wearily. 'We tried to get through to you earlier, while it was still dark, but we couldn't make it. There's trees down all over the place; fishing boats blown a mile inland. It's a muddle, I can tell you. If only the blasted wind would drop – beggin' your pardon, Ma'am. But we'll get you out now, don't worry.'

Nikos' head came up sharply.

'Out?' Cathy asked.

'Of course. They've opened up an emergency centre at the school. You'll be safe enough there.'

'We're safe enough here.'

The man looked from one to the other. He had not slept for twenty-four hours. Stubborn civilians he could do without. 'There's another high tide at midday,' he said. 'You might not be so lucky this time.'

Cathy said the first thing that came into her head. 'We can't leave Bert.'

'You don't have to leave him. We'll take him too. He'll get attention at the centre.'

'Just getting him to the centre will almost certainly do him more harm than good. Mr Becket – I'm sorry, I know you mean well, but truly we'd as soon stay here. If the waters should rise any further we can always move upstairs. I don't want to abandon the house; if the floods should reach it there are things I don't want to lose, things I'd need to move out of the way. There's a year's work here –' she gestured towards the sitting room. 'I can't afford to have it entirely ruined. As you can see, we're safe and well provisioned. We can look after ourselves, I promise you.' She smiled reassuringly. 'Would you like another cup of tea?'

'Please.'

Cathy refilled their cups.

'The water supply may become contaminated.'

'I'll fill the bath,' she said, calmly. 'That'll give us enough for a couple of days at least if it should be necessary.'

The man shrugged tiredly. 'I suppose it's up to you, Mrs Kotsikas. If you really want to stay –'

'We do.'

'– then we can't force you to leave.'

'It's kind of you to have made the effort,' she said, gently, and meant it.

He stood up, reached for his cap. 'Best we get going, then.'

As the boat puttered away through the grey, choppy water Cathy, watching from the window, said, 'You should have gone with them. You're due back in town. You'll be missed. You can't just disappear.'

'I'm not leaving you here alone.' He came up behind her, put his arms about her. She leaned her head upon his shoulder. 'In fact I don't want to leave you at all. Ever.'

'You'll have to. Sooner or later.'

She sensed his shaken head.

'You should have gone with them,' she said again. 'What will you tell Leon? How will you explain?'

He moved away from her, started to clear the table. 'From what your Mr Becket said it sounds as if the whole coast is in chaos, through to London and beyond. Pa's out of the country. Miss Hooper lives on the coast near London – Canvey Island, is it called? Didn't he say there are reports that conditions in Essex are as bad if not worse than here? I very much doubt that she'll make it to the office until this lot clears. The trains probably aren't running anyway. For once, no one knows where *I* am. For once the gods are on *my* side. And I'm going to take advantage of it.' He put the dirty cups in the sink and came to her, cupping her face in his hands. 'Another day. Perhaps another two. Time together. Who knows when we'll get such a chance again?'

She covered his hands with her own. 'It's dangerous,' she said. And wrong. That she did not say; it was too late. 'What if someone should suspect?'

'I have every right to be here.' He gathered her to him, spoke into her hair. 'Don't make me go. Please.'

'I can't,' she said. 'You know I can't.'

The dangerous midday tide, still wind driven, crept only a few inches up the garden. It was bitterly cold and snow swirled in flurries about the cottage. Watching from the window Cathy allowed herself a sigh of relief. 'It's OK. It's going down I think.'

Nikos came to stand beside her, surveying the wastes of water, the wrecked and sodden countryside. In the distance a small flotilla of boats cut through the flood, heading

towards the village. 'I suppose there must have been casual-
ties,' he said.

'Yes.' She was sombre. 'Not everyone can have been as
lucky as we were.'

He turned her to face him. Kissed her. 'Are,' he said. 'As
lucky as we are. In every possible way. So don't let's waste
what the gods have bestowed. Go and check on Bert. Then
hurry back. I have plans for the afternoon.'

They saw no one for twenty-four hours, except for the
occasional small boat in the distance. The wind died a little
at last though it remained bitterly cold. Gradually, very gradually, the waters started to recede. Cut off as they were they
might have been alone in the world, and they delighted in it.
It seemed to Cathy that the bizarre situation in which they
found themselves served only to stimulate their need for
each other. She found herself living each minute, each hour
with an intensity that drove from her mind all thoughts of
past or of future; the moment was all, and in this strange
small kingdom of theirs, lapped and isolated by the floods
that had devastated others' lives, they were safe. As they
made love, and talked, as they dreamed by the fire and made
love again it was for those few precious hours as if the hostile world, that would – rightly she knew – condemn and
revile their love no longer existed. Soon enough he would
leave. Soon enough she would be alone. Soon enough she
would have to face the enormity of what she had done. The
long, tender night she spent in his arms, listening to the
wind and the lapping of the waters, touching him, being
touched, loving him, being loved; storing memories for the
empty future. For no amount of self-deception could entirely
defeat logic, or conscience. She knew, even as he mused and
played the game of imagining there could be a life they
could somehow share together, that she must send him
away. But not yet. Not just yet. Moment by moment she
hoarded her happiness, as a miser hoards his gold; the silk of
his skin, the smile in his eyes as he looked at her, the

murmured words in the darkness, all of these things were her treasures, her defence against cold reality.

Until, that was, the moment that she stood at the bedroom window looking out into the bleak February afternoon and saw a boat approaching, a boat that did not, as others had, veer away from their small island, but chugged steadily and inexorably towards it. And from which, when it had safely beached by the garden gate stepped the tall, handsome, absolutely unmistakable figure of her son, Adam.

'God Almighty!' For a moment shock paralysed her; then she flew to the bed, shook the long-limbed, naked, slumbering figure that lay upon it. 'Nikos! Nikos, wake up! It's Adam! *Nikos!*'

He mumbled and turned, reaching for her. 'No! Nikos – wake *up!*' Frantically she tore herself from his grasp, began dragging her clothes on. 'Nikos, please –!'

At last her urgency reached him. He sat up, sleepily. 'What? What's the matter?'

'It's Adam. Nikos – please – wake up – *Adam's* here!'

He stared at her for a moment longer before rolling from the bed and reaching for his trousers. 'Jesus Christ.'

She had pulled on jumper and slacks and was thrusting her feet into her shoes. She reached for a brush, dragged it through her wild hair. 'I'll go down. I'll keep him talking. You stay up here for a minute or two.' She fled to the door and down the stairs. As she went into the sitting room there was a crisp rap on the door. She glanced around. The room was neat and tidy. The fire was almost out. She ran to it and threw a couple of logs on it, opened the kitchen door. The remains of lunch, clearly for two, stood upon the table. The faintest chance of keeping Nikos hidden faded. The knock came again. She took a deep breath, pulled back the curtain, opened the door. 'Who on earth – Adam! Adam, darling! What are you doing here?'

Her son stood grinning, a young man in fisherman's jersey and heavy waterproof trousers behind him. 'The Seventh

Cavalry, Ma'am,' he said, 'or I suppose to be more accurate The Seventh Company of Lifeboats. Rescuing fair maidens and elderly ladies our speciality. I managed to get through to the village. They told me you were still here. I found Jerry here and persuaded him to bring me to check you were OK.' He kissed her cheek lightly. 'See how I worry about you?'

'I'm fine. As you see. Absolutely fine. But come in – come in.'

Adam and his silent companion followed her into the room. Her son shook a finger at her. 'You shouldn't have stayed, you know. It's a bit extreme, even for you, under the circumstances.'

She shook her head mildly. 'I didn't know what the circumstances were, not until too late. And even if I had done there was Bert. He's been really very unwell. I couldn't leave him.' The excuse echoed hollowly in her own ears.

'Oh, come off it.' Her son's words were easy, and dismissive. 'You can't fool me. I know why you wouldn't go.'

She looked at him, blinking, her heart in her mouth.

'You wouldn't leave your blessed Sandlings to the sea. You'd stand on the doorstep like Canute yelling at the waves before –' he stopped.

The door to the stairs had opened, and Nikos stood there, hair ruffled, eyes sleepy. 'Adam!' he said, 'Adam – what on earth are you doing here? I heard voices –' Apologetically he turned to Cathy. 'I'm sorry. I guess I must have dozed off.' He turned back to Adam, self-deprecating and rueful. 'We haven't had much sleep these past couple of days.'

Cathy felt deep, guilty colour rise in her cheeks. She could not look at him.

Adam's attention had been understandably distracted. He was staring at Nikos. 'Never mind about me – what the hell are *you* doing here?'

'Didn't they tell you in the village?' Cathy answered for him, very swiftly. 'Nikos is the other reason I didn't leave. With him to help me I felt perfectly safe. Come in the kitchen. It's warmer in there.' She led the way into the kitchen, cleared the table as they sat down and dumped the dishes in the sink. 'I'll make a cup of tea.'

Adam was still watching Nikos. 'But – how did you get here? The whole of the coast is chaotic. It took me hours to get through.'

Nikos glanced at Cathy, a gleam of desperation in his eyes.

'He was here when it happened,' Cathy said, rapidly. She filled the kettle, set it on the stove. 'He – heard that conditions were going to be bad and came to warn me. On Saturday night. He'd been staying with friends in – Ipswich, didn't you say?' she asked Nikos.

He nodded, dumbly.

'Unfortunately he got here too late. By the time he arrived it would have been more dangerous to try to get ourselves and Bert out than to stay. Then by next morning – as you see – we were thoroughly cut off so there wasn't a lot we could do anyway. By the time the coastguard came it was fairly obvious that the cottages were safe, so it seemed best not to leave. Nikos stayed to help me look after Bert and the house. He's been a Godsend.'

Adam was looking puzzled. 'How did you know?' The question was addressed to Nikos.

'I'm sorry?'

'How did you know? That conditions were going to be that bad? There were no real warnings. Everyone's outraged; there've been questions in Parliament. There were no warnings given, not of any significance, anyway, and not until far too late. The floods have caused huge damage. Half the east coast is under water and there are apparently hundreds of people dead or still missing –'

'There were warnings of high tides,' Cathy broke in, and Jerry, still silent, nodded.

'But not of the kind of flooding that actually happened. It was a freak. No one was prepared. Did your friend in Ipswich have a crystal ball?' Again the question, light-hearted enough, but demanding of an answer, was addressed to Nikos.

Nikos shook his head. 'No, of course not. He just thought that there might be flooding, and that this part of the coast was vulnerable. Since I was so close I came to warn Cathy. To check that she was OK. That's all. I'm sure you'd have done the same.'

Adam shrugged, apparently satisfied. 'I suppose so. And flooding there certainly was, and not just here. The Low Countries caught it too. It's been absolutely devastating. Have you heard any of the news at all?'

Cathy shook her head. 'The electricity went off Saturday afternoon. When the wind got up. I haven't heard a newscast since.'

'Just as well. It's been pretty grim.' Adam sat back in his chair, his hands behind his head. 'And it's not going to get any better for some time. They said in the village they're working day and night to repair the breaches – there are more high tides due in a week – but they don't know how long it will take. It's no good, Ma – you're going to have to pack up and come back to town with me.'

'No,' Cathy said. 'I can't.'

'Why not?'

'Bert.'

He shook his head impatiently. 'If he's that bad he should be in hospital.'

'From what you say the hospitals have got enough to deal with. The water's going down. It's inches lower than it was. I've stuck it out this long. I won't give up now.'

'Oh, for Christ's sake!' Adam shook an exasperated head. 'This isn't some sort of competition! Supposing it happens again?'

'I should think that's very unlikely.' Cathy's panic had subsided. Suddenly she found herself thinking clearly and coolly. Composedly she poured the tea and handed the cups round. 'As you say it seems to have been some kind of freak.

The likelihood it will happen again must be very slight.' She looked at Jerry, smiled her most beguiling smile. 'I could do with some supplies. Would you be able to fetch some for me?'

'Ma!'

'Adam, I shall be perfectly all right. It was very good of you indeed to come out to find me. I do appreciate it. But I'm fine, and I shall stay. If you wish I'll promise that if there is the slightest danger of the floods rising again, I'll leave. As things stand it would be silly. Bert isn't well, though he is a bit improved. Everything I own is here, my work is here. I suppose you could say my life is here. I don't want to abandon it.'

'I still think –'

'No.' She was gentle but obstinate. 'I'm staying. Now that's settled. Still,' she glanced at Nikos and away, 'I think you should take Nikos back with you. He ought to have left before.'

'No,' Nikos said, quickly, 'I'm sure Adam would agree. I don't think you should be left here alone. If I go you should come too.'

'I can't. You know I can't.'

Adam cast resigned eyes to the ceiling. 'Give up, old boy,' he said. 'My mother is the most stubborn animal this side of a mule. You won't move her.'

'Then I'll stay.'

'No,' Cathy said. 'There's no need.'

Only she guessed that the colour that rose in his thin, dark face was bred of anger. She held his eyes. 'Please, Nikos. The danger is past. You should go. There's the business to manage. And Miss Hooper to find.' She turned back to Adam. 'Mr Bentley said that Canvey was badly hit?'

'Completely under water. Everyone evacuated. Forty or so dead.'

'Oh, Lord – that's dreadful! Nikos – you must go and make some enquiries. She lived alone, didn't she?'

He nodded. His eyes, hooded beneath his lashes, were fierce as a hawk's.

She would not meet them. 'Well then – you really must get

back to town and see what's going on. You'll need to report to Leon when he gets back. Now –' she stood up '– if you don't mind I'm just going to pop next door to check on the patient. After that, since Jerry has been kind enough to say he'll replenish my supplies tomorrow then I can offer you the last of the eggs and bacon if you'd like.' She reached for her coat.

Nikos stood up. 'I'll come with you,' he said, his voice brooking no protest. 'To say goodbye to Bert.'

Outside he caught her arm angrily. 'Why? *Why?* Why are you sending me away?'

'Because there's no possible justification for your staying. Because sooner or later there's the chance, if you did, that someone will add two and two together and make four.' At Bert's door, protected from the wind, she turned to face him. 'Because we've had our time together, my love.' She reached to touch his face, feather-light, before she let her hand drop to her side. Inexpressible sadness held her mute for a moment. 'Whatever happens Adam mustn't suspect any-thing. And you really should check that Miss Hooper is all right. We have no choice. You must go.'

'No!' The word was agonised.

She leaned to him for a moment, her arms about him, her head bowed to his shoulder. He crushed her to him.

'Nikos –'

'I can't! I won't! You love me. You know you do. You said you do –'

'Nikos, stop it!' She pulled away from him. 'I said other things too. I said it couldn't last. I said we must never, never do this again –'

'You didn't mean it. You couldn't have meant it!' He caught her arms, not noticing how she flinched at the force of his grip. 'Cathy, come away with me. Anywhere. Anywhere! I have a little money –'

'Nikos, don't be silly. You know it's impossible.'

'It wouldn't be. Not if you loved me the way you say you do –'

She tilted her head back, suddenly tired. 'Nikos – contrary to popular belief love doesn't conquer all.'

'Don't be so bloody cynical.' He was close to tears.

'I'm not being cynical. I'm being realistic.'

He let her go so suddenly she stumbled back against the door. 'Realistic?' his voice was bitter. 'Is that what you call it? You don't mean by any chance "Thanks, but no thanks and goodbye?"'

'Nikos!'

He turned from her in despair. 'You don't love me,' he said.

'That isn't true.'

'Then let me stay!'

She shook her head. 'It would look – odd. Can't you see that?'

'I don't give a damn how odd it might look!'

'Then you should,' she said, quietly. 'Nikos – have you any idea – have you given it the slightest thought? – how your father might react if he suspected there were anything going on between us?'

He stared at her in miserable defiance. Suddenly he looked very young.

'He'd kill us both,' Cathy said, very quietly. 'You know it.'

'Now you're being melodramatic.'

'Am I?'

He said nothing.

'I suppose,' she added, 'that it could be said he'd have every right to.'

'No.'

'I'm his wife. You are his son. His much-loved son.'

'Both of whom come second to his bloody business.'

'Nevertheless –'

'Nevertheless nothing!' He would not let her finish. When she tried to turn from him to the door he caught her wrist. 'Oh, no. Look at me. Will you look at me?' He waited until her eyes met his. 'Tell me you don't love me. Tell me you don't want me. Tell me that the past days haven't been the most wonderful experience of your life.' His grip tightened. *'Tell me!'*

She shook her head. 'I can't. You know I can't.'

'Tell me you love him and not me. Tell me you wish it hadn't happened.'

Cathy opened her mouth to speak, shut it again, shaking her head.

'Then let me stay!'

'No.'

He let go of her. Stepped back. 'All right,' he said, his voice shaking, 'I'll go. But don't you try to tell me you love me. Not ever again. I'll never believe it. Never!' He turned and left her. At the corner of the house he turned back. 'I love you,' he said, harshly, his young face savage, 'I'll always love you. I hope you can live with that. I'll have to,' and he was gone.

Cathy closed her eyes for a moment, steeling herself against the sudden welling of tears. She leaned against the door in the swirling, salt-laden wind, her head bowed. She had known from the start that it could only end in pain. She just had not been prepared for the depth of that pain. It was several full minutes before she straightened, took a breath and put her hand to the latch of the door.

Nikos, silent and coldly polite, left with Adam a couple of hours later. Watching him Cathy was torn between love and fury. She could not bear it that they should part in such a manner, with no private word, no chance to heal the rift between them; yet, too, his inability to hide his feelings, his refusal, it seemed, even to try, was so dangerous that it strung her nerves almost to breaking point. She made eggs and bacon for Adam and Jerry, plied them with questions about the floods, tried to keep Adam's attention from Nikos' black mood. In the end when the time came for them to leave it was almost a relief; but only until the little boat, in which Nikos sat rigid, looking ahead, refusing to turn, refusing to wave, chugged away, the sound of its engine dying, Adam's one last cheerful wave the last thing she saw before the little craft disappeared into the late afternoon dusk. She stood at the bedroom window, straining her eyes after it. The house was very quiet. She had never known it feel so empty. She had never in her life felt so alone. Miserably she turned from the window and walked to the bed; sat on it, staring straight ahead.

He had gone. It was finished. It had to be finished.

'But it hurts,' she said, softly, aloud, into the silence. 'Oh, God, it hurts!'

The memories – so recent, so warm, more real than the present – were all about her. Almost she expected to see him walking across the room to her, almost she expected to hear his voice, his laughter.

The silence echoed, mocking in her ears.

The fire was dead in the grate, the room was chill. She felt suddenly, overwhelmingly tired and cold to the bone. It was as if all warmth, all feeling, had drained from her. As if the essence of herself had been drawn like a will o' the wisp across the grey waters behind the little craft that had taken Nikos from her.

She reached for a pillow. It was the one on which Nikos' head had rested. She hugged it to her, let herself fall sideways on to the bed, the pillow clutched to her, eyes wide and looking into space. She lay for a very long time in the darkening room, trying not to think, trying not to feel, trying to convince herself that the world had not ended. And in the end, practical as always, she had to concede that it had not; not for other people anyway. A thump on the wall that adjoined with the next cottage told her that her much improved patient considered, quite justifiably, that it was time for supper. Stiff and shivering with cold she hauled herself off the bed and went downstairs to the kitchen.

PART TWO

Chapter Eleven

'There you are, Guv. Bein' a bit careful this afternoon, are we?' The bookmaker grinned in impudent fashion at Adam; a small roll of banknotes changed hands. 'Another day you'd 'a' broke me with that one.'

Adam shrugged, noncommittally, took the money and tucked it into his pocket. As he turned from the booth the man behind him slapped his shoulder. 'Sinclair! How goes it? Winning as usual?'

Adam blinked at a barely familiar face, hid his irritation beneath a meaningless smile. 'Of course. What else am I here for?'

'Got a tip for the next one?'

'Rosy Lee's probably the best each way.'

The man's grin broadened. 'Bugger off, you shyster. She doesn't stand a chance.'

Adam shrugged, still smiling, already moving into the crowds. 'Please yourself, old man. Please yourself.'

The loudspeakers were announcing the line-up for the next race. Adam caught a glimpse of a rider's silks as a horse picked its way through the swarms of people in the saddling enclosure. Two wins, small, but better than nothing. If the next one came in he'd risk a bit more on the last. He had a real hunch about that one. His hand went to his breast pocket, patting, checking. The thin roll of notes crackled beneath his fingers. Yes; another win and he could risk taking a bit of a chance. Whatever happened at least now he could afford to eat tonight. If he couldn't con someone into feeding him for free, that was. As he shouldered his way through the crowds he found himself once more fighting that stomach-churning combination of anger, resentment and apprehension that had been his almost constant companion since the terse interview a week or so ago during which he had been told, briefly and in the most humiliating of terms, that his services at Bates and Associates were no longer required, and that under the circumstances no notice would be given and no references provided. No notice and no references? After he'd slaved his guts out for that parsimonious bunch of know-nothing bastards? And what 'circumstances'? A malicious web of rumour and insinuation, not a shred of evidence to prove a thing. He'd done nothing that everyone else didn't do. Anyone who knew anything knew that. He'd get even with them somehow, that was for sure. They'd find they couldn't treat Adam Sinclair like this. They'd regret it. He'd see them broken, the lot of them.

He elbowed his way through to the rail, leaned on it watching as the jockeys took their frisky mounts to inspect the first fence; the low, late February sun glowed on the multicoloured silks and burnished the already gleaming pelts of the horses.

Adam reached into his pocket for his cigarettes. Oh, yes, he'd get his own back. Especially on that spineless, arselicking pipsqueak Walters; he could deny it till he was blue but Adam knew which crawler had blown the whistle on him. But – first things first – meanwhile there was the small matter of a living to be earned. The dismissal and loss of salary could not have come at a more difficult time.

He tapped his cigarette on the box, put it between his lips.

'Allow me.' Within inches of his face a lighter – a very expensive-looking gold lighter – clicked into flame. 'Mr Sinclair, isn't it?' The voice was very soft. And very cold. The hand that held the lighter was clean, white-skinned and rock steady.

Adam glanced at the man. He was big-built, well groomed, a little overweight, very well dressed. His overcoat fitted him snugly and his trilby hat was set firmly and squarely on his smooth hair. His face was like granite, the eyes grey, expressionless and as cold as the voice.

Adam's heart had begun to thump. A group of men had apparently aimlessly moved up beside and behind the stranger. Adam was aware of movement behind him. He was hemmed in. The men turned to the racecourse, apparently absorbed in the start of the race. 'We'd like a word,' the stranger said, softly, smoothing back on to his hand the well-fitting leather glove he had removed to handle the lighter. 'Just a word, you understand?'

'Who are you?'

The neat head shook. 'You don't need to know that, now do you? It's who we represent that matters. Isn't it?'

'I don't know what you mean.'

The head shook again, reproachfully. 'Oh, Mr Sinclair. I think you do. It can't have escaped your notice that you're – shall we say a little overdrawn? – in certain accounts?' The wire was up. The horses started forward. The stranger turned to watch them. 'I hope you're having a good day?'

Adam stood rigid and in silence as the horses thundered past. His skin was crawling with sweat. The shouts of the excited punters beat in his ears like a punishment.

The man leaned to him, confidentially. 'Certain parties,' he said quietly, 'are getting a little impatient. A little worried, even. They feel you aren't trying quite hard enough to repay what they were good enough to lend you. There's someone who feels that you might be taking advantage of his good nature. Not a good feeling, that, not for the gentleman concerned. I'm sure you'll agree. The problem is, you see, it sets such a bad precedent. You can understand that, I'm sure? I'd be reluctant to talk about making examples but . . . He let the words trail into the noise around them.

Adam drew nervously on his cigarette, aware that his hands were shaking, hating himself for it. 'It's only temporary,' he said. 'I'm a bit strapped for cash at the moment, that's all.'

'Oh, aren't we all, Mr Sinclair?' the other man said, sympathetically. 'Aren't we all?'

'I'll pay. Soon.'

The chill grey eyes turned to him. 'Oh, yes, Mr Sinclair. You will. One way or another. That I can promise you.' The man doffed his hat, smiling gently. 'I wish you a good day's racing, Mr Sinclair.'

He and his silent escorts moved away through the crowd; watching them go and with the sound of that quietly menacing voice still in his ear Adam found himself fighting against the rise of pure panic. He gripped the rail, forcing himself to calm. He'd find a way. He'd talked himself out of tighter corners than this. He'd do it again. Somehow. And meanwhile – he reached into his pocket for his race card – there was still the last race to go.

The train chugged through the flat, rural landscape; a landscape parts of which, despite a nation's best efforts, were still marked and scarred by the aftermath of the terrible flooding of a month before. Fields were silt-covered, farm buildings had collapsed, trees still lay where they had fallen in the worst gales in living memory. Cathy closed her magazine and rested her chin on her hand, looking out of the window. The countryside might well take years fully to recover from the havoc that the January storm had wreaked. Square miles of rich arable land had been inundated by salt water; towns, villages and hamlets were still counting the cost in shattered streets, disrupted services and wrecked buildings. The network of coastal defences had been overwhelmed and destroyed by the very force they had been set up to control; in some places the land would never be recovered. Whole streets in some coastal villages had simply disappeared overnight, lost to the perennial hunger of the sea. Cathy, in the days that had followed that dramatic and disastrous night had thanked the gods more than once for that usually almost unnoticed lift of land that had saved Sandlings from the flood. As she had worked with others in the village, organising and delivering supplies and necessities to those many families who had lost everything – including in some cases a precious life – she had come to realise very quickly how lucky they had been, she, Nikos and Bert, isolated on their small island. In a race against time most of the breaches had been patched up before the following week's high tides, and the waters never had reached the cottage. Drained, now, its hedgerows and woodlands battered, the countryside around the house looked forlorn and desolate. Given her state of mind, Cathy had found it a fitting place to live during these past few weeks.

The first twenty-four hours after Adam and Nikos had left she barely remembered, so torn had she been between an ever-growing and sometimes almost crushing feeling of guilt and a deep and debilitating unhappiness. It had taken a furious effort of will to shake off the wretched and self-centred misery which, cut off and alone, she had almost allowed to overwhelm her. It had been the realisation of the disaster that had touched the lives of others that had eventually wrenched her from her self-preoccupation. The community had been shattered; there were a million things to be done. In involving herself with the organisation and administration of help to those whose plight was so much worse than her own she had come at least to some kind of peace, some kind of resolve. She had heard nothing of Nikos, apart from indirectly, through his father. Just a week after he had left Sandlings he had gone to Greece on company business, and stayed for ten days, during which time Cathy had visited Leon in London and stayed at the flat with him. Just days after returning Nikos had left again, this time for an extended trip to New York, where he still was, the trip a combination of business and pleasure, partly to represent his father in some delicate negotiations, partly finally to wind up his grandmother's estate, partly a holiday to visit old friends and acquaintances in the city. He was not expected back for at least a fortnight, that she had established before agreeing to go to London again. There had been no communication between them since that bitter exchange before he had left. The message was clear; and Cathy told herself, time and again, that she was glad of it. What was done could not be changed, however much they both might wish it. The future was a different thing. Obviously Nikos had come to the same conclusion that she had; they must not see each other again. The memory of those days they had spent together must be totally and ruthlessly expunged. It had not happened. It must most certainly never happen again.

She turned again to the passing countryside. She had another problem to occupy her. Leon was becoming more and more insistent that her place was in London with him, until such time as the Greek house was ready. For her husband the events of a month ago had been the final straw. In vain she had argued that the storm had been an isolated one, the first to cause such danger or damage in generations. In vain she had pointed out the improvements being made to the sea defences, the determination that such a thing should never happen again; Leon had made up his mind. They had narrowly avoided quarrelling about it the last time she had visited the capital. He could see no reason why she would not give up Sandlings. She could see no reason why she should. The problem was insoluble.

Sighing, she went back to her magazine.

The visit started well enough. With Leon busy at the office all day Cathy took the opportunity to visit museums and art galleries, to stroll in the capital's parks and by the riverside. The first evening they ate out, the second they went to a concert. Cathy began to breathe a little easier. Not once had Leon mentioned her leaving Sandlings. Perhaps he had after all come to understand what the place meant to her. He seemed preoccupied, a little distant. On the one occasion that they made love it was a brief and for Cathy at least a deeply unsatisfactory exercise after which her husband rolled on to his side and was snoring in minutes. Cathy lay quiet beside him in the darkness, distancing the sound of traffic, listening for the sea.

The next day, unexpectedly, Adam telephoned. Leon had just left for work, Cathy was pottering around the flat tidying up and running a bath; the well-appointed bathroom was the one luxury in which she revelled. The shrill of the phone took her by surprise.

'Adam!' She was delighted to hear his voice. 'How lovely to hear from you. How are you?'

'I'm fine. Fine. Couldn't be better. Listen – I wondered if you might care to meet me for a spot of lunch later?'

'I'd love to! What a nice idea.'

'Fancy anywhere particular?'

She laughed. 'Oh, don't be silly! You know me and London. I'll leave it up to you.'

'Right. Tell you what, I'll pick you up at the flat – say about twelve-thirty?'

'Perfect.'

He was spot on time. The fine weather that had brought almost a taste of spring to the capital had given way yet again to the soot-laden fog that had so plagued the city during this long winter. Stepping into the restaurant, however, was like stepping into another world. Softly lit and plushly furnished, the place was warm and elegant, glittering with crystal and silver, the white damask tablecloths and napkins crisp and fresh. Adam was greeted with deference, they were escorted to a small table in an alcove. A piano played softly in the far corner of the room.

'Like it?' Adam asked, accepting the wine list from a hovering waiter.

'Love it,' she answered frankly, smiling. 'Very cosmopolitan. I'm surprised they let a country bumpkin like me across the threshold.'

Adam laughed, easily. 'Don't be so daft. Now – sherry to start? Or would you prefer Champagne?'

The meal was excellent, the wine plentiful and very good. Adam, at his most attentive and entertaining was an easy and charming companion. Yet it took a very short time in his company for Cathy to sense that all was not entirely well with her son. She had seen the signs before, too many times, both in him and in his father. He was too bright, too brittle. His face was a little drawn. He smoked constantly. The light-hearted chatter held no substance, and nothing of the personal. She was not entirely surprised when, after falling to silence for a moment over coffee and brandy he lifted his bright, forget-me-not eyes to her face and spoke abruptly. 'Ma – could I ask you a favour?'

She toyed with her brandy glass, watching him. 'Of course.'

He could not sustain her steady gaze. His own eyes dropped to his nicotine-stained fingers that were curled around his glass.

'Money?' she asked at length.

He nodded.

'Adam!'

His head came up sharply. 'I'm not asking you. I would, I'm not pretending I wouldn't. But there's no point. Ma – this time we're talking real money, more than you could manage. I need bailing out. I'm in real trouble.'

She stared at him, her stomach suddenly churning uncomfortably. 'If I can't let you have the money then what do you want me to do?'

'Talk to Leon. Ask him to fix it for me. I'm sure he can. I'll work for him to pay it back. I'll do anything –'

'But Adam –'

'Ma, please! Don't argue. Don't ask. Just tell me, yes or no. Will you ask Leon for me?'

'Adam, I don't know how much ready money Leon could raise anyway –'

'He has contacts. Banks and things. He must have. Jesus Christ, I met someone the other day who swears he's bought a shipping company lock, stock and barrel, cash on the nail –'

'Oh, Adam, you can't believe every silly rumour you hear! Leon certainly hasn't got that kind of money.'

'Well, he's got access to it.' He was stubborn. The telephone call he had received that morning had terrified him. 'I don't know where or how, but he has. Ma, please! Try for me?' He lifted the glass, but his hand was shaking too much for him to drink. He slammed it savagely back on to the table. 'I've had a run of bad luck, that's all. I've no job –'

'What?'

His eyes flickered to hers and away. 'The firm I was working for went bust. Nothing left. Not even a month's notice.' His face was taut. 'I owe – some people some money. They're getting pushy.'

'You've been gambling again,' she said, bleakly.

He shrugged, said nothing.

'Adam, will you never learn?' Her voice was very quiet.

He would not look at her.

'I could let you have –' she thought for a moment '– at a pinch – a thousand pounds?'

He shook his head. 'Not enough.'

'God Almighty!'

'I told you. I've had a run of bad luck.'

Concern and anger made her sharper than she had intended. 'No, Adam. You've had a run of stupidity.'

His mouth tightened, but he did not speak.

Cathy took a few moments to marshal her thoughts. 'Adam – if I did speak to Leon – wait –' she held up her hand as he lifted his head sharply '– wait. I say *if* I did – and even so I'm not convinced he has the kind of money you're hoping for – but if I did – would you make me a promise?'

Too readily he nodded. 'Of course.'

Her heart sank. In that moment he looked and sounded more like his dead father than he ever had. Knowing herself defeated before she started she said, 'Promise me you'll stop gambling.'

'Oh, I will. I promise.'

She pushed aside her untouched brandy, reached for her bag. 'Then I'll try. I promise I'll try.'

Adam tilted his head and drained his glass. 'Thanks. I'd appreciate it.'

'I'm still not sure that Leon has the kind of money you think he has.'

Adam surveyed her with a small, precarious smile. 'Well, you're the only one who isn't, Ma,' he said. 'Perhaps it's time for you to find that out.'

Leon, slowly and with obvious enjoyment, unwrapped his cigar, fingered it, cut it, lit it, tilted his head to let the fragrant smoke drift to the ceiling. Cathy's fingernail clicked against her coffee cup. In candle- and firelight the apartment seemed warmer, more homely than usual.

The silence lengthened. Then, 'So,' Leon said, 'you have no idea of exactly how much he needs?'

Cathy shook her head. 'More than a thousand. I offered him that, and he said it wouldn't be enough.'

'I see.'

'Leon – even if you can't lend him the money – would you please consider giving him a job? Taking him into the firm? Keeping an eye on him?'

The smoke rose again. 'Oh, I'd do that,' Leon said, softly.

'I'm worried sick about him.'

'I think you probably have every reason to be.' Her husband poured another brandy, lifted his sharp, dark eyes to hers. 'Of course if you spent more time in London you could keep a better eye on him yourself.'

She drew a deep breath.

'Well?' he asked, gently. 'Isn't it so?'

'I – suppose so.'

Leon leaned forward, covered her hand with his. 'Kati, my dear, it's time for you to join me. I need you. It can't have escaped your notice that the business, like a child, grows day by day. I need a home. I need a wife. Is it too much to ask?'

Cathy said nothing.

'You want me to help Adam. I'll help him. I'll lend – I repeat "lend" – him whatever it takes to get him out of trouble. I'll give him work; and he will have to work, we carry no passengers, as Nikos has found. But in return . . .' He let the words trail into silence.

She sat, rigid. 'In return you want me to give up Sandlings.'

'Not give it up. I wouldn't expect you to sell the house. But at least spend less time there. You can still play with your children's books –'

Her mouth tightened, and she bit back angry words.

'– though you must know you no longer need to earn money. Things are changing. Changing dramatically. Adam needs my help. I need yours –'

'What sort of help?'

He shrugged. 'I need a home – a home where I can entertain customers and associates. I need a wife who will do that for me. A wife who will support me, back me up –'

'A hostess,' she said, bleakly.

'Yes. Amongst other things, yes. The presence of a woman –' he put a finger beneath her chin and lifted her head, forcing her to meet his eyes '– of a very attractive woman – can, shall we say, oil the wheels of commerce. You could be a great asset, my Kati, if you would give up this ridiculous life of yours and join me. Here, in London, and in the Greek house when it is finished you would be a great ornament in my life.'

'An ornament,' she repeated, quietly, and in despair. 'An *ornament*?'

He appeared not even to have heard her. 'You'll see, *koukla mou*. I've told you – we have money now. We can afford to spend a little. We can afford a home – a home like this –' he gestured, indicating the luxury of their surroundings. 'You will soon forget your primitive little Sandlings. Come to London. Help me to find an apartment. You shall furnish it yourself, I promise. Anything you want . . .'

She had leaned her chin on her hand and was regarding him, steadily and in question. 'Adam was right,' she said.

'Oh?'

'He said you had more money than I thought you had. And it's true. You agree to bail him out without even knowing how much it will take to do it. You talk about renting a place like this and furnishing it as if it were going to cost the small change in your pocket. Leon – where is all this money coming from?'

He leaned back in his chair. Smoke drifted between them, veiling his expression. 'I've made some good deals these last few months. Made some killings. There is money to be made, my Kati – I've told you that before –'

'Doing what?'

'Why do you keep asking? Why do you bother your head so? Your husband is a successful man.'

She picked up her brandy glass, surveyed him thoughtfully over its rim. 'My husband is a secretive man,' she said.

He smiled, as if she had paid him a compliment, tapped the side of his nose with a finger. 'It pays, my Kati. It pays. Now . . .' He leaned forward again. 'You wish me to speak to Adam? You wish me to help him?'

'You know I do.'

'Then – you will consider what I have suggested?'

The silence lasted for perhaps a dozen heartbeats. 'Yes,' she said, very quietly.

'Splendid. Splendid! It will be fine, you'll see. So now – we go to bed. To celebrate.' He stood up, his bulk looming above her in the flickering candlelight.

'You go ahead,' she said, 'I'll clear away first.'

'Do it in the morning.'

She did not look at him. 'I'd rather do it now. I can't stand dirty dishes in the morning.'

She sensed the quick anger in him, sensed the effort he made to control it. 'Very well, *koukla mou*. But be quick, eh? Be quick.' He turned and left her.

Cathy sat like a statue until the bedroom door had closed behind him. Then she got up, switched the light on, blew out the candles, began to carry the dirty dishes out to the kitchen. The curtains were drawn back. The lights of the city reflected into the foggy sky. The constant movement and noise of the still-busy streets penetrated the quiet of the room. Somewhere in the apartment block a telephone shrilled. The long, deserted beaches of Suffolk seemed suddenly to belong to another life. Another world. A world she was losing.

'I'm in trouble this time, Ma,' Adam had said quietly as he had held the taxi door for her. *'Real trouble. Please don't let me down. There isn't anyone else.'*

She dumped the dishes noisily into the sink, ran the water on to them.

The doorbell rang.

Cathy nearly jumped out of her skin. Drying her hands she went back into the sitting room, and out into the hallway.

'Kati?' Leon called from the bedroom. 'Who is it?'

Nikos, standing on the threshold, did not take his eyes from Cathy's face. When she stood in stunned silence he raised his voice: 'It's me, Pa. Sorry to wake you. I forgot my key.'

'Nikos! Nikos, my boy!' Wrapped in a dark silk dressing gown Leon had appeared in the doorway. He advanced on Nikos, clapping him on the shoulder, hugging him. 'What are you doing here? We weren't expecting you until the week after next –'

Nikos wrenched his gaze from Cathy's face, hauled his suitcase into the hall, shut the door behind him. 'A friend of mine was coming to London. I'd done what needed doing so I decided to come back with her. Sorry – I should have let you know – I didn't realise –'

'Oh, don't talk nonsense, my boy! This is your home. You come and go as you please. Come in, come in! Kati – what can we give him? The boy looks exhausted.'

Hastily Nikos shook his head. 'No, truly, I don't want anything. Just a good night's sleep. It's been a long trip.'

'A drink. A drink at least. Come tell me about the trip. Did you see Galliano? What will he take?' Leon ushered his son into the sitting room.

Cathy hung back. Nikos' eyes flickered to her and away as he followed his father; and in them she saw what she knew he must have seen in her own. The sheer shock of the sudden and unexpected confrontation had left her trembling, and in that briefest of moments had stripped her of all her carefully constructed defences. 'Are you sure you couldn't eat something?' she asked, astounded at the steadiness of her voice.

'No. Thank you.' He was, as always, quietly courteous.

She stood uncertain, gestured, vaguely. 'I'll leave you two together, then,' she said. 'You've obviously got a lot to talk about. But Leon, don't keep Nikos up too long. He looks very tired.'

Leon patted Nikos' cheek; Nikos pulled back a little. 'See what a little mother she is?' Leon chuckled. 'Don't worry, Kati. I won't keep him from his bed for too long. Off you go. I'll come later. Now – Nikos – tell me the news –'

Cathy went into the bedroom, shut the door and leaned against it. She could hear the murmur of the men's voices. Leon laughed. Cathy closed her eyes for a moment, seeing again the expression on her stepson's face when she had opened the door to him.

When Leon came to bed an hour or so later she was apparently fast and peacefully asleep. He turned out the light, settled himself beside her, tentatively put out a hand to touch her. She breathed deeply and slowly. Heavily he turned from her, and in a very few moments was asleep.

Chapter Twelve

Cathy was in the kitchen washing the dirty dishes from the night before when she heard the door open behind her. She knew without turning who it was that had entered the room. Meticulously carefully she stacked a plate on the draining board.

'Cathy,' Nikos said, quietly. 'How are you?'

'I'm well.' Her voice was neutral; she did not turn her head. 'And you?'

He did not reply.

A door opened. 'Kati? Did you see what I did with my blue tie?' Leon's voice, bellowing.

Cathy raised her own. 'On the right-hand side in the wardrobe. With the white shirts.'

'Cathy –' Nikos began again, softly.

'I've looked there.' Leon was plaintive. 'I've found the pale one. It's the dark one I want. Kati –?'

Cathy sighed, dried her hands. 'I'm coming.' She turned. Nikos was standing a couple of feet behind her. 'I'm sorry,' she said, rapidly and quietly. 'I didn't expect you back so soon. If I'd known you were coming I'd have made sure not to be here. I'll leave as soon as I can make an excuse –'

'Kati!'

'I'm coming.'

Nikos stepped back to let her pass. 'You don't have to leave because of me.'

She held his eyes for a moment, steeling herself against anything she might see – or want to see – in them. 'Oh, I think I do,' she said, very composedly. She had had a long and all but sleepless night to prepare for this. And to consider Leon's ultimatum – for that it surely had been – concerning Adam. In those dark hours she had come to two very firm resolutions; or rather, perhaps, had realised that in neither case did she have a choice.

'*Kati!*'

She left him standing there.

Over breakfast Leon, his dark blue tie neatly knotted and his good temper restored, took to some heavy-handed teasing. 'So, Nikos – who is this young lady that you told me of last night? The one who tempted you home from New York? She's pretty? Rich?'

Nikos flushed to the roots of his hair. 'She's – very nice.'

'Nice? Nice? Nice you don't need, my boy.' Leon chuckled. 'Rich and beautiful. That's what you need.'

'She is pretty. But she's not rich. Not so far as I know, anyway.'

'How does it happen she flies from New York to London?'

'It's her job. She's a freelance journalist and photographer. Mostly to do with fashion. She's working on an article. She needed to come to London, and then she's going on to Paris. I'd finished my business. I was at a loose end. She'd never been to London before. I offered to fly back with her, show her the ropes. That's all.' Nikos was studiously avoiding Cathy's cool, unblinking gaze.

'So you're seeing her while she's in London?' Cathy asked, sipping tea.

'I'm – yes. I'm seeing her tonight, actually. For dinner.'

'That'll be nice. If she's staying for long enough you'll have to bring her here for a meal.'

'Excellent idea.' Leon stood, brushing crumbs from his jacket. 'Nikos – you come to the office with me. You give Miss Hooper the notes on Galliano, and then as I told you last night I have something to discuss with you. We need to expand. We need more staff. Reliable staff. As I said, Adam wishes to join us – this is good – but perhaps not enough – we'll see, we'll see.' He dropped an absent-minded kiss on Cathy's hair. 'I'll be a little late, *koukla mou*. I have a meeting at six.'

'We can eat in,' Cathy said. 'Will eight do?'

'Eight will be fine.'

'You're sure? I can make it later –'

'No, no. Eight will be fine.'

Cathy glanced at Nikos. 'You're eating out?'

'Yes. I'll go straight from the office. We're going to the cinema first. I'll be late, I expect.'

Cathy felt for one awful moment that if she opened her mouth again she might scream. How could Leon not sense the tension beneath the trivial exchange? How long before he did? When the door finally closed behind father and son she sank into a chair and buried her face tiredly in her hands. She felt fraught and exhausted. She lifted her head. 'I love him,' she said, aloud. 'I thought I could deny it, but I can't. I love him. And I want to go home. Oh, God, I do so want to go home!' For a second her hard-held control deserted her and she laid her head on her arms, tears burning in her eyes; but only for a second. If she started crying now, she told herself grimly, she might well never stop. 'Best not to, then,' she told the butter dish, on a long, shaky breath, and set about clearing up.

The telephone rang a couple of hours later. Cathy was sitting at the kitchen table sketching. She laid down her pencil, went into the sitting room, expecting to hear Adam's voice when she answered it. 'Hello?'

Coins dropped in a call box. 'Cathy.' Nikos' voice was

quiet. He spoke very quickly. 'Cathy – I must see you – talk to you properly –'

'No.'

'*Please!*' The word was anguished.

'No!' She was shaking. 'Nikos, leave me alone. Go away and leave me alone!'

He was still speaking when the handset clattered back on to the cradle.

She walked in Hyde Park for most of the afternoon, wandering aimlessly along the walks beneath the giant, leafless trees, solitary amongst the dog-walkers, the pram-pushers, the lovers. It was very cold. The air, even here in the capital's largest open space, smelled of traffic fumes and stung her eyes. She tried, unsuccessfully, not to think. Tried not to admit to herself that she was afraid to go back to the apartment; afraid that Nikos might come, afraid of what might happen if he did; tried above all not to remember those days they had spent together at Sandlings, the things they had said, the things they had done, the bond they had forged. She was chilled to the bone when she got back to the dark and empty flat. She ran hot water into the bath, pinned her hair up and climbed in, lying back in the steam. The water lapped about her body, the warmth lulling her. She had hardly slept all night. Her eyelids drooped.

She awoke to hear the clock striking in the sitting room. The bath water was stone cold. Shivering and disorientated she scrambled out of it, wrapped herself in a towel and reached for her watch. Seven o'clock. 'Seven o'clock? Dear Lord, it *can't* be! There's a fire to light, a dinner to cook – oh, *blast* it! What an idiot!' She was clumsy with cold and the catnap had left her if anything even more ill-temperedly tired than she had been to start with. The fire refused, sullenly, to light and she cut herself peeling the potatoes. By ten to eight, however, with Leon still blessedly absent, the apartment was tidy, the fire at last beginning to draw, the table was laid and the

supper, late but smelling good, was in the oven. Relaxing a little, and breathing a small prayer that Leon might not turn up
for ten minutes or so to give her time to recover from the rush
she poured herself a small sherry and settled down to wait.

An hour later, with the meal close to spoiling and the
sherry bottle half empty she was still waiting. She eyed the
telephone. Wherever Leon was, there surely must be a telephone? She picked up the handset to check the line was live.
It was. She tossed aside the magazine she had been reading
and went in to the kitchen to salvage the meal.

By ten o'clock she was truly worried, convinced that
something quite terrible must have happened. She had by
then tried the office number, in case Leon had gone back
there after his meeting, but there was no reply. There was
nowhere else to try; she had no idea where he might have
gone – he could be anywhere in London. She couldn't phone
every hospital in the city. There was nothing to do but to
wait, and to worry.

It was nearly half past eleven when she heard a key in the
lock. By now beside herself with anxiety she rushed to the
door.

Leon, smiling beatifically, swayed a little. *'Kalispera sas,
koukla mou.'*

Cathy stared at him.

'You are looking –' he raised a finger, waved it as if con-
ducting an orchestra '– very beautiful.'

'You're drunk,' she said.

He shook his head. 'No. No. A little merry, yes. It was a
good meeting. We celebrated a little afterwards.' He shut
the door behind him, reached for her. 'Aren't you going to
give your husband a kiss?' He smelled of cigar smoke,
whisky and something subtle and flowery.

Trembling with anger she moved her head so that his lips
brushed her ear, pulled herself from his grasp and stalked
into the sitting room. 'And where was this meeting?' she
asked, coldly. 'On the moon? In Outer Mongolia?'

He frowned, puzzled. 'What do you mean?'

'It was obviously somewhere that hasn't yet acquired a telephone system.'

He shrugged, threw off his overcoat. 'I was busy, Kati.'

'And I was worried. Worried sick! You said you were coming home to dinner. You said you'd be here by eight –'

'I told you –' his volatile temper was, inevitably, rising to match hers '– I had a meeting.'

'At six o'clock! It's now getting on for midnight! I don't care where you've been. Or what you've been doing. I care that you didn't bother to ring me and tell me you weren't coming home –'

'I'm home now, aren't I? What kind of a greeting is this I get?'

'The same kind of apology you're offering me. None at all.' The clipped and angry words seemed to come from someone else's tongue; she could put no brake on them. 'Leon, you are the most self-centred person I have ever met! Did it even occur to you to ring me? Did it even occur to you that I was sitting here alone worrying myself half to death? That I had cooked you a meal? That I was waiting for you?'

'Of course it did.' Irritated he turned from her, walked to the table upon which stood bottles and glasses, reached for the brandy. 'I thought you would understand –'

'Oh, I understand. All too well. I understand that I'll always come second to the other priorities in your life – whatever they may be. I understand that if I give in and come and join you in London I'll spend half my life –'

'Give in? Give in?' He tossed back the drink and turned on her, interrupting her, his voice suddenly hard. 'What is this you're saying? That I'm forcing you to come to live with me?'

The silence was taut, and suddenly perilous. But in her anger and unhappiness she could not pull back now. 'Well, aren't you?' she asked.

He stood, glowering, a pulse beating in his heavy jaw. 'I

offered you a home with me,' he said, very quietly. 'I asked you to leave your pathetic backwater and come to live *here*. With *me*.' He emphasised the words with a furiously pointed finger.

Like the sudden blaze of a heath fire the quarrel had from one moment to the next run totally out of hand. 'In return for helping Adam. You can't deny it. Your trouble, Leon, is that you're coming to believe you can buy anything,' Cathy heard herself say, furiously and stubbornly, and knew she had gone too far.

Shaking his massive head he reached for his overcoat. 'No, my Kati, no! I have just found something I can't buy, have I not? A loving greeting when I come home. A wife who is pleased to see her husband –'

'You're nearly four bloody hours late!' Suddenly, tears of temper and misery running down her face, she was screaming like a fishwife. 'What do you expect me to do? What do you expect me to say? "Hello my darling, I didn't want dinner anyway"? Where the hell do you think you're going now?'

Leon had flung his coat back on. 'Out,' he said. 'Out to where I know I'm welcome. Out to see people who will be pleased to see me.'

'Well, you'd better take your key,' she snapped. 'I shan't be waiting up.'

'Why would I expect you to?' A moment later he was gone, the door, all but shaking the substantial building, slamming thunderously behind him.

Cathy threw herself on to the settee, sobbing, all control finally lost. She cried until she could, physically, cry no more. Curled up in a tense and trembling ball, her knees to her chest, for a space of time she never afterwards measured she abandoned herself totally to her confusion and misery. Until, at last, exhausted, she cried herself into a disturbed half-sleep.

And that was how Nikos found her.

It had not been by any measure a successful evening. He had not remembered Lois being quite so strident, quite so overpowering in New York. She was, so much he understood, one of those people who counterbalanced a basic lack of self-assurance by an occasionally nervewracking show of over-confidence. He thought everyone in the restaurant must have heard her none-too-thinly veiled invitation over dinner, to say nothing of her cutting displeasure at his refusal. In fact he had almost been tempted; the thought of going home to the apartment, of seeing Cathy and his father together, of knowing them in the intimacy of the marriage bed together was almost more than he could bear. Yet the thought of not seeing her, of missing any opportunity to be near her, was worse. He fitted his key into the lock and pushed the door open.

Cathy was lying curled up, fully dressed, on the settee. Her hair was tumbled, damp with sweat, about her blotched face, her eyes, even in sleep, were swollen with crying. Her breathing was uneven, as if with no volition she wept still. The apartment was darkly silent, and obviously empty. The fire was almost out. He knelt beside her. 'Cathy? Cathy, what is it? What's happened?'

She stirred a little.

He put a hand on her shoulder, shook her. 'Cathy.'

She opened her eyes. Sat bolt upright, covering her face with her hands. 'Nikos. Go away. Please go away.'

'What is it? My darling, what's wrong?'

'Everything. Everything's wrong.' The miserable tears had started again. Her shoulders shook.

Nikos sat beside her, drew her gently to him. Unable to resist she lay against him, her head on his shoulder. His arm tightened about her. 'Tell me what happened.'

She struggled to control her voice. 'Leon didn't come home till nearly midnight. He didn't call. He didn't attempt to let me know he wasn't coming. He might have been dead for all I knew. When he did arrive he breezed in as if nothing had happened. I've had a wretched day. I lost my temper. We quarrelled. He walked out.' She pulled away from him, sniffing.

Wordlessly he pulled a handkerchief from his pocket and offered it to her.

Calmer now, she mopped at her face, blew her nose. 'Look at the state of me.'

'I love you,' he said, his voice very soft and very certain.

Tears welled again. She shook her head. 'Nikos, you mustn't. You mustn't say it, mustn't think it.'

'Mustn't feel it?' he asked, quietly. 'How can I not? Do you know where the switch is to switch it off? You're with me every moment of the day, wherever I am, whatever I'm doing. You're in my blood. In my heart. Tell me how to stop it and perhaps I will.'

She stared at him in helpless silence. Her swollen eyes were red with crying, her hair wild as a bird's nest. He reached a hand, rested the back of his curled fingers on the burning skin of her face. 'I love you,' he said again. 'I can't fight it any longer. I love you and I want you. I don't care if it's right or wrong. I don't care what anyone thinks. Because whether you like it or not I think you love me too. Don't you?'

She ducked her head, fiddling with the handkerchief.

'Cathy?'

'Yes. I do.' The words, separated by a small hiccough of a sob, were scarcely audible.

'Then let's start from there. At least we're being honest with each other.'

She lifted her head to look at him again. 'But not with anyone else.'

'To hell with anyone else.' His voice was still gently patient. 'I'm talking about us. A pact. A promise. Whatever happens we won't misunderstand each other again. We've problems enough without making them worse for ourselves.'

'You were the one who quarrelled. At the cottage.'

'I know. And I'm sorry. I thought you were sending me away.'

'I suppose I was. I couldn't think of anything else to do.'

He took her hand, lifted it to his lips, kissed the tips of her fingers. 'And now?'

She shook her head wearily. 'I still can't think of anything to do.'

'What do you want to do?'

'I want to kiss you.'

He smiled. 'I'd taken that as read. Apart from that.'

'I want to go home.'

'Then do it. Go home. I'll come to you there.'

She took a quick breath to reply, but then said nothing.

'I won't let you go,' he said, simply. 'Not now that I know you still love me. Go home. I promise I won't take risks. But I will come. I will see you.'

She closed her eyes, suddenly remembering. 'I can't.'

'Can't what?'

'I can't go to Sandlings. That was the other thing Leon and I quarrelled about. Adam needs help. He's lost his job and he's in debt. Leon agreed to bail him out – but only if I came to live here in London –'

Nikos leaned forward, her hand still trapped between his. 'Forget Adam. He's old enough to look after himself –'

'He's my son.'

'You think I don't remember that? Look – I'll talk to Pa. I'm sure he'll help. He's already talked to Adam about coming into the business. He wants him to. He won't let a quarrel with you spoil that, I'm sure. Go home to your cottage. Give yourself time to think. But don't think yourself out of loving me. Please don't do that.'

She lay back tiredly, her head tilted back on the cushions. 'No. I won't. I promise.'

He settled himself beside her, drew her head on to his shoulder. She lay peaceably for a long, quiet time before she said, softly, 'Nikos? Are you going to make love to me?'

'No.'

She lifted her head to look at him.

'Not here. Not now. I want you to myself. I don't want you worried, or listening for interruptions. Pa could walk back in at any minute. I won't risk that for you. It isn't that I don't want to; you know that. But I'm ready to wait.'

She touched his lips with her finger. 'And I thought the young were always so impatient.'

He smiled. 'That's the first time you've joked about it.'

'What?'

'The difference in our ages.'

She flushed a little.

He kissed her. 'Tired?'

'Yes.'

'Do you want to go to bed?'

'No. Not if you can't come with me.'

'Then stay here.' He reached for a cushion, laid it on his lap. 'Cuddle down. Get some sleep. I'll wake you if Pa comes back.'

For the few hours that were left of the night he kept watch over her as, despite her best efforts to stay awake, she slept. His own near-exhaustion he ignored, indeed he hardly noticed it. As the quiet hours ticked on he rested, quietly, with her. His mind, at last, had cleared. The New York trip had served only to demonstrate to him how much he loved her. The familiar places had been cold and empty. Memories had been simply that; something to remember, not something to live for. He had found the only thing he wanted to live for, and it was here. What the future might bring he dared not contemplate. All he knew, as Cathy, her face still puffy and tear-marked, slept like a tired child on his lap, was that for the moment he was happy.

Leon did not return that night. Tired and fuzzy-headed the next morning Cathy packed to go home.

'Pa'll be at the office.' Nikos leaned in the doorway, watching her. 'What will you do? Phone him?'

She shook her head. 'No. If he'd wanted to speak to me he could have phoned here. I'll leave him a note.'

He grinned suddenly. 'I'll grant that Adam's right about one thing.'

'What's that?'

'You are as stubborn as a mule, aren't you?'

'Yes.' She flashed him a tired smile. 'Be warned.'

He came to her, gathered her into his arms, laid his cheek upon her hair. They stood so for a quiet few moments. 'I'm still officially on holiday,' Nikos said. 'Pa agreed I should have some time off. I came home early from New York. There's no reason why I can't come to the cottage in a couple of days' time. I can say I'm taking Lois away for a few days.'

Cathy shook her head a little. 'Lies. I hate lies. They have a nasty habit of biting you back.'

'If lying is the only way we can be together then I'll do it,' he said, evenly. 'And smile.'

'I wish we didn't have to.'

'If wishes were horses –'

'– then beggars would ride. I know.'

'You want me to come?'

'Yes.'

'Then I will. Expect me on Friday.'

'How long will you stay?'

'I don't know. For as long as I can.'

She lifted her mouth for his kiss.

The doorbell rang.

'Blast.' She stepped back from him. 'The taxi. Would you ask him to wait for a moment? I have to write my note.'

A keen March wind blustered in the street. 'Let me come to the station with you,' Nikos said.

Cathy shook her head. 'Best not. I'll see you in a couple of days.' She smiled with the words, and his heart turned over.

'Liverpool Street, did you say, Missis?' the taxi driver asked.

'Yes, please.' Cathy turned back to Nikos. 'You'll speak to your father about Adam for me? Promise?'

'Of course I will. Don't worry.'

'It's important.'

'I know.'

They stood for an odd, uncertain moment. Then she brushed his cheek with her lips. 'I'll see you on Friday?'

'Yes.'

She climbed into the taxi, waved as it pulled into the traffic. Nikos stood looking after it. 'Oh, yes,' he repeated softly.

Adam sat, apparently relaxed, legs crossed, the smoke from his cigarette spiralling to the dingy ceiling. He had been surprised at the unpretentious premises of Kotsikas and Son; knowing Leon as he thought he did he had expected something a little more flamboyant.

The silence had lasted for rather longer than was comfortable. He shifted a little in his chair.

Leon lifted his head to fix him with a dark, contemplative gaze but disconcertingly still did not speak. With an effort Adam kept his face schooled and his eyes steady. For Christ's sake – was the man never going to say anything?

Leon got up from behind the desk, walked to the window and stood looking down into the street. 'It's a lot of money,' he said at last.

'Yes, I realise that.' Adam was tense as a coiled spring. He needed the money; desperately he needed it. If Leon were to refuse to help him he would be in deep and dangerous waters indeed.

'A lot of money,' Leon repeated, thoughtfully.

Adam leaned to the desk, ground out his cigarette in the ashtray. 'I'll pay you back. I promise that.'

Leon turned, smiling a little grimly. 'You won't be able to avoid it. You'll be working for me, remember?'

The younger man smiled a lop-sided, disarming smile. 'Of course.'

Leon perched on the desk, leg swinging. In the silence he loosened his tie, undid the top button of his shirt. Adam saw the glint of gold against his dark, muscular neck. Absent-mindedly Leon fingered the icon. 'I rarely – I would say never – give something for nothing. You can understand that?' he said at last, softly.

The blue eyes that met his were wary. Adam said nothing.

'So, I would ask – supposing I wanted something in exchange for this loan?'

The frown on the fair, handsome face was puzzled. 'What sort of something?'

'Supposing I wanted you to use – shall we say your influence? – with your mother?'

It took a moment for the import of that to sink in. As it did Adam sat back, relaxing a little.

'She's very close to you,' Leon added, pensively. 'And I know you can be very persuasive.'

'You want her to leave Suffolk,' Adam said.

Leon nodded. 'I want her to leave Suffolk. I want her here, with me. And when the time comes I want her to come to Greece with me, as a good wife should.'

'Is that all?' Adam was rueful.

Leon slipped his hand into his breast pocket and pulled out a cheque book; sat tapping it idly into the palm of his hand. 'That's all,' he said. 'Is it a bargain?'

Adam shrugged. 'I can but try.'

'Don't try, Adam. Do it.' His stepfather held up the chequebook. 'Half now. Half when your mother tells me she's coming to London. Fair enough?'

'Leon – I don't know if I can –' Adam stopped, shrugged. He recognised a corner when he was driven into one. 'Fair enough,' he said.

Chapter Thirteen

In a pale, cool sunshine that encouraged belief in an early spring they walked the shingle beach hand-in-hand, their feet crunching on the stones, the dogs racing and bounding excitedly around them. The sky was vast, and clear as crystal, the air lucent and salt-smelling. The coast stretched ahead of them, spacious and deserted. A few small boats, their paintwork weather-beaten, lay empty, hauled high above the reach of the tide. In the distance a huddle of tumbledown fishing huts was the only sign of human habitation. 'It's like being alone in the world,' Cathy said.

Nikos squeezed her fingers. 'As far as I'm concerned we are. There's no one but you.'

She smiled, but did not reply. Sandy trotted hopefully to them, a piece of driftwood in his mouth. Nikos took it and threw it for him, into the waves. Cathy groaned. 'You've had it now. He'll never give up.'

The tide was ebbing, leaving the shingle washed and glittering in the sunlight, the browns and blacks, golds and ochre yellows of the pebbles contrasting with the mother-of-pearl sheen of shell and the dark and gleaming green of seaweed. Cathy stooped to pick up a smoothly rounded pebble, rolled it between her fingers. 'Just feel how smooth it is. It never ceases to amaze me that water can do this to stone.' Their fingers touched as she handed it to him, and both smiled.

They linked hands again, scrambled up to where a small boat lay, upturned. Cathy perched herself on it, Nikos leaned against it and reached for his cigarettes, turning away from the wind to light one. Cathy was sitting, eyes half closed against the dazzling light, looking pensively into the spray-smudged distance of the horizon, where a few small fishing boats rocked on the heaving, pewter-grey sea. For a long moment neither of them spoke. Then, 'I can see why you love it so,' Nikos said.

She turned, took his hand and held it to her cool cheek, rubbing her face gently against it. 'Can you? Can you really? It's so very different from what you're used to. And I suppose nowhere near so conventionally beautiful.'

'It grows on you. And anyway – it's a part of you. How could I help but love it?'

She kissed the palm of his hand. 'It's so wild. There's so much space. So much sky. You can breathe here. You can shout, and sing, and no one can hear you.'

'And I'll bet you do?'

She grinned a little. 'It's been known.' She leaned her face against his arm, still holding his hand. 'Nikos?' Her voice was quiet, the laughter gone. The question she had determined not to ask came from nowhere: 'What are we going to do?'

He did not answer for a long time. 'I don't know,' he said, at last. 'I only know that now I have you I'm never going to let you go. That I'm not going to waste a single moment that I have you with me in regret, or guilt, in caring about other people. I know that I love you and that you love me. That's enough.'

She shook her head a little. He felt the movement against his arm, caught her shoulder so that she lifted her head to look at him. 'Yes!' he said, fiercely. 'How can you doubt it? As long as we love each other then nothing else matters.'

Cathy bowed her head, picking absently with her

fingernail at the rough, oily stitching of the fisherman's jersey she wore.

'As long as we love each other,' he repeated, very firmly, 'then nothing else matters. The world can't touch us.'

'Oh, my darling,' she said softly, 'you are so very –' She stopped.

'What?'

She said nothing.

'What? What am I?'

Cathy lifted her wind-tangled head and smiled. '– fierce,' she said.

'That wasn't what you were going to say.' His jaw had set stubbornly.

She looked back down at the jersey.

'Was it?'

She jumped from the boat, brushing sand off her trousers.

'You were going to say "young". Weren't you?'

She reached for his hand. 'I suppose I was, yes.' Her voice was gentle.

He turned her to face him, holding her by the shoulders. 'Well, I can't deny it. I am young. That doesn't mean I don't know what I'm doing. I've told you before and I tell you again; you are the only woman I've ever loved, the only one I ever will. I won't – I can't live without you. Age doesn't come into it. I'm yours. I'm going to love you for ever. I want to look after you. I'd die rather than see anyone hurt you –' He stopped. 'Cathy? What is it? You're crying?'

She pulled free, laid her head on his shoulder. 'No. Of course I'm not. It's just the wind. Let's go home.'

The world, inevitably, and despite Nikos' fierce confidence that it would not, caught up with them three days later. It had been an idyllic few days; even Cathy had come to believe that for a week or so at least they might be left alone; in the event it was Bert who was the unwitting messenger of possible disaster, and their equally unwitting saviour. He had borrowed Cathy's bicycle to go to the shop. An hour or so later he was banging on the door again. 'Cath? Letter for you.'

Cathy opened the door. 'Hello again. Come in. Cup of tea?'

The dishevelled old head shook. 'Best get on.'

'OK.' Cathy knew better than to try to persuade him. She held up the envelope. 'Thanks.' She turned from the door, looking at the letter. Adam's writing. She tore it open as she went into the kitchen.

Nikos was sitting at the table, leafing through some of her sketches. 'These really are –' He lifted his head 'What's that? Cathy, what's the matter?'

'Damn it! Damn and *blast* it!'

'What?'

She passed the note to him, dropped on to a chair, put her head into her hands.

He read it. Read it again. Laid it down on the table and looked at her. 'Ring him. Tell him he can't come.'

She shook her head. 'I can't. How can I? What possible excuse could I give?' She picked up the letter and glanced at it again. 'Thank God Bert went down into the village! Adam wrote this nearly a week ago. It's been waiting at the post office for days. I can't just ring him now and say no, can I? It would look very peculiar.'

'I'll stay,' Nikos said, calmly. 'Why shouldn't I? I've as much right here as he has.'

'No!' She flung herself from her chair. 'No,' she repeated more quietly. 'Oh, Nikos, think! You're supposed to be in the Lake District with Lois. Adam knows that. It would mean more lies. More deception.'

It would mean seeing the two of you together, and that, at the moment, I could not bear. She knew better than to speak the words.

She turned, leaning against the stove. 'I'm sorry, my darling. You'll have to leave. You mustn't be here when he comes.'

'You want me to go.' His young face was mutinous.

'*No!* Of course I don't! But we don't have a choice. Oh, Nikos, please – don't quarrel about it. Not again. I couldn't bear it.' She came to him, bent to lay her face on his hair. 'You can't be any more disappointed than I am. But Adam will be here tomorrow, and you mustn't be here when he comes. Nikos – we have to be careful –'

'I know.' He turned his head, his voice muffled in the folds of her jumper. His hand cradled her breast. 'I know. I just hate it.'

'You can't hate it any more than I do.'

'Don't make me go now. Let me stay till the morning. Please.'

'Of course,' she said.

That night, for the first time, his lovemaking was so fiercely unrestrained that he hurt her. Afterwards he lay heavily upon her, his face buried in her shoulder, his fingers still tangled into her hair. 'Cathy – please – *please!* – don't make me go.' His breathing was heavy, his voice a whisper.

Cathy stroked his hair and said nothing.

The next morning she walked with him up the track to where the black Austin stood in the lane. He kissed her gently, touched her bruised lip with his finger. 'I'm sorry.'

'Don't be silly.'

The cold March wind whispered around them. The scrubby trees were budding palely green. 'I'll write,' he said.

'Yes.'

'And we'll see each other again soon.'

'Yes.'

'We must.'

She kissed him again. 'Yes.'

He drove away blindly, tears blurring his eyes, the pain of leaving her so acute that he could barely breathe.

And Cathy, as she watched the car out of sight, felt the now familiar flood of guilt, fear and an unhappiness that came close to despair that inevitably filled the vacuum left by his going.

Heavy-hearted she went back to the cottage to prepare herself to face her son.

'Thanks, that was great.' Adam put down his knife and fork and leaned back in his chair, replete. 'I don't know how you manage it on that old thing.'

His mother reached for his empty plate. 'Don't be rude to my stove. It's my best friend,' she said, mildly. 'Would you like a piece of pie?'

'Yes, please.' He watched as she busied herself with the pie, reached for the jug of custard. 'Ma?'

Cathy laid the plate in front of him. 'Mm?'

He picked up his spoon, tinkered with it. Small rivers of custard enclosed the islands of crisp pastry. 'You do know you can't go on like this for ever, don't you?'

Her face suddenly expressionless she straightened. 'I don't think I understand what you mean,' she said at last, carefully.

He jerked his head, indicating his surroundings. 'Living here. Like this.'

Cathy rested both hands flat upon the table and leaned to him. 'As I believe you well know,' she said, her voice dangerously quiet, 'I like living here. Like this.'

He could not meet her eyes. He applied himself to the pie. Cathy turned to the sink.

'Leon's found an apartment,' Adam said after a moment. 'Not far from Nikos'. In Kensington High Street.' He waited for her to speak. The silence was ominous. He ploughed on. 'In one of those big old mansion blocks. It's very nice –'

'I'm sure it is.' The words were clipped.

'Ma –'

She turned. 'Adam, you worry me when you call me that. It almost invariably means you want something.'

'That's not fair.'

'Isn't it?' She eyed him repressively. Slow colour rose in his face.

'It's only that Leon wants you to come up to London to look at it, that's all. It doesn't seem much to ask.'

Cathy sucked her lower lip for a moment, looking at him. 'There's no point,' she said, quietly. 'I've quite made up my mind. I'm staying here. If Leon wants an apartment I'm sure he's quite capable of finding one –'

Adam's spoon clattered into his plate and he pushed it from him, his face tight and bright with anger. 'You can't do that! You're married to Leon –'

'Adam. It is none of your business!' She articulated the words with a ferocious clarity. 'You are my son. And I love you. But that doesn't give you any right whatever to interfere so –'

'I'm *not* interfering!'

'I think that's exactly what you're doing. I'm a grown woman. I will not have you telling me what I should or should not do! I will not have you conniving with Leon to make me do something that I don't want to do, that I have never pretended I wanted to do. It's my business, and Leon's. It's nothing to do with you.'

'And if Leon has made it my business?' he snapped. And could have bitten his tongue off the moment the words were out.

She eyed him in sudden, caustic understanding, leaned back on the stove, arms crossed. 'I see.'

'No. You don't.'

She gave not an inch. 'Then explain.'

With a quick, almost violent movement he pushed his chair back from the table and stood up. 'I can't. You wouldn't understand.'

She stayed silent, watching him.

'Look –' He spread his hands appealingly. 'All he asks is that you come to see it –'

'No,' she said. 'That isn't all. And you know it.'

Two days before, Adam had met a man, by arrangement, in a bar. A man who had informed him in brutal detail what might befall him if the rest of his debt were not paid off in very short order. A muscle twitched, irritatingly uncontrollable, in his cheek. 'You're not being fair,' he said. 'Leon works bloody hard. He's making money. He wants you with him –'

'To help him spend it?' she interrupted, drily. 'Oh, I think not, Adam. Yes, I know Leon works bloody hard. Something tells me he plays bloody hard, too. And I'm sure one of his – playmates –' the word was acid '– will help him spend his money if that's what he wants. I will not be treated like a chattel. I will not sit twiddling my thumbs in bloody London while he disappears for hours – days – weeks at a time without telling me where he is or what he's doing. I will not be the *ornament* he so fondly thinks I could be.' The emphasis on the word was savage. 'I will not dance to his every whim. And I will *not* have him use my son as a messenger boy to bring me to heel –!'

Once again Adam flushed furiously. 'Now you're being ridiculous.'

'You think so? Well, I think not. If you want to take a message back to Leon then you can take one; and it's this. He knows where I am. If he wants to talk to me then we do it here. I've heard not a word from him for nearly two weeks. The last I heard from or of him was a slammed door. Well, now it's up to him. No, Adam, I am not going back with you to London. And that's flat.'

Adam stood for a moment in silence, breathing heavily. Then, very precisely, he tucked the chair on which he had been sitting neatly back under the table. 'This is absolutely silly,' he said, his voice very controlled and very reasonable. 'There's no reason in the world for us to quarrel.' He glanced at his watch. 'Look – the pubs are open. I'll pop down to the village for a pint. Give us both a chance to cool down. Ma – I promise you – the last thing I want is for this to come between us –'

The taut line of her shoulders softened a little. She took a long breath.

Adam reached for his coat from the hook behind the door, slung it over his shoulder, turned wide, blue, beguiling eyes upon her. 'Just think about it. That's all I ask.' He crossed the room and kissed her lightly. 'I won't be long.'

He covered the short distance from the house to the lane where he had parked the car in long, angry strides, threw open the car door, flung himself into the driving seat and reached for his cigarettes. He had to cup one hand with the other to keep the flame steady. He drew on the cigarette deeply, tilting his head, screwing up his eyes. 'Shit!' he said aloud. 'Oh, *shit!*'

Cathy heard the roar of the car's engine, the spin of its wheels as it pulled away, too fast. The quiet of the house closed about her, broken only by the peaceful ticking of the clock. It was a long time before she moved.

The public bar of the Lion and Lamb was quiet. A couple of scruffily dressed old men sat at a corner table silently engaged in a game of dominoes, their pints in front of them, and a grizzle-haired man in corduroys and boots leaned at the bar. He nodded and grunted a greeting as Adam entered.

'Hello, love.' The landlady was plump and dark-haired. Her eyes brightened at this unusual break in routine. 'What can I get you?'

'Pint of bitter, please.' Adam fished in his pocket for change. Fool! What a fool he'd been to anger his mother so. He had to mend his fences. He couldn't afford to antagonise her. On the other hand the last thing he could afford was to fail to persuade her at least to go up to London to look at the apartment. Once there it was surely up to Leon to control his own wife? 'Thanks.' Absently he accepted the proffered, dripping glass. The dominoes clicked in the corner.

'Lovely day.' The woman took his money, the till tinkled.

'Yes.' How to do it, that was the problem. He knew Cathy

too well to imagine she could be moved easily. It must have been one hell of a quarrel.

'Spring's just round the corner. Bulbs'll be up any minute.'

'Sorry? Oh – yes. Thank you.' He took his change, moved away from the bar, lit a cigarette, stood brooding, looking out of the window into the breezy, sunny day.

The door opened again. Heavy boots clattered on the flagged floor. 'Afternoon, Bill. All right?'

'Fine, Iris, just fine.'

'The usual?'

'Aye. Thanks.'

'The wife all right?'

Adam detached himself from his surroundings and thought, ferociously. There were two alternatives. Either he succeeded in the task Leon had set him and he was home and dry, or he failed and would have to trust to Leon's good nature to bail him out of the bloody mess he found himself in. The more he thought about the second option the less he liked it. His recent contacts with his stepfather had not encouraged any belief in Leon as a Good Samaritan. He drove a hard bargain, and expected always to gain by it. So Adam, in order to make certain of his own salvation, had to change his mother's mind. He took a long swallow of the warm, bitter beer. There was one way. Not a comfortable way, but surely a way? If his mother knew how desperate the situation was, then surely she couldn't refuse? If he spoke to her – explained honestly the bargain he had had to strike with Leon –?

'Afternoon. It's Mr Sinclair, isn't it?'

The friendly voice at his shoulder made him jump. He turned. A vaguely familiar figure had joined him at the window, a tankard of ale in his huge fist. The man smiled widely, seaman's eyes crinkling, when he saw the startled expression on Adam's face. 'Bill Becket,' he reminded him. 'Coastguard. We've met a couple of times over the years.'

'Oh, of course. I'm sorry. I was miles away.'

'Down for a holiday, are we, sir?'

'Sort of, yes. A bit of a break, that's all.'

'You'll be stayin' up at Sandlin's with your mother o' course –' The man settled himself foursquare on his booted feet, rocking a little. Adam's heart sank. Conversation with a stranger, however pleasant or well meaning, was the last thing he needed at the moment. 'She's a lady an' a half, your mother.' The big man chuckled a little. 'Well, you'd know that, o' course. There's many a one in this village had cause to thank her for her work after the storm. She was lucky, mind you, that the water didn't reach the cottage.' He laughed again. 'Not that it would have made a ha'p'orth of difference if it had. She made it clear that afternoon that she wasn't goin' to leave. Adamant she was, an' the young man too –'

Half listening Adam let the man run on, smiling an automatically charming smile, struggling with his own demons. How much danger was there in telling his mother of the scrape he'd got himself into? She'd been mad before, but she'd always helped him in the end.

'– well, they were snug enough. An' at the time we didn't realise how bad it was goin' to be, or p'raps I'd have tried harder to persuade them to leave, Bert an' all. It was a mercy the tide missed them. I've often thought I should 'ave made 'em leave, but that early in the day I couldn't 'ave known, now could I?'

He'd have to risk it. He'd try once more to persuade her, but if she wouldn't budge he'd have to explain. She wouldn't let him down. She couldn't.

'That was a night and a half that was.' The man nodded his head ruminatively, 'Oh, yes. A night an' a half.'

'I'm sure it was.' Adam tilted his head and poured the rest of his beer down his throat almost without swallowing it. The decision made, he wanted to implement it. Putting it off wouldn't make it any easier. He put the glass down on a stained table, extended his hand. 'I have to go, I'm afraid. Nice to meet you again, Mr Becket.'

The man's own hand was huge and rough as sandpaper. 'And you, Mr Sinclair. You'll give my regards to your mother.'

'Of course.'

Adam drove slowly back to the cottage, sat in the car for a few minutes marshalling his thoughts. When he let himself quietly in the back door Cathy was sitting at the table reading a book. She looked up, unsmiling. He slipped his coat off and hung it on the back of the door, crossed the room to drop a kiss on to the top of her head.

'I thought you'd be longer,' she said.

He shrugged. 'I only had a pint.'

There was a small and slightly strained silence. Then both spoke at once.

'Adam –'

'Ma –'

Both stopped. Adam smiled, reached for his cigarette case. 'After you.'

She closed the book, folded her hands upon it. 'Darling, I don't want to quarrel with you. It's the last thing I want. But – you must understand – what's happening, or not happening, between Leon and me is our business. We have to work it out ourselves. Now, I don't know what he's said or done to make you so partisan –'

'Ma!'

'No. Listen. As I say, I don't know why you so much take his side, but I have to tell you this: if you keep on interfering then it is going to come between you and me. And I don't want that.' She paused for a moment, choosing her words carefully. 'I don't want to leave Sandlings. I don't want the life that Leon wants. You have no right to try to force me into it.' Obdurately she ignored the cutting blade of conscience. She wasn't lying. She wasn't! Nikos had nothing to do with this. Nothing.

Adam sat down opposite her, his expression for a moment obscured by a wreath of smoke. 'I think I'm going to have to tell you something, Ma,' he said.

*

For a long time after he stopped speaking his mother sat in silence, her face buried in her hands. He watched her uneasily. 'Ma? For Christ's sake, at least say *something*.'

She lifted her head, shook it. Her expression was bleak. 'I don't know what to say. Apart from "How could you be so stupid?" and "How dare Leon use you in this way?" and other such totally unhelpful things.' She left the table and went to the stove to put the kettle on. Adam reached for his cigarettes. 'You smoke too much,' she said. 'I don't think it can be good for you.'

'Ma –!'

She spun on him. 'Adam, I'm sorry! I don't know what to say. I don't know what to do! You'll just have to leave me to think –'

He stared at her in growing disbelief. 'Think?' he echoed. 'What's there to think about?'

'Me,' she said, quietly. 'There's me to think about, Adam. Had that not occurred to you?'

'Look – Ma –' He came to her, caught her urgently by the shoulders. 'Just go along with it for a while. Come back with me. Help me get these gorillas off my back. I'll pay Leon back, I swear I will. Then you can do as you like –'

'Adam, I am already doing as I like. Why should I allow Leon to blackmail me through you? For, make no mistake, that's what he's doing.'

'It's only because he loves you. Because he wants you with him. What's so wrong with that? For God's sake – I've told you before – you're married to the man.'

'I'm well aware of that.' The words were very cool.

He struggled to contain his rising panic. Above all things he must not antagonise her further. 'Please, Ma,' he said.

Cathy took a long breath. 'I'll write to him,' she said. 'Tonight. You can take it back with you tomorrow.'

'I don't think that will do any good.'

'At least let me try. He's got to be shown he can't just order everybody's lives as he thinks fit.'

Adam shook his head in despair. 'You don't know him, do you?'

She held his eyes, thoughtfully. 'I'm coming to believe not.'

Cathy sat at the table later that night, after Adam had gone upstairs to bed, staring into space, a blank piece of notepaper in front of her. She had spoiled the boy. She knew it. In the shocked and guilt-ridden aftermath of his father's death she had indulged and overprotected him. She had seen the incredulity and anger in his eyes that his squalid story had not made her cave in to his demands without question. He was nearly twenty-five years old. Surely it was time he grew up? Surely it was time he began to take responsibility for his own actions?

You're fooling yourself, said a cold, clear voice in her head. You know it. Lying to the world is one thing. Lying to yourself is the worst of folly.

Her mouth set in a miserably stubborn line, she reached for a pen.

Upstairs, Adam prowled the small bedroom like a restless cat. A letter? What the hell good was that going to do? And what the devil had got into his mother lately? 'What a bloody mess!' He took off his jacket, hung it in the small wardrobe, rummaged on a shelf for his pyjamas. How much time did he have? A week? Less?

With a small clatter something fell from the shelf and skittered across the floorboards where it lay glinting in the firelight. He bent to pick it up, recognising it immediately. Nikos must have lost it the last time he was down. He picked up the cuff link, slipped it in his pocket and went back to his worrying.

The following day Adam's every misgiving was confirmed. Leon read the letter in silence, tossed it on to his desk, steepled his fingers and regarded the younger man impassively over them. 'Not good enough, Adam. I told you. I want her here. And soon. I'm planning a trip to the Greek house in a week or so. I want her with me.'

'Then why don't you ask her? Why don't you go to see her?'

The other man's face darkened. 'I have better things to do,' he said, very quietly. 'This time, she comes to me. And this time she stays. I have had enough. We have a bargain, Adam, you and I. If you want the rest of the money you need then your mother comes to *me!*' Adam jumped as a massive hand came suddenly down on the desk. 'Go back to her. Tell her. I want her here.'

Adam's shoulders slumped. 'Leon, she won't come.'

His stepfather leaned forward. 'Try again, Adam. Try again.'

Adam spread helpless hands. 'OK. I'll try. But I can't go until the end of the week. I'm due down in Bristol for the meeting with Biggs tomorrow – with Nikos still away I'll have to go – I'll be back in London by Thursday at the latest. I'll drive down to Suffolk on Friday. But –'

'No "buts", Adam.' Leon reached for a heavy folder, opened it and began to leaf through it. 'No "buts". Do it. Ask the good Miss Hooper to come in on your way out, eh?'

Friday was a day for lovers; bright, springlike and beautiful. Even preoccupied as he was, Adam could not help but see it. Hedge and tree were cloaked in misty green as the tender new leaves opened to the sun. In the cottage gardens bright crocuses bloomed and celandines glinted in the roadside ditches. As the turning for Sandlings came up he slowed down, reached into his pocket for his cigarette case and flicked it open, one-handed. As he had thought, supplies were very low; given the likely nature of the coming clash with his mother the thought of running out was not a happy one. He picked up speed again and drove past the lane and on to the village shop.

Half an hour later, slowly and with a thoughtful frown on his face, he was driving up the narrow lane towards the cottage. In all of his life, at least as far as he could be certain, he had never known his mother to lie. So why had she lied about this? About something so silly? So unnecessary? And why had Nikos lied with her? For he did not doubt that they had; the old bag in the shop might be a nosy old gossip, but he could see no reason on this occasion for her to be telling anything but the truth. As she had pointed out herself the weekend of the storm was etched firmly in every detail on everyone's memory. In a conversation that had started as a casual exchange of pleasantries she had at first mentioned – and then, when questioned, firmly insisted – that Nikos had arrived on the Friday afternoon, not the Saturday night as Cathy and Nikos had said. And even as he had questioned her he had suddenly remembered the one-sided conversation with Becket, the coastguard, in the Lion and Lamb the other day. Hadn't he said that he had first seen Cathy 'and the young man too' – early on Saturday afternoon? So Nikos had been there for the whole weekend. And they had lied about it. Why?

He negotiated a bend, then slipped a hand into his jacket pocket and brought out the gold cuff link he had found in the bedroom. There was something odd about this, too. It wasn't until he had found it in his trouser pocket on the night he had gone back to town that he had suddenly been certain that he had seen Nikos wearing these links just the week before. He always noticed them, since they were so much like his own, given by Leon at New Year, and, thinking about it, he was ready to swear that Nikos had been wearing them on the evening that he and Adam had escorted the dreadful American Lois to the theatre. If that were so, how had it come to be at Sandlings?

He had come to the track that led to the cottage. He turned off the engine, rolled quietly to a halt. Folded his arms on the steering wheel and laid his chin on them, looking pensively through the windscreen; at the battered bike that his mother so ridiculously insisted on riding, and at the dusty black Austin Princess parked beside it. After a moment he got out of the car. The air was still, and riven with birdsong. The sound of the sea sifted in the background.

He closed the car door very quietly.

Nikos was sitting at the kitchen table watching Cathy as she prepared lunch. She glanced at him, and smiled to catch his eyes on her. 'I do love you,' he said.

She stood the heavy saucepan on the hotplate, came to him, slipped her arms about his neck and laid her cheek on his hair. 'And I you.' She laughed a little. 'Though I still think it's naughty of you to have turned up again so soon.'

'I couldn't stay away. You aren't angry with me?'

'Of course not.' She turned his head gently towards her and kissed him on the mouth. 'How could I be?'

Sandy dozed, twitching, by the stove. Suddenly he lifted his small head, the beginnings of a growl in his throat.

'Poor Sandy's chasing dream-rabbits,' Cathy said.

Nikos put his hand up to hold her, to stop her moving away from him, drew her mouth back on to his. Neither of them heard the door swing very quietly open.

'Well,' Adam said, softly, one shoulder propped against the door jamb. 'There's a cosy little scene.'

There was a moment of total silence. Adam's eyes flickered to Nikos. 'Get out,' he said, his voice calm, his face very white.

'No,' Nikos said.

Cathy, her eyes on her son, put her hand on Nikos' shoulder. 'Nikos. Do as he says. Please.'

'No,' Nikos said again, flatly.

'I want to speak to my mother. Alone.'

Nikos did not move. Beneath her hand Cathy could feel his shoulder tense as a steel spring. 'Come in, Adam,' she said. 'Shut the door.'

Adam closed the door and leaned against it, his eyes

flicking from one to the other. 'No excuses?' he asked, quietly. 'No protestations of innocence?'

'No.' It was Nikos who answered. He stood up, moving between Cathy and her son. 'There's nothing to excuse. I'm glad you've come. Glad you know. At least it's out in the open. I love Cathy. And I'm not ashamed of it.'

'How touching.' Adam, still lounging against the door, folded his arms. 'Not ashamed of it you say?' he mused. 'I wonder – what exactly is the definition of incest? Do you know?' He looked directly at his mother, watching her flinch.

Cathy moved around Nikos, put out a hand to touch her son's arm. 'Adam – I'm sorry – I know this must be very difficult for you –'

Adam pushed himself fiercely away from the door, striking her hand down as he did so. Nikos took a sharp step forward. 'Difficult? *Difficult?* I should think that rates as the understatement of the year, don't you? Ma, how could you? *How could you?*'

'I love him.'

Adam stared at her, his face that had been as pale as death suddenly suffused. 'You're pathetic,' he said. 'The pair of you. Pathetic!' To Cathy's horror the blue eyes were suddenly bright with tears.

'Adam – please –' Once again she attempted to touch him. Once again he pushed her angrily away, and this time she stumbled a little.

'Don't do that, Adam.' Nikos' voice was hard. 'Don't touch her again.'

'You bugger off, you little bastard.'

'Adam!'

He spun on her. 'Get packed. Now. You're coming to London with me.'

She eyed him steadily, fighting for calm, trying not to let the panic that was beating like a pulse in her throat sound in her voice. 'And if I don't?'

'You will. You have absolutely no choice in the matter. And you know it. Because if you don't I shall simply have to go back alone. And when Leon hears that you refused to come – and why you refused – I should think there's a fair chance that he'll kill you. Both of you. And by Christ I'd give him the gun or the blade to do it.'

Nikos started forward. Cathy put out a restraining hand. 'So – if I do come, then what?'

'Not just come. Stay. If you agree to do as Leon wants. And if you promise me never – never! – to get near this disgusting little creep again then I'll keep your sordid little secret. But I warn you – if I ever catch the two of you so much as looking at each other again then I'll tell Leon what I know.'

'Supposing we denied it? It would be your word against ours. What makes you think Leon would believe you?'

'I wouldn't deny it,' Nikos said, very quietly. 'I couldn't.'

Adam watched his mother, his face hard. 'Are you willing to take the chance? What do you think your husband –' he emphasised the word bitterly '– would do to him –' he jerked his head contemptuously towards Nikos '– if he so much as suspected that he'd touched you? And supposing I could prove that he spent the whole weekend of the storm with you and you both lied about it? Supposing I showed him this –' he put his hand in his pocket and produced the gold cuff link '– and told him where I found it? Do you know where I found it? I found it upstairs. In my bedroom.' The words were so savage that Cathy physically flinched from them. 'Oh, no, Ma. I think it would be just a little more than my word against yours. Get packed.'

'Cathy, no.' Nikos turned to her, caught her by the shoulders. 'Listen. I won't let you go. I won't. Come with me. I love you. You know it. Come away with me –'

'Get away from her, you conniving little bastard –'

'Please, Cathy –'

'I said get away from her!' Adam caught Nikos by the shoulder and threw him against the table.

'Adam – stop it! Nikos!' Cathy flung herself between them. The two young men stood glaring at each other, breathing heavily.

'Get packed, Ma,' Adam said.

'He's blackmailing you.' Nikos' face was drawn as if with pain. 'Are you going to let him?'

'You bet she is.' Very slowly Adam turned his head to look at his mother. 'Don't think that now I don't see why you wouldn't help me. All that highfaluting talk of independence. What a joke. When all you really wanted was to shack up with him. And for that you were ready to drop me in the shit.'

'No.' Cathy closed her eyes and shook her head.

'Don't fool yourself. Look at yourself straight. And tell me that what you see doesn't disgust you.'

'*No!*' The word was agonised.

'Cathy – darling –'

'*Will you get the hell out of here!*' The sheer, unadulterated violence in the words froze them all. Adam was shaking. '*Leave my mother alone, you snivelling little sod!*'

Helpless tears had begun to stream down Cathy's cheeks. She took both Nikos' hands in her own. 'Nikos, please go. Adam's right. It's over. It was always going to happen, we both knew it –'

'No!'

'Please, Nikos – you're just making things worse –'

'Tell me one thing.'

She waited, watching him with drenched eyes.

'Do you love me?'

'You know I do.'

'*Out!*' Adam, by far the stronger built of the two, grabbed Nikos by the coat collar and hauled him towards the door. Nikos' flailing fist caught him a glancing blow on the cheekbone. Adam swung round and slapped him, open-handed, twice, across the face, rocking his head.

'Adam! Stop it!'

The two struggled for a moment, crashing back against the table. Sandy danced and yelped excitedly about them. They drew apart, panting.

'Nikos, please.' Appalled, Cathy was truly sobbing now. 'You have to go. Adam's right, you know he is. Your father would kill you if he knew. We have to finish it.'

He turned to her. His mouth was bruised, a narrow trickle of blood seeped down his chin. 'My father kills me if I stay with you. You kill me if you make me leave you,' he said. 'Don't do it, Cathy. Please don't.'

Cathy said nothing. Adam stood watching them both, his face grim as death.

Nikos studied Cathy's face for a long moment. Then, 'I see,' he said. 'All right. If that's what you want I'll go. For you. Only for you. Remember that. Remember it always.' He picked up his coat, slung it over his shoulder. Cathy watched, mute with misery as he opened the door. He left without looking back.

'Get some things together,' Adam said. 'We're leaving too.'

'I'll have to take Sandy next door.'

'I'll do it. Just get yourself bloody packed, will you?' Adam lit a cigarette with a shaking hand. In the distance they both heard the sound of the Austin's engine starting. Cathy shut her eyes for a moment, then turned abruptly and left the room. Adam dropped into a chair, rested his elbows on the table. To his own surprise he was fighting tears; yet beneath the anger and the real sense of betrayal the spark of self-interest still glowed bright. He was safe. Leon would have to give him the money now.

Upstairs, numb with anguish, shock and humiliation Cathy packed her bag to go to London.

Chapter Fourteen

'You're losing weight, *koukla mou*. Too much weight. It doesn't suit you.' Leon eyed Cathy over the top of his newspaper. 'We must feed you up.'

Cathy sipped her coffee. 'I'm all right. I just don't get so hungry in town, that's all.'

Leon folded his newspaper, noisily and untidily, and tossed it on to the table. 'Kati, no one ever suggested you couldn't go back to the country occasionally. Why don't you pop down to Suffolk for a couple of days?'

'No.' She spoke very quickly. 'No. I don't want to. The break is made. It's been a month. It would unsettle me to go back. As a matter of fact I'm thinking of letting Sandlings. If I can find anyone mad enough to want to live there, that is.'

'And Sandy? What of him? Will you bring him to London?'

She reached for the paper and folded it meticulously, smoothing the pages, not looking at him. 'No. There's no point. It wouldn't be fair. He'd be desperately unhappy. And if we're going to spend a lot of time in Greece I couldn't take him anyway. I've written to Bert. He's agreed to keep him. So –' she looked up at him and smiled, very brightly '– that's that. You're stuck with me for good.'

'I'm sorry about the little dog,' he said, unexpectedly gently, and as so often lately, caught off her guard she felt the sudden, mortifying threat of tears.

She cleared her throat. 'Don't be silly. He's only a dog. And an ill-behaved one at that. You'd better be off. It's getting late.'

Leon hauled his bulk from the chair. 'I have an idea. For once I am not so busy today. Meet me for lunch. We'll start to put some flesh back on your bones at Dmitri's. One o'clock, yes?'

Cathy, halfway to the kitchen with the breakfast plates, hesitated. 'I –'

'What?' He was jocular. 'You don't want to lunch with your husband? You'd rather take your ration book down to the butcher's and slave over a hot stove?'

'Of course not – it's just that I was thinking of –' she stopped. What had she been thinking of doing? Nothing. Another aimless, empty day. A drift around the art galleries to find a picture to go over the mantelpiece. A solitary sandwich in a corner house. A visit to Harvey Nichols, perhaps, or Debenham and Freebody's to buy something she neither needed nor particularly wanted –

'Never mind what you were thinking. You meet me at Dmitri's. At one.'

She shrugged. 'OK.'

With Leon gone and the breakfast cleared she stood at the window of the elegant first-floor apartment looking into the street below. It was a relatively quiet cul-de-sac. The roar of the traffic in Kensington High Street was a background as, at Sandlings, had been the roar of the sea. For a moment she could almost see the gleaming, tide-washed strip of sand between the shingle and the creaming water, hear the haunting screech of the gulls, feel the small wet nose pushed affectionately into her hand. She closed her eyes, feeling the familiar, agonising ache in her heart. The ache of

homesickness. The ache of a lost love. The ache of hopeless-
ness. It astounded her sometimes that no one appeared to
see it, that everyone acted as if the world – as if she – had not
changed. She sometimes felt that she was living in two
places at once; in the busy, noisy, inhabited world of others,
and at the same time in the shadowed and joyless place to
which her soul had retreated during that awful journey back
from Suffolk with Adam. They had barely spoken. She had,
she supposed, been in a state of shock, her mind and emotions in a turmoil, incapable, almost, of speech or of rational
thought. The break had been so sudden, so brutal, so sham-
ing that she had felt physically ill. Fixed indelibly in her
memory had been the look on Nikos' face, the sound of his
voice: *'My father kills me if I stay with you. You kill me if you
make me leave you. Don't do it, Cathy. Don't!'* She had sensed,
too, beneath her son's grim silence, his triumph, and had
detested it. In the intervening weeks she had avoided Adam
as far as she could, and Nikos had avoided her almost
entirely; although inevitably there had been the odd occasion
when their paths had crossed. Cathy leaned to the window,
pressing her forehead on to the cold glass. She did not want
even to think of it, could not bear to contemplate the perfect,
cool politeness so at odds with the disturbing look in the
golden eyes, that had once spoken of love, but that now she
was terribly afraid might speak of hate, or – worse – contempt. On the one occasion they had been left momentarily
alone together, at a bleak little cocktail party given by a society harridan whom Leon, for some reason, was assiduously
courting, he had snubbed her utterly, turning and walking
away from her without a word or a glance and before she
could open her mouth. Like her he had lost weight, and –
unlike her, she well knew – it suited him. The delicate planes
and angles of his face had sharpened and hardened, the line
of his long mouth, too, was less soft. There were permanent,
smudged shadows beneath his eyes that, far from detracting
from his attraction, somehow served only to add to it; every

young god's face should, she supposed, wearily, have a hint
of decadence behind it. And that was not too far from the
mark. For Nikos, to his father's open delight, had taken to
drink and, with an even more single-minded dedication, to
women.

'At last!' Leon had chuckled when two mornings in a row
Nikos had turned up for work in a state of some delicacy
and looking as if he had not slept for a week. 'The boy has
discovered he is a Greek! Is good. The influence of the old
dragon is fading. He will be the son of his father yet!'

Cathy had said nothing, had tried to ignore the raw knife-
wound of jealousy. The thought of Nikos with another
woman – worse, with a beautiful girl – was unendurable.
But then the whole situation was unendurable; unendurable
and inescapable. She was trapped. A little surprisingly the
only time her spirits had lightened had been during their
short trip to Greece, when Leon had taken her to see the
nearly finished house. Almost against her will she had been
enchanted by it, and the challenge that it had offered had
been hard to resist. The weather had been mild and it had
rained a little, but almost every day the spring sunshine had
broken through, and the promise of summer was clear. As, in
the ancient pre-war car that Leon kept on the island, they
had jolted along the unmade road that led up the mountainside towards the village the deadening depression had
begun to lift and she had started to relax. The hillsides were
freshly carpeted with spring flowers, the mountain gorse
was in full golden bloom. The streams and springs were full
and running with the winter rains. In tiny hamlets stately
women, black-eyed and swarthy-skinned, an infant on the
hip, a child held by the hand, watched in unsmiling curiosity as the car laboured past. Old men with walnut faces
rested within the olive groves, hunkered on their heels with
their midday meal of bread and cheese. A shepherd boy,
barefoot and dressed in greasy fleece, trilled and whistled to
his flock as the scrawny animals scrambled up a steep track.

Cathy's artist's eye, that over the past weeks had dulled, grew sharper and more interested at every turn. Here and there, dotted about the hillsides, she saw the gleam of azure and gold, barbaric and beautiful in this rocky landscape; the domes and steeples of tiny churches nestling within their glossy-leafed groves of orange and lemon. The car had rattled through yet another small village and then on up a steep track that after a while levelled, then plunged precipitately down towards a small cleared area that ended in what looked alarmingly like a cliff edge. Sensing her sudden movement Leon laughed. 'Is all right, Kati. Is not as bad as it looks. See – there's the house – beyond the big tree –'

Cathy looked. All she could see, almost on a level with the small piece of clear ground, was a roof, part tiled, part what looked like a kind of thatch. For the moment she was rather more concerned with their perilous descent. Ridiculously she found herself clutching at the sides of her seat. A fat lot of good that would do her if the car didn't stop! When the vehicle did roll to a halt she discovered that she had been holding her breath. Her husband's deep laugh rang out again. 'You'll have to get used to it, *koukla mou!*'

She wondered, a little wearily, and for far from the first time, if Leon knew how irritating she found it to be called his little doll – and if he would understand if she tried to tell him. 'I doubt I ever will.' She climbed out of the car, stood, stretched, and then found herself catching her breath as she took in the beauty of what lay before and beneath her. The house was nestled into the hillside below; all that could be seen of it from here was the roof and a low stretch of windowless whitewashed wall, around which a narrow rocky track, cut into the hillside, curved. The tops of the trees of the grove in which it was set were several feet below where she stood. The view was spectacular: a wide, fertile valley dotted with tiny farms, villages and churches, beyond which rose the shadowed foothills of another range of mountains, that lifted to the west. To the left, along the run of the valley and around a spur of hillside, the sea glittered. From this height she could just see the clustered roofs of the little port of Karystos in which they had disembarked that morning. For the moment the sky was a cloudless blue, the air dazzlingly clear. Far above her two huge birds circled lazily.

'Eagles,' Leon said, his voice very soft. 'Look at them. Kings of the air. The birds of Greece.' They stood for a moment listening to the mountain silence, that was punctuated by the trilling of birds and the running of water. Then, 'Come,' Leon said, briskly, 'let's see what progress has been made. If any.'

In the event even he had been pleasantly surprised. The house – which was in fact two dwellings knocked into one – was perfectly habitable, if Spartanly furnished. It was quite literally built into the hillside behind it, the back walls of the lower rooms being simply roughly rendered living rock. These downstairs rooms, that had once been the winter home and summer shelter for the family's animals, had been turned into four shady, serviceable bedrooms and the tiniest and most primitive of bathrooms, with a wide verandah running across the front of them. The upstairs accommodation – kitchen, dining room, large sitting room and a half-finished terrace that overlooked the valley – was reached by an outside staircase that curved up from the verandah. The only access to the house was by a gate on the upper level which opened from the lane directly on to the terrace. The ground dropped away from the house through stepped groves of olives and lemon trees and from the terrace Cathy caught sight of a tiny building huddled some hundred yards or so from the house. 'What's that?'

'It's the original shepherd's hut.' Leon was tossing logs into the iron stove that ran almost the length of one side of the large kitchen. 'The first house that stood on this land. I didn't want to pull it down. It seemed a good idea to keep it. Tell me –' He straightened. A curl of blue, fragrant woodsmoke wreathed about him, and for the first time in years she saw in his eyes a touch of uncertainty. 'What do you think of the house?'

'It's lovely,' she said, and meant it. 'It's upside down, but it's lovely.'

'You mean the bedrooms being downstairs and the living rooms up?'

She nodded. She had wandered to the window. Smudged cloud had built up over the hills, and cloud-shadows chased themselves across the valley.

'It's simple good sense.' Leon had moved to a small cast-iron pump that was set in a wide, shallow sink of stone. 'The bedrooms, windowless and buried in the rock, are cool and dark in the summer and cosy and easy to heat in the winter. The living rooms are light and breezy by day in the summer and catch any winter sunshine.' He levered the pump handle. Water spurted. He caught some in a cup and brought it to Cathy. 'And, as you see, there is the most spectacular view. Taste that.'

She sipped. It was so cold it almost sparkled in her mouth. She drank deeply. 'It's delicious!'

'It comes directly from the spring a little way up the hill. The spring is famous – there is a little church – I'll take you there, perhaps tomorrow.'

Cathy now, penned above the Kensington traffic, remembered those few peaceful days that had followed with a faint twist of longing. Whilst Leon had spent most of his time instructing his workers, arguing with suppliers and drinking and discussing the ways of the world in the local taverna – an activity which appeared to be mandatory upon the whole of the male population of the area – she had roamed the hillsides, or sat beneath the olive trees in the half-finished garden, watching the distant sea, happy to be alone, the peace and quiet lulling her senses, calming her nerves, easing her sore heart. She had even started to think about the garden; so far as Leon was concerned only the construction was up to him, the rest was to be her concern. The land that dropped away from the house already consisted of ancient terraces in which grew equally ancient trees, gnarled and twisted by time and the elements. Cathy was glad to have come in time to prevent the enthusiastic mass felling that Leon had had in mind. Looking at the grotesque patterns etched upon the bark of an old olive tree she found her fingers itching for a pencil. With both Nikos and Adam what seemed half a world away she had half persuaded herself that happiness, or perhaps to be more realistic simple contentment, was not after all entirely beyond her grasp. Here, relaxed and in his own environment, Leon had been genial and good-tempered. He had, she knew, enjoyed showing off his achievements – of which she quickly came to understand she was one – to the people amongst whom he had grown up, and for most of whom nothing had changed – or was likely to change – since the time of their grandparents, and to her his standing in this community in which respect came very hard-won.

Then they had returned to London, and the fragile peace of mind she thought she had achieved had, like a mirage, proved to be of no substance whatsoever. Nothing had changed.

She supposed, bleakly, that nothing ever would.

Dmitri's, Leon's favourite restaurant, was crowded. As the wife of one of the proprietor's best customers she was welcomed with deferential smiles and greetings and shown to a small table in the window. Inevitably Leon had not yet arrived. Cathy ordered a dry sherry and sat, chin on hand, watching the busy street outside. Just before she had left the apartment her editor had phoned; everyone was delighted with the illustrations for *The Sea Magician*, and would she be interested in another commission? Not very well paid, but prestigious – would she care to come and discuss the project? Cathy had prevaricated. Since she had left Sandlings she had had neither the heart nor the inclination to pick up a pencil. But then – perhaps this was what she needed? Something of her own to occupy her, to force her to pull herself together? She couldn't go on like this, adrift on a sea of self-indulgent misery – she caught her breath. Striding along the crowded pavement towards the restaurant were two tall, familiar figures, deep in conversation. For a moment a wave of something close to panic choked her. Why hadn't Leon told her? She glanced around. It was too late to leave. By the time she had retrieved her coat they would be here.

She saw from the sudden shock in Nikos' eyes when he caught sight of her that he had no more expected her than she had him. She watched as the two of them wove between the tables towards her, accepted her husband's peck on the cheek in greeting. 'See what a surprise I've brought you. The boy was mooning about the place like a lost soul. I offered him lunch to cheer him up.' Leon leant to her and added in a stage whisper that could be heard halfway across the room, 'He's had a fight with the latest flame. Be kind to him.'

'Pa –' Nikos said. 'You didn't tell me you were meeting Cathy. You don't want me –'

'Nonsense, boy, nonsense. Sit down. I'll get the waiter to lay an extra place.' Leon clicked his fingers.

Nikos remained standing for a moment longer before pulling out the chair opposite Cathy and sitting down. The place was laid, the orders given. To her horror Cathy discovered that she was trembling. With great care she put her glass on the table, folded her hands in her lap. Leon was telling a long, complicated and slightly salacious story involving a business rival. Nikos sat, eyes downcast, absently tinkering with his fork, the shadowed sweep of his lashes veiling any expression. He looked tired and drawn. Cathy ached, physically ached, to put a hand out to him, to touch him, to hold him. She laced her fingers together, clenching them so tightly that they hurt. Leon talked on.

The next hour seemed to Cathy the longest and most painful she had ever endured. Not once did Nikos look at her, and only when it was totally unavoidable did he speak to her. In the end she herself lapsed to silence, leaving the conversation to husband and son. Yet try as she might she could not keep her eyes from Nikos' face, could not still the echoes in her mind. She ate mechanically, picking at her food, hardly tasting it.

'*Baclavas*,' Leon said, having demolished a plateful of lamb and pasta stew. 'Dmitri makes the best *baclavas* in London. No, I insist –' He had correctly interpreted Cathy's attempt to protest almost before she had opened her mouth. 'I told you this morning. Lately you don't eat enough to keep a sparrow alive. Is not good enough. What good is a skinny woman to a man, eh?' He glanced slyly at Nikos. 'What you think, Nikos? She needs to put more flesh on the bones, yes?'

For the first time Nikos' eyes met hers. They were expressionless. 'It's up to Cathy,' he said. 'Isn't it?'

'Sir –' A waiter had appeared beside Leon, bent to his ear, 'A telephone call. A Mister Kariopoulos. He says it's urgent.'

Leon mopped at his lips with his napkin, pushed his chair from the table. 'Excuse me. I won't be a moment.'

Left alone Cathy and Nikos were silent. Around them a babble of conversation rose and fell.

'I'm sorry,' Nikos said at last, his voice the voice of a polite stranger; cool and neutral. 'I really didn't realise you were going to be here. I would never have come if I'd known.'

'I realise that.'

'How are you?' There was no warmth in the question, no real enquiry.

She swallowed. 'I'm well. And you?' This was madness. Utter madness.

'OK.'

'Leon says you're –' she struggled for a moment '– you're having a good time.'

He shrugged.

The silence between them was heavy, hanging between them, dense as a muffling curtain. Cathy picked up her wine

glass, put it down again, turning it around and around on
the tablecloth, watching it as if it were the most absorbing
sight in the world. At the bar on the far side of the room
Leon was talking volubly into the telephone, waving his
hands. 'There's so much to say,' the words were barely audible, 'and no way to say it.'

'There's nothing to say.' Nikos' voice was harsher than
she had ever heard it. 'I'd really rather you didn't try.
Excuses? Lies? Spare me.' As her startled eyes met his he
leaned forward over the table, and she flinched from the
expression on his face. 'It was your choice, Cathy. Always
remember that. You sent me away. I was ready to stand and
fight. Fight the bloody world if necessary. You made it very
clear that you weren't prepared to do that.' His mouth
twisted to a bitter smile. 'So much for love.'

'That isn't fair –!'

He watched her steadily, his young face hard. 'Nothing's
fair in this life. If I've learned anything I've learned that.'

'Nikos -!'

'Tell Pa I had to go, will you? I've got a meeting this afternoon.' He pushed his chair from the table and stood up. 'I
wish I had never set eyes on you,' he said, very quietly.

A knife in the heart, she thought strangely detachedly,
could not have hurt more. For a long time after he had left
she sat quite still, her face calm, her eyes distant. The situation was intolerable. Every nerve she possessed screamed at
her to get away. But how, and to where? Sandlings was out
of the question, no matter how she yearned for it; Adam and
Leon between them would make sure of that. But since the
trip to the Greek house with Leon the thought had begun to
take root in her mind; now there was somewhere else.
Sunlight and clear skies. The hum of bees on the mountainside. A place where no one knew her, and she knew no one.
Peace.

'I have ordered the *baclavas*.' Leon's voice made her jump.
'Where is Nikos?'

'He had to go. He said he had a meeting. Leon – I wanted to talk to you about something –'

'Hm? We have retsina with the *baclavas*.' Leon lifted a hand.

'I've been thinking. I'd like to go to Greece. Back to the house. Now – as soon as possible. There's so much to do, and I'd like to get the house painted and at least a part of the garden planted before the heat of the summer –' She stopped as Leon's great, expansive smile was turned upon her.

'You really want that?'

'Yes.'

He took her hand. 'Then we have Champagne with the *baclavas*,' he said, softly. 'I have waited a very long time for this. Give me a couple of days to organise things. I will send for Yannis. He will take care of you until I can join you at Easter.'

'Thank you.'

'Kati – you're sure?'

'Yes,' she said.

Cathy liked Yannis Vasilios from the moment she met him. He was waiting for her as she stepped off the ferry that had brought her from the mainland, his scarred face wreathed in a wide smile. '*Kiria* Kotsikas! Welcome! You have had a good journey?'

She greeted him, shook his hand, winced a little. 'Tiring,' she admitted, laughing.

'But yes. Come.' He picked up her case. 'I take you home. Everything is ready for you.'

To her surprise everything was indeed ready for her. She had steeled herself to find a house still full of workmen and their attendant mess; instead it was obvious from the moment they walked through the door that the place, though still in its raw state and far from being truly homely, was neat as a pin. A mouthwatering smell drifted from the kitchen upstairs. Yannis called from the verandah. 'Anna? Anna!'

A girl of perhaps thirteen or fourteen came running down the stairs, stopped, hands folded, and smiled shyly. She was dressed in the full skirt, white blouse and colourful scarf of the village girls. Her black hair was smoothed to a neat coil on her neck.

'This is Anna. She is to look after you. She's a good girl.'

Cathy held out a hand. '*Kalispera sas,*' she said, carefully.

The child did not take her hand but bobbed a little curtsey and to Cathy's surprise replied in heavily accented English, 'Good afternoon, Madam.'

'She is a good girl who speaks English,' Yannis said with his broad smile. 'She learns with Father Vangelis, the local priest. He tells me she is his most promising pupil.'

Cathy smiled. 'Perhaps you'll help me with my Greek? I'm ashamed not to have learned more.'

The girl blushed a little, gestured with her hand towards the house. 'If you would like, I have cooked for you.'

Yannis, it seemed, had organised everything, and organised it well. Anna came to the house at seven in the morning and left at six in the evening; initially she was dismayed that Cathy would not hear of her sleeping in the kitchen at night, as had first been planned, but gently and firmly Cathy insisted. As much as anything she had come to Greece to be alone, to restore her own peace of mind, and not even Anna's silent, smiling presence could be tolerated all the time. Embarrassingly it was some days before Cathy discovered that Anna was cooking for her food that, due to the strict observance of the Lenten fast, she would not dream of eating herself. Yannis had also ensured that the decorating materials had been purchased and stored in an outhouse. Four men from the village came each day – or at least almost each day, which was testament to Yannis' powers of persuasion – to help her; she was amused at their mild consternation when she insisted on working alongside them. The bright blues and greens she had chosen for the doors and shutters, the subtler washes of lemon and terracotta for the walls, transformed the interior, whilst a coat of white-wash on the outside walls and on the Shepherd's Hut gleamed in the sunshine and shone from the shadows of the little grove. It was a little under two weeks to the start of Holy Week, when Leon would come to join her. The women of the village were already deep in the preparations for the greatest feast of the Orthodox calendar. The mornings and the evenings were cool, the days bright and sunny. The sun-sets, seen from the now finished terrace, were spectacular. Cathy picked flowers on the mountainside, explored the paths and fast-running streams, went occasionally to the vil-lage shopping with Anna or with Yannis – who was lodging in the local taverna, an arrangement that Cathy just occa-sionally thought might be a little too convenient. She knew she was the object of great curiosity; the Foreign Woman, the outsider, and for the moment judged it best to remain aloof. Like the village women themselves she was always polite, and always ready with a greeting, but for now she was happier not to trespass on others' privacy, and not to have them trespass upon hers. She was aware that this was a very different society than the one to which she was used; too much damage could be done by misunderstandings and misconceptions. There would be time later to explore this new world of hers. She began to sketch again, building up a small portfolio, mostly of the flora and fauna of the moun-tains. She even began to toy with the idea of a studio – the Shepherd's Hut, she realised, would be perfect; separate from the house, wonderfully quiet and with a view down the valley towards the sea that could only be described as inspirational. A little surprisingly, however, Yannis did not greet this idea with his usual unreserved enthusiasm for anything she suggested, not being certain, he explained apologetically, whether Leon already had other plans for the little building. Cathy shrugged and acquiesced. She was sure she could persuade Leon when he came to join her.

A few days before Leon was due to arrive Yannis escorted

her on the boat to Athens. Despite her determination that the house should be furnished in traditional style – to which end she had commissioned work from a skilled carpenter in Karystos – there were some things unavailable on the island. She needed, too, to talk to Leon, to ask him to bring with him some personal possessions, and the best place to do that, given the cheerful and relentless unreliability of the telephone system, was from his office in the city. The trip was a delight, a pleasant two or three hours across waters so unlike that other sea with which she was familiar they might have been those of a lake. Shimmering in the sunlight and as blue as the lucently clear sky, there was no affinity here at all with those long, grey, spume-topped rollers that crashed incessantly upon the shingle beaches of Suffolk. The waters lapped gently in tiny golden coves and at the feet of bird-haven cliffs. The boat chugged steadily on, carving a way through the glassy sea, her wake spreading wide and unbroken behind her. They never once lost sight of land; always, on either side, sometimes close, sometimes distant and misted, the mountains rose, mysterious and shadowed in the sunlight. They passed the occasional fishing village climbing the hillside behind a small natural harbour, its houses freshly whitewashed for the spring. Often Cathy saw little groups of fishing boats, working together, the crafts bobbing like corks as the larger vessel passed them. The breeze in her face was very soft and carried with it the scent of flowers from the mountainsides.

Athens was hot, and very crowded. Four years after the end of a bitter civil war it gave the impression of a city still not quite at peace with itself. Yet despite this and despite the all-too-obvious signs of recent conflict that still marked the streets and buildings the urge to trade and commerce had quickly reasserted itself. Cathy had little difficulty in finding the fabrics and household effects she had come to buy, albeit at a price. The telephone call to Leon had been booked for three that afternoon; it was, inevitably, delayed, and when it did come through the line was terrible.

'Yannis – he's looking after you –?'

'Wonderfully.' Despite herself Cathy could not resist the urge to shout. 'Everything's going very well. Leon – can you manage to ship the gramophone and records that I wanted?'

The reply was inaudible, fading into the crackling background. Cathy strained her ears in frustration. Then the sound surged again. '– next Tuesday. We will take the afternoon boat to Karystos –'

'We?' Cathy's heart had begun to thud, slowly and painfully. 'Leon? Leon – who's we?'

The line was breaking up entirely, Leon's heavily accented voice was distorted. Cathy heard Adam's name, and Nikos'. Had Leon said 'fortunately' or 'unfortunately'? 'Leon!' she was gripping the heavy telephone so tightly her fingers ached. 'I can't hear you! Who did you say was coming with you?'

More atmospherics. Then '– Tuesday. The afternoon boat –' The line was dead.

Very precisely she replaced the handset.

'Is OK?' Yannis had materialised beside her, smiling his crooked, piratical smile.

'Yes. Fine. He'll be here on Tuesday. He's taking the afternoon boat.'

'Good. We will go down to the harbour and meet him, yes?'

'Yes. A good idea.' Not him. Them. Who? Who was coming with him? Not Nikos, surely? It couldn't be Nikos.

She was thinking the same thing – had been thinking it for all these past, tense days – as she sat beneath a perfumed flowering tree outside a taverna sipping ouzo and watching the small ferry approach the shore the following Tuesday. There was the usual crowd awaiting its arrival; relatives and friends meeting their loved ones, idle onlookers, people with bundles of every shape and size taking the return trip to the

city, small, barelegged children who shrieked and dashed
about, their bare feet silent in the dust. There were shouts,
greetings and laughter from ship to shore. A rope was
tossed, casually caught, wound around a capstan; the gang-
plank was lowered.

And there they were, as somehow she had known they
would be: Leon and Nikos, both still in their city suits, both
carrying cases. Nikos' eyes rested upon her over the heads of
the crowd, and the discipline, the self-control, the hard-won
peace of the past couple of weeks were wiped out in a single
moment. Her heart all but stopped. And in a terror that was
bizarrely mixed with happiness she knew that nothing had
changed. Worse; that no matter how she tried to lie to herself, she was fiercely – joyously! – glad they had not.
Whatever his reasons for coming, whatever the pain his
presence might bring, she was so happy to see him she could
have wept for it.

Chapter Fifteen

The stuffy little room was so dark, the air so thick with smoke that beyond the light that hung low above the card table the silent, intently watchful figures that had gathered about the players were like shadows in a pit. Adam hardly noticed them. He felt the familiar anticipatory frisson of excitement as he reached for the cards. His heartbeat lifted, the adrenaline sharpening his brain, churning in his stomach. One more. That was all he needed; just one more good one. The pile of chips in front of him had grown steadily. Only one other man at the table had had as good a run: a middle-aged, stocky man, snappily dressed, his thick, swarthy fingers heavy with gold, a soft felt fedora pushed to the back of his sleek black head. Adam held the hand for a superstitious moment, face down, as he drew on his cigarette. Never hurry the cards. Schooling his face he turned them, fanned them out very slowly in his long fingers.

An eight. Another. And another. His heart flickered in his chest; eyes downcast he forced himself to calm, slid the other two cards out; kept his expression carefully blank. In a long night of good luck, this was the best yet.

Piles of chips were being stacked in the centre of the table. Cards were pushed over to the dealer; the man's big, raw-boned hands were deft as he collected them, dealt out others. Fedora, Adam noted, exchanged three cards. That was a good sign. A long-faced man with a Southern drawl who picked at his teeth with a sharpened match as he spoke said, 'I guess I'll stick with what I've got.' That wasn't.

'One,' Adam said, sliding a card face down across the table. It didn't matter. It really didn't matter.

Fedora pushed a small pile of chips into the centre of the table. 'A thousand,' he said, equably. The minimum bet.

'See your thousand. Raise you another.'

It went on, the tempo quiet at first. Early on a hand folded, the cards tossed face down on to the table. 'Too damn' strong for me,' said a big, red-faced man, his accent pure downtown New York. Fedora was leaning back in his chair, his face mask-like as he surveyed his hand from beneath lowered lids. The players waited, watching him. For the most fleeting of moments he appeared to hesitate and then with the faintest of shrugs he picked up a stack of counters and set them neatly beside the growing piles. Five thousand dollars.

Adam tucked his cigarette between his lips, half closing his eyes against the smoke. Matched the bet, and raised again. 'Six.'

Black eyes flickered to him and away. Fedora tilted his chair on to its back two legs.

'I'm out.' A few minutes later another man pushed his chair back and stretched, yawning. There were great sweat-patches on his shirt, under his lifted arms.

'Me too.' The dealer tossed his cards on to the table.

The match-chewer, impassive, raised again. The flat, coloured counters, smooth and dull with handling, piled higher under the light.

Another round, and the stakes even higher. Excitement was singing in Adam's brain, stinging in his blood. This was the big one. 'Ten,' he said, calmly.

'Shit.' The word was mild. The match-chewer tossed his cards back to the dealer. 'I'm done.'

Fedora leaned forward, slid first one pile and then another

very precisely into the centre of the table. 'Your ten,' he said, softly. 'And I raise you –' he paused, 'twenty-five.'

The room was very quiet. Someone let out an audible breath. Adam glanced down at the diminishing pile in front of him. He had already staked most of his evening's winnings. For a fraction of a second his confidence wavered. Blue smoke wreathed in the harsh light of the bare bulb. Black eyes held his, expressionless. To hell with it. No one ever got rich without taking risks. He counted the chips into a pile, pushed them forward. 'I'll match you,' he said, 'but it looks as if I'm out of the readies. You'll take an IOU?'

Five long and nervewracking minutes later Fedora counted out the last of his stake, dumped it on to the pile on the table, that had long since slithered into an untidy heap. 'Time to call it a night. I'll see you.'

Adam was sweating. There was a fortune on that table. A bloody fortune. Very precisely, one by one, he snapped his cards on to the table. A king. And four eights.

For the space of a couple of breaths Fedora looked at the cards thoughtfully. Then, very gently, he fanned out his own and laid them on the table. A murmur ran round the room. 'Lucky bastard,' someone said, in grudging admiration. 'Fucking lucky bastard.'

Surprisingly soft-looking and well-manicured fingers riffled across the cards. 'A royal flush. In spades.' Fedora's full lips curved to a smile. He pushed the hat further to the back of his head. 'Hard luck, old boy.' The mimicking of Adam's English accent was mocking. 'Mine, I think.' The stubby dark hands reached for and cupped around the pile, pulling it towards him. Gently he extracted several scraps of paper from the slithering counters. Held them up. 'You'll honour these, of course?'

'Of course.' Adam felt as if he were choking. Bile rose in his throat, tainted his mouth. The only hand that could have beaten him. The only sodding hand! 'If you'll excuse me?' Blindly he turned and pushed his way through the dozen or so onlookers that stood between him and the door.

He did not see the flickering glance that passed between Fedora and the dealer.

He just made it to the foul-smelling toilet before he was spectacularly and gut-wrenchingly sick.

'Why did you come?' Cathy asked, very quietly.

Nikos kept his narrowed eyes on the distant glitter of the sea. 'I had no choice.'

Despite herself she felt a small twist of pain. It had not been the answer she had looked for. 'You mean Leon –?'

'No,' he interrupted her, very calmly. Still he would not look at her. 'No, not Pa. I could have made an excuse. You. I had to see you.' At last he turned his head a little, to glance at her. 'However much it hurt. However much I wished I could hate you. I discovered, after you left, that I didn't. I hadn't realised, I truly hadn't, how much I loved you. When you left –' He turned his veiled gaze to the sea again, shrugged a little. 'I hadn't realised,' he said again, 'how terrible it is to be in one place when your heart is in another. Terrible, and empty.'

Cathy sat quite still, her hands clasped loosely in her lap, trying to control the warm and joyful tide that was lifting within her, melting the chill barrier she had so carefully constructed about her heart and her soul. A terrace or so beneath them her husband, in shirtsleeves, was helping to move a large rock. His voice and those of the workmen echoed up to them. Leon's lusty laughter bellowed, and birds flew from the trees.

'I tried,' Nikos' quiet voice continued beside her. 'I truly did. I tried to hate you. Tried not to want you. Tried not to love you. But I couldn't. In the end I had to admit it; I would rather accept the pain of being near you than the agony the bereavement – of being apart.'

'Nikos –'

'Don't worry,' he said, swiftly. 'I'll do nothing to hurt you. I don't ask for anything. I just wanted to come. That's all.'

There was a long moment of silence, then, 'I'm glad,' she said, simply. 'I'm so glad.'

'I thought you might be angry.'

She shook her head.

'Cathy?'

She turned to look at him, her green, slanted eyes beneath the tilted brows very wide, and he saw there were fine new lines of strain beneath them. The cheekbones in her too-thin face were delicate and razor-sharp. In the warmth of the day she had pinned her thick, unmanageable hair untidily up. Sweat-damp strands clung to her neck. For a moment he could barely breathe. From the hillside beneath them came the musical chime of bells, the bleating of goats, the clicking of hooves on the rock as a small herd clattered past, its hunched and ancient guardian toiling behind them up the steep and winding little path that led from the village below past the house and on up the mountain. 'Do you love me?' Nikos' voice was very quiet.

Leon called a greeting to the goat-herd, who leaned on his crook for a moment and exchanged a few words across the low stone wall that encompassed the garden.

'Yes,' Cathy said; and thought, with a painful twist of the heart that the smile that very slowly lit his face was the sweetest she had ever seen.

Woodsmoke drifted down from the house, from where Anna was cooking in the kitchen. The goat bells chimed again as the animals stopped to graze.

'That's all I need to know.'

'Hey – Nikos! Lazy one! Come and give a hand –' Leon waved. He was stripping off his shirt, exposing his massive shoulders and the thick grey tangle of hair on his chest. A small bright arrow of light reflected from the icon at his throat.

Nikos lifted his own hand in reply, stood up. 'These last weeks have taught me something,' he said, very quietly.

She smiled up at him. 'Oh?'

'They have taught me that I am perhaps more Greek than I thought myself to be. I find I believe in fate.' His own smile was wry. 'And you are mine. For better or for worse.' He slipped off his jacket and laid it on the seat beside her. She watched as he joined the group on the terrace below. Leon's teeth showed bright in his brown face, and they bent once more to their labours. Ten minutes later the terrace was cleared, and the wine-cask was broached. Ten minutes after that Yannis arrived, leading on a tether two kids; tiny, soft mouthed, their big eyes sadly knowing.

Cathy eyed them in some dismay. She had been in Greece for long enough to know that these were no pets. And she was right. 'The Pascal feast,' Yannis announced, tethering the pair under an olive tree. 'Tender as the dawn. They will make fine eating.'

That evening, over a Lenten meal of salt cod, courgettes and tomatoes that tasted a good deal better than Cathy had expected – Anna, she noticed, since Leon's arrival, having quietly reverted to the traditional dishes of the season – Cathy broached the subject of the Shepherd's Hut. '– it would make a perfect studio. If I could just enlarge the window a little –'

'No.' Leon shook his massive head in adamant refusal. 'The building must not be changed. The father of my grandfather built this. It must stay as it is. There are many places, Kati, that you may use for your painting. But the Hut stays as it is. It is –' he hesitated '– my *patriko* – my family home. It is a symbol. Of what was, of what is now. I make you a studio. You'll see. But the Hut – no. Is best left alone.'

The next day Cathy found herself agreeing to the conversion of a small outhouse on the far side of the house, and wondering how the devil it was that Leon always, it seemed, got his own way in the end. She wandered down to the Shepherd's Hut late in the afternoon. The sun gleamed on the white walls and glinted on the tiny windows. The roof, like that of part of the house, was constructed traditionally of two layers of heavy timbers between which were sandwiched olive branches, and on top of which soil had been laid and rolled and left to bake in the sun. Inside the little house, which consisted of a single long, narrow room, it was warm and very quiet. A blackened fireplace with a flagstoned hearth stood empty at one end of the building. A bluebottle buzzed heavily at the window. There were a few antiquated agricultural tools lying around, a small broken chair, an empty olive barrel, an ancient box-bed in one corner, still filled with straw. She turned to look out of the door; the view was breathtaking, directly down the valley and to the sea. A pity. It really would have made a lovely studio; but she could see Leon's point. Here were his roots, and to leave them unchanged was to tell the world how very far he had come. She leaned in the doorway, watching the sun dip, red as fire, through a heavy streak of cloud above the western foothills. It had been a very warm day. She wondered if there might be a storm.

Movement caught her eye. Someone was coming from the house, winding their way down through the olive grove, the occasional glimpse of a white shirt flashing through the tracery of dusty leaves. Cathy stood quite still, watching him come. He stopped a couple of yards from her. The silence that enveloped them both rendered words entirely unnecessary. Nikos stepped past her into the shadowed interior of the hut, slipping his hand into hers as he passed and drawing her after him. They stood, hands linked, still silent, watching each other. As the sun sank lower a shaft of light, blood red, suddenly illuminated Nikos' face, polishing the dark skin, the smooth and shining bone. His kiss was cool water in the desert; light in darkness. An opiate to a pain she had buried so deep that it had festered to agony. She leaned against him, for the moment aware only of the feel of his body against hers, the possessive strength of his arms about her, the tender insistence of his lips on hers. She could feel the effort he was making to be gentle, sensed the urgency, the leashed strength. He laid his cheek on her hair, held her to him so tightly that she could not look up into his face. 'Pa's just come back from the village,' he said, quietly. 'There's a message from Adam.

He's back from New York. He'll be here the day after tomorrow, in time for Easter.'

She moved a little, trying to pull away. His arms tightened
further, holding her still.

'That only leaves us tomorrow. Once Adam's here it's
unlikely we'll be able to meet.'

'Nikos – we *can't* –'

She felt him stiffen. Still she could not move. He stood for
a very long time in silence; she could feel his trembling. Then
he released a long, sighing breath, let her go abruptly and
stepped back. 'I'm sorry. That was unforgivable. Of course
we can't. Shouldn't.'

'Mustn't,' she said.

He shrugged, his face bleak. 'Forgive me. Please forgive
me. I promised you – promised myself – that I wouldn't do
this – it's just that when I realised Adam was coming –' He
shook his head, and the expression in his too-bright eyes cut
her to the heart. 'I'm sorry,' he said again, and turned.

He was at the door when she spoke. 'Nikos. Don't go.
Please.'

He stopped, his back to her, silhouetted against the angry
red sky. Great drops of rain were beginning to drum an
uneven tattoo upon the dirt roof, pattering heavily through
the leaves of the trees, setting them shivering. On the shadowed hillside the tree frogs had begun to call.

'Nikos?'

He would not turn.

'Please. Don't be angry. I can't stand it.'

He bowed his head; the thick black hair fell across his forehead. 'I'm not angry.' The words were so quiet they were
barely audible.

There was a long silence. Then, 'It's starting again, isn't
it?' she asked, close to despair.

His breath of laughter was bitter. 'It never stopped,' he
said. 'You know it. It never will.' He turned, suddenly fierce.
'Cathy, I have to see you. I have to! Just once. Please!'

'But –'

'Listen. You know the little church by the spring – *Aghia Magdalena* –?'

'Yes.'

'If you follow the path on past it, through the woods and up on to the mountain you'll find a little hut not unlike this one. It's been abandoned since before the war. No one goes there. I'll be there tomorrow morning. I'll wait. Will you come?'

She hesitated only for a moment. 'I'll try.' She joined him at the door. The sudden, heavy shower had passed, yet the air was still heavy, the sky ominous. A lone cicada called from somewhere nearby and set the tree frogs squawking dementedly again. The swift mountain dusk was falling.

'This was my mother's favourite time of day,' Nikos said unexpectedly. 'Winter and summer, whatever she was doing she would stop and watch the sunset.' He lifted his face to the sky for a moment, his eyes intent.

Cathy slipped an arm through his. 'You must find it hard,' she said. 'To come back, I mean. To the place –' she stopped.

He shook his head. 'Funnily enough, not as hard as I thought. Pa's right, I suppose; it's past and done. He's changed it all. It's nothing like it was. It's just sometimes like now – I can see her. Hear her. It's as if she's close –'

Cathy half laughed, shook her head. 'Don't! God alone knows what she'd think of me!'

'She'd love you as I do,' he said, with young and perfect confidence. 'How could she help it?'

Cathy shook her head again, but said nothing.

He looked down at her. 'You will come? Tomorrow?'

'I'll try. I promise I'll try.'

He left her then, striding through the rough, dampened grass, disappearing into the olive trees.

In a last florid blaze of light the sun slid from the blood-stained sky and disappeared beneath the shadowed lip of the mountain.

*

'I do believe,' Cathy said, tracing the line of his eyebrow with a square finger, 'that poor little Anna has fallen for you.'

Nikos shifted a little in the rustling straw, smiled lazily, shook his head. The morning sun was high and through the gap where a door had once hung an eagle soared across a sky clear and cool-looking as crystal.

'Oh yes.' Cathy leaned above him, tickled his nose with a straw. 'Believe me. I know the symptoms.' She grinned a little ruefully. 'I should, for heaven's sake.'

'Don't be silly.' He caught her head, burying his fingers in her hair, bringing her mouth back down on his. She relaxed for a moment, then struggled free. 'It's no good, my darling. Look at the time. We have to go.'

'Oh, shit.'

'Quite.' Cathy was pulling on her shirt and slacks.

Nikos sat up, drawing his knees to his chin, watching her. 'I hate this.'

She paused for a moment, then brushed her hair briskly, not looking at him. 'No more than I do. But – we have no alternative. You know it.'

For a moment his mutinous face looked very young. She bent to him and kissed him lightly. 'Don't be cross,' she said, softly. 'Don't spoil it.'

He took her hand. 'No.'

She hunkered down beside him, her face very serious. 'Your father in some ways is very – unpredictable,' she said. 'You know it. If he found out about us I don't know what he might do. To either of us. Nikos, we must be careful.'

'I know. I just hate it. That's all.'

She squeezed his hand and stood up. 'I have to go. Wait an hour. I'll see you back at the house.' A swift kiss and she was gone.

Nikos stood and went to the door, watching her as she swung off down the mountain path into the woods. She did not look back.

*

Cathy and Leon met Adam off the little ferry the next afternoon. Immediately and instinctively Cathy knew there was something wrong; Adam was too bright, too talkative, his laughter was too loud and his smile was brittle. The minute he joined them he reached for the ouzo bottle. Cathy studied him as he answered Leon's questions about the journey from London and about his recent visit to New York. Despite his apparent high spirits he looked pale and tired and there was a worrying nerviness about him that set her teeth on edge. On the way back to the house as Leon concentrated on manoeuvring the old car around the occasional battered and war-scarred truck or bus, the plodding donkeys and the ancient carts that made the dusty mountain road an obstacle course, Adam fell silent, gazing from the window with pre-occupied eyes. As at last they bumped along the track that led to the house he turned and caught his mother's eyes upon him and, oddly, he flushed a little as if caught doing something wrong. 'Are you all right?' Cathy asked, and immediately the brilliant, meaningless smile lit his face.

'Fine. I'm fine,' and as if to prove it, began to whistle softly between his teeth.

Cathy sighed and sat back in the sagging leather seat. The next few days were not going to be easy.

Anna – to her own disappointment, Cathy suspected, given that there were now two eligible young men in the house on the mountain – was spending most of Easter with her own family, though she had insisted on not leaving to join them until Saturday. During the past days she had worked as diligently as any housewife to ensure that the traditions of the feast would be observed in the Kotsikas household. In the week leading up to the festival Cathy thought she had never seen such scrubbing and cleaning; even the doorstep was freshly whitewashed. Flowers were gathered from the fields, candles acquired from the stall in the village, ready for the midnight service on Saturday night. On the day of Adam's arrival the *hasapis* – the village butcher came – to the house to slaughter the two kids. As tradition demanded the animals were killed by the door of the house and the sign of the cross drawn in their blood on the wall, to bestow good luck and a happy Easter upon the household. On Good Friday evening – the whole household apart from Adam but including Anna herself having attended the solemn morning service – Anna cooked the traditional frugal meal abstaining, for this one day of the year, even from using olive oil. 'We'll fade away, girl!' Yannis grumbled good-naturedly, toying with his lemon-dressed salad.

'Is good for the soul.' She smiled shyly, delighted with herself as she scolded him. 'And makes an appetite for Sunday!'

Yannis grinned as he reached for the wine bottle. 'At least the good Lord doesn't expect us to do without a drink!'

Cathy, elbows on the table, put her chin in her cupped hands, glancing from face to face. She was sorry Adam had not accompanied them to the village church that morning; she herself had been deeply moved by the service. The solemnity of the day, the dark splendour of the interior with its sad-eyed saints and heavily carved and gilded wood, the melancholy tolling of the bell as the flower-strewn bier was carried three times around the church had been counterbalanced by the constant comings and goings of a congregation for whom the church was as much part of everyday life as the kitchen or the taverna. Children had been kept biddable by Easter biscuits and sweetmeats, men and women gossiped quietly, grandmothers in their best black-and-white murmured over their beads whilst keeping an all-seeing eye on the behaviour of the little ones. Later she had stood with Nikos at his mother's grave, and had been oddly shocked to realise how young she had been when she had died; only in her early thirties. Neither had commented on the fact that Leon had been too busy talking to a man in a sharp business suit that immediately invoked Athens and money, to join them. At that moment her eyes met Nikos' across the table in the flickering lamplight. He smiled gently.

Adam, face expressionless, tossed back his wine and held out his glass for more.

The next day, before she left for home, Anna prepared the *magiritsa*, a dish made from the offal of the slaughtered kids; one that was eaten in every household as they broke the Lenten fast after the midnight service on Holy Saturday. Cathy, a little queasily, watched this exercise with less than wholehearted enthusiasm. The intestines, heart, lights and fat were packed into a huge casserole with onions, leeks and other green vegetables, topped up with water and set on the stove to simmer. 'Will be good,' Anna promised, earnestly.

'I'm sure it will be.'

'Now –' Busily the girl opened cupboards, set things upon the table: Easter bread, plaited and baked about red-dyed eggs, a large bowl of these eggs – *kokkina avga* – and a great plateful of sweet Easter buns. A huge bowl of salad and a dish of *tzatziki*. Cheese, and peppers. Lettuce and olives and dishes of fruit. 'These are for tomorrow. You are sure you can manage?' The young face was solemn. Cathy had long ago realised that Anna's regard for her employer's housekeeping skills was justifiably low.

'Yes. I'm sure I can. Thank you, Anna. You've worked so hard.' Cathy handed her a small, gaily wrapped package. 'A little present for you, from us all.'

The girl's face flushed with pleasure. 'Thank you, *Kiria*. And see – I have something for you –' From yet another cupboard she produced a wreath of living flowers, intricately woven. 'For the table, tomorrow.'

Delightedly Cathy thanked and kissed her. 'Now you must go. It's getting late. Your family will be expecting you.'

For the midnight service it had been decided that they would go not to the village church but to the tiny *Aghia Magdalena*, up the track by the spring. It was an utterly delightful setting. The verdant cleft that gave rise to the spring cut into the hillside a mile or so above the house. The stream, clear and cold, bubbled from the mountainside into a rocky basin, and thence on down the mountain. The little stone-built church, erected in thanksgiving for the life-sustaining waters, was perched on a rocky ledge beneath a spread of ancient trees, within sight and sound of the water. The building itself was too small to hold an Easter congregation, so they gathered outside, murmuring quietly, the leaves over their heads rustling as counterpoint to the sound of the running stream. At midnight all torches and lanterns were extinguished. There was a moment of dramatic quiet. Then from the church issued the small procession of priests and acolytes carrying the lit candles that symbolised the Resurrection.

'*Christos anesti!*' Christ is risen. The cry was joyful.

Candle was lit from candle, hand to hand. Greetings and kisses were exchanged. Then the candles were nursed carefully back down the mountainside, for it was considered ill luck indeed for them to go out before being taken through the door of the house.

Adam stumbled a little. He had been drinking steadily all day. A little way ahead of him a group of children were singing an Easter hymn. The candle he carried guttered and nearly died. Bad luck if it did. He found himself grinning, grimly. Bad luck? He might as well blow the bloody thing out himself.

Cathy had laid the big table in the kitchen before they had left. Schooled by Anna she had made sure there was a polished red egg by every place; schooled by an ebullient Leon and Yannis they set to cracking each other's eggs with gusto. The bread was broken, the *magiritsa* taken from the stove. To Cathy's surprise it was utterly delicious. Through the open door they could see and hear the flash and crack of fireworks from the valley below, and distantly the sound of music. He clapped with the others as Leon and Yannis, arms linked about each other's shoulders, performed an impromptu dance about the table, stamping and twisting, handkerchiefs held high. The bottles emptied; wine at first, and then ouzo, milky-white and strong with the taste of aniseed. Yannis sang a song, and Leon and Nikos joined in. Adam's eyelids drooped a little. At last Cathy pushed her chair away from the table and let out a small, explosive breath. 'Goodness me! I'm full as a fisherman's cat! And it's two o'clock in the morning! No, No –!' She held up her hands, laughing and shaking her head as Yannis tried to pour her another glass of wine. 'I've had quite enough! I'm going to have to clear my head before I go to bed as it is! It'll be lunchtime before we know it. I'll take a wander outside and then I'll go to bed. The clearing up will have to wait till the morning.' She stood up, smiling around the circle of faces. 'Good night.'

'*Kalinihta sas, Kati mou.*' Leon caught her hand and pulled her to him for a kiss.

Nikos, eyes downcast, dissected an Easter cake to a mess of crumbs on the scrubbed tabletop.

As Cathy left the room Leon reached for another bottle of ouzo. 'Now the drinking really begins, eh?'

Nikos' head came up sharply. 'Honest, Pa, I couldn't.' His smile was disarming. He ignored the sudden narrowing of Adam's eyes. 'Like Cathy says, there's tomorrow to contend with yet. I really guess I'd better turn in.'

'Nikos, Nikos!' Leon shook his head in mock sorrow. 'And here I was thinking I'd made a true Greek of you!'

His son held up his hands, palm out, in an exaggeratedly placatory gesture. 'Tomorrow, Pa, tomorrow. I'll be as Greek as you like. Right now, I'm bushed.'

Leon unexpectedly roared with laughter, banging the table so that the cutlery jumped. 'Off you go, then, little one.' He was gently caustic. 'Don't let your wicked papa keep you from your beauty sleep.'

Nikos stood up. Adam firmly followed suit. And was surprised when, in a quite different tone of voice Leon said softly, 'No, Adam. You stay.' His smile was bland as ever, but the dark eyes were suddenly very steady and far from laughter. Leon gestured with the bottle. 'We have another drink,' he said, flatly.

'Leon – I really am very tired –' Adam watched Nikos leave the room, turned back to the table.

'Tired, tired – suddenly everybody's tired –' Leon leaned back in his chair, gesturing expansively. His voice was still soft, yet there was a note in it that Adam knew all too well. He sat down again, alarm bells ringing. What the hell did Leon want of him now? Christ alive, he wished he hadn't drunk so much.

Leon splashed ouzo into the three glasses, pushed the water jug towards Adam. The fireworks had stopped, and the distant music was quieter. 'Yannis.' Leon was looking not at Yannis but at Adam as he spoke. 'Shut the door, eh? It's getting cool in here.'

In fact with the stove still glowing through its bars the room was far from cool. Adam tipped water in the glass, sipped his drink. Suddenly queasy, it occurred to him that Leon might have found out about Nikos and Cathy. Shit! Suppose Leon asked him what he knew? Which would be most to his advantage – to confirm, or to deny it? The room had already become very close. He was sweating. He loosened his collar. If he admitted that he'd known for weeks and done nothing about it —

'I want to have a little chat, Adam,' Leon said. 'About New York.'

Taken completely off guard Adam stared at him. 'New York?'

With elaborate patience his stepfather nodded. 'New York,' he repeated.

Adam shrugged. 'Why sure. But – I don't know what I can add to what I've already told you.'

Leon reached into his top pocket, extracted some pieces of folded paper, leaned forward and smoothed them on to the table. 'Try these, Adam,' he said.

There was a very long silence. Leon's eyes were steady. Yannis ostentatiously pared at his fingernails with a matchstick. Adam cleared his throat.

'Well?'

'I –' Adam's long, fair lashes flickered as he glanced at Leon and then, flinching a little, back to the scraps of paper.

'You recognise them?'

'Yes.'

'You accept that is your signature?'

'Yes.' Shaken to the core Adam once again forced himself to meet the other man's eyes. 'Are they – are they settled?'

Leon deliberately let the silence lengthen before answering. 'Yes. They're settled.'

Adam let out a long breath.

'– so now you owe me. Again.'

The room was very warm. Leon loosened his tie and opened the collar of his shirt. A sheen of sweat stood on the dark skin of his forehead. The icon at his neck, that a woman had given him to keep him from harm, shone dully in the soft lamplight.

Adam picked up the IOUs, tidied them and stacked them neatly on the table again. 'How – where did you get them?'

'I met a man,' Leon said, gently. 'In church. That's all you need to know.'

'I should thank you.'

'Yes. You should. And you will. By doing something for me.'

'What do you want me to do?'

Leon smiled for the first time, a smile wide, and peaceably amused. 'I want you to do what you like to do best. I want you to gamble, Adam. For me. I have made – an arrangement. But, Adam, you will do exactly as you are told. No more, and no less. And if I find that you are cheating me – by, for instance, gambling for yourself – I will throw you to some very fierce lions indeed. And they will tear you to very small pieces. Is it understood?'

'I – suppose so.' Once again Adam wished fervently he had not had so much to drink. What the hell was going on? What exactly was Leon talking about?

'Not so much as a side bet. Not so much as a penny. Or should I say a dime?' Leon raised a strong, stubby finger, jabbing it in the air. 'The stakes are too high. Swear, Adam, that you will not so much as turn a card except on my orders. That you will never – never! – do this again –' His fingers flicked at the IOUs.

'I swear. But I still don't understand.'

Leon put his hand into his pocket and brought out a large metal key, which, his eyes still on Adam's face, he handed to Yannis. 'Yannis has something to show you, Adam,' he said.

He sat after they had left, pensively picking his teeth. A promise is a promise. But there are many ways of keeping it.

The two figures in the cave-like darkness beneath an ancient olive tree stood so close they might have been one. They were still as statues as Yannis and Adam passed, the torch that Yannis carried flickering in the darkness. 'Where are they going?' Cathy whispered.

Very gently Nikos laid a hand to her lips. 'Ssh.'

They waited. When the two men were out of earshot Nikos brought his lips to her ear. 'We must go. Before they come back.'

Cathy was staring in puzzlement into the night, to where the small light of the torch still flashed and bobbed. 'They're going in the direction of the Shepherd's Hut. What on earth can they be doing?'

Nikos' laughter was very soft. 'They're men, my darling.'

'What's that supposed to mean?'

'There is a certain brotherhood, after a night of drinking, in relieving oneself in the open air.'

Ridiculously Cathy found herself blushing. 'Oh.'

Nikos' lips brushed hers. 'Happy Easter, my love. Now go.' And as she let go of his hand and stepped quietly through the rustling branches his last words whispered behind her. 'I love you.'

Chapter Sixteen

Cathy woke to the smell of woodsmoke and the sound of laughter. She was alone. Beyond the partly closed shutters a golden gleam of sunshine beckoned, though the low-ceilinged bedroom was, as always, shadowed and cool. The sound of a barking dog echoed up from the valley to be answered nearer at hand by the hiccoughing bray of a donkey. She lay for a moment, warm and sleepy, before throwing back the covers and padding barefoot to the window and pushing the shutter wide. On a terrace just below the house a cooking fire glowed. On two spits above it the young goats were roasting. All the men were there, each of them obviously taking turns at the spit; as Cathy watched Leon took over from Adam, laughing uproariously at something Yannis said. The wine, she noticed, was already flowing. Across the valley the bells were ringing. It was Easter Sunday, the most joyful day of the year. No cloud marred the perfect sky, no shadow fell across the perfect, festive day. Cathy was never to forget that. The Easter table was spread beneath the trees, the smell of roasting meat delicious and mouthwatering on the air. By the time Leon, with some ceremony, tore off a piece of meat and, declaring it well and truly cooked, offered it to Cathy a couple of wineskins had already been emptied. They ate the tender meat with their fingers, as tradition demanded. The bread and salads and *tzatziki* that Anna had so painstakingly prepared were demolished. When the exuberant strains of music floated up to them from the tiny village square below Leon and Yannis were immediately on their feet, dragging the two laughing younger men with them, demonstrating the complicated steps of a dance as Cathy clapped in time. Later Yannis danced alone, arms outstretched, slight, sinewy body erect as a knife-blade, a wooden chair held between his teeth; a feat that made Cathy's jaw ache just to watch it. Over and again the toast was drunk: '*Christos anesti!*' – 'Christ is risen!' – and over the valley and the mountainsides a fragrant pall of woodsmoke drifted in the clear air as the people celebrated with about equal fervour the deliverance of their Saviour from the cold hand of death and the end of the Lenten fast. The air was sweet with the smell of blossom. At the setting of the sun the fires leapt and blazed in the shadows, and voices sang in the darkness.

'*Christos anesti!*' The forces of evil are vanquished. For the moment.

The next morning they were all deservedly heavy-headed. This was the last day of the holiday – the menfolk were off the following day; Leon and the two boys back to London and Yannis on some unspecified expedition of his own. Anna came up from the village to help clear up after the festivities, shyly presenting each of them with a dyed and painted egg; the most colourful and elaborate, Cathy noted with a hidden smile, being reserved for Nikos, together with a guileless and dazzling smile. In the afternoon they sat in the garden with the last of the wine watching the sun dip towards the mountains, the inevitable sense of anti-climax subduing them.

'Come,' Leon said, suddenly, lifting his glass. 'A last toast.'

Adam surveyed him with a mordant eye. 'If Christ rises again,' he said, with mild acrimony, 'it'll be to the great detriment of my head. He's worse than a bloody yo-yo!'

Leon laughed. 'No, no. We drink to when we shall all be here together again. To the next festival.'

Adam put his head in his hands in mock despair. 'Good God! Not another one!'

'Another one. In two or three months' time it will be the festival of *Aghia Magdalena* – of Mary Magdalene, the patron of our little church by the spring. There are great festivities in the village – processions and fireworks, music and dancing.'

Adam's blue eyes had moved, lazily, to his mother. 'Mary Magdalene,' he said, thoughtfully, and with a sudden, dangerous smile. 'Tell me – wasn't she the lady that was – as they say – no better than she should be?'

Cathy saw Nikos' head come up sharply.

Leon chuckled. 'The repentant whore. That's the one. So we make it a date. Whatever else may happen we will all be here to celebrate her name day on the twenty-second of July. Yes?' Taking their assent for granted he raised his glass. '*Aghia Magdalena*.'

Adam raised sardonic eyebrows and, smiling, toasted his mother.

They had already agreed that Cathy should stay in the house, with the proviso that she would join Leon in London for a couple of weeks in early June, for the Coronation. There was the rest of the decorating and the furniture to organise, the garden to plan and plant. With Anna to help her she was confident that she could do without Yannis' assistance. She hardly admitted even to herself that the decision was made easier by her discovery that Nikos was to liaise with the Athens office and would be likely to visit fairly frequently.

With the men gone, and more especially with Leon's flamboyant and egotistical presence removed, the house was a haven of peace and quiet. Cathy had not herself realised quite what a strain these past days had been. And whilst she longed for Nikos she also – in what she well understood was an exercise in self-deceit – felt a degree of relief that the temptation of his physical proximity had, for the time being at least, been removed. She imagined that she was not the first, and would not be the last, to discover that guilt was the most wearing and exhausting emotion of all. Nor could she have been the first to attempt to comfort herself with the flawed argument that to sin in the mind was less culpable than to sin in the flesh. The look in Adam's eyes as he had raised his glass to her haunted her for days afterwards; but there again, the tiresomely honest voice of what she could only think of as her conscience pointed out, that did not stop her from writing to Nikos, nor from living for the letters he wrote to her. Twice a week she would walk down the path to the village to catch the battered bus into town – to shop, and to collect and post her mail. The sight of Nikos' writing on an envelope – a lean, oddly and indisputably American scrawl – brought a lift of delight as addictive as any drug. On those days when the pigeonhole was empty, however, the corresponding disappointment was cruel.

The weather grew steadily hotter, though on its perch on the hillside it was rare that a breeze did not cool the now finished terrace of the house. Cathy loved the occasional brief but splendidly spectacular thunderstorms that crashed their way from the mountains, growling and glaring from a billowing slate-grey sky. To her delight the wind-up gramophone arrived unscathed as did her precious store of records. With Anna's quick and willing help her Greek began to improve, and during the course of their idiosyncratic conversations in which Greek and English were blithely and perfectly intelligibly mongrelised she found herself becoming increasingly intrigued with the structure of the village society in which the girl's life was rooted. In which, she was coming to understand, despite his success and urbanisation, Leon's life was rooted; and from which cradle Nikos had sprung. She learned without surprise of the importance of 'the house' in village life, the term being used to describe not simply the physical structure but the immediate family who lived within it. Great and often violent rivalries could grow between houses – even between those closely related by blood. Once a man found himself head of a household of his own, that household became his life, his pride, his honour and his responsibility, and savage quarrels could rise between brother and brother, cousin and cousin, even father and son. As in all small and insular communities gossip, envy and petty jealousies could be and often were the sparks to ignite an inferno.

Anna had lived in the village all of her life and knew the ins and outs of every feud and vendetta for the past twenty years; and there were a startling number of them. Her own cousin had been killed by a neighbour who had accused him of swindling him over the ownership of a patch of land. On the other hand, any threat from outside the community would be faced with a solidly united front. The society as a whole was almost totally male-dominated; to an outsider's eyes the women had little freedom and their lives and behaviour were strictly circumscribed, hostages to their menfolk's honour, though within 'the house' their influence and power was strong. A man's home was considered, almost literally, to be his castle; within it he was respected and on the whole obeyed, in the outside world he was expected to defend it and those who lived in it to the last, and it was this tradition that led to the phenomenon known as *egoismos* – the flamboyantly self-assertive attitude that so characterised the behaviour of the men and which could lead so easily to quarrels and even bloodshed; to lose face was a disaster for a man. Anna's own family were something of an exception – not many girls of her age would be allowed to work outside her own home. Her father had been killed in the last days of the civil war, leaving her mother with Anna, her two very small brothers and a new baby. 'Life is hard for my mother,' Anna said. 'She is not old; yet she must dress in black, must not sing, or dance or wear jewellery. She never gets invited anywhere. It is hard for a woman alone, and with little ones to feed. We must have money. So –' She shrugged and smiled her peculiarly sweet smile. 'I come here. And it is good.' Anna herself knew – and cared not a jot – that her working

for 'the foreigner' jeopardised her standing and reputation in
the village, at least amongst the older generation.

Nikos' first visit was a flying one, three weeks after Easter.
He came for one day, and stayed overnight. The night was a
long one, and not without its tears. Watching him leave the
next day Cathy was moved almost to despair. How could
they go on like this? And yet – how could they not? For a couple of days she was depressed and listless; then the letters
began again, and the anticipation of their next meeting – a
longer one, this time, he had promised; three perhaps four
days – was too great to allow for doubts or fears. She quite
deliberately cultivated a day-by-day philosophy, forcing herself to take each moment as it came and to avoid at all costs
looking too far ahead. The next glimpse of Nikos with his
golden eyes and polished skin was as far as she wanted to see.

In the month before she visited Leon in London Nikos came
to the house twice more. Their days were circumspect, Nikos
going about his father's business and being careful not to
arouse any suspicion that his devotion to his stepmother was
anything other than filial. In this he was helped by two
things – the fact that the house itself stood alone and not
actually within the bounds of the village with its many sharp
ears and prying eyes, and the fact of Anna's growing infatuation. So blinded was she by her own feelings she had little
time, when Nikos was around, for anyone else's; and anyway, much as the girl liked and admired Cathy, in her young
eyes her employer was an old woman and long past the
painful joys of love. The nights, however, were a different
thing. Cathy loved the long, warm evenings when they sat
together, alone, on the terrace eating supper, listening to
Mozart, or Mahler or the majesty of Beethoven, sometimes
talking, sometimes in a silence so intimate that it spoke
louder than any words. As the blaze of the sunset first sharpened the mountain skyline to an operatic backdrop of fire
and shadow and then, dying, smudged it to faded pastels

that paled slowly to darkness their fingers would touch, or
their eyes meet, and without a word Nikos would reach to
pick up the lamp and draw her behind him down the curving
stone stairs to the bedroom below. She grew to know exactly
the moment when his need for her overcame his content simply to watch her, to share her company, to listen to the music
and to her voice. He loved her, she knew that with utter certainty, but he wanted her too, and made love to her with an
ardent young strength that not only left her in no doubt of it
but fed her own desire for him as dry bracken feeds a forest
fire. And each time he left the pain grew worse and the ensu-
ing guilt more terrible.

She returned to a London consumed by Coronation fever.
Nothing, it seemed – not even the typical unreliability of the
capricious English weather – could quell the enthusiasm of
the New Elizabethans for their young queen and her family.
The darkness of the desperate years of war was lightening,
the gloom of austerity lifting. There was a new air of confidence abroad in the country; taxes were being cut, rationing
coming to an end. The proper moment had come at last, it
seemed, to draw a line on the bad times and look forward to
the good. Two million people braved the rain to cheer the
monarch to Westminster Abbey and back, twenty million
more, historically, watched the ceremony on television –
many sets bought simply for that purpose, intrusive guests
that having been invited to a party would remain for a life-
time and influence a generation. To add to the nation's pride,
on the very day of the crowning came the news that Everest,
the highest mountain in the world, had at last been con-
quered and by a British expedition; though, as Adam pointed
out a little tartly, quite how such a feat accomplished by a
New Zealander and a Himalayan Sherpa, however gallant,
reflected full glory on the United Kingdom was a little hard
to fathom, coronation or no coronation. Adam too had
returned for the festivities from a long spell in the United

States. He had lost weight and there was a nervy edge to him that worried Cathy a little. The days were long gone, however, when she could express such concerns and expect him to confide in her so she held her peace. In the ten days or so she spent in London she saw little of Nikos – a snatched word or two, a single clandestine lunch in a small restaurant in Soho that somehow served only to make things more rather than less difficult, and – disastrously – a visit to the theatre with Leon to which Nikos, agonisingly for Cathy, escorted a pretty, likeable and animated girl called Patsy with whom he was obviously on warm and easy terms, and whose name she had never before heard him mention: a fact she struggled hard and wholly unsuccessfully not to invest with dire significance.

Two days before she left to return to Greece Leon drove her down to Suffolk, to check on the tenant of Sandlings and to visit Bert, Paddy and Sandy. The visit was not, for Cathy, a success; she spent the entire journey back to London fighting tears and trying not to remember Sandy's frantic greeting and urgently happy tongue, nor his struggles when Bert had leashed him to prevent him from running after her as she had left. On the whole it was with little regret that she packed her bags and left a still damp and cool London for the warmth and sunlight of Greece. She did not try to contact Nikos, nor did she make any special effort to bid him goodbye; a perhaps inevitable constraint had fallen between them – Cathy, despite her best efforts, finding it impossible to forget or ignore the shock of seeing him with the girl Patsy and Nikos, knowing it, and having only done it with the best of intentions, equally stiff-necked and sore at her reaction and resultant apparent coolness. They did not quarrel; perhaps it would have been better if they had. Later – much later – Cathy came to believe this to be true. But for now it was almost a relief to escape from him for a while.

And Nikos, sensitive to her every mood, knew it, and brooded.

*

He followed her within days, without consultation or warning, in the process clashing stormily with his father on the need for yet another trip to Athens. 'Am I in charge there or not? For Christ's sake, Pa, stop looking over my shoulder every five minutes! I need to go myself –'

'Your telephone wire's been cut?' Leon suggested caustically. 'The post no longer works? In the war we used homing pigeons; I should buy you some? You still haven't explained to me what's so urgent?'

'Why should I? You've given me a job. Let me do it my own way. Or do it yourself.' The challenge was open.

His father's eyes glittered for a moment, then Leon shrugged. 'Very well. Go. But –' a stubby finger pointed sharply '– I hope something comes of it, boy. Airplane tickets don't come free.'

Cathy was alone on the terrace when he arrived. It was a sleepily warm June evening. Earlier there had been a storm, there were still puddles on the stony ground and on the paving. The air was laden with the scents of rosemary, thyme and the freshly abundant wild flowers of the mountain that had not yet been fully subjected to the punishment of a high summer sun. Cathy was reading, a lamp lit against the fading light, Verdi's *Requiem* playing softly in the background. Over the chirruping cicadas and the rasp of the tree frogs she heard the swift footsteps on the stone steps and lifted her head, watching the curve of the stairs. That was his first sight of her, alert but not frightened, the slanting, cat-like eyes wide in the gloom; and wider still when she saw him.

'Nikos!' Her voice was a breath. She was alarmed now, that was clear in voice and face. Expecting a stranger she had not feared; seeing him had triggered trepidation in her. She held up a quick hand, as if to ward him off, to hold him where he stood. Already high-strung the thought infuriated him. Two long steps took him to the table. He spread his hands upon it and leaned to her, capturing her mouth fiercely before she could speak. For the briefest moment he felt the familiar flame of response, then, frantically, she pushed him from her. 'Nikos – what are you doing here?'

'What do you think?' Against her whisper his voice sounded unnaturally loud in the quiet. 'I came to see you. To find out what the hell –'

'Sssh!' She flinched from the sound, covered her own mouth with two cupped hands, her eyes flickering in signal beyond him to the house. '*Yannis is here.*' The words, desperately urgent, were barely audible. And were too late.

'Nikos?' The voice came from the shadows of the room behind them. 'That you, boy?' Yannis appeared, moving silently at the edge of the circle of lamp light.

Nikos straightened. Cathy sat frozen. Yannis strolled to them, hands in pockets, an unlit cigarette dangling from the corner of his mouth. He held out a hand to Nikos. 'What are you doing here?'

Nikos relaxed a little, took the proffered hand. 'I was in Athens. Thought I'd pop over and make sure Cathy was OK.'

'She's OK,' Yannis said, poker-faced.

Cathy's glance flickered from one lean, lamplit face to another. How much had Yannis seen? Even the words – '*I came to see you. To find out what the hell –*' were hardly the conventional greeting under the circumstances. Especially spoken as they had been. Yet Yannis' face, his gleaming dark eyes, betrayed nothing. She pushed her chair back briskly. 'Yannis and I have eaten. But there's cold meat, and bread. And cheese if you'd like. I'll make up a bed in the spare room – help yourself to a glass of wine –' Thankfully she slipped into the house, stood for a moment by the door, listening.

'How long are you here for?' Nikos' voice, admirably casual.

'Just a couple of days. I leave tomorrow. Cigarette?' A pause, whilst Nikos accepted. 'How's the old man?'

'Exhausting as ever.' The words were genuinely rueful.

Yannis laughed. Cathy took a long breath. A close shave. A very close shave.

And somewhere in the depths of her treacherous heart she did not care. He was here. Nikos had come. What else truly mattered? 'Dear God,' she asked the fresh-baked loaf softly and uneasily, as she carved a chunk from it. 'Are we asking to be found out?'

The two of them had no chance to talk until the following evening, with Yannis safely gone and Anna, reluctantly, sent home at a decent hour. Once certain they were alone Nikos gathered Cathy into his arms and held her against him. She leaned to him in silence, her head resting on his shoulder, her eyes on the distant mountains, red-lit in the evening light. 'Why did you come?' she asked at last. 'And why so angrily?'

'To see you. And – I don't know – I was afraid – I had imagined –' He stopped.

She lifted her head to kiss the sharp line of his jaw.

His arms tightened painfully about her. 'Tell me you love me.'

'I love you.'

'Again.'

'Nikos – you're being silly –'

'*Again!*'

'I love you.' She was gentle, 'I love you, I love you, I love you. There. Does that satisfy you?'

'Nothing will ever satisfy me but having you to myself.'

She closed her eyes and drew a long breath.

He put her a little way from him, holding her by the shoulders, his eyes intent upon hers. 'Cathy, come away with me. Please. I can't stand this. I can't stand the lying, the deceptions. I can't stand to be away from you.' His voice harshened and his fingers bit deep. 'I can't stand to have you living with Pa.'

'He's my husband.'

He released her so suddenly that she stumbled a little. 'And I'm your lover. And that's the way you want it to stay.'

His face had darkened with anger, the pale eyes blazed with it.

'Nikos! For God's sake – what are you trying to do? Are you determined to quarrel?'

'I'm trying to tell you that I love you.' He was making a physical effort to control himself. 'I'm trying to tell you that I want you to leave Pa and come away with me. I want you to myself. I want to live with you, care for you –'

'Oh, Nikos – can't you see that's impossible? Where could we go? How would we live?'

'We'd manage somehow.'

'And Adam?'

'It's nothing to do with Adam.'

'*Of course it is!*' Cathy clenched her hands, fought to keep her voice even. 'Nikos – darling – you can't simply ignore other people! Adam is my son. My *son*. I can't lose him. I can't!'

He turned his back on her, felt in his pocket for his cigarette box. She watched as he extracted a cigarette, lit it with a shaking hand. 'The truth is,' he said, very quietly, 'that you don't really love me.'

'No!'

He tilted his head. Smoke curled into the warm air. 'If you did,' he was stubborn, would not look at her, 'you wouldn't care. You'd come away with me and tell the world to go to hell.'

She moved behind him, put her hands on his shoulders and laid her face against his back. 'Darling, darling Nikos – don't you see? Life's more complicated than that. What of your father? Could you really hurt him so much?'

His laughter was harsh. 'Aren't you splitting hairs just a little?'

'It may seem so, but no, I don't think I am. Think what it would do to him. To his pride. You know him well enough.'

He turned then, very slowly, looked at her searchingly. 'You still love him.' It was not a question.

'I'm very fond of him. How could I not be?' She hesitated for a moment before adding very quietly, 'Are you telling me you feel nothing for him? Are you telling me you feel no guilt towards him, no sympathy for him?'

'Of course not. But –'

'Oh, Nikos!' She turned and walked to the low stone parapet, stood looking into the gathering shadows. 'You think I don't dream of it? Of our being together? Of course I do! But you know as well as I do that it simply isn't possible. Apart from anything else you know Leon would never let me go. I'm his. Part of his life, one of his possessions. He never gives up anything he considers to be his. You know it. It isn't in him.'

The sudden silence was telling.

'What are we going to do?' Nikos' quiet voice, shockingly, was suddenly unsteady. She turned. He looked away, but not before she had seen the too-bright eyes.

The night chorus had started. Somewhere a dog barked.

She walked to him, put her arms about him and held him very tightly.

But she did not answer his question; because she could not.

They sat long into the night; giving up on reality, weaving dreams. They would live at Sandlings, spend their days walking the beaches, flying kites, skimming stones. They would go to America, to the south-eastern shores where the Gulf Stream warmed the waters and life was slow and kind. They would find a farmhouse halfway up a mountain in Italy and live on spaghetti and tomatoes. Or perch on a cliff in Brittany and fish for their supper. At last he relaxed, and she saw him smile again. It was very late when at last he reached for her hand and drew her to her feet. On the way down the stairs he asked, in sudden curiosity, 'What was Yannis doing here, anyway?'

'Oh – I don't know. He's a law unto himself is Yannis. He comes and goes as he pleases. Stays a day or so, then disappears again.' She paused on the bottom step, looking up at him. 'Can you stay for long?'

He shook his head. 'I'd better get back to Athens for the day after tomorrow at the latest.'

'You've got business there?'

'No.' He shrugged and lifted a hand in a way that suddenly and uncomfortably reminded her of his father. 'You are my business here.'

'Nikos –'

'I know, I know. I'll be careful. I promise. I know you're right.'

'When will I see you again?' The bedroom was cool and dark. The lamplight playing on the rough-plastered walls sketched moving shadow-demons.

'At the festival.' He drew her to him, began to unbutton her shirt. 'Not even I can manufacture an excuse to come back before then. And it's going to be the worst kind of torture, with everyone here. But at least I'll be near you. That's all that counts.'

'Now,' she said, softly. 'You're here now! *That's* all that counts.'

The feast of Saint Mary Magdalen, whilst in no way comparable to the Easter festival was nevertheless kept in some style in the village. *Aghia Magdalena* was patron saint to the church by the spring, and her name day was a day to celebrate. There would be processions and services, musicians and fireworks. Flowers and ribbons decorated the church and the doors of the village houses. The baking and the sweet-making began a week before. Cathy too was busy, taking more of a hand herself this time in organising the festival, and making sure that the finishing touches were put to the house in good time. A week or so before the feast, during a shopping trip to Athens she spoke to Leon on the telephone.

'– the agent says the table and chairs you've shipped from London will be arriving next week. Mr Gikas here at the office says he'll get it shipped straight on to me, so that's all arranged and it should be ready in time. I've bought mosquito nets for all the beds. Oh, and some lovely hand-made pottery for the house. Once the furniture arrives then the dining room's finished. Anna's very impressed. She tells everyone in the village that we have a room just for eating in. Oh, and I've finished painting the kitchen. It really does look nice.'

Leon laughed. 'It sounds as if you've been busy. Do you need any more money?'

'No, I'm fine.'

'Just ask Gikas if you need anything.'

'I will.'

The line crackled and for a moment her husband's voice broke up. '– he'll be with you a couple of days early, to help.'

'Sorry? I didn't hear you –?'

'Nikos. I've given him a couple of days off. He'll be with you early next week. Kati? Are you there? Do you hear me?'

She recovered herself. 'Yes. Yes, I heard you.'

'Adam and I will follow on Friday. We're coming together. We'll be on the evening boat. Nikos can meet us with the car.'

'Fine. That's fine.' The hand that held the telephone had clenched to a fist. Very carefully she relaxed it.

'I thought I might take a little holiday. A week. Perhaps a little longer. Would you like that?'

'Yes. Of course.' She was hardly listening. Nikos, here, for three – perhaps four? – days. The world seemed suddenly warm and bright.

'Good. So I'll see you next week.'

They said their goodbyes. Cathy replaced the handset and stared out of the grubby window into the hot, bustling streets of Athens. The gods were smiling again. Nikos was coming.

She was climbing the precipitous path from the village to the house when she saw the boat in the distance, chugging across the glittering bay like a tiny toy across a gleaming pond. She stopped in the shade of an olive tree beside the running stream that here followed the track of the path and watched as the little vessel drew closer, and disappeared behind the mountains and into the harbour. Nikos was coming. If all had gone well he would be here within the hour. Hot and breathless from her climb she sat on a rock and bent to splash cool water on to her face and neck. A small tortoise plodded its way across the stony path at her feet and she smiled. 'Hello, little fellow.' She straightened her back and sat for a moment, elbows on knees, looking out across the valley and regaining her breath. The path here was very steep, zig-zagging through the rocks and the olive groves out of sight both of the village and of the house above. It was very quiet, and utterly peaceful. From a distant hillside came the melodious sound of bells as a herd of goats grazed. The air was warm and heavy with the heady scents of the mountains. It was a perfect day; the sky a vivid cobalt blue, brilliant with sunshine. The distant sea sparkled and danced in the diamond light.

Nikos was coming.

Cathy stood, slung her bag back on to her shoulder, and set off up the last quarter-mile of scrambling ascent to the house.

'For you, Anna.' Nikos handed the girl a wooden cigar-box, smiling. 'A young friend of mine doesn't need them any more.'

Blushing deeply, Anna took the box and opened it; gasped with pleasure. ' Oh – *Kirios* Nikos! For me?'

'For you.' He watched as she touched with a gentle finger the rolls of brightly coloured silken ribbon that were tucked into the box.

The eyes that lifted to his were brilliant with thanks and as adoring as a puppy's. 'Thank you! Oh, thank you. They're beautiful!'

'Well, you've certainly made that young lady very happy,' Cathy said later, smiling a little after Anna had said her good-nights, and more effusive thanks, before taking her booty home.

'It seemed a shame to throw them away. Such things are

still hard to come by. The daughter of a friend of mine has decided she's too grown up for plaits and to her father's despair has had them cut off. As I say, it seemed a pity to waste such pretty things, and I thought of Anna, that's all.'

'And a very kind thought it was too. Would you like a drink while I'm finishing off supper?'

'That would be nice.'

'Wine? Ouzo?'

'Wine please.'

Cathy filled his glass. 'Have you seen much of Leon?'

'Not over the past couple of days. He's been off on one of those mysterious trips of his.'

'He's all right?'

'He seems fine.'

She filled another glass. 'Food won't be long. I've got time to have a glass with you before I do anything else.'

They sat in silence, bathed in the glow of yet another spectacular sunset. 'We're so lucky,' Cathy said, 'that the house is on the west-facing side of the valley. I'd much rather have sunsets than sunrises.'

'Yes.' He was not watching the glories of the sky, he was watching her, his mouth crooked in a small smile, his eyes narrowed lazily on hers. He reached a hand across the table, palm up, and curled his fingers a little.

She nibbled her lip, her own eyes alight with love and mischief. 'Supper,' she said.

'Damn supper.'

Still she teased him. His long fingers moved, invitingly.

'I haven't finished my wine.'

'Bring it with you. Bring the bottle. Bring two bottles.'

'Good God! My mother warned me about men like you. You're trying to get me tiddly so you can take advantage of me! What kind of a girl do you think I am?'

'The kind of girl that's going to come to bed with me now, and make love, and then have supper and then make love again. That kind of girl.'

Cathy stood, moved round the table to him. 'Got it in one,' she said. 'Nobody loves a smart arse, you know.'

He caught her hand, drew her down to kiss him. 'You do.'

'Yes. I do.'

He picked up the wine bottle and led the way downstairs. The bedroom was coolly shadowed. The shutters, half closed, let in a single, blindingly brilliant shaft of fading sunlight that dazzled the eyes. Nikos put bottle and glasses on the small table by the bed, slipped off his jacket and turned. Cathy's fingers were at the buttons of her skirt. 'No,' he said. 'Come here. I want to undress you.'

She moved through the bar of light to him. He unbuttoned her blouse, slipped it from her shoulders, bent to kiss the curve of her neck. She raised her arms, pressing her breasts against him, her fingers loosening his tie, undoing the top button of his shirt.

His hands moved gently on her lifted breasts. She let her head fall back, closing her eyes, savouring every moment, every touch.

There was the faintest of movements in the shadows by the opened door. Nikos lifted his head sharply. The dagger of light from the window, blood red now, dazzled him for a moment.

A dark bulk loomed in the doorway. 'Well,' said Leon, his harsh voice savagely and perilously quiet. 'It seems that after all I owe Yannis an apology.'

Chapter Seventeen

For the briefest of moments the shocked silence was absolute.

'Nothing to say?' Leon enquired, still softly. 'No protests? No denials? Well –' his smile was contemptuous '– perhaps not. Not in the circumstances.'

'Leon –' began Cathy.

'Quiet, woman. Cover yourself.' Leon's intent, unblinking gaze was fixed upon Nikos. He still had not raised his voice. 'Perhaps I should have left my interruption for a few moments longer? Would the entertainment have been worth such restraint?'

Nikos' olive skin had paled to ivory. His head was up, the bones of his face braced and stark.

'Lost your voice, boy?' Leon asked. In contrast to the softness of the words his huge, threatening hands were clenching and unclenching very slowly at his sides.

Nikos stepped towards him, out of the shadows, away from Cathy. 'No, Pa. I haven't lost my voice.'

'Your wits then?' His father thrust his great head forward like a bull. 'Your sense of honour? You've lost them?'

'Pa, listen. Please. I'm sorry. I'm truly sorry. I love you. You know it. But I love Cathy more. And she loves –'

He was not allowed to finish. Leon's massive hand caught him, flatly, across the cheek and sent him spinning across the room to crash painfully into the table.

'*Leon! No! Please –*'

Leon ignored Cathy's cry. In two quick, surprisingly agile steps he was beside Nikos and had hauled him to his feet by the front of his shirt. He slapped him again, very hard. Nikos' head rocked. Blood sprang brightly upon his cheek-bone. He made no attempt to defend himself. Leon raised his hand again.

'No!' Cathy launched herself across the room and caught his arm, clinging to it. 'Stop it!'

He shook her off as if she had been a kitten. The next blow took Nikos almost off his feet and he staggered, and went down on one knee, putting a hand to his bloodied mouth.

Again Cathy tried to stop Leon, and again was sent reeling. Leon stood over his son, hands fisted at his sides. 'Get up. At least fight like a man.'

Dizzily Nikos got to his feet, stood swaying. 'I won't fight you, Pa. Not like this.'

'You'd better, boy. Or I'm going to kill you.' A fist in the stomach doubled Nikos up again, and again he was on his knees, retching.

Leon stepped back, breathing hard. Cathy, shaking and sick with terror, stepped between them. 'Leon – please listen – it isn't Nikos' fault –'

'Get out of the way. I'll deal with you later.'

'No! You'll listen to me now – you must!'

At last his eyes rested fully upon her, and she flinched at what she saw in them. He caught her wrist in a brutal grip. 'I said get out of the way.' The words were unnervingly quiet. With no effort he threw her from him, on to the bed, turned again. 'Up, boy.'

'Leon, what good will it do to hurt him any more?' Tears were running down Cathy's face.

Once again Nikos staggered to his feet. 'Pa –'

Leon seized him by the hair, straining his head back viciously. 'Don't "Pa" me!' The words were a snarl. With his free hand he reached to his own throat and lifted the gold icon from the folds of his shirt, dangling it before Nikos' eyes. 'Once you would have had this. I have always carried it in trust for you. A token of your mother's love. Of the woman who died in this very yard, protecting us. You spit on her memory!'

'No!'

'You spit on my fatherhood. On your family. You are not my son – do you hear? *You are no longer my son!* You are nothing! A dog, who copulates!' Every word he accentuated with a shake of the hand that was twisted into the thick black hair.

Nikos gasped in pain. Cathy scrambled from the bed and stood frozen, watching. For a moment the pair were still. The icon spun, gently and lazily between them. 'Leon, listen to me,' Cathy spoke very rapidly, 'the fault is mine. Mine. Not Nikos'. He's a boy. I –' she was shaking uncontrollably '– I led him on.'

'No!' Somehow Nikos found the strength to break his father's grip. He spun to face her, swaying. Blood drenched the front of his shirt, his right eye was almost closed. He put the back of his hand to his mouth to wipe it, shook his head a little. 'Don't say that. Don't lie. I can't bear it if you lie.'

'I'm not lying.' Cathy was keeping her eyes steady on Leon's, willing him to believe her. 'I'm not. From the start it was my fault. I was lonely. I was angry with you. Nikos was –' she stopped, unable to go on.

'Nikos was my son!' Leon came slowly towards her, face and eyes darkly venomous. '*Nikos was my son! Whore!*'

She flinched at that but said nothing.

Nikos launched himself at his father, fists flailing. 'Stop it! Leave her alone –!'

With a roar Leon turned on him. In a moment the boy was on his knees again, panting, winded, his arms crossed over his stomach, a fresh cut opened on his brow.

'Leon, enough!' Cathy said.

He turned his head to look at her. 'Enough, you say? Enough? He should be dead. He has betrayed me.'

'No,' she said, steadily, 'I have betrayed you. Nikos is a boy. And a not very experienced one.' She lifted her head, setting her jaw, refusing to look into the dawning disbelief in the young face that turned sharply to hers. 'He believed me,' she said quietly, 'when I told him I loved him. Why should you blame him for that?'

'Cathy, no!' Nikos' voice was full of pain.

'I told you, the fault is mine,' Cathy continued steadily. 'And has been from the start.' She knew the risk she was taking; fear was pulsing in her blood and turning her stomach to water. Leon was watching her with murderously fierce, narrowed eyes. 'You've punished him enough. Let him go.'

Nikos shook his head, winced. 'I won't go.'

Cathy schooled her face to look at him. 'Yes you will. It's over, Nikos. Over.'

'No!'

'Get up.' Leon hooked his hand into Nikos' shirt collar and hauled him to his feet. 'Listen to what she's saying. The voice of Eve.' He glanced at Cathy, contempt in his face. 'You've been had, boy. We both have.'

'I don't believe you,' Nikos said, flatly, to Cathy.

In some odd dispassionate corner of her mind Cathy found herself registering the fact that the pain in her heart was physical, an agony that constricted the flow of blood and stopped the breath. 'Believe me,' she said. 'It's over.' She glanced back at Leon. 'Let him go,' she said again. 'He's guilty of nothing but stupidity.'

Leon raised his voice. 'Yannis!'

'Cathy, stop this,' Nikos said. 'You love me. You know you do. You can't send me away. You can't! Not again!'

She managed, somehow, to face calmly his hurt and bewildered gaze. His young, damaged face was smudged with blood and bruises. 'I am sending you away. And –' she hesitated only for a moment before aiming very carefully the final blow '– I don't love you, Nikos. Not the way you wanted me to. There is a difference between love and infatuation. The one lasts, can sustain any blow. The other can't. You have to go. My place is here.'

There was movement at the door, and Yannis slipped into the room. Cathy cast him one bleak glance; he returned it, coolly expressionless.

'Yannis,' Leon said. 'Get this puppy out of here. Take him to the boat. Make sure he's on it when it leaves. And – Yannis – drop a word in the ear of Captain Makris – tell him to spread it – the young bastard's not to be allowed back. Not under any circumstances. I'll have the guts – and the boat – of anyone who brings him.'

'I won't go,' Nikos said, stubbornly desperate.

'You'll go,' his father said quietly. 'Or, by Christ, I'll finish what I started.'

Cathy turned her back on all of them, folding her arms tightly across her breast. 'Cathy?' Nikos asked, despairingly.

'Go,' she said.

There was a long moment of silence, followed by movement. Then quiet fell again. Cathy could sense the presence behind her, menacing. 'I'll deal with you later,' Leon said at last, very softly, 'when the temptation to cut out your deceitful heart has eased at least a little.'

She heard the door close, heard the turning of the key in the lock. The sun had at last sunk behind the distant horizon, and the blood-red glow in the sky was dying.

He came in the middle of the night, after she had at last fallen into a fitful nightmare of sleep, involuntary sobs still shaking her. He had been drinking. She sensed rather than saw him in the darkness; so long and so hard had she wept she could barely focus her eyes, and her head ached as if it would split. Leon struck a match, unsteadily set it to the wick of the lamp, loomed above her for a moment before

with a swift movement reaching to strip the light bedcover
from the bed. Cathy sat up, scrambling away from him, curling her legs beneath her, pushing herself back against the
wooden headboard, her heart hammering in her throat. With
a shaking hand she clutched at the neck of the shirt that was
her only covering.

'So,' his voice rasped in the silence, 'you bare your body to
my son and you try to hide it from me.'

She was incapable of speech; sheer, primitive fear locked
her tongue. She stared at him with unblinking eyes.

'Nothing to say?' He was unbuckling his leather belt, slipping it from the loops that held it; with a terrible fascination
she watched as he wound the buckled end around his hand
and swung it, threateningly, across his shoulder. He was
breathing heavily. 'No pleas, no apologies? No excuses?'

She pressed her back harder against the headboard.

'*Speak, will you!*'

Still she said nothing. She saw his knuckles whiten as he
gripped the belt, and tensed herself against the first blow,
turning her head a little, unable for all her efforts to prevent
herself from flinching.

'You are a whore. A harlot. You have betrayed me, shamed
my name. You have dishonoured me. I should kill you. No
one would blame me.'

Tense and trembling she looked back into his face. The
grim gleam of tears in the fierce, dark eyes all but broke her.
'Leon – please – don't cry –'

'Cry?' He bent his head to her, thrust his face into hers.
'Cry, whore? These tears should be blood! You hear me?
Blood!'

Cathy bowed her head and covered her face with her
hands.

'Beg for your life, woman.' His voice, close to her ear,
cracked and dropped to a whisper. '*Beg for it!*'

Numbly she shook her head, gasped as he buried his hand
in her hair and dragged her head back, forcing her to look at

him. The tears were running down his unshaven face, chan-
nelled into the deep grooves about his mouth. The smell of
ouzo was strong enough to make her gag. With a sudden,
violent movement he flung her from him, stood swaying
above her. 'You've – shamed – me,' he growled, and lifted his
arm. The heavy belt swished through the air; Cathy gasped
as it struck the bed an inch from her face. Leon bent close,
thrust his face in hers. 'God damn you, woman,' he said,
very clearly, 'God damn you for a squalid whore. You've
stolen my honour and my son. Look for punishment, for it
will come.' Then he left her, crashing the door behind him
and turning the key in the lock. Cathy heard his heavy tread
on the stone steps, heard him stumble and regain his balance. Shaking and exhausted she was beyond tears. The
lamp guttered. Shadows leapt about her. Lying where he
had left her, she stared into them in despair.

Cathy kept to her room for the next twenty-four hours,
pleading a sickness that was not entirely feigned. The
trauma had taken its toll of her, both physically and mentally, and the misery of guilt and remorse was merciless.
Anna tutted and fussed about her, bringing trays that left the
room as laden as they had entered it. 'You must eat, *Kiria*,'
the girl scolded, 'or you will not get well. The festival is
nearly here. Your son is coming. What will he think, to find
his poor Mama has fallen sick?'

Adam. Dear God – Adam was coming. She had forgotten
it. She laid back on her pillow, her forearm across her aching
eyes, letting Anna chatter on. Nikos. Where was Nikos? What
would he do? Where would he go? He had the money his
grandmother had left him, and still had friends in America.
Often he had asked her to go there with him. One thing was
certain. She would never see him again. She fought tiredly
against the tears that brought. Had he believed the things
she had said that she had said to save him? She feared so.
Always he had hovered on the edges of disbelief – of distrust.

Finally, late in the afternoon, she dozed at last, falling into a heavy, exhausted sleep from which she was awoken by the opening of the door.

She narrowed her eyes against the evening gloom; fear started within her. 'Leon?'

Her husband did not answer. He closed the door behind him, walked to the bed, stood for a moment looking down at her. Then, very deliberately, his eyes hard and steady on hers, he began to undress.

She turned her head away. 'Leon – no. Please.' The words were barely a breath on the warm and dusty air.

Still he did not speak. She closed her eyes, hearing his movements, the rustle of his clothing as he dropped it at his feet. She felt his weight, the deliberately cruel strength of his hands about her wrists and on her breasts, smelled the wine on his breath as his mouth covered hers, not kissing, but biting, inflicting pain. He took her brusquely and in anger; an exercise in brute force, in humiliation. Quickly spent, he rolled from her, panting. A moment later he stood, naked in the dim light, the massive torso with its mat of greying hair sheened with sweat. He bent to pick up his clothes. Straightened.

She watched him, pale as death except where the blood stood on her lip.

'Tomorrow,' he said, the words heavy and even, 'you will get up. You will resume your duties in the house. You will prepare for the festival. You will not, however, leave the house. Send Anna on any errands that may be necessary. You will make amends, Kati, for what you have done. You will ensure, above all things, that no one ever knows what happened between you and my son. One word –' he held up his huge hand, put his finger and thumb together with barely a space between '– one small word – and I will kill you with my bare hands. And Nikos with you, if I have to hunt him to the ends of the world to do it. I promise you. Adam comes the day after tomorrow. You will by then have everything ready. You will act as if nothing has happened.

We will attend the procession and we will celebrate, as planned, the feast of the fallen woman.' The words were ironically emphasised. 'Afterwards you will return to London with me. Is that understood?'

Her pale eyelids drooped. He leaned to her, grasping her chin, forcing her face to his. '*Is that understood?*'

'Yes,' she said. 'Yes.'

He walked, naked, to the door, left without looking back, padding up the warm stone of the staircase softly as a stalking animal.

Cathy stared, unblinking, at the planked wooden ceiling, heart, mind and aching body empty of all but pain.

Such is the resilience of the human spirit that, against all her expectations, Cathy slept deeply that night, and woke if not refreshed at least ready to bear the burdens of the day as best as she might. Leon went down into the village early and did not return until evening, having spent the best part of the day in the taverna, drinking and playing dominoes. Cathy supervised the preparations for the coming festival with an empty mind and an aching heart. She and Leon ate the evening meal in a heavy silence. The meal finished, Cathy cleared away the dishes and came back to the table on the terrace. Leon's eyes brooded upon the distant skyline; smoke from his cigarette drifted lazily in the still air.

'I'll go to bed if you don't mind,' Cathy said, quietly.

He grunted, without looking at her.

She took it for assent, and turned.

'Wait,' he said.

'Yes?' As calmly as she could she turned back to face him.

'Adam comes tomorrow on the evening boat. I shall meet him and bring him home. I shall tell him that Nikos has been called away, and will not be here for the festival. You will do nothing and say nothing to make him suspect that anything is wrong. You understand?'

'Yes.' Her mind sheered away from the question of what

Leon might do if he ever discovered that Adam already knew what had been going on.

His expressionless eyes studied her face for a moment, then, 'Go,' he said, and reached for the wine bottle.

Unusually – in fact extraordinarily – Anna was late the next morning. She arrived at last, flushed and out of breath from running. 'I'm sorry, *Kiria* – my little brother is sick – I had to go for the doctor –'

'That's all right, Anna. Nothing serious, I hope?'

'I don't know, *Kiria* – he has a very high temperature and a bad cough. Please – may I go home for an hour a little later to see how he is?'

'Of course. There isn't a lot to do. I can manage.' She was actually relieved when, at lunchtime, she packed the girl off with a small bag of cakes and sweetmeats for the sick child. She needed time on her own, time to collect herself, time to think. She poured herself a glass of wine and wandered on to the terrace. How had everything gone so wrong? How could she face the future, day after long day, week after long week, living like this? 'Nikos,' she said aloud. 'Nikos!' and for a moment concentrated every ounce of will and energy into the name, as if she could force him to hear her, force him to understand. Would the pain ever ease? She supposed it would in time; she supposed it must, or surely neither of them would be able to bear it? Would Leon ever forgive? Doubtful; and who could blame him? A movement in the bushes drew her eye. A small black and white cat detached itself from the shadows, leapt on to the parapet and sat regarding her with lambent eyes. They watched each other in silence for a moment. Then, 'Lucky cat,' Cathy said. 'No past, no future, no heart, no memories.' She tilted her head and drained her glass. 'Lucky little cat.' She turned and went into the kitchen to prepare the vegetables.

The cat looked after her, unmoved and unblinking, before lifting a delicate paw and proceeding to wash it with a neat pink tongue.

*

Any fear that Adam might sense or notice the strained atmosphere between his mother and her husband was dispelled almost as soon as he arrived. It was with sinking heart that Cathy recognised the symptoms of an intolerably bad mood. Morose and monosyllabic, he ate little and matched Leon glass for glass of the strong red wine.

Cathy studied him. 'Adam? Is something wrong?'

He lifted his head. 'What? Oh – no. Of course not. I've just had a bitch of a week, that's all. And the flight was late. I'm bushed, that's all.' He did indeed look tired, and his face was drawn.

'Get to bed, boy,' Leon said. 'A good night's sleep will sort you out.'

Adam hesitated.

'Tomorrow we stroll down into the village, to the taverna,' Leon said. 'A game of dominoes, a glass or two, you'll be a new man.'

Adam half smiled, but his eyes stayed sombre. 'Yes,' he said, and stood up, stretching. 'Perhaps I will turn in. I'll see you in the morning.' He bent to peck a kiss upon his mother's cheek. She covered his hand in hers and was surprised at the tension she felt in it.

After he had left Cathy glanced at Leon. For the past couple of nights he had slept in Nikos' abandoned bed; to do so with Adam in the house would certainly not go unnoticed, however self-absorbed Adam might be. Desperately she hoped he might leave her alone, but instinct told her it was unlikely. She had to know. 'Leon?' she asked, directly. 'Where will you sleep tonight?'

He bent a dark, oppressive gaze upon her. 'You are my wife,' he said. 'Where else would I sleep but in your bed?'

She lowered her eyes and tried to suppress the rebellious stab of anger that the words unexpectedly triggered. She would not quarrel with him. Not until she was certain that Nikos was well away and out of his reach. Quietly she stood and began to clear the table.

The following morning was an especially glorious one. The sun flooded the mountainside in golden light, the vaulted, forget-me-not sky was cloudless. The faintest of breezes, in from the sea, stirred the leaves of the trees and touched the petals of the bright mountain flowers. A shepherd called and whistled to his flock and on a far hillside a man tended to his beehives. The little, fast-running stream that dashed past the house from the spring rippled and sang in its deep and rocky gully and the scent of bougainvillea hung on the air.

Mid morning the two men set off for the village below. Cathy, standing on the terrace and watching them tramp off down the steep path that followed the stream down the mountain, and then lifting her eyes to the distant, shimmering, sunlit hills, wondered if her heavy heart would ever allow her to appreciate such beauty again. It was, she thought, as if she saw everything – what was that evocative biblical phrase? – through a glass, darkly; the light, the peace, the colour, all that she had loved, all were marred. She drew a long, sighing breath, unaware that the stamp of her unhappiness was clear upon her face.

'Kiria?' The soft voice beside her made her jump. 'Shall I put the fish in to soak before I sweep the steps?' Anna's eyes, huge and dark, held a look of gentle enquiry, and of unexpected sympathy.

'What?' Cathy shook herself from her reverie. 'Oh, yes, Anna. Please. I should have done it earlier –' She cast one last look at the lovely view, then turned to the house and her domestic chores.

She was resting in the darkened bedroom in the oppressive heat of mid afternoon when she heard a hammering on the gate upstairs and the sound of a man's voice, shouting. She sat up, startled. It was rare indeed to receive an uninvited visitor, let alone one who made so much racket. She swung her feet to the floor, groped in the gloom for her sandals.

Beyond the open door a shadow flitted, a footfall

sounded. Her heart jumped, then, 'Anna?' she called. 'Is that you?'

There was no reply.

The peremptory hammering on the door came again.

'Anna! There's someone at the door –' The words were sharper, a little nervy.

Again the shadow flickered, hovering beyond sight.

Cathy shoved her feet into her sandals and stood up, screwing her eyes against the glaring sunshine beyond the door. 'Who is it?'

A tall, broad figure loomed against the light for a moment, then slid into the shadows of the room. Adam leaned against the wall, his head back. Even in this light she could see the bloodless pallor of his face. She took a hesitant step towards him. 'Adam? What is it? What's wrong?'

He bowed his head and passed a hand over his face.

'Adam – please – what is it?' She moved to him, putting out a hand to touch the broad chest. Catching her breath in horror at what she touched. 'Adam! You're hurt!'

On the terrace above Anna spoke and a man's voice answered, quickly, vehemently and at some length.

Adam took her by the shoulders, his fingers biting deep. When he spoke his voice was low, and desperately urgent. 'No. Not me. I'm OK. Ma, listen to me. Don't let anyone know I'm here. Please! I didn't mean it. I swear it. It was an accident. But no one will ever believe it. Help me. Help me!'

'What have you done?' Her voice was a breath of dawning terror. 'Adam, what have you done?'

He was crying now, suddenly and helplessly, the tears running unchecked down his face. 'I didn't mean to,' he said again, 'I didn't! It was an accident, I swear it – he drew that bloody knife of his – I don't *know* how it happened – Ma, it was an accident –'

Upstairs, Anna let out a small, shrill scream.

Adam's tear-bright, distraught eyes held hers, his hands still holding her agonisingly tightly; a support without which she might have fallen. 'Don't tell them I'm here, Ma. Please don't. Give me a chance. To get away –'

'*Kiria* Kati! *Kiria* Kati!' Anna's voice held the fraught edge of hysteria. She was coming down the steps, stumbling awkwardly. Adam slipped away from his mother into the deeper shadows of the room.

Cathy rubbed her hand frantically upon her skirt before she ran from the door into the sunshine.

Anna was standing halfway down the steep stairs, her hands wringing in her apron, her face distorted. When she saw Cathy she shrieked again, buried her face in her apron. '*Kiria* Kati!'

'What is it? What's happened?' Cathy raced up the steps, caught at the girl's arm. 'Anna! Tell me!'

By way of answer the girl gestured mutely up towards the terrace. Cathy pushed past her and took the rest of the steps two at a time. At the top she stopped. The man who stood there, a shepherd from the look of him, thick-set, grim-faced, unshaven, took off his cap. Dark eyes were intent upon her. 'What is it?' Cathy asked. Behind her, Anna was sobbing.

He spoke in Greek, thickly accented, gesturing towards the path that ran beside the garden and on down the mountainside. Cathy understood not a word.

'Help me, Anna. I don't know what he's saying.' She was astounded at the calm of her own voice. Resolutely she put from her mind the picture of the bright, fresh stains on her son's shirtfront.

Her breath catching in her throat Anna said, 'Is *Kirios* Leon. He says – he says –'

'What?' Anna turned on the girl, took her by the shoulders and shook her. 'What does he say? *Tell me!*'

'He says he is on the path below. In the stream. He says he is – dead! Murdered! He says – oh –' The words ended in a wail. Anna once more threw her apron over her head and resumed her frightened sobbing.

Shock had rendered Cathy unnaturally calm. 'No,' she

said, evenly. 'That isn't possible.'

The shepherd spoke again. Cathy looked at Anna. The girl struggled to control herself. 'He says there is blood. And a knife. Oh, *Kiria* –!'

Cathy closed her eyes for a long moment. For one, awful instant she thought she would never move again. Then she found herself saying, still calm, still perfectly contained: 'Ask him to take us there, please, Anna. It has to be a mistake. I must see for myself.'

The girl shook her head, pleadingly.

'Please, Anna.' Cathy realised that she had begun to tremble, and that in the warmth of the sun her skin was ice-cold. 'I must see for myself,' she said again.

Chapter Eighteen

Leon was lying, face down, beside the stream, where the shepherd had left him after he had pulled him from the water. Even lying so there could be no mistaking the huge frame, the leonine head with its springing shock of grey hair. Anna took one terrified look, shrieked and hid her face in her hands, sobbing hysterically. The rocky path widened here, and was edged with thorny brush. Bloodstains, already blackened in the sun, marked the stones where Leon had apparently crawled or dragged himself across them. An area of vegetation had been trampled down. A few yards from the body lay a knife – Leon's own; Cathy recognised it from the barbecue at Easter, the very one with which he had carved the kid. She had once questioned him about his reason for carrying it in a sheath on his belt whilst here in the house and he had laughed, and given the answer he had given so often before: 'Once a peasant always a peasant, my Kati. You don't survive long in these mountains without a means to hunt and a means to eat.'

She dropped to her knees beside him, laid light fingers upon the broad, hirsute wrist. Nothing. Looking at the way he lay she had expected nothing. She stood up, put a hand to her forehead, rubbing at the pain that suddenly hammered there. 'Anna, please, stop it. Anna!'

Anna's frightened sobs subsided a little. Cathy forced her mind to work, quelled the sickness that was roiling in her stomach with an effort of will that seemed to drain the blood from her veins and the marrow from her bones. 'We must get the police,' she said. 'Anna – ask him if he'd be willing to go back down into the village and call them. Tell them what has happened and say we need someone up here, quickly. The taverna has a telephone.'

Anna backed away from the body, keeping her eyes on the shepherd's face. After she had spoken the man grunted and nodded.

The shock that had held Cathy calm was wearing off. Somewhere not far from the surface hysteria hovered. Grimly she fought it off. Whatever happened she must keep her head. Anna had started to wail again. Cathy somehow resisted the urge to slap her. 'Anna, go find the priest. Ask him to come.' Anything to get the girl away.

Helplessly Anna shook her head. '*Kiria* – I can't leave you here – alone –' She glanced towards Leon's still form and the great sobs started again.

'Bring the priest,' Cathy said. 'I'll stay with him. Go.'

The girl and the man left, scrambling and sliding down the path. As the sound of their departure faded Cathy stood very still, the heat of the sun hammering mercilessly on her unprotected head. A fly buzzed. She bent to brush it away. 'Leon. Oh, Leon!' She sank to her knees beside him, her hand resting on his still one, and as she bowed her head above him the tears came in an irresistible and shocking onslaught. She heard a cry so primevally animal-like that she did not recognise it for a moment as her own. Yet still as that first fierce tide of grief and terror ebbed, somewhere within her she knew the need for control. She sat back on her heels, the shuddering sobs quietening a little. The fly buzzed again, and another. She lifted her head; and froze, staring.

The mountainside sloped steeply above her, dotted with bushes and trees, sculpted with outcrops of rock. But by a bizarre chance the Shepherd's Hut stood out clearly above her, open to view. The door stood open. And the movement that had caught her eye had been Adam, coming from the dark interior, carrying what looked like a heavy bag. He stopped, stood silhouetted for a fraction of a second looking down at her. Even from this distance she could see that he had changed his clothes.

'Adam!' The cry had escaped her lips before she could smother it.

Her son, face working, stood for a moment longer, then he hefted the bag into his arms, turned and disappeared from her sight. She stood for the space of a breath, tense as a spring. Then: 'Run, Adam,' she whispered. '*Run!* But – where will you go? What will you do? Oh, God – how could you do this? And why? *Why?*' She sat on a rock not far from the sprawled body and dropped her face into her hands. Nothing made any sense. Nothing. Dully she stared down at the rocky ground. It took a long moment or so before she noticed the glint of gold in the sunshine. She reached a hand to the broken chain that lay half-hidden in the dust beneath a crushed sage bush. She would have recognised it anywhere. She glanced around, searching for the icon. Obviously the chain had been broken in the struggle. Had Leon known it? It was of substantial strength; had he felt the chain break and been distracted, knowing the icon to have fallen? Was that how Adam, unskilled and untrained, had in one split second been able to overcome his stepfather, who had more than usual experience in defending himself? If it were so it was a terrible irony. Leon had been Greek enough, and superstitious enough, she knew, truly to believe in his good luck charm, and the protection he believed that it afforded him. She scuffed at the stones with her sandalled foot, but for the moment at least the thing was gone. Best, perhaps, to let it go, she thought, wearily. It had not, in the end, proved any safeguard from this worst of evils.

From the path below came the sound of footsteps, the murmur of voices. The swift village telegraph had done its work.

In a moment a group of men appeared, carrying between them a wooden door. Dark, watchful eyes met hers, then bent upon the sprawled body. To a man they doffed their caps. Their leader looked at Cathy. 'Constantine – *astinomia*,' he said, miming a running movement.

The police station. Constantine must be the man who had found Leon. She struggled to concentrate. 'We must not –' she searched for a moment for the Greek word '– move him. He must stay until they come.'

The man grunted and nodded.

'Will you wait with him?' She reinforced her appeal with her hands, not trusting them to understand her ill-accented Greek. 'I – go to the house. To prepare. You will stay?'

There was a general murmur of assent.

Cathy dashed a hand across her tear-stained face. 'Thank you.' She climbed away from the little group as fast as she could. Would Adam still be there? Surely not. But she had to check. Whatever he had done she could not bear to lose him too.

The house was quiet, and empty. She could hear the sound of voices floating up from the path. 'Adam?' she called, her voice a whisper in the shadows. 'Are you there?'

No reply.

In the kitchen the stove was roaring. She lifted the lid. All that was left of a bundle of clothing flared and collapsed into a glowing heap of ashes that, as she watched, disappeared into the burning logs. She slammed the lid down. Ran to the door. She was crying again, the hot, exhausting tears running down her face, dripping on to her shirt. Her throat ached with them and her nose was running. She stood for a moment, listening. Nothing. Adam had gone. She went back into the kitchen, reached for her handbag that lay upon the table and opened it, looking for a handkerchief.

The note rustled as she reached into the bag. She opened it. It was hastily scrawled, in some places all but unreadable. '*Ma – I didn't mean it. I swear I didn't. He attacked me. I –*' she could not entirely make out the next word, but she thought it might be 'pushed' – '*him, and he fell. I tried to help him. I pulled the knife out. Believe me. I didn't mean to kill him.*' It was unsigned.

With careful, shaking hands she tore the note to shreds and consigned it, too, to the fire. Then she dropped into a chair, sat unmoving, hands lying still and lightly clenched on the table before her, waiting.

'He won't get off the island.' Yannis, leaning in the doorway, his eyes on the distant hills, lit a cigarette. 'And if he does, I'll find him.'

'Yannis, please –' Cathy was sitting at the table, a glass of wine untouched before her. Her voice was hoarse with exhaustion. '– he's my son.'

'And Leon,' Yannis said evenly, his voice like granite, 'was my friend. More than my friend. He was my brother.' He drew on the cigarette. The sounds of the evening drifted to them. 'Tell me the truth. Did you see him?' His eyes were unfriendly.

She hesitated for only a second. 'No.' It was the story she had told the police. It was the story that wolves and wild horses would not make her change. She had neither seen nor heard from Adam since he and his stepfather had set out for the village on the morning of the murder. She had listened in silence to the story, repeated word for word by more witnesses than anyone could possibly need – of the drinking and of the fierce quarrel that had followed in the taverna – no one knew the reason for the sudden flare-up, the argument being conducted in English, though most seemed to agree it was something to do with money – of Adam lunging at Leon and of Leon using those huge fists, as he had upon his own son, to defeat and humiliate him. Of Adam shouting, threatening, pleading; and finally storming off up the mountain path. Where, as was undeniable from all the evidence – and as she knew from Adam's own words – he had lain in wait for his stepfather. And killed him. His fingerprints were on the knife. And he had disappeared. She rested her forehead on her clenched fist. 'No,' she said again, softly, 'I didn't see him. He didn't come here. Why would he?'

The police had believed her. Two days had passed and no sign had been found of him. Two days in which she had hardly eaten and slept not at all. Two days when momentarily she had expected news of his capture. She was exhausted, emotionally and physically. Yannis' unexpected arrival had all but broken her. At least from everyone else she had received some degree of sympathy. Yannis' hard-eyed, uncompromising – and she had to admit justified – judgemental antagonism had been hard to bear.

He pushed himself now away from the doorjamb and without a word left her. She closed her eyes, and as always opened them again immediately, fighting off the image that imprinted itself in that glinting darkness; of the arrival at the house of the sombre little group who had carried Leon home, lying on the door, eyes open and sightless in the brilliant light, the great bloodstain spread across his chest, all the vivid, intemperate life of him gone. They had laid him upon this very table, and she had covered him with a sheet. Then had come the questions. The terrible explanations. The awful thing was that the knife wound was not, in the end, what had actually killed him, though almost certainly he would not have survived it. Left mortally wounded in the searing heat he had crawled to the water, and then collapsed, rolling down the steep-sided gully and sliding into the stream unconscious. Bereft of the protection of his golden icon, Leon had drowned within a few hundred yards of the place that the woman who had given it to him had died, equally horribly. Leave it, she had said, leave it. Don't look for it. The luck it bestows is worse than bad.

She stared into the wine. It glimmered in the gathering dusk, red as rubies. Red as blood. She turned her face away.

'You're a liar,' Yannis said, softly, from the doorway.

She started, turned to him, eyes wide.

'You're a liar,' he repeated.

'No.'

'Adam was here.'

She wrapped her hands about the glass to still their trembling, kept her eyes wide and steady on his face. 'What makes you say that?'

For a moment he watched her with those narrowed, sceptical eyes, then he said softly, 'You still don't know, do you?'

'What?'

He was silent for a moment, still studying her.

'Yannis – what? What don't I know?'

'Why your son murdered your husband.'

She closed her eyes in pain. 'No. I don't.'

'Come with me.'

Puzzled, she stood up, followed him out on to the terrace and down the steps into the garden. As she realised where he was leading her, her heart began to thud uncomfortably.

It was dark in the Shepherd's Hut, and it took a moment for her eyes to adjust. She looked around. So far as she could see it was as it had always been. Dust lay thick. The place was airless and hot as an oven. Sweat started the moment she entered, dampening her shirt.

Yannis moved to the fireplace and picked up a rusty crowbar that leaned against the wall. Cathy watched in uncertain silence as he slipped the thing between two flagstones and, one handed, levered one of the stones up until he could reach a hand beneath it and swing it up on smooth, well-oiled hinges. Snugly beneath it nestled a metal box, massively padlocked. Yannis slipped a hand in his pocket and brought out a key. The heavy lid yawned. 'There,' he said, quietly. 'See what he died for. As others have before him.'

Cathy knelt beside the hole, reached into the box. It was almost empty, but her groping hand found something; a small bag that was much heavier than she expected as she lifted it out. It chinked weightily in her hand. She glanced back into the box; there were perhaps three or four more of its like lying there. Yannis reached for it, undid it and tipped some of its contents into her palm. The gold gleamed in the sunlight that fell through the door. She picked up one of the coins and held it to the light. It was not one she immediately recognised, though she could see that it was English. On one side was depicted the portrait of George V, on the reverse, St George and the dragon. 'What is it?'

'A sovereign. A golden sovereign. Now, as always, negotiable anywhere in the world.'

Cathy sat back on her heels, shaking her head. 'But – what are they doing here? How did they get here?'

Yannis reached to take the coins back from her, dropped the bag back into the box and lowered the lid. 'Come back to the house. I tell you.'

'In the war, as you know, the Germans and the Italians invaded and occupied Greece.' Yannis poured himself a glass of wine, turned a chair around and straddled it, across the table from her. 'But Greece never submitted. We fought in the cities and in the countryside. We were an army, a real army and we resisted to the end.' He fell silent for a moment. Cathy sipped her wine and watched him, intrigued despite herself. This part of the story at least she already knew something of. Yannis lifted his head. 'The problem was that we were not one army, but two.'

'Loyalist and Communist,' Cathy said. 'Leon often spoke of it. I believe he hated the Communists more than he hated the Germans.'

'Exactly. And with good reason – for while we, who were fighting for our king and our country expended our lives, our arms and our gold to free Greece, the Communist pigs waited, hoarding their coin and their arms, like vultures who watch the death throes of lions in order to feast in safety later.' His normally good-natured face had hardened suddenly to hatred, the long scar stood livid on his cheek. The civil war that had followed the departure of the vanquished Axis powers had been more bitter by far than the occupation itself, for brother had fought against brother, and father against son. Many families in Greece were still torn apart by the wounds of the conflict.

'And the gold?' Cathy asked.

'The British Government supported the Partisans – with arms, with specialist agents – and with gold. Gold meant to be used to fight the Germans. To buy arms and explosives, to bribe, to feed the ragged army in the mountains.' Yannis tilted his head and drained his glass at a swallow. 'The problem was that whilst the loyalists put the gold they received to the purpose for which it was intended the Reds hoarded any they could lay their hands on. For future use. Against us, their brothers.' The words were bitter.

None of this was new to Cathy. She waited, watching him.

Yannis hunched his shoulders and reached for the bottle before he started to speak again. The story in the end was a simple one: 1949, the civil war drawing to a close, ELAS, the pro-communist guerrilla army on the run, and every man for himself. Leon, Yannis and some of their loyalist comrades had been following the trail of a party of ELAS men known to be carrying partisan gold. The two groups had met in the mountains to the north of the island and a particularly bloody clash had ensued; the clash that had put Leon out of the war for good, with a wound that had nearly killed him.

'And the ELAS men?' Cathy asked.

Yannis lit a cigarette, scraped the chair back from the table and wandered to the door, stood with his back to her. 'They died.'

There was a long moment of quiet. 'All of them?' Cathy asked.

'All of them.'

Once again the silence hung heavily between them. Yannis turned, his face in shadow. Smoke drifted lazily into the air. 'It was war,' he said. 'These men had done terrible things. There was too much bad blood.'

'And – there was the gold' Cathy said, trying, unsuccessfully, to keep the dawning horror from her voice.

He came back to the table. His face was expressionless. 'No. There wasn't. The gold had disappeared. Into thin air, it seemed. At the time there was nothing we could do – we had to get Leon and our other wounded comrades to safety. But he never forgot, and neither did I. When the fighting was finished we agreed that I should try to follow the trail. It had to be somewhere. Obviously they had hidden it before we caught up with them. It was a long task –'

'But you did it.'

He shrugged. 'I did it. I traced them at last to a small village in a valley deep in the mountains. Nothing much. A few huts. A church. They had hidden there for some days. As with every other location I had found there were three possibilities; the gold was never left there in the first place, it had been hidden, discovered and stolen, or –'

'– or it was still there,' Cathy offered into the silence as he let the words trail off.

'Yes. At first it was not promising. I talked to the peasants, and to the priest. The peasants knew nothing. The priest was young, and had been in the village but a few months. The trail was cold. Until a few months later – at the end of last year – I traced the priest who had been at the church when the terrorists were there. He remembered them. He remembered them well. It was the only time the war had touched the village. And he was surprised – the Communists showed more respect for mother church than he had looked for. A terrorist, sadly, had died.' Yannis' lips twitched into the faintest, bleakest of smiles. 'He conducted a funeral service.'

'A funeral service,' Cathy repeated. And then – 'You mean – the gold?'

'The gold. They buried it with full rites, a fallen comrade, dead for the cause.' The words were sardonic. 'It was worth a try. And I had heard rumours. Someone else was on the trail, not far behind me. I flew to London –'

'Christmas,' Cathy said.

'I'm sorry?'

'Christmas. That explains Christmas. Why Leon didn't come.' Why I was left alone. Alone with Nikos.

Yannis lifted a shoulder, drew on his cigarette.

'So – Leon joined you and you discovered that it was the gold that was buried there?'

'Yes.'

'How did you do it? Didn't anyone object? What of the village? Wasn't there gossip?'

He smiled that small, hard smile again. 'Everything has its price, and the place was well chosen. Isolated, self-concerned. Silence comes a little expensive, but it comes. There are sons being educated, and daughters with dowries. And a small matter of reprisal should lax tongues wag.'

Out of her depth, she pondered that. 'And of course there is the respectable firm of Kotsikas and Son,' she said at last, quietly bitter. 'Founded on the strength of stolen gold.'

'Stolen? How is it stolen? To whom does it belong? Who had a greater right to it?'

She was silent.

'And it was for this,' Yannis added, quietly, 'that Adam killed Leon.'

Her head came up fiercely. 'How can you *know* that? The evidence is purely circumstantial – what makes you think that Adam even knew about all this? How could he?'

He leaned across the table, palms flat, face very close to hers. 'Because I told him. I showed him the gold. On Leon's orders.'

'Why? *Why?*'

'Because we needed a way to exchange a – shall we say a commodity that might raise some questions? for one that would raise none. There are organisations in America, organisations with power and influence. An arrangement was made. It worked. No one questioned Adam's gambling –'

'Jesus!' Cathy said, and dropped her face into her hands.

There was a long silence. She lifted her head. Yannis was watching her. 'Did you know,' she asked, very calmly, 'that Adam's father was a compulsive gambler?'

He made a small, dismissive gesture with both hands.

'Did you know that Adam's father – because of the gambling – committed suicide?' Her voice was very calm, very quiet.

He shook his head.

'Leon knew,' she said. And then, again, forcefully, 'Leon knew!' A promise made. A promise terribly broken. '*I will watch over your son for you as if he had been my own.*' Oh, the irony of that!

'What we know, and what we don't know,' Yannis said, after a moment. 'How does it signify? One thing I know. Adam killed Leon.'

The lift of her head was challenging. 'How can you be so certain?'

'The key,' he said, quietly and reasonably.

'What key?'

'The key to the chest. Gold has been taken. A fair amount; as much as a man could carry. Do you think I wouldn't know? It was my charge. But the padlock was not broken. It was open. Unlocked. Only three people knew of the existence of that box. Myself, Leon – and Adam. And there were only two keys. Mine. And Leon's. There was no key on Leon's body. It had been taken. By the one who killed him.' He studied her shielded face. Unexpectedly he said, softly, 'I am sorry.'

She shook her bowed head, said nothing.

'Where is he?' he asked.

'I don't know.'

He questioned no further. Lifted his head. 'Someone is coming.'

A moment later Cathy heard it too; the sound of a motor car approaching the house up the narrow road. 'The police again, I expect,' she said, tiredly.

Yannis had a keener ear for an engine than hers. 'I think not,' he said.

A door slammed, and in the quiet footsteps approached down the steep path from the parking place. Yannis lounged to the door and waited. 'Ah,' he said, softly, as the gate on to the terrace opened. 'I wondered how long it would take for the puppy to coming sniffing again.'

Nikos' face was drawn. Seeing Yannis he lifted his chin and stared defiantly.

'Who is it?' Cathy asked, and joined Yannis at the door. Nikos, ignoring the other man, stepped forward, took her hand.

'I was in Athens. I read it in the papers. Pa –' He stopped. Tears welled in his eyes.

'You were told not to come back,' Yannis said.

'Oh, for pity's sake!' Cathy flung round on him, shaking suddenly with a rage she had until this moment contained, 'His father is dead! Give him leave to come home to grieve!'

Yannis looked at her levelly for a moment before, with the characteristic half-shrug, he turned and left them, vaulting over the stone wall on to the mountain path and setting off for the village without a backward glance.

Silence held them for a moment. The tears had spilled from Nikos' eyes and were running unheeded down his face. With no word Cathy held out her arms, and like a child he came to her, burying his face in her shoulder, his body shaking with sobs. It was a very long time before he calmed. She held him still, for a moment, comforting and soothing; beyond tears herself she found his all but unendurable. He lifted his head at last. 'What happened? It said in the paper that Adam –?'

She took his hand, led him to the table. 'Come, sit down. I'll tell you.'

They did not see Yannis again, though certain it was that he returned at some time during the night, for by the morning the box beneath the floor of the Shepherd's Hut was empty of the last of its burden. 'I'm glad,' Cathy said, standing at the doorway of the hut and looking out at the distant sea. 'I want nothing to do with the filthy stuff.' A wild wind had risen in the night and died with the dawn, but the far-off waves were still rough and white-capped, as a swell ran on to the shore.

'What will you do?' Nikos asked, quietly, from behind her.

She shook her head. 'At the moment I can do nothing. There are things to be done. And the police have asked me not to leave yet. But as soon as I can –' She turned to him, walked into his arms and laid her head tiredly on his shoulder. '– I want to go home,' she said.

Later that day a sober-faced policeman called. Nikos was on the terrace, Cathy in the kitchen making coffee. She heard their voices and came to the door. The man glanced at her, continued speaking rapidly to Nikos. She looked from one face to another, trying to follow the conversation. Nikos' face was grim. The policeman sketched a salute, and left. Nikos turned to Cathy.

'What is it?' she asked. 'Nikos? What's happened?'

He came to her and took her hand. 'A boat was stolen last night. From a fishing village on the north of the island.'

Her heart leapt. 'They think it was Adam?'

'They're fairly sure of it. A child saw someone answering his description in the mountains near the village. The kid didn't think to say anything until after the boat was taken.' He saw the beginnings of hope in her eyes and shook his head fiercely, his hand gripping hers painfully. 'No, Cathy. Hear me out. The boat was found this morning. In a cove further up the coast. There was a bad squall last night. The thing had run on to the rocks.'

'And – Adam?'

'There was no sign of him.' His voice was soft. 'Cathy. I'm sorry. I'm so sorry.'

She shook her head fiercely. 'It doesn't mean anything. Not necessarily.'

He said nothing.

'The gold?' she asked, after a long silence.

He shook his head. 'That must have gone, too. The police would surely have mentioned it had it been found.'

'A liferaft worthy of Midas,' she said, softly and bitterly.

Nikos gathered her to him in silence, held her until at last the tears came. In the distance the sea had calmed, and lay shimmering beneath a relentlessly burning sky.

Epilogue

The police investigation, it seemed to Cathy, was brief, and less than painstaking; baldly, the case was open and shut, the only suspect missing, presumed drowned. Logically she, of all people, knew it to be true, yet the very brusqueness of it all was painful. Not knowing whether Adam were alive or dead was the worst part of what was already a nightmare. All that she wanted to do was to go home; the one thing the authorities for the moment would not allow her to do. There were still formalities to be gone through, an enravelled skein of red tape to be untangled. Without Nikos beside her, she thought she might have despaired or gone mad.

Leon was buried in the village graveyard, beside the first wife who had died for him. Cathy was glad of it; it seemed right. The funeral was an ordeal. Wife to the victim, mother to the murderer, the bizarre situation took every ounce of her strength to face on such a public occasion. The whole village attended, and ferry after ferry brought people from the mainland, from Athens and beyond. There were very few faces she recognised as she accepted handshakes and condolences; the day passed in a nerve-strung daze; by the time she escaped at last she was weary beyond rest and beyond tears.

Yannis did not come, and for that at least she was grateful.

Over the next few days life, as it has to through even the worst turmoil of grief and regret, returned to something approximating normality at last. Not for the first time Cathy had good reason to be grateful for the isolation of the house: at least she did not have to endure the glances and whispers that would surely have followed her if she had been in the village. Numb and exhausted she shut herself away, relying on the subdued but still ever-helpful Anna to run any errands that were necessary. Nikos stayed, to all outward appearances an attentive and dutiful son. But by night their bodies sought each other in ever increasing desperation, obsessive in their need for each other.

With the funeral over Nikos went to Athens to begin the mammoth task of taking up the reins of the business. He came back a day or so later, worn out, and with a briefcase full of papers over which he pored for most of the night. Cathy set a fourth cup of coffee beside him, laid a hand on his shoulder. 'Come to bed?'

He sighed, rested his cheek on her hand for a moment. 'In a little while. There's so much to do.'

'How long can you stay?'

'Just for tomorrow. Then I'll have to go back for a couple of days. We're getting there. Gikas is very good, very efficient, and the London office seems to be coping. We'll sort it out, you'll see.'

She tilted her head back, closed her eyes. 'Oh, God, I wish we could go *home!*' she said, suddenly intense. 'I'll die if I can't get away from here, I swear it!'

He stood up, turned to her, took her in his arms. 'Come on, now. Bear up. It won't be long now. They'll let us go soon. A few more formalities and we can put it all behind us.' He put her from him, regarding her with sober eyes. 'And then you're going to have to make a decision.'

She held his gaze steadily.

'I won't leave you. But I won't lie. Not any more. Never again. You either live openly with me or you send me away. I won't pander to other people's prejudices and opinions any more. I want you openly to be mine.'

She bent her head to lay her forehead on his shoulder, her untidy curls brushing the skin of his cheek. 'We'll talk about it later. When we get home. Leave it for now. Please.'

He dropped a kiss on to her head. 'I will. For now. But you have to think about it.'

'I know,' she said, softly, 'I do know.'

The next day he was gone again, promising to return in two days. 'I'll start to pack,' Cathy said. 'They have to let us go soon. There's so much to do, I might as well at least get started. And it will keep me occupied.'

'Good idea. I'll be back on the evening boat on Wednesday.'

Aware of Anna's eyes upon them she kissed his cheek. 'Take care.'

A little later, with Anna gone to the village for supplies she took a break from her labours to sit for a while in the shade of an olive tree, a cup of coffee to hand and her sketch book on her knee. But, as so often recently, her pencil soon stilled. Images invaded her mind; Adam, a small child, bright, precocious, gleaming with mischief. The young man, the deft charm of him already apparent, beguiling his way through life with laughter and a quick tongue. The sudden tempers, the disarming apologies. The turn of his head. The timbre of his voice. Dead. Could he really be dead? A murderer. How could it be? But unstable, the ever-present voice of honesty argued, braced against pain. His father took his own life, Adam took another's. Not so very different. The seeds were always there.

The sound of footsteps coming up the stony path by the garden wall was a welcome distraction; Anna's mother, black-clad, three small children at her skirts, was trudging up the steep slope. She smiled shyly as she saw Cathy, and on impulse – anything to break this terrible chain of memory – Cathy walked over to the wall. 'Good morning, *Kiria*. How are you? Is the little one recovered from his sickness?'

'*Kiria* Bouyoukas has had her baby. A little boy.' Anna was at the sink, peeling potatoes. 'She had a hard time so they say. I met her mother in the bakery.'

'Is the baby all right?'

'Oh, yes.' Anna fell to silence.

Cathy watched her for a moment, then on impulse said, 'Anna? Are you unhappy with me because of what's happened? You don't have to stay with me if you'd rather not, you know –'

'Oh no!' Anna's head came up sharply. 'I like to work for you.' She regarded Cathy with wide, alarmed eyes. 'Are you not satisfied with me?'

'Of course I am. It's just – you've been very quiet lately and – well, I just wondered if there were something wrong. Something you hadn't told me.' Anna was chewing her lip, worriedly. Cathy laid a hand on her arm. 'I spoke to your mother this morning,' she said, very gently, 'I asked about your little brother. She said he hadn't been ill – Anna, darling what is it?' The knife had clattered into the sink, and the girl's face had drained of colour. Still she stared at Cathy in silence. Cathy put an arm about her shoulders. 'Is it a young man? Have you been meeting someone? Oh, don't worry – I said nothing to your mother – you know I wouldn't do that. I simply said I must have been mistaken.' She could feel the slender body trembling within the circle of her arm. 'Anna, tell me what's wrong –'

'He said he would tell you,' Anna said. 'He promised me he would tell you.'

'Who? Who promised?'

'*Kirios* Nikos.' The words were barely audible.

There was a long, puzzled silence. Then, 'I don't

understand,' Cathy said, still gently. 'I think you had better explain.'

She had two days and a long night to absorb the significance of the story Anna told. By the time Nikos returned from Athens she had thought herself round in circles so often that she did not know what to believe. Nikos came on the evening boat; she watched it, as she had so often before, as it steamed across the bay to dock at the little port. He arrived at the house hot, thirsty and tired. 'God, let me get into something more comfortable!' He shrugged off his jacket, slung it over his arm, kissed her. 'Pour me a drink?'

She did so in silence. Minutes later he had rejoined her on the terrace, wearing open-necked shirt and light slacks. He threw himself into a chair, accepted the drink she offered, lit a cigarette and then cocked his head questioningly, watching her. 'Cathy? Is something wrong?'

'Yes,' she said. 'Something is.'

'What? What's the matter?'

She drew a long breath. 'Anna's mother came up the mountain the other morning. She was going to the beehives to collect some honey. I spoke to her.'

He blew out a long, calmly drifting spiral of smoke, eyebrows raised.

'Anna had told me her little brother was sick. It was an excuse for being late. She also went home – or so she said – a couple of times to help nurse him. I enquired about the child. He was never sick. Anna was lying.'

He had become very still. The drink stood untouched on the table.

'I asked her about it,' Cathy said, very quietly. 'I asked her if she had been meeting a young man.'

'And she told you,' Nikos said, very evenly, 'that indeed she had been meeting a young man. Me.'

'Yes.' Her head came up, and her eyes were blazing.

'Why didn't you tell me? You were here on the island all along! You didn't arrive from Athens that night –'

'Yes I did.' He held out an assured hand. 'Come and sit down. I was going to tell you. Later.'

'Tell me now.' She folded her arms obdurately.

'I wouldn't leave you. I couldn't. I was afraid for you. Afraid of what Pa might do. I couldn't stay away, no matter what Pa said. I hitched a lift with a fisherman from the mainland who dropped me in the north of the island. I was back here by the following day – but I knew I had to keep out of sight, both of Pa and of Yannis. I slept in the deserted hut, up the mountain there –'

'The one we made love in,' she whispered.

'Yes.'

'Why didn't you let me know you were here?'

'I was going to.' He was patient. 'But I told you – I had to be careful. I was afraid for you. Well, I have to admit it, for myself as well. You know how violent Pa could be –'

She turned from him.

'Cathy?' he said, quietly, behind her. 'What are you think-ing?' She heard his movement, felt him come to her.

She turned to face him. 'I don't know what to think.'

His eyes narrowed. 'I see.'

'Explain to me,' she said. 'Explain what happened.'

'You obviously know what happened. Anna has told you.'

'You tell me.'

He shrugged. 'I waylaid her that morning. I wanted to know you were safe. And I needed help; food, water. She agreed to help. The girl isn't stupid, and she'd do anything for you –'

'Or you,' Cathy said.

He shrugged. 'She knew something was very wrong. She knew you were unhappy. That Pa was treating you badly. She said you were sick. She said he wouldn't let you out of the house.'

'That was true.'

'So I simply decided to bide my time until I could get to see you –'

'But why didn't you let Anna tell me you were here? Why didn't you send a message?'

'Darling, I know you too well! I *know* how stubborn you can be once you make your mind up. And once I'd had time to think I knew – of course I knew! – that you'd lied about not loving me. And I understood why. I was afraid if you knew I was there you'd defy Pa and come to find me. I wanted to protect you, not make matters worse, can't you see that? I thought sooner or later he'd have to leave. That was what I was waiting for. I intended to persuade you to leave him, to come away with me, for good and all. To America, perhaps. Anywhere. I didn't care. But meanwhile I didn't want to do anything to make him angrier than he already was. He was capable of killing you, you know he was.'

She said nothing.

'Darling, don't doubt me.' He put his arms about her and laid his face on her hair. 'Please don't doubt me. I can't bear it.'

'When you heard what had happened,' her voice was muffled against his chest, 'why didn't you come straight away?'

He put her from him, looked down at her. 'Think,' he said. 'Yannis knew what had happened between us. He knew what my father had done to me. What if he had discovered that I had been on the island that day? I heard the commotion, heard some of what was said, and I panicked. I didn't realise then that Adam had been involved, or that the police had no cause to look for anyone else. All I knew was that Pa was dead – murdered, for Christ's sake! – and that I was where I shouldn't be. I went back up north, crossed to the mainland the same way I had come and slipped back to Athens. The news was in the papers by then. The rest you know.'

She leaned against him tiredly. 'I was afraid –' she said,

and stopped.

'What? What were you afraid of?'

She shook her head. 'I don't know,' she whispered.

'Look at me.'

She raised her eyes to his.

'Do you love me?'

'You know I do.'

'Then trust me.' His voice was very quiet, his hands firm upon her shoulders, his eyes unwavering. 'Trust me,' he said again.

'I do. Of course I do. I'm sorry. It was just – when Anna told me – it was a shock, that's all. That you could have lied to me.'

He pulled her to him again, and held her gently, a hand in her hair. 'I would have told you,' he said, 'if I'd really thought it was necessary. But to be honest, by the time I got back to Athens I was thoroughly ashamed of myself for panicking and running away. I still am. I can't believe I did such a thing – leaving you to face that horror alone. I wish with all my heart now that I had stayed. And I suppose that's why I didn't want to talk about it. I didn't want you to know what a coward I had been. I didn't want you to be disappointed in me. That's all. I swear it. You've had such a lousy time lately. I just want to put it all behind us.'

'And go home,' she said.

'Yes.' He tilted her chin and kissed her. 'And go home. We will. Soon.'

It was another long week before the news finally came that they were free to leave; the relief was so great that Cathy wept. The lethargy of grief which had afflicted her during the seemingly endless wait dropped away, and she was galvanised into a frenzy of packing and organisation. They were to travel by sea, a brief relaxing break before they faced the problems of the future; for problems there would be, she had no doubt of that. For now she simply wanted to get

away, to give herself a chance to come to terms with the double tragedy of Leon's and Adam's deaths. She wanted cool
winds and summer rain. She wanted the wide skies and the
space of the Suffolk coast. She wanted – needed – peace, and
a chance to heal.

She wandered from room to room. Most of the packing
had been done; the place already seemed empty, unlived-in.
Leon's dream was finished, done to death as surely as Leon
himself had been. She went out on to the terrace, watching
for the evening boat. It had been windy all day, and it was
rising still. The boat was late. She went down the steps to the
bedroom. Here too most of the packing had been done, only
the last of their personal possessions left. She opened the
empty wardrobe, to check nothing had been missed, went
through the equally empty drawers. In Nikos' room she
checked methodically that all was ready for the morrow's
departure.

Home. They were going home.

Through the sound of the wind she heard the ferry's whistle as it ploughed round the headland and into the bay.
Nikos was coming.

She opened another drawer. This one still had some
clothes in it; neatly folded shirts and jumpers, waiting to be
packed. She must remind Nikos to clear it tonight. She tried
to shut it, and the thing skewed and jammed. She rattled it
impatiently, trying to free it. 'Blast it!' It was wedged tight.
She pulled it, and with a suddenness that made her jump it
freed itself, swinging in her hand, cracking against her knee,
spilling the contents all over the floor. 'Blast the thing!' she
said again, rubbing her damaged knee before bending to
retrieve the scattered clothes.

She almost missed the gleam of gold; for ever after she
wished that she had. Very, very slowly she reached for the
small bright object that had been concealed within the folds
of a pale blue shirt. It lay in her hand, heavy and familiar.
She stared at it for what seemed a very long time,

marshalling thought, trying to suppress a dawning dread.
The missing icon. The talisman that had lost its power to
protect; that had been wrenched from the neck of a dead or
dying man.

How had Nikos come by it? The police had spent two
days scouring the scene of the murder; the icon had not
turned up then.

No matter how she fought, it was impossible not to follow
the path down which her thoughts were leading her. Nikos
had lied to her once. In God's sweet name – was the deception greater than she had imagined? Her mind sheered from
the thought.

Adam had stabbed Leon – by accident, she did believe
that – and left him for dead. Mortally wounded Leon had
dragged himself to the stream and, too weak to save himself,
had drowned. Those were the facts. Or were they? Had Leon
dragged himself to the water? Or – terrible thought – had he
been dragged? No one had looked for such signs; there had
seemed to be no need. With Adam fled, a self-confessed
murderer, who else was there to suspect?

Who indeed?

She shook her head once, and then again, fiercely. 'Adam
killed Leon,' she said aloud, firmly. 'He told me so himself.
Adam did it.'

Then what of this? Her hand closed upon the icon.

'*If you love me,*' Nikos had said, '*then trust me.*'

And on the heels of that, Leon's voice rang suddenly in
her head, clearly as if he were there in the room with her;
'*God damn you, woman. God damn you for a squalid whore.
You've stolen my honour and my son. Look for punishment, for it
will come.*'

She closed her eyes for a moment. 'Adam killed Leon,'
she said again, and even she could hear the dreadful edge of
doubt in her voice.

The ferry whistled again as it approached the shore.

With enormous care she fitted the drawer back on to its

runners, folded the clothes and put them back. She stood for a long, still moment, the trinket that she knew had meant as much to the son as it had to the father still in her hand. What superstitious impulse – what fear? – had led to the breaking of that chain? And under what circumstances?

'*If you love me, then trust me.*'

How had it come here?

One day she would ask him. But, she knew, not now, not yet. Not until she was certain she was strong enough to face the answer. 'How did I never realise,' she asked into the empty, oppressive silence of the room, very softly, 'what a terrible thing – a truly terrible thing – love can be?'

After a long moment she tucked the icon carefully back into the folds of the shirt and shut the drawer.

The ferry would have docked by now. Nikos was coming.

They were safely away and on the high seas when the earthquake struck, two days later. At the heart of the monstrous upheaval whole villages were destroyed as the treacherous earth convulsed beneath them. The mainland and the farther islands, however, escaped more lightly, though the tremors were enough to terrify and to bring down the odd building. Though Cathy did not discover it until later the house on the mountain was, oddly, the only one in the village to be damaged. As the earth slipped so the structure slipped with it, beams cracking and walls leaning drunkenly, the waters of the stream washing across the terrace and through the wrecked garden. In a few violent moments Leon's pride was destroyed. Only the Shepherd's Hut remained, whole and untouched, small and solid upon its outcrop of rock.